She'd been attracted to Colt since she was old enough to feel attraction, and apparently that hadn't changed one bit. If anything, that kiss had made it a heck of a lot worse.

Mercy, he'd gotten even better at this since they were teenagers. Not that she'd expected anything less. With those hot cowboy looks, he'd no doubt had a lot of practice. That thought was something to cool the heat down just a bit.

She definitely didn't want to be another notch on Colt's bedpost.

Yes, they'd made out before, but they'd never gone further. Elise figured it was a good idea if that remained true. And the best way for that to happen was for the kiss to stop.

He pulled back, his gaze snapping to hers, then lowering right back to her mouth. "That was a mistake."

Then, he dropped another of those scalding kisses on her mouth. He cursed some more, backed away from her. "And it's also proof of why I need to put you in someone else's protective custody."

Merry held grimly onto that sliver as the days
wore towards... Not that she'd expected too many
to... With these hot cowboy looks, he'd no doubt
had a lot of practice. That thought was somehow
to override that creepy little bit...

She demanded when he wanted to another notch on
that's bedpost.

Yes, she'd made out before, but they'd never
gone further. Gave lie and it was impossible to
...imagine her true, and the best way for that to
happen was for the kiss to stop.

He pulled back his gaze snapping to hers, then
to his right eyes to her mouth. "That gave a
moment..."

Then, he dropped another of those scalding kisses
on her mouth. He curved one hand back away
...son her. And it's also kind of why I have to tell
you it's actually a... saying an awful...

8

THE DEPUTY'S
REDEMPTION

BY
DELORES FOSSEN

Published in Great Britain 2015
by Mills & Boon, an imprint of Harlequin (UK) Limited,
Eton House, 18-24 Paradise Road, Richmond, Surrey, TW9 1SR

© 2015 Delores Fossen

ISBN: 978-0-263-25298-9

46-0315

Harlequin (UK) Limited's policy is to use papers that are natural, renewable and recyclable products and made from wood grown in sustainable forests. The logging and manufacturing processes conform to the legal environmental regulations of the country of origin.

Printed and bound in Spain
by CPI, Barcelona

Delores Fossen, a *USA TODAY* bestselling author, has sold over fifty novels with millions of copies of her books in print worldwide. She's received the Booksellers' Best Award and the RT Reviewers' Choice Award, and was a finalist for a prestigious RITA® Award. You can contact the author through her webpage at www.dfossen.net.

Chapter One

Deputy Colt McKinnon caught the blur of motion from the corner of his eye.

He hit the brakes, not hard, because there was likely some ice on the road, and he pulled his truck to a stop on the gravel shoulder.

There.

He saw it again.

Someone wearing light-colored clothes was darting in and out of the trees. Since it was below freezing and nearly ten at night, it wasn't a good time for someone to be jogging.

Colt took a flashlight from the glove compartment and got out, sliding his hand over the gun in his belt holster, and he tried to pick through the darkness to see what was going on. Thankfully, there was a full moon, and he got another glimpse of the person.

A woman.

She was running and not just an ordinary run, either. She was in a full sprint as if her life depended on it.

Colt hurried down the embankment toward her to see if anything or anybody was chasing her. There were coyotes in the woods, but he'd never heard of a pack going after a human. However, before he could see much of anything else, the woman ducked behind a tree.

"I have a gun!" she shouted.

Ah, hell.

He instantly recognized the voice. Elise Nichols. A voice he darn sure didn't want to hear at all, much less her yelling about having a gun.

Her house was a good five miles from here, definitely not close by enough for her to be on foot. So what in the Sam Hill was she doing running in the woods in the middle of the night?

"It's me—Colt," he said, just in case she thought he was a stranger.

"I know exactly who you are." Her voice was loud but very shaky. "And I have a gun."

"So do I," he snarled, and Colt drew it to prove his point.

Colt hadn't exactly expected a warm, friendly greeting from Elise, but he hadn't thought she was to the point of threatening to do him bodily harm.

"What the heck are you running from?" he asked.

She didn't jump to answer. The only sounds were the February wind rattling through the bare tree branches and his heartbeat pumping like pistons in his ears.

"I'm running from *you*," she finally answered.

Colt jerked back his shoulders. That sure wasn't the answer he'd been expecting. Nor did it make a lick of sense.

"I'm a deputy sheriff of Sweetwater Springs," he reminded Elise just in case she was drunk or had gone off the deep end and couldn't remember what was common knowledge around these parts.

And he reminded her also because her comment riled him.

"People generally don't feel the need to run from

me," he added with a syrupy sweetness that she would know wasn't the least bit genuine.

"They'd run if you were trying to kill them."

He tried not to let his mouth drop open, but it was close. "And you think that's what I'm trying to do to you?"

"I know you are. You ran me off the road about fifteen minutes ago."

He glanced around, didn't see another vehicle. But there was a road not too far away, and it would have been the one Elise would likely take to get to and from her place located just outside town. It was possible someone had sideswiped her and maybe she'd hit her head during the collision. That was the only explanation he could think of for a fish story like that one.

"Come out so I can see you," Colt told her, "and I'll drive you to the hospital."

She didn't answer.

Didn't move, either.

Fed up with Elise herself, her story, the butt-freezing night and this entire crazy situation, Colt huffed. "Get out here!" he ordered.

"Right. So you can kill me," she accused. "Then I can't testify at your mother's trial."

Good grief. Colt figured that subject would come up sooner or later. But he hadn't expected it to come up like this, with Elise accusing him of trying to kill her. His mother, Jewell, was the one about to stand trial for murdering her lover twenty-three years ago.

And Elise would be the key witness for the defense.

That alone was plenty bad enough because Colt figured his mom had indeed killed the guy. Anything that Elise would say in Jewell's defense could be a lie at best, and at worst it could tear his family to pieces.

Because Elise was expected to testify that not Jewell but rather Colt's father, Roy, had committed the murder.

No way would Colt or his brothers let that happen.

His father wasn't going to pay for Jewell's sins.

But there was also no way Colt would murder a witness to stop that testimony from happening. The badge he wore wasn't for decoration. He believed in the law. Believed that his mother, and Elise, would get what was coming to them.

Without his help.

"Come on out here," he repeated. "You probably got sideswiped by a drunk or something."

"A drunk driving a truck identical to yours," she countered.

That sent a bristle up his spine, and that bristly feeling went up a significant notch when Elise finally stepped out. He didn't see a gun, but from her stance, she looked as if she were challenging him to a gunfight in an Old West showdown.

"Call the county sheriff or the Texas Rangers," she insisted. "I know they won't try to kill me."

Colt huffed again and turned the flashlight on her. He prayed she didn't do something stupid and pull the trigger of the weapon that she claimed she was holding. It was a risk, but he figured Elise was only a liar and not a killer like his mother.

He moved the light over her face and then her body. She was wearing a pale blue coat and a stocking cap, but wisps of her light brown hair were flying in the wind and snapping against her face like little bullwhips.

And yeah, she had a gun.

Pointed right at him.

That didn't help his racing heartbeat. Nor did the

white-knuckle grip she had on the weapon. There were a lot of nerves showing in that grip.

"Put down the gun," Colt insisted.

"Call the county sheriff," she insisted right back.

Neither moved. Colt certainly didn't turn to make that call, but somehow he had to convince Elise to surrender her weapon. And he didn't want to have to wait the forty-five minutes or so that it would take the county sheriff to get out here.

"It's not like when we were kids, huh?" Elise said. The corner of her mouth lifted, but it wasn't a smile. "We used to play cops and robbers with toy guns. You were always the cop. I was the bad guy. Remember?"

In too perfect detail. Once, way too many years ago, Elise had been his best friend. The first girl that he'd kissed. Okay, she'd been his first love.

But he darn sure didn't feel that way about her now.

Hadn't felt that way in a long time, either. He wanted to ring her neck for trying to drag his dad into the middle of this murder trial mess.

Colt drew in a long, weary breath. "Look, can we just have a truce? Besides, you really do need to see a doctor. If you were run off the road, you could have bumped your head."

She touched her fingertips to her temple, just beneath the edge of the stocking cap, and Colt was stunned to see the dark liquid.

Blood.

That did it. He cursed and walked toward her. Colt lowered his gun to his side, just so she'd feel less threatened, but it was clear she was injured and needed help. Even if she didn't want that help from him.

Elise didn't lower her gun, however, and she backed up with each step he took. Colt kept watch to make sure her finger didn't move on the trigger. It didn't. And when he got close enough to her, he dropped the flashlight and snatched the gun from her hand.

He expected her to try to get it back. Or curse him for taking it, but she turned and ran.

Hell.

Not this.

He really didn't want to be chasing an injured woman through the woods at night, but Elise was the job now. She'd become that when she'd accused him of attempted murder and pointed the gun at him.

Colt shoved her gun in the back waist of his jeans, grabbed the flashlight and took off after her. For a woman with a bloody head and dazed mind, she ran pretty fast, and it took him several moments to catch up with her. He snagged her by the shoulder, spun her around and pinned her against a tree.

It didn't put them in the best position. They were now body to body and breathing hard. But at least she wouldn't be running anywhere.

Colt reholstered his gun so he could use the flashlight to get a look at her head. Yep, there was an angry-looking gash at least two inches long. Not a lot of blood, but she would have taken a hard lick to get that kind of injury.

"Did you hit your head when you went off the road?" he demanded.

She opened her mouth. Closed it. "I'm not sure." Her eyes were wide. Startled. But Colt couldn't tell if it was because she was still afraid of him or because of her injuries.

"The air bag deployed," she said a moment later. "The windshield broke."

So, something could have come through the glass and smacked her. "What happened then?"

Her mouth started to tremble, but she clamped her teeth over it. She also met him eye to eye, nudged him several inches away from her and hiked up her chin. No doubt trying to look a lot stronger than she felt.

Yeah, that was Elise.

"After I crashed, I heard someone get out of the truck," Elise finally answered. "The man was armed. Dressed like you."

Her gaze drifted from his Stetson to his buckskin coat. And lower. To his jeans and boots.

His *uniform* for this time of year.

"*Exactly* like you," she added.

"Plenty of people around here dress like me." Well, except for the badge. "Plenty of people drive trucks, too. In the dark most trucks look the same."

There was no indication whatsoever that she believed anything he was saying. Elise just kept staring at him as if trying to piece things together. But Colt figured that was better worked out at the hospital after a doctor had examined her.

Of course, he'd have to file a report. *Of course.* And he'd have to say that a witness in an upcoming murder trial had accused him of doing her bodily harm. He wasn't looking forward to having to explain himself, especially when he'd done nothing wrong. Still, that was part of the job, too.

"Come on." This time Colt hooked his arm around Elise's waist and got her moving. He was thankful when she didn't resist. Or collapse. Though she suddenly looked ready to do just that.

"I'll drop you off at the hospital," he explained, "and

then come back and have a look at your car. Where exactly did you go off the road?"

"Just a few yards from Miller's Creek. I crashed into the guardrail."

He knew the exact spot and winced. That creek was deep and icy this time of year. If her car had gone over, then she might have gotten a lot more than just a bloody gash on her head. She could have drowned or died from exposure, especially since there likely wouldn't have been anyone to come along and rescue her.

He leaned in to smell her breath. No scent of booze. But she did scowl and shoved her elbow against him to get him out of her face.

"I'm not drunk," she grumbled. "Or crazy. I know what happened, and I know what I saw."

Yes, and sometimes what a person saw wasn't the truth. But Colt kept that to himself. No sense getting in an argument about this particular incident.

Or the trial.

Though he was positive Elise hadn't seen what she thought she'd seen all those years ago, either.

"So, you crashed into the guardrail," he repeated while he continued to lead her to his truck. "What happened then?"

She took a deep breath. Paused. "I managed to bat down the air bag, and I got out on the passenger's side. I just started running."

Colt was about to remind her that she could have run for no reason. But he didn't get a chance to say anything.

The slash of lights stopped him.

Since the road was only twenty yards or so away, it wasn't unusual for a vehicle to come this way. But Elise obviously didn't feel the same.

"Oh, God." She turned and pulled him behind one

of the trees. Elise also reached down and turned off his flashlight.

Colt kept his attention on the truck. It was indeed the same model and color as his. And it wasn't going at a normal speed. It was inching closer as if the driver was looking for something.

Probably Elise.

And not for the killer-reasons that she believed but maybe the driver was trying to find her to make sure she was okay.

Still, Colt stayed put. Watching. Waiting. Wondering if he, too, had lost his bloomin' mind to hide behind a tree instead of just trying to have a chat with whoever was behind that steering wheel.

Next to him, Elise's breath was gusting now, and she had her hand clamped on his left arm like a vise. Every part of her was shaking.

The truck pulled just ahead of Colt's. Stopped. And the automatic window eased down. It was too dark for him to see inside, but he could just make out the silhouette of a driver. A man, from the looks of it.

The driver turned off his headlights.

That didn't help the prickly feeling down Colt's spine.

Nor did the other thing he saw.

He stepped from his truck, taking slow cautious steps while he looked at the ground.

And the man was carrying a gun.

Chapter Two

Oh, God. The man was back, and he would no doubt try to kill her again.

Elise didn't have any idea who he was, but at least she now knew that it wasn't Colt who was trying to murder her.

Not at the moment, anyway.

She'd seen the hatred in his eyes. Felt it, too, but thankfully that hadn't put him in a killing rage.

"Don't go out there," she warned him in a whisper when she felt Colt move.

Colt stopped but drew his gun. And he kept watch. Just as she did.

Elise's heart was in her throat now, every part of her geared up for fight or flight. She was hoping it was a fight that she could win, but it was hard to think straight with her head pounding like a bad toothache.

The man walked from the front of Colt's truck and down the shoulder of the road. Toward them. But he wasn't looking exactly in their direction. His gaze was firing all around him.

So, maybe he hadn't seen them, after all.

Part of her wanted to run out there and confront him, and the other part of her just wanted to see what he planned to do. She figured he wanted to finish what he had started on the Miller's Creek Bridge.

"Is that the guy who ran you off the road?" Colt asked, his voice barely making a sound.

"I'm pretty sure it is."

Elise had only gotten a glimpse of him. Or rather a glimpse of his clothes, specifically the midnight-black Stetson that looked identical to the one the Colt had worn since he was a teenager.

Maybe a coincidence.

But with everything else going on, she wasn't so sure. She had only been back in Sweetwater Springs for a month. Had barely unpacked her things at the house that'd once belonged to her grandparents. But since Elise had arrived, she'd known she wasn't exactly welcome in town.

"Had you seen him before tonight?" Colt continued, sounding very much like the lawman that he was.

"Earlier today, I saw someone watching me from the parking lot at the grocery store. I thought it was you."

He made a sound in his throat to indicate it hadn't been. "I need to bring him in for questioning. This could be just some kind of misunderstanding. I heard something about your previous tenant not being happy about having to give up the place when you moved back."

No, he hadn't been. In fact, the guy had trashed the house and left a rude message for her. "I know the tenant, and he's not the guy."

Colt stayed quiet a moment, watching the man walk closer to them. "Stay put," he told her.

And that was the only warning she got before Colt stepped out from cover. "I'm Deputy Colt McKinnon," he called out. "Who are you?"

It was hard to see much of anything with just the

watery moonlight, but the man didn't lift his gun in their direction, and he stopped, staring across the narrow clearing at Colt.

"Toby Gambil," he said, practically in a growl.

She repeated the name under her breath, trying to remember if she'd ever heard it. But she hadn't. And she didn't recognize that voice, either.

Elise wished she had her laptop handy so she could do a quick check to see what she could pull up on him. It was something she did almost daily. Her job as a corporate security analyst gave her access to all sorts of dirty little secrets.

And she had a bad feeling this guy had some.

"Any reason you're out here this time of night?" Colt pressed.

"Yeah. Some bimbo ran me off the road. I suspect she was drunk, and I came looking for her."

Elise frantically shook her head, but if Colt realized what she was doing, he gave no indication of it.

"You know this woman you claim ran you off the road?" Colt asked.

"Never saw her before in my life. I was just out here in Sweetwater Springs looking for an old army buddy. Got lost. Then, when I tried to get across the bridge not far from here, she smacked right into me with her car." He tipped his head to the front of his truck. "I want to find her because I'll need to make an insurance claim."

The man made it sound so innocent. As if it was all her fault. And it wasn't.

"You ran *me* off the road," Elise shouted out to him. Colt glanced back at her, scowled, but that didn't deter her. "You acted like you were trying to kill me."

The man took his time answering, and if he had any outward reaction to her accusation, he sure didn't show it. "Well, little lady, it seems we have a difference in opinion as to what happened."

His condescending nickname irritated her almost as much as his smug attitude.

"Just give me your name, and I'll be on my way," the man added. "I'll let the insurance company sort it all out."

"You already know my name," she snapped. "Because you were watching me at the grocery store earlier today. It's Elise Nichols."

Again, he didn't jump to respond. "Seems you're mistaken about that, too. It's my first night in town. Never been here before in my life. Maybe you're not thinking straight after the little wreck you caused."

Again, he was cocky. And that tone chilled her even more than the night air. It must have done the same to Colt, because he stepped in front of her.

"Let's drive back to the sheriff's office on Main Street," Colt ordered. And there was no mistaking the fact that it was an order given by a man with a badge. "I'll follow you. I can get your statement and call for a medic to come and check out Elise."

The moments crawled by, and Elise figured the guy would flat-out refuse. But he didn't. Gambil finally nodded, then shrugged and, as if he didn't have a care in the world, he strolled back to his truck.

"Just follow the signs to town," Colt instructed Gambil. "It'll take you straight to Main Street."

Colt got her moving again, staying just slightly ahead of her so that he was between her and Gambil. Once the man was inside his truck, Colt practically stuffed her inside his and hit the master switch to lock her door.

"Any chance what he's claiming is true?" Colt asked, taking out his phone. He didn't reholster his gun, and he didn't take his eyes off the other vehicle that was parked just a few yards ahead of them.

"No chance whatsoever," Elise insisted. "He ran into me, and when he got out, he was coming right at me with a gun."

"But he didn't shoot? And he didn't say anything to you?"

"No."

That's where her explanation ground to a sudden halt. Because he'd certainly had time to shoot her. Or at least verbally threaten her. She'd had to get out from beneath the air bag, exit on the passenger's side and then start running.

He could have put a bullet in her at any time.

So maybe this had all just been an accident. Except it hadn't felt like one.

And still didn't.

Colt started the engine and turned on the heater full blast. Until the warm air started to spill over her, Elise hadn't realized she was shivering. He also punched a button on his phone.

"Reed," he said a moment later. Reed as in Deputy Reed Caldwell from the Sweetwater Springs Sheriff's Office. "I need you to run a license plate." And Colt rattled off the number of Gambil's truck. Waited.

Looked at her.

Of course, no look from Colt was ever just a mere look.

They shared too much history for that, and those bedroom blue-gray eyes always had a way of cutting right through her. Elise tried not to let that happen now. In fact, she tried not to think of anything from their past—including the sizzling-hot attraction that'd once been between them.

No.

Best not to think of that.

Even though her body always reminded her of it whenever she was within breathing distance of him. Thankfully, over the past decade or so there had been plenty of distance between them, but she couldn't rely on that any longer. Not with them both in the same small town.

"Toby Gambil," Colt repeated. "Yeah, that's right. Anything suspicious on him, like maybe an arrest warrant?"

She couldn't hear what Reed said, but judging from the way Colt's mouth relaxed, the answer was no. Nothing suspicious. Well, nothing except for his behavior after he'd crashed into her with his truck.

"I'm on Ezell Road right now. I'll be bringing both Gambil and Elise Nichols in to take their statements about a car accident," Colt said to Reed. "Run a quick check on Gambil for me. And have a medic come to the station." He paused. "No, but Elise might need a few stitches."

She certainly hadn't forgotten about the cut on her head. It was still throbbing. But a few stitches were the least of her concerns.

Colt ended the call, put his truck into gear and flashed his headlights to let Gambil know they were about to leave. Elise held her breath, to see what the man would do, but Gambil eased out onto the road, and Colt followed right behind him.

It seemed, well, normal.

"You think I'm crazy," she mumbled. Heck, she was beginning to think that, too.

But the words had barely had time to leave her mouth

when she heard the sound that she didn't want to hear. Tires screeching on the asphalt.

Ahead of them, Gambil's truck sped away.

"Hell." Colt tossed his phone into her lap and slammed on the accelerator, too. "Call Reed. Tell him we might have a problem."

Elise didn't have time to feel even an ounce of justification that she'd been right about this situation. Ahead of them, Gambil fishtailed, his back tires skirting across the wintery road, but he quickly corrected the truck and went even faster.

Colt was right behind him.

"Let Reed know that I'm in pursuit of Gambil's vehicle," Colt said, his attention nailed to the road and the truck.

Even though her hands were shaking, Elise managed to pick through the numbers and find Reed's. The deputy answered on the first ring, and she began to relay Colt's message.

"Tell Colt to back off," Reed said before she'd even finished talking. "I believe Toby Gambil is an alias. I don't know who you're dealing with."

Elise knew. They were dealing with a man who'd tried to kill her. A man who was now trying to flee the scene. A man who'd likely given a fake name to a deputy sheriff who was questioning him.

There weren't many good reasons for a person to do that. She relayed what Reed had said to Colt.

"He could be dangerous," Reed added. "I'm on my way out there now, and I'll see about setting up a roadblock."

The moment Elise pressed the end call button, Gambil slammed on his brakes. Colt cursed again, hit his brakes, too, but had to swerve into the oncoming lane to stop himself from plowing right into the back of Gambil's truck.

"Don't you dare say I told you so," Colt grumbled.

The thought hadn't crossed her mind. Right now, she was only worried about what Gambil might do next. After all, the man was armed, and Colt's and his trucks were now practically dead level with each other. Gambil could fire right into the cab and kill them both.

That's probably why Colt threw his truck into Reverse to drop back behind Gambil. But they didn't hold that position for long. Gambil hit the accelerator again, shooting forward like a bullet.

"Go after him," Elise insisted.

Yes, she was scared. Terrified, actually. But if he got away, they might never know who he really was and why he'd come after her like that.

Colt seemed to have a split-second debate with himself about what to do, but she must have convinced him, because he took off after Gambil.

"Watch for Reed," he told her.

She would. And she'd also try to watch for other cars. Elise prayed that everyone in Sweetwater Springs had stayed in tonight because with the way Gambil was driving, he could run into someone who happened to be in the wrong place at the wrong time.

There was a flash of red ahead of them. Gambil's brake lights. And he turned onto another road. But not just any road. The one that led to Miller's Creek Bridge where he'd first rammed into her.

"Why's he doing this?" she mumbled. "Why would he go back there?"

Colt only shook his head and kept following the man. However, they had only gone about a quarter of a mile when she heard the sound. As if the truck had backfired.

Almost immediately, Gambil started to swerve. And it got worse. His truck pitched to the right, heading straight for the ditch.

"Hold on," Colt said just as he put on his brakes. He had to careen around Gambil, but he somehow managed to avoid another collision.

Gambil wasn't so lucky.

His truck left the road, going airborne when it vaulted over the raised shoulder, and the front end slammed into a cluster of small trees.

Elise had braced herself for something bad to happen, but she certainly hadn't expected *that*.

Colt and she sat there. Breaths sawing. Her heartbeat going like crazy. But Gambil didn't get out of the truck.

"Call Reed again," Colt told her. "Let him know where we are." And with that, he shifted his gun and opened his door.

"You're not going out there." However, she was talking to the wind because Colt was indeed going out there.

"If you move, I'll arrest you," Colt growled at her. He also shot her a warning scowl to go along with that and started toward Gambil.

Only then did Elise remember that Colt still had her gun, and she didn't like the idea of him not having some kind of backup.

Not that she would be of much help.

At best she was a lousy shot, a disgrace for someone raised on a Texas ranch, but if Gambil came out with guns blazing, she might have been able to scare him by firing over his head or something.

Now, she didn't even have that option.

With her stomach churning and her heart in her throat, she watched as Colt approached the truck. He took slow, cautious steps, his attention pinned to the driver's side.

His gun, too.

He had it pointed right at Gambil.

Gambil's headlights were still on, cutting through the silvery fog that was drifting from the nearby creek. That, along with the moon, gave her plenty of light to see Colt's expression when he threw open Gambil's door. He froze for a moment when he looked inside.

Colt's head snapped up, his gaze no longer on Gambil but on the road. And on her.

"Get down!" Colt yelled.

Elise froze, too, wondering why the heck Colt had told her that and why he was sprinting back toward her. He jumped into the truck, threw it into gear and hit the accelerator as if their lives depended on it.

A split second later, Elise realized that it did.

Because Gambil's truck exploded into a giant ball of fire.

Chapter Three

With his phone sandwiched between his shoulder and ear, Colt waited on hold while he watched the medic put some stitches on the side of Elise's head. She didn't even wince. Didn't even seem to notice.

Because her attention was nailed to Colt.

She was no doubt on the edge of her seat, waiting for answers about why this nightmare had happened, but Colt figured those answers might be a long time coming.

Especially since their suspect was dead.

Now he needed to find answers to a couple of whys. Why had Gambil come after Elise in the first place? And why had the explosives been in the truck?

Colt had only gotten a glimpse of the device on the ceiling of the truck, but he'd recognized the type of explosive and figured it was time to get out of there. He'd been lucky that he'd gotten far enough away to get only a few nicks and cuts from the flying debris. A couple of seconds later and he would have been a dead man, too.

Yeah, he definitely wanted to know why, and that started with learning everything about Gambil that there was to know.

There was a slight sound on the other end of the line to indicate he'd been taken off hold, and he heard Reed's voice. "It's not good, Colt."

Hell. Colt had already had his fill of bad news for the night and didn't want more. "I'm listening."

"We just fished Gambil's body from the rubble, and it looks as if the explosion wasn't what killed him. He already had a gunshot wound to the head."

Colt was about to say that wasn't possible, but then he remembered the sound that he'd heard right before Gambil ran off the road. A sharp pop. He'd thought it was the truck backfiring, but it could have been a gunshot.

"Check the area for any sign of a shooter," he told Reed.

Elise stood even though the medic was still trying to put a bandage on her head. Her gaze locked with his, and Colt clicked the end call button so he could fill her in on something that she wasn't going to want to hear.

"Looks like somebody shot Gambil," Colt explained.

She released her breath as if she'd been holding it. "So, all of this is real." She swallowed hard and caught onto the edge of his desk when she wobbled.

Colt went to her in case he had to stop her from falling or fainting, but the grip on the desk alone seemed to steady her enough. Still, it probably wasn't a good idea for her to be on her feet. He thanked the medic after he finished the bandage, dismissing him, and Colt took Elise by the arm and put her in the chair next to his desk.

"I know I asked you this already, but do you have any idea why Gambil wanted to hurt you?" Colt insisted.

She was shaking her head before he even finished the question. "I never saw him before today."

That didn't mean there wasn't a connection, and even though it was getting late and Elise would need to crash soon, he wanted to find out as much as he could while the events were still fresh in both their minds.

"What about your job?" Colt asked, trying for a different angle. "Are you working on anything controversial? Maybe running a background check on somebody who didn't want you to find something?"

Elise didn't immediately dismiss that. Not good. Because so far Colt hadn't been able to rule out anything. He wanted to be able to check something off his list, and he apparently wasn't going to be able to do that by eliminating anything work related.

"I'm working on two cases right now." Elise idly rubbed her head and winced when her finger raked over the freshly bandaged stitches.

"Want something for the pain?" he asked.

Elise looked at him. Maybe a little surprised by his concern.

"I just need you to have a clear head right now," he clarified. "Figured that wouldn't happen if you were in pain."

The corner of her mouth lifted for a split second, but there was no humor in it. He wasn't normally a jackass, but he also didn't feel too friendly toward someone who'd soon try to mess over his dad in a really bad way.

"Back to these two cases," Colt continued. "Did any red flags come up that could be connected to Gambil?"

"Nothing that immediately jumps to mind." She paused. "I'll have a second look, though. But this seems a little extreme for someone who might just be upset over a background check that I'm doing on them for a job."

Ah, he knew where this was going.

Right back to his family.

Colt was about to remind her that he and his brothers were all lawmen and not into witness intimidation, but there was another possible player in all of this. Best to stick to business rather than snarky comments that he really wanted to make.

"Could Gambil be connected to Buddy Jorgensen, the tenant who gave you all that trouble?" Colt asked.

She hesitated again as if surprised by the turn in the conversation. Another head shake. "I haven't heard from Buddy in nearly two weeks."

That didn't mean it wasn't connected. "He was furious about you moving back and threatened you."

And not just a threat. He'd tried to buy the place for double its value, but Elise had refused.

The rumor Colt had heard was that she planned to make the old place a small working ranch again where she could raise and train cutting horses. Ironic since Elise had been in such a big hurry to get off that ranch and out of town when she'd turned eighteen.

In a hurry to get away from him, too.

"After all of that happened, I did a background check on Buddy myself," Elise explained. "There wasn't anything that popped up that would indicate he has violent tendencies toward other people. Obviously, he didn't have quite that same level of respect for property because he spray painted graffiti on some of the walls."

Yeah, Colt had read the report that she'd filed after the incident.

Colt figured the background check on Buddy Jorgensen had been thorough since it was Elise's job. When it'd first come up that she'd be moving back to town, he'd checked on her job and learned she did investigations on potential high-level employees for several large companies. She had a solid reputation for identifying people who could be risks.

That, however, didn't mean she hadn't dropped the ball with Buddy.

And that's the reason Colt had already sent a text to Cooper, his brother, who was also the town sheriff. Cooper planned to get Buddy in for questioning first thing in the morning. In the meantime, Colt would look for some kind of connection between Buddy and Gambil.

"Have you found out anything else about the explosion?" she asked.

"Not yet. The registration for the truck leads to a dead end. No known address. But they were able to get Gambil's prints." From a couple of fingers, anyway. "Reed's already sent them to the Ranger lab, and they'll be analyzed. We might be able to get a match and find out if Toby Gambil was his real name."

Well, they would be if the prints were good enough. The explosion had done a lot of damage not just to the truck but to the man himself. Still, maybe the crime lab would be able to come up with something.

The front door flew open, bringing in a gust of the bitter-cold air and a leaf that went skittering across the floor. A man came right in with it, his pricey leather shoes crushing the leaf to bits.

Their visitor was Robert Joplin.

His mother's attorney and not someone who should be paying a visit to the sheriff's office this time of night. Judging from the scowl that he sent Colt's way, this was not going to be a pleasant conversation. Of course, pleasant and Robert Joplin had never gone together so far, and Colt figured that wasn't about to change.

"Elise," Joplin said like a concerned father. He hurried to her, plopped down his equally pricey briefcase next to her chair and caught onto her shoulders. "How badly were you hurt?"

"I'm okay, really." And she stood, easing away from him before she stepped back.

Colt didn't miss the shift in her body language. Not only had she put some distance between Joplin and her, but she also folded her arms over her chest. Like Elise, Colt had known Joplin his entire life and had no doubt seen Elise with him before, but this was the first time Colt had witnessed them together since she'd come back to testify for his mother.

Something that had pleased Joplin to the core, of course.

Before Elise and her statement, Joplin had to have known that he was defending a client who would almost certainly be found guilty. And probably still would be. However, Elise and what she'd supposedly witnessed on that day twenty-three years ago was now a game changer.

That made Elise Joplin's star witness.

But from the looks of it, an uncomfortable one.

Ditto for Joplin. His mouth tightened after she backed away from him. "I heard someone tried to kill you."

Elise lifted her shoulder. "A man tried to run me off the road, but he'd dead now."

Joplin aimed his index finger at Colt. "This is your fault. Yours and your family's. You've created a hostile atmosphere in Sweetwater Springs that's now made Elise a target."

Since things were about to turn real ugly, real fast, Colt got to his feet, but Elise stepped between them.

"I was mistaken when I called you earlier and told you that Colt was watching me," she said to Joplin. "It was this other man, Toby Gambil. He dressed like Colt and drove the same kind of truck."

So, that likely explained the weird body language

from both Joplin and her. Joplin thought he had some kind of proof of Colt's wrongdoing, and Elise was eating a little crow.

"It doesn't matter that Colt didn't do the deed himself," Joplin challenged. "He probably stirred up some of his cowboy friends to do this."

Colt moved out from behind Elise so he could face this idiot head-on. "I didn't stir up anybody. I damn sure didn't encourage anyone to kill her."

"You don't want her testifying for your mother."

"True enough. But that's only because I don't think the memories of a nine-year-old kid are reliable enough to tip the verdict of a murder trial. Especially since she didn't even tell anyone about those memories for twenty-three years."

"I didn't tell anyone what I saw because I didn't think it was important," Elise snapped, and when she swiveled toward Colt, there was some fire in her eyes. "It was only after Jewell was charged with Whitt Braddock's murder that I remembered what I saw that day."

"And what she saw was your father coming out of the Braddock cabin." Joplin punctuated that with a satisfied nod that made Colt want to smack him.

This was old news now, but it ate away at him just as it did when he'd first heard it two months ago. According to Elise, she'd been playing by the shallow creek near her grandmother's house and had seen Colt's father, Roy, leave the very cabin that all these years later would be labeled a crime scene. It'd taken that long to have all the evidence retested, the DNA identified, and the district attorney had used that to reopen what had been a missing person's case.

But now Whitt Braddock was officially dead.

Murdered.

And the only suspect had been his mother. Only her DNA and Whitt's had been found in the cabin. But Elise's eyewitness testimony could put his dad there, too.

Yeah, it ate away at him.

Because a lawyer like Joplin could maybe convince a jury that his father had just as much motive to kill Whitt Braddock as his mother did. With Elise's testimony putting his father at the scene, it might be more than enough to sway a jury and get charges filed against his father.

"I need Elise's testimony," Joplin said, stating the obvious. "I'll do whatever it takes to protect her. And more. I'll do your job, too. I've hired two private investigators to comb over every inch of the Braddock cabin and grounds again. They're looking for anything that might help with your mother's case, but the bottom line is that Elise is the best defensive weapon I have right now."

Colt wasn't disputing that, but it didn't mean he liked it, either.

Joplin huffed. "Look, I know you hate your mother because she abandoned you and your brothers—"

"She abandoned my dad, too," Colt interrupted. "Jewell walked out on her family because she couldn't bear living with the guilt of murdering her lover. But then, you've always had stars in your eyes when it comes to her, so I doubt you'll see her for the person she really is."

The anger bolted through Joplin, tightening all his muscles. "Because she's a good woman and doesn't deserve the way her so-called family has treated her."

"Enough!" Elise shouted. No stepping between them this time. She moved several feet away and glared at both of them. "Arguing about this won't help. That's what the trial is for. You can finish this debate there."

Great.

Now he had a victim scolding him like a third-grade

teacher. Of course, he shouldn't have gotten in any kind of contest with the likes of Joplin—even if everything Colt had said was true. The lawyer was crazy about Jewell, and Colt figured Joplin would do just about anything to clear her name.

Maybe even try to sway a someone's memory.

"You should go home, get some rest," Joplin said to Elise, sounding not only calmer but chastised, as well. "I can drive you there."

She motioned to Colt, or rather in his general vicinity. "I need to give a statement about what happened. That could take a while."

"Then, I can drive her home," Colt offered.

That earned him another huff from Joplin, but he didn't say a word to Colt. Instead, Joplin looked at Elise. "Call me when you're done, and no matter what time you finish, I'll come and get you."

She shrugged. Then nodded eventually. Colt was betting dollars to donuts that she wouldn't call. Nope. She was riled at both of them and would figure out her own way to get home.

Joplin picked up his briefcase and shot Colt one last warning look before he headed out.

"You actually told that jerk I was following you?" Colt asked.

That brought her gaze snapping back to his. "Because I honestly thought you were."

But the snapping and the fiery eyes didn't last. With a weary sigh leaving her mouth, she sank back down into the chair and buried her face in her hands.

Winced again, too, when she touched the stitches.

Colt didn't ask her about the pain this time, but he snatched up the phone, called the medic who'd just left and insisted that he bring some meds over for her right away. The hospital was just a few blocks up, so it wouldn't take long for him to arrive. She might need those meds just to get her statement done.

"What's going on between Joplin and you?" Colt came out and asked. "And don't say it's nothing because I detected more than a hair's worth of tension between you two."

A huff, but again no fire. "Sometimes I get the feeling that he'd like for me to say more."

Colt did a mental double take. *"More?"*

"He wants me to go through hypnosis to see if I can recall more details about Roy." Her gaze came back to his. "Like maybe blood on his clothes or looking disheveled, as if he'd just been in a fight with Whitt."

The sound that Colt made started out as a groan but got much louder. "This is a witch hunt. The only DNA found in that room was my mother's, along with a whole boatload of Whitt's blood."

"But your father was there the day Whitt went missing," she mumbled.

"So says you."

"Have you actually asked your father if he was there?" Elise challenged.

"No. I don't have to. If he'd killed Whitt, he would have owned up to it. He wouldn't have run. He darn sure wouldn't have abandoned his family."

But his father had admitted being more than just drunk that day and having some gaps in his memory. Of course, he'd just learned about his wife having an affair. And not just any ol' affair but with his sworn enemy. A man who'd been a thorn in his dad's side since they were young boys.

Colt went closer to her so she wouldn't miss a word. "If my father had killed Whitt, he would have almost certainly gotten blood on him. And when he sobered up, he would have seen it and gone to the sheriff."

He paused. "Have you actually asked Jewell about this?" Colt threw right back in her face.

The breath she took was thin and long. "Yes."

"And what did she say?" But he had to ask that through clenched teeth.

Elise made him wait several long moments before she answered. "Nothing."

Which sounded like a boatload of guilt to him. Innocent people usually spoke up to defend themselves.

Something Jewell had yet to do.

In fact, from all accounts, she wasn't even cooperating with her own attorney. Hadn't even hired him. Joplin had volunteered pro bono and had refused to back off even when Jewell had asked him to.

Because Elise and he were in the middle of an intense staring match, Colt nearly jumped out of his skin when the sound shot through the room. Elise gasped.

But it was only the phone.

Talk about losing focus.

"It's me," Reed said the moment that Colt answered. "The Rangers got an immediate hit on Gambil's prints."

That got his attention. Because that usually meant the prints were in AFIS, the national fingerprint database. "Gambil had a criminal record?"

"Oh, yeah. His real name is Simon Martinelli, and I just talked to one of our criminal informants about him." Reed paused, cursed. "Martinelli wasn't in town to scare Elise."

Mercy. There went the bristly feeling down his spine again. "Then why the devil was he here?"

"Because Martinelli's a hit man," Reed answered "He was sent here to kill Elise."

Chapter Four

"You know that I'm staying here with you tonight, right," Colt said when he pulled to a stop in front of her house.

Elise was certain that wasn't a question, and she wanted to insist that she didn't need a babysitter.

But she was afraid he'd disagree.

Because someone wanted her dead. Had even sent someone to end her life. And that someone had nearly succeeded.

She'd hoped the bone-deep exhaustion would tamp down the fear. It didn't. She was feeling both fear and fatigue, and that wasn't a good mix.

Nor was having Colt around.

However, the alternative was her being alone in her house that was miles from town or her nearest neighbor. And for just the rest of the night, she wasn't ready for the alone part. In the morning, though, she would have to do something to remedy it. Something that didn't include Colt and her under the same roof.

For now, that's exactly what was about to happen.

They got out of his truck, the sleet still spitting at them, and the air so cold that it burned her lungs with each breath she took. Elise's hands were still shaking, and when she tried to unlock the front door of her house, she dropped her keys, the metal clattering onto the weathered wood porch. Colt reached for them at the same time she did, and their heads ended up colliding.

Right on her stitches.

The pain shot through her, and even though Elise tried to choke back the groan, she didn't quite succeed.

"Sorry." Colt cursed and snatched the keys from her to unlock the door. His hands definitely weren't shaking.

"Wait here," he ordered the moment they stepped into the living room. He shut the door, gave her a stay-put warning glance and drew his gun before he started looking around.

Only then did Elise realize that someone—another hit man maybe—could already be hiding inside. Waiting to kill her.

Sweet heaven.

When was this going to end?

And better yet, why was it happening in the first place?

Elise glanced around at the living and dining rooms. The house wasn't big, so she had no trouble seeing directly into the kitchen. Colt checked it out and then headed to the back hall where there were three small bedrooms and a bath. She'd always felt so safe here. But at the moment, every shadow looked like someone lurking and ready to jump out and attack.

She held her breath, waiting, trying not to panic. The pain certainly didn't help, and even though she wanted to keep a clear head, she might have to resort to the meds that the medic had brought to her at the sheriff's office.

"Keep the curtains closed and stay away from the windows," Colt insisted. He reholstered his gun as he made his way back toward her. "You got a security system?"

She shook her head. Her grandparents would have

found it laughable that she needed such measures since there was usually no crime out here to speak of, but first thing in the morning Elise would definitely look into getting one.

"Do you have any friends from Dallas you can stay with for a while?" he asked.

Elise was about to assure him that she did, but she heard the judgmental tone in his voice. Or maybe that was her imagination working overtime, but she figured the tone was there. In Colt's mind, and likely everyone else's in town, she wasn't part of Sweetwater Springs anymore. She had chosen the city life, and while that didn't exactly make her an outcast, it didn't make her welcome, either.

"I have someplace I could stay," she answered, but then had another look around the house. No, correction.

Her home.

For two years she'd been making plans to come back here, and she'd finally gotten the chance. Not only because of Jewell's trial but because she finally had scraped together enough money to try to make the place into a working ranch again. It'd been her grandmother's dream.

Elise's, too.

And now someone was trying to snatch that away from her.

Yes, she could go running back to Dallas, to her friends and her job, but there was no guarantee that the danger wouldn't just follow her there. Maybe her best bet was to make a stand here. Of course, that might not turn out to be the safest way to go, and she'd be betting her life on it.

"You okay?" Colt walked back toward her, and he was sporting a concerned look on his face.

That's when Elise realized she was massaging the side of her head just above those stitches. She wasn't anywhere near okay, but saying it would only confirm what Colt already knew.

"Swear to me that your family didn't have anything to do with what happened tonight," she said.

Colt's eyes narrowed, clearly insulted. "I swear," he snarled. Then, he cursed. "And you'd better not accuse me of hiring that hit man to murder you."

No, she wouldn't accuse him of that. But it didn't mean the hit man hadn't been connected to Jewell's upcoming trial. The problem with that was figuring out who exactly involved with that trial would want her out of the picture.

They stood there. Gazes held. A little too close for comfort in the small living room. Of course, miles might be too close, considering how he felt about her. And how she felt about him.

Except her feelings were all over the place right now.

Elise blamed that on the pain and spent adrenaline— and the fact that Colt had saved her life—but her body wasn't going to let her forget that her childhood flame was just inches away. There'd always been an attraction between them, and she'd had that attraction verified on multiple occasions over the past decade when she'd been visiting her grandmother and had run into Colt.

Of course, the timing had always been wrong for her to act on that attraction.

He'd either been involved with someone or vice versa. Plus, there was him resenting her running off to another life. Which she had indeed done. Chasing that greener grass that hadn't turned out to be so green, after all.

Elise had always figured the attraction would just fade away. But she was rethinking that now.

Nope, it was still there. On her part, anyway.

Colt reached out, and for one heart-slamming moment, Elise thought he was reaching for her. Her stomach did a little flip-flop, and she felt something else.

That trickle of heat.

A trickle that she tried to cool down fast. But Colt cooled it for her when he didn't touch her but instead reached around her and locked the door.

"What?" he questioned, doing a double take when he looked at her face.

She saw the exact moment when it registered that it was not a question that he wanted answered aloud, and he didn't want her feeling anything for him. Didn't want to feel anything but contempt for her, either.

Elise was pretty sure they both failed at that.

It didn't mean anything would happen between them. It wouldn't. No way would Colt let something like an old attraction play into this when his father's life was essentially at stake. However, even that didn't cool the old fire that'd started to simmer again.

His mouth tightened, and he tipped his head to the sofa. "I'll need a blanket and a pillow."

"I have a guest room," she offered.

He shook his head, fast. "The sofa's fine."

Maybe because the guest room was right next to hers. Or maybe because he wanted to keep an eye on the front door in case another would-be killer showed up. That reminder didn't help with the fear or the throbbing in her head.

"It's just a precaution," Colt added, as if he'd read her mind. "Since you don't have a security system or a dog, I'd rather be out here where I can hear if anyone drives up."

She nodded, forced her feet to get moving to the linen

closet in the hall, but Elise had only made it a few steps when Colt's phone buzzed. Just like that, her heart went to her throat again, and she pulled in her breath, praying that nothing else had gone wrong.

"Reed," Colt said, answering the call.

He didn't put it on speaker, and Elise figured it wasn't a good idea for her to get close enough to him to hear what his fellow deputy was saying. However, judging from the way Colt's jaw tightened again, this wasn't good news.

"He did what?" Colt answered in response to whatever Reed had said. "No, I'll call Cooper," he added and then ended the call.

"What happened now?" she asked when Colt just stood there, glaring at the phone.

"It's Joplin. He's claiming that the attack on you is grounds for a mistrial, and he wants the charges against Jewell dismissed."

It wasn't totally unexpected news, but clearly Colt blamed her at least in part for what Jewell's lawyer was doing.

"There's more?" she asked when he just glared at her.

"Yeah, there's more." Colt pressed a button on his phone as if he'd declared war on it. "Joplin convinced the county district attorney to look into charging my father with your attempted murder."

COLT STARED AT the coffeepot, willing it to brew faster than it was. He needed another hit of caffeine now. Maybe, just maybe it'd get rid of the cobwebs before Elise finished her shower and hit him with the questions that she no doubt would have.

Questions that he still couldn't answer.

All these hours later, everything was still up in the

air. They had no leads on the identity of the person who'd hired the hit man, Simon Martinelli, and so far, Cooper hadn't managed to convince the county DA that his father was innocent.

That riled him to the core.

His dad had been through too much already what with Jewell's return to Sweetwater Springs. Now his father might not only be charged with Elise's attempted murder but also the very homicide that Colt was certain Jewell had committed.

Well, almost certain.

But even if it hadn't been her, then his father damn sure hadn't been the one to kill Whitt Braddock. That meant Colt had to figure out a way to keep his dad out of jail along with making sure Elise wasn't attacked again. It would help to find out who was behind the attempt to kill her. If he could prove his father had no part in that, then the county DA would back off.

He hoped.

Of course, there was still the problem with Elise's testimony itself. With those old memories, she could put his father at the crime scene, and because Roy had been drunk, there was no way he could refute it.

"Is that scowl for me?" Elise asked.

Colt cursed and nearly scalded his hand with the coffee he was pouring. He'd been in such deep thought about his dad that he hadn't heard her come into the kitchen. Hardly the vigilant lawman that he needed to be right now, and that seemed to be a particular problem for him anytime he was around her.

"Yes, it's for you," he mumbled.

But that lie died on his lips when he looked at her.

She was dressed simply in jeans and a red sweater, but every bit of the fear and worry was still etched on her face. Coupled with that bandage on the side of her head and the dark circles under her eyes, it was obvious that her night had been as bad as his.

Maybe worse.

After all, no one had tried to kill him in the past twelve hours.

Elise made a soft sound of frustration and stepped around him to get a cup from the cabinet. "Well, I would scowl back, but the stitches hurt when I move my face." She added a dry smile and winced to prove it.

Colt hated that attempt at bad humor, not only because he wasn't in the mood for any kind of humor but also because he knew that it had indeed hurt. Too bad the man responsible for those stitches and her pain had been blown to smithereens and couldn't give them any answers.

However, Martinelli wasn't the only way to get to the bottom of this. It would take some good old-fashioned detective work.

"I'm having inquiries made about the two people you're doing background checks on," Colt let her know, and he tipped his head to the paper on the table that he'd been using to make notes.

Obviously, she hadn't expected that because her eyes widened just a fraction. "But I didn't give you their names yet."

He gave her a flat look, tapped his badge. "Meredith Darrow and Duane Truett. I got the names from your boss when I called him in the middle of the night."

Yet something else she hadn't expected. And obviously didn't approve of. Her boss hadn't cared much for the late-night call, either, but the man had cooperated after he'd learned that Elise could have been killed.

"I knew you'd finally taken some pain meds, and I

didn't want to wake you up to get the names, so I called him. I needed to get a head start on the investigation."

That was the only apology Colt intended to issue about doing his job.

Elise walked to the table, looked over his notes and her attention stayed on the first name he'd jotted down. "'Buddy Jorgensen,'" she read off. Her former tenant. "I already told you that I ran a check on him. He doesn't have as much as a parking ticket."

"Neither do some serial killers before they're caught." Extreme, yes, but he was trying to make a point here. "It won't hurt to run another check. Is that Buddy's handi-work on the side of the barn?"

She nodded but didn't even glance out the window, though the barn was only about ten yards away and clearly visible from this side of the house. The morning sun practically spotlighted the paint that'd been splat-tered like blood across the gray-weathered boards. No words or drawings, just the red eyesore. Apparently, Buddy had done the same to the interior of the house, but Elise had already painted over it.

However, she couldn't paint over or dismiss the hostility that was now between Buddy and her. Buddy hadn't wanted to leave the place that he'd rented for over five years. But then he'd been more than just a tenant. He'd worked the ranch, reseeding the pasture and bring-ing in some livestock.

All gone now.

Buddy had taken them with him, but there were signs that Elise was planning to bring in her own cattle along with making some much-needed repairs. There was a stretch of land already marked off with stakes and small flags where she apparently intended to build a stable for the cutting horses she wanted to raise.

"I think Buddy left town, because I haven't heard from him since the paint incident," she explained. "He also apologized for the vandalism and paid for me to have it repainted."

"That's not going to get him off the suspects list," Colt insisted. "Why didn't you have the paint taken off the barn?"

"Because I'm having that one torn down. It needs a lot of repairs, and it was cheaper just to build a new one. It would be a waste of money to repaint it."

Still, it couldn't be easy to look at that every day. It wasn't a threat, but it was a reminder that someone had gotten close enough to vandalize her home and property.

Colt tapped Meredith's name. "Any reason she'd be upset with you?"

Elise paused. "No reason that she would know of yet." Another pause. "I'm not exactly giving her a favorable background check, but it'll be at least another day or two before she learns about that. I just finished my report on her yesterday. But from what I uncovered about her, she could end up facing criminal charges for misusing corporate funds."

So, that could be motive, but there hadn't been enough time for her to have hired a hit man. Well, unless Meredith had already gotten word of what would be in Elise's report. It was definitely something Colt wanted to find out.

"And what about him?" Colt asked, tapping Duane Truett's name.

"Nothing. He's squeaky clean."

Colt would still put the man under the microscope. There was a reason someone had come after Elise, and he wanted to know who and why.

"Really?" Elise said, looking at the last name on the list. "You suspect Joplin hired Martinelli?"

Colt hadn't just added it as an afterthought, he'd also underlined it. "He's got motive. If he slings enough mud at my father, or at me and my brothers, then he could get a mistrial."

And Jewell could go free.

Colt wouldn't care about that as long as going free meant Jewell left town and that there were no charges or allegations made against the rest of his family.

That wasn't likely to happen, though.

If Jewell was cleared, the blame for Whitt's murder would almost certainly fall right on his father.

"I called Joplin before I got in the shower," Elise said after she had a long sip of coffee. "I told him to back off on arresting your dad."

Colt had to replay that in his head. "And?"

She lifted her shoulder, sighed. "I don't think it did any good. Joplin's looking for a way to get the murder charges dropped against Jewell, and he thinks this is his best shot at making that happen."

"Yeah, by arresting an innocent man."

When Elise didn't argue with his *innocent* declaration, Colt glanced at her. Hard to miss her expression since they were both right in front of the coffeepot and practically elbow to elbow. He moved away from her but not before his arm brushed against her, and he felt that blasted kick.

Oh, man.

Too bad he was in between relationships right now because he would have liked to have turned this bad fire in a different direction. As it was, it went straight to Elise.

"Another scowl," she mumbled.

And he hoped she didn't ask him what this particular one was about. Best not to remind her of an attraction that he was trying hard to forget.

"Hey, I'm only testifying about what I saw," she went on. "Your father coming out of the Braddock cabin around the time that Whitt Braddock went missing. I didn't see Roy commit a murder or any other crime other than maybe trespassing. And that's what I'll say when I take the witness stand."

Colt just stared at her.

"Oh." Elise suddenly got interested in staring at her coffee. "*That.* I thought the scowl was for your father."

"It was." Not a total lie. It mostly was. "And the *that* isn't something we're going to discuss. Old water, old bridge."

It sounded good, but judging from the way Elise quickly dodged his gaze, that water and the bridge weren't quite as old as they wanted them to be.

His phone buzzed, finally, giving him a timely distraction and hopefully some good news in the process. "Cooper," he answered when he saw his brother's name pop up on the screen.

"The FBI will question Dad here in about an hour," Cooper said, skipping any greeting.

They weren't wasting any time. "I'll be there soon."

"With Elise?" Cooper immediately asked.

Colt had to think about that a moment. Best not to leave her alone until she'd worked out some other arrangement or until he'd gotten someone else to watch her. "Unless you got a better idea."

"No. Bring her. I want to talk to her."

Oh, mercy. That wouldn't be good for Elise or the investigation. And it might look as if the McKinnons were ganging up on her. Joplin would only use that to put the screws to their father.

"She's hurt and still in pain," Colt added. "She'll come with me, but I'd rather keep her out of this."

Cooper's silence was long and unnerving in a way only an older brother/boss could have managed. "Bring her," Cooper ordered and hung up.

"I heard," Elise said before Colt could fill her in. That put some steel in her cool blue eyes. "No matter what Cooper or anyone else says to me, I'm not changing my testimony."

"Good." And he meant it. "Because despite what you think of us, we're not into obstruction of justice or witness tampering."

She made a sound to indicate she didn't fully buy that. "I'll get my purse, and on the way to the sheriff's office, I can make some calls and find a safe place to go."

Colt hoped that a safe place was possible for her. Still, it wasn't his problem.

Even if it felt as if it was.

While she went back into the bedroom, he downed the rest of his coffee and reached for his coat. But reaching was as far as he got.

Something caught his eye.

Some movement out the window.

He stepped back, his gaze combing over the grounds. And he finally saw something that he definitely didn't want to see.

"What's wrong?" Elise asked the moment she came back into the room. She had obviously noticed his body language and that his attention was nailed to the barn.

"Are you expecting any workers or ranch hands today who would have a reason to go into your barn?"

"No," she answered on a rise of breath. "Why?"

"Because somebody's in there."

Colt drew his gun and headed for the front door.

Chapter Five

Elise reached for Colt to stop him from going outside, but it was already too late. He unlocked the door and hurried out onto the porch before she could tell him to wait for backup to arrive.

"Stay put," Colt insisted. "And call 911 and have Cooper get someone out here."

Just like that, her pulse revved up, and the fear returned with a vengeance. After what'd happened the night before, she figured this wasn't some coincidence.

A killer could be in her barn.

Elise made the 911 call, and the emergency dispatcher assured her that help was on the way.

The question was—would help arrive in time?

Her house wasn't exactly on the beaten path, and it would take the sheriff or one of the deputies at least twenty minutes to get out to this part of the county. That might not be nearly soon enough, and Colt was out there alone, maybe about to face down yet another person who'd been sent to murder her.

She hurried into the kitchen and took the gun from the cabinet near the fridge before she went back to the window to keep watch. She wouldn't be much backup for Colt, but maybe he'd be able to diffuse the situation before it turned violent.

Maybe.

She didn't see any movement in the barn. Didn't see Colt at first, either, but then Elise caught a glimpse of him on the side of the front porch right before he jumped down next to some shrubs. He waited, obviously listening, with his attention nailed to the gaping hole where there'd once been a barn door.

"I'm Deputy McKinnon," Colt called out, taking aim. "Come out with your hands in the air."

Elise gulped down her breath. Waited, too, and just when she thought Colt was going to have to go in after the intruder, she saw someone in the doorway of the barn. She lifted her gun. Took aim, as well. And watched as the sandy-haired man stepped out from the shadows.

Buddy.

What the heck was he doing here?

She groaned, releasing her breath and lowering her gun. But Colt certainly didn't lower his. He kept it pinned to her former tenant.

"No need for that gun," Buddy snarled, but he did keep his hands raised in the air. Even though he had a loud voice, she opened the window so she could hear him better. "I just came here to get the rest of my things."

"You're trespassing," Colt insisted.

"I'll only be here long enough to pick up a few things," he answered. Of course, that didn't explain the trespassing accusation. "After I'm finished, I'll be leaving town."

He'd told Elise that nearly two weeks ago, so either something had delayed him or he'd lied to her. She didn't like either possibility.

Buddy eased his hands down to his sides, but he didn't drop the glare that he was giving Colt. And her. Buddy snagged her gaze through the window screen, and she had no trouble seeing that he was still past the point of being angry at her.

After the night that Colt and she had had, the last thing she needed was Buddy showing up with more demands and a surly attitude. Feeling pretty surly herself, Elise shut the window and went out onto the porch so she could confront Buddy face-to-face. Obviously, though, Colt didn't like her being outside, because he shot her a split-second glare of his own.

Tough.

She stayed put.

"Got the law sleeping over here with you now?" Buddy asked her.

It wasn't just a simple question. Maybe he'd heard about the trouble from the hit man or maybe he was just trying to goad her by implying that Colt and she were having an affair.

"It's my house," she answered. "I can invite anyone I want to come here. Or sleep over. But I definitely didn't invite you."

"Didn't figure I needed an invite to get my own things," Buddy snapped.

"Well, you were wrong." Elise made sure she added her own dose of surliness to that.

Of course, it wasn't a bigger dose than Colt's.

"Go back inside," Colt warned her. Glared at her, too. "And call Cooper again to tell him I don't need backup. I can handle this on my own. But let him know that Buddy's here and that I want somebody to run a quick check on him to find out why he's still in town."

Elise debated the wisdom of him handling this alone as well as her going back inside, but Buddy didn't appear to be armed. Despite the bitter cold, he wasn't even wearing a coat, and the frayed drab gray sweatshirt hugged his beer gut enough that it didn't seem he was carrying a concealed weapon.

She made the call to Dispatch to cancel the backup and to ask for the check on Buddy, as Colt had requested, but Elise stayed put on the porch.

Oh, yes. That made Colt's glare even worse.

"You've already picked up all your things. Why'd you come back?" she asked Buddy.

He hitched his thumb toward the hayloft. "I forgot about a box of stuff still up there."

Colt glanced back at her to see if that was true, but Elise had to shrug. The ladder leading to the loft was rickety at best, and she hadn't gone up there since her return. There was no telling what was up there.

"Get the box," Colt told Buddy. "But if you remember anything else you left, call first and get permission from Elise."

That caused Buddy's nostrils to flare. "This place is my home, you know. Lived here over five years while Elise was off gallivanting in the city. If it hadn't been for me, this barn and that house would have probably fallen down by now."

"I wasn't gallivanting." Elise thought her nostrils might have flared, too. "I was working. And you were paid for any repairs you made."

She had the proof, too, since Buddy had sent her the bills, and she'd deducted the cost from his rent.

"You can't pay a person for making a house into a home," he snarled.

"And this isn't your home. It's Elise's," Colt reminded him. "It's been in her family since well before any of us were born."

"Home," Buddy repeated like profanity. His attention drifted to the place that she had staked out for a new stable. "She'll run it into the ground. She's all city now. No way can she make a go of this place."

It wasn't exactly the first time she'd faced that attitude, probably wouldn't be the last, either. But it wouldn't put her off. Especially not coming from Buddy.

"Where were you last night?" Colt demanded.

That didn't help with Buddy's angry body language, and he didn't jump to answer. "Any reason you're asking?"

"Because Elise ran into some trouble. I hope that trouble didn't come because of you."

"Not a chance. I don't want her here, but I didn't do nothing about it. If she had trouble, she probably brought it on herself."

Colt made a skeptical sound. "Or you could have helped it along. Where were you last night?" he repeated. "This time, I want an answer. If not here, then you can answer it at the sheriff's office."

"You're serious?" Buddy barked.

"Oh, yeah. Now answer me."

Buddy's glare eased up a bit, and after he did some mumbling, he scratched the scruff on his chin. "I started the night off at the Outlaw Bar, had a few drinks and left around midnight, I guess."

The incident with Martinelli had happened nearly two hours earlier, which meant Buddy wasn't involved. Well, if he was telling the truth, that is. Elise hadn't exactly trusted the man before this latest incident, and she certainly didn't trust him any more now.

"Were you with anybody at the Outlaw Bar who can confirm you were there?" Colt pressed.

Buddy shook his head. "Didn't know I'd need somebody to vouch for me."

"Well, you do."

That got Buddy cursing again. "You might be wearing a badge, Colt McKinnon, but that doesn't give you any right to talk to me like this."

Colt was no doubt about to dispute that, but Elise spoke before he could.

"Did you try to have me killed?" Elise came out and asked despite Buddy's latest round of profanity.

Colt shot her another back-off glance, which she ignored. She'd been dealing with Buddy for weeks now, and she thought she might be able to tell if he was lying. Or at least she might be able to push a button or two to get him to come clean.

"Kill you?" Buddy questioned. And his mouth twitched as if threatening to smile. "Wasn't me. But I guess you got more than just me ticked off at you, huh?"

Maybe. But Elise wondered if this was all truly connected to Buddy and his venom over her not selling him the place? She'd been so quick to pin the blame on Colt's family and the testimony that she would give for Jewell, but Buddy was certainly acting like a guilty man.

"Since it's pretty clear this isn't going to be a friendly chat, I'll get that box and leave," Buddy grumbled. "If I do any more talking to you, Deputy, I should probably have a lawyer with me so you don't try to pin any trumped-up charges on me."

With that, Buddy turned and went into the barn.

Colt huffed and moved back onto the porch with her. "I really don't want you outside with Buddy still here," he insisted.

She understood Colt's concern, but she wanted to show Buddy that she wasn't afraid of him.

Even if she was.

Either the man was mentally unstable or he had a strange attachment to her childhood home.

"If you won't go inside, at least move into the doorway," Colt pressed.

Because he was genuinely concerned about her safety. Elise was, too. So, she moved back.

"Did you see Buddy's truck anywhere?" Colt asked her.

Elise had another look around the grounds. "No." And she could see clear to the end of the road that led to her house. There weren't any motels or rental properties nearby, so that likely meant Buddy had parked on the main road itself.

Where his truck wouldn't be seen.

A man with nothing to hide wouldn't do that.

"If he'd knocked on the door and asked to get the box from the barn," she said, "I would have let him. So why all the secrecy?"

"Because maybe he wants more than just that box." Colt shot her another warning glance. "And that's another good reason for you to go inside."

Since he was right, and she was tired of arguing, Elise huffed again and stepped just inside the living room. That way, she could still see the barn and help Colt keep watch but without being right out in the open.

As Colt was.

Of course, he'd argue that it was his job to take risks like that, but Elise hated that he was essentially risking his life for her.

It didn't take long for Buddy to come back out of the barn, and he was indeed carrying a cardboard box. Thankfully, he had both hands around it, which would have made it hard for him to pull a weapon.

"Walking far with that box?" Colt asked. He went down the side steps of the porch, heading straight for

Buddy. Elise moved back into the doorway so she could hear Buddy's answer.

"Not far. Just up the road." Buddy called out. He kept walking, but he glanced over at her. "I figured I'd be in and out before Elise even got out of bed. If I'd driven up, the engine might have wakened her."

Elise wasn't buying that. Of course, maybe there was nothing sinister about this and Buddy simply hadn't wanted to run into her this morning. After the argument they'd just had, she could understand why he'd want to avoid something like that.

Still...

Colt caught up with Buddy, and he had a look in the box. Elise couldn't see what was inside it, but it didn't seem to alarm Colt any more than he already was.

"It's just papers and old magazines!" Buddy yelled. "I'm not taking anything that's not mine."

Colt stepped in front of Buddy, forcing the man to stop. "Then you won't mind if I check."

He didn't wait for permission. Colt rifled through the box while Buddy's shoulders and back got even stiffer. Colt must not have found anything because after a thorough look, he stepped aside. Buddy grumbled something that she didn't catch and continued walking up the road.

Colt kept his attention on the man, but he came back onto the porch. To stand guard, she quickly realized. Protecting her again.

"I'll make some calls," she volunteered. "And get some security arrangements started. Maybe I can even get a security system installed today."

Colt huffed. "But you're insisting on staying here." He tipped his head toward Buddy. "What if he shows up again? Or what if another hit man does?" Colt didn't wait for her to answer. "Look, I know it's uncomfortable for you having me here, so I'll call the Rangers and have them send out a protection detail."

"I'm less uncomfortable than I was," she mumbled. She no doubt should have kept that to herself. "Well, about some things, anyway."

That, too. No way should she have said that aloud to Colt because he knew exactly what she meant.

He looked over his shoulder at her, and despite the fact that they'd just had the adrenaline-spiking encounter with Buddy, she saw something else in his eyes. The reason why she shouldn't put up even a smidgen of a fight about having someone guard her.

Those McKinnon eyes—and pretty much the rest of him—were playing havoc with her body.

Colt gave Buddy another glance, no doubt to make sure the man was indeed leaving. He was. And Colt took her by the arm and moved her deeper into the living room before he shut the door. He opened his mouth, closed it and opened it again only to curse.

"Hell," he mumbled, reholstering his gun.

In the same motion, he leaned in and put his mouth on hers.

Elise wasn't sure who was more surprised by that, her or Colt. She felt the tightness of his lips. For a second, anyway. And then no more tightening. It turned into a full-fledged kiss.

One that she instantly felt.

The heat rippled through her. Mouth to toes. Warming her. Then, firing her body in a really good-bad way. It brought to the surface all those feelings that she'd been trying to pretend didn't exist.

Well, the pretense was over.

The feelings existed, all right.

She'd been attracted to Colt since she was old enough to feel attraction, and apparently that hadn't changed one bit. If anything, that kiss had made it a heck of a lot worse.

Mercy, he'd gotten even better at this since they were teenagers. Not that she'd expected anything less. With those hot cowboy looks, he'd no doubt had a lot of practice. Something that cooled the heat down just a bit.

She definitely didn't want to be another notch on Colt's bedpost.

Yes, they'd made out before, but they'd never gone further than that. Elise figured it was a good idea if that continued. And the best way for that to happen was for the kiss to stop.

He pulled back, his gaze snapping to hers. His gaze then lowering right back to her mouth.

"That was a mistake," he informed her.

Then he dropped another of those scalding kisses on her mouth. He cursed some more, backed away from her. "And that's also proof of why I need to put you in someone else's protective custody."

Elise couldn't argue with that, even if that's exactly what her body wanted her to do. However, she didn't get a chance to say anything one way or the other because Colt's phone buzzed.

"It's Reed," Colt said, glancing down at the screen. He took the call, but he also looked out the front window. So did Elise, but she could no longer see Buddy.

Despite the heat and the tension still crackling between them, Elise moved closer so she could hear what Reed was saying. And she heard, all right. Something she didn't want to hear.

"We got a problem," Reed said.

"Hell," Colt mumbled. "What's wrong now?"

"I just got the results of Buddy's background check. If he's still there, you need to bring him in now."

Chapter Six

Colt glanced through the report that Reed handed him, and he cursed. Something he'd been doing a lot of lately, but he might do a lot more before this was over.

Elise, too.

Standing beside him in the sheriff's office, she shook her head when she looked over the report on Buddy. Her attention landed on the same thing that'd caught Colt's eye.

That Buddy had been in juvie lockup when he was fifteen for assault with a deadly weapon.

And that his cell mate had been none other than Simon Martinelli, the now-dead hit man.

"Sweet heaven," she mumbled, and she dropped down in the seat next to Colt's desk. Judging from the way she rubbed her head, it was still hurting, and this sure wouldn't help matters.

"This didn't come up during the background check I ran on him," Elise added.

"It wouldn't have," Colt assured her. "Juvenile records are sealed."

She looked up at Reed and him, volleying glances between them. No doubt wondering how they'd managed to get the records unsealed, but Colt just shrugged.

"Reed has a few connections that he uses on occasions like this."

Reed nodded. "After the stunt Buddy pulled vandalizing your place, I thought it was strange that he didn't have a record. So, I kept digging."

And the digging had paid off. It'd given them a direct connection between Buddy and Martinelli. But there was just one problem with that.

Buddy was nowhere to be found.

The moment Reed had told him what was in the report, Colt had gone after Buddy, but the man had practically disappeared. There was an APB out on him, though, and Colt figured he would show up sooner or later. He just hoped that Buddy didn't show up around Elise. She'd already been through more than enough.

That blasted kiss included.

She darn sure didn't need any more complications to her life, but Colt had added a big one by kissing her. Twice! Heck, he'd added a big complication for himself, too, because now he was personally involved in something and with someone he shouldn't be. Especially considering he had so many other things that should be holding his attention.

"We'll find Buddy," Colt told her. "In the meantime, we'll keep searching for proof that he's the one who hired Martinelli. Unless Martinelli owed Buddy a huge favor and worked free, we might be able to get a court order and find a money trail for payment."

Elise lifted her head, looked at him. "Buddy has money. About a hundred thousand dollars. It's an account in his late mother's name, but since he was on the account, he still draws funds from it. The last time I checked, he'd withdrawn thirteen hundred."

Now it was Reed and Colt's turn to look at her. "I have connections that I use on occasions like this," she repeated.

"Legal connections?" Colt pressed.

She stared at him. "You really want to know?"

He groaned. Colt didn't mind her bending the law but not in this case. "If it's legal, we can skip the court order and try to connect that money to Martinelli."

"You'll need that court order," she confirmed. "The source I used won't own up to helping me. It wasn't illegal. Not exactly," Elise added in a mumble. "But my source could have cut a few corners."

Great. So now they needed to go about this in a way where they could actually build a case against Buddy.

"Thirteen hundred," Reed said. "That's not a big sum for a hit man, but killers have been hired for less."

Colt didn't like the way that caused Elise to cringe, but this was possibly a piece of evidence that could end in Buddy's arrest and put a stop to the danger. Not just for Elise but for his father. If Buddy had indeed done this, then it would clear his father's name.

About this, anyway.

They'd still have to deal with Elise's testimony, but Colt decided to take on one battle at a time.

Battles that involved keeping his mouth away from Elise's.

"I need to call Cooper," Colt said, taking out his phone. "He's at the county jail right now where the FBI's about to start questioning my dad."

"I'll do that for you," Reed volunteered. He tipped his head to the two messages that were waiting on Colt's desk. "You need to call them back."

Colt had already glanced at the message on top. It was from the Texas Rangers, and he was supposed to contact them with a time and place for them to take over protection detail for Elise. She glanced at the message, too, her eyebrow lifting, and Colt was about to make that call when he looked at the next message.

It was from Robert Joplin with a message to contact him ASAP.

"Did Joplin say what he wanted?" Colt asked.

Reed glanced at Elise. "Joplin made her an appointment to see a hypnotist this morning. So he can find out what else she remembers about what she saw at the cabin."

At best, the timing sucked. At worst, it was flat-out dangerous for Elise to be going to any appointments. With Buddy's money and criminal connections, he could simply hire another hit man to come after her.

Or come after her himself.

Either way, Colt didn't want to make this easier for him, and having Elise out and about was a good way to do that.

"Joplin's pressing hard," Reed commented, and he stepped aside to make the call to Cooper.

Colt hoped that pressing hard was all the man was doing. "Joplin's already put in for a mistrial, and he's looking for anything to clear Jewell's name. *Anything*," he repeated under his breath.

Elise stared at him. "Not *that*."

It was spooky that they were on the same wavelength. Of course, Colt hadn't bothered to hide his disdain for Jewell's lawyer since the man seemed hell-bent on pinning the murder charge on anyone but his client.

"Why not?" Colt asked.

She huffed and got to her feet. "Because I refuse to believe that Joplin would have me murdered all for the sake of getting a mistrial."

"Maybe murder wasn't the plan. Not your murder, anyway. He could have hired Martinelli to run you off the road but not kill you. It would have accomplished the same thing—it would have made it look as if me or someone in my family was trying to obstruct justice. Then he could have eliminated Martinelli."

Obviously being on the same wavelength didn't mean Elise agreed with him. "Joplin has never said or done anything threatening toward me. Now you think he's capable of murder?"

"Murdering a piece of scum like Martinelli—yes. And he'd be saving his client in the process."

Of course, Elise could have been seriously hurt. Or worse.

"It would also explain why Martinelli didn't just shoot you when he ran you off the road," Colt added. "And Joplin could have had those explosives set to make sure that Martinelli never told anyone who hired him."

She was shaking her head before he even finished, but the head shaking stopped, and she sank down into the chair again. "You believe Joplin could do this because he's in love with Jewell."

Oh, yeah. "They were high school sweethearts, and from everything I've heard, he didn't take it too well when she dumped him to marry my dad. He could see this as his chance to get her back and get my dad out of the picture."

Elise didn't jump to deny that. She sat there, obviously giving his theory plenty of thought. "Still, it would mean he committed murder."

Okay, so there was the denial, after all. Except she did take several more moments to think about it. "I'll call Joplin and have him cancel the appointment with the hypnotist," Elise finally said, reaching for the phone.

Good. At a minimum, it would keep her away from Joplin until Colt had more time to get to the bottom of this. And just in case it was Buddy behind the situation and not Joplin, canceling the appointment would also keep her from going someplace where she'd be easy pickings for another hit man.

Elise and Reed started their calls, and Colt was about to press in the number for the Rangers when he spotted a tall, thin woman making a beeline for the sheriff's office. Elise obviously noticed her, too, because she quickly ended the call with Joplin and got to her feet.

"You know her?" Colt immediately asked.

She pulled back her shoulders. "We haven't met, but I recognize her from her pictures. That's Meredith Darrow."

The woman Elise had recently run a background check on. A less-than-favorable one from what Elise had told him, but Meredith wasn't supposed to know about that report for another couple of days.

Judging from her tight expression, the woman had learned early. Colt figured her coming here wasn't a coincidence.

Meredith stepped inside, unwinding a pricey-looking scarf from her neck and removing her equally pricey-looking shades. Her gaze landed on him, and his badge, before her frosty green eyes went to Elise.

"Elise Nichols, I presume," Meredith said, her voice as frosty as the rest of her. Her pale blond hair, bleached-out skin and stark white coat reminded Colt of an icicle. "I drove out to your house first looking for you, and when you weren't there, I decided to come into town. Someone at the diner said they thought they'd seen you come into the sheriff's office."

Colt figured that same person could have also told

Meredith about Elise nearly being killed. Trouble of that sort didn't stay under wraps long in a small town.

"What can I do for you?" Elise asked, her tone a lot more polite than their visitor's.

"You can stop telling lies about me, that's what." Meredith shoved the shades and the scarf into her purse as if she'd declared war on them. Declared war on Elise, too.

"I don't know what you mean," Elise insisted.

"Of course you do. I read the report you sent to Frank Wellerman, the owner of the company where I applied for a job. All lies, and those lies cost me big-time. Now I could end up facing charges. I'm not going to jail because of some pencil pusher like you."

Since Colt didn't like the crazy look in Meredith's eyes, he tried to step between them, but Elise would have no part of that. Even though she obviously wasn't feeling well enough to be standing toe-to-toe with this irate woman.

"They weren't lies," Elise answered. "I was very careful and thorough with my research. I'd be happy to go over each area with you. In private."

"You think I care if this cowboy cop knows the lies you told about me? I don't," Meredith snapped. "I only want you to call Frank Wellerman and tell him that it was all a mistake. That you gave him the wrong report. Then he'll back off, and I won't end up facing charges."

"It wasn't a mistake." Elise paused. "And how'd you get the report, anyway? Mr. Wellerman assured me that he wouldn't talk to you about this until Monday, two days from now."

Meredith's chin came up. "It doesn't matter how I found out."

Which meant the woman had likely done some

hacking or at least something unethical to get her hands on that report.

"All that matters is this situation will be corrected *now*," Meredith insisted. "And you'll be the one correcting it."

Colt had heard enough of these threats. "What exactly do you think Elise lied about?"

The woman spared him a glance but kept her attention pinned to Elise. "She claimed there were some irregularities with the accounts of my current job. There's nothing wrong with those accounts. Then she implied the so-called missing funds might be linked to my brother."

"Leo Darrow," Elise explained to Colt. "He has a criminal record under an alias. I found it and included it in my report since Leo's record is for misappropriation of funds and embezzlement."

"You had no right to dig into his past," Meredith insisted.

"But I did. Companies pay me to be thorough." Elise looked at Colt. "I thought it was a red flag that her brother has been trying to do business with Frank Wellerman's company for months now but has never been able to get his foot in the door. I was concerned that maybe he was using his sister to help with that."

Meredith stabbed a perfectly manicured nail in Elise's direction. "Leo served his time, and you should have never brought him into this. *Never!*"

Since Elise had already admitted that she bent the law when searching financials, Colt didn't ask her how she'd gotten the information on Meredith. Besides, he had a bigger fish to fry.

"Someone ran Elise off the road last night," Colt tossed out there. "What do you know about that?"

Meredith made a sound of outrage.

"Well?" he pressed.

"I know nothing about it, and I resent the implication that I had anything to do with that."

"Yeah, yeah," he grumbled and turned back to Elise. "Does the ice princess have the funds to hire someone to do some dirty work?"

"She does," Elise answered without hesitation.

Colt nodded and made sure the stare he aimed at Meredith was all lawman. "Then I'm going to ask if you knew a man named Simon Martinelli?"

"Of course not." Meredith didn't hesitate, either, but again that didn't prove she was telling the truth.

"I'll do some checking," Reed volunteered. "I'll see if there's a connection, and if there is, I'll arrest you."

That clearly didn't please Meredith. "I'll be back with my lawyer, but I'm warning you, you'd better back off. I'm obviously not the only one you've managed to upset. Well, it serves you right."

Elise shook her head. "What do you mean?"

Colt wanted to know the same darn thing.

"I saw your barn," Meredith said as if that explained everything.

"You mean the red-paint splatter?" Colt asked.

"Splatter?" Meredith repeated, shaking her head. "This was more than just that. Judging from what I saw, someone obviously wants you dead."

Chapter Seven

Elise dreaded what she would see when she got home. Of course, with everything else that'd happened, nothing should surprise her. However, she figured there was plenty that could make her even more afraid than she was now.

And angry.

She was sick of feeling like the victim. Sick of having someone throw her life into upheaval this way. And especially sick of having to rely on Colt. Yet here he was again, driving her home to face heaven knew what.

Meredith had said there were death threats scrawled on the barn. Better than having someone try to run her off the road, but it was still another attempt to upset her and maybe try to force her to leave town.

"Thank you for doing this," she mumbled to Colt.

"No need to thank me. No way would I have let you come back out here by yourself."

Nor would Elise have come alone. As sick and angry as she was about the incidents, she wasn't stupid and didn't want to make herself an easy target for another attack, and coming alone would have done just that.

Colt glanced at her, but then he continued those lawman glimpses all around them. No doubt making sure that someone wasn't following them. Elise was trying to make sure of that, too, because after all, someone could have used this as a ruse to get them back out in the open. That's the reason that Reed was following behind them in his truck. That, and because they weren't sure what they were about to face when she got home.

The death-threat graffiti might not be all they'd have to deal with.

There could be someone waiting to try to kill her.

And that brought her right back to their suspects.

"Buddy could have made a return visit," she said. In fact, he was the most likely candidate since he'd already vandalized the barn once.

Colt made a sound of agreement. "We'll find him, question him. We'll also question Meredith again since she admitted to being out here."

Yet something else that was unnerving. The woman obviously despised her and had come all the way out to her home to threaten her. Of course, that led Elise to the next thought.

"If Meredith did this, wouldn't she know she'd be an automatic suspect?" she asked.

"Yeah, but she might have seen the other paint splatter and thought she could blame it on someone else. A sort of reverse psychology."

True. "Joplin might be trying to use reverse psychology, as well. Especially since this wasn't a physical threat against me." But she hated to think that Jewell's lawyer or anyone else would go to such extremes. Of course, someone had gone to an even bigger extreme than this by hiring a hit man.

Elise paused. "Do you think anyone in Whitt Braddock's family could be behind all this?"

Colt shrugged. "I don't see why. His wife and kids probably don't care who's convicted for his death. They just want justice. None of them have said a thing about you returning to testify for Jewell."

She had to agree with that, and a mistrial was the last thing they'd want. If fact, Whitt's family might be glad that her testimony could implicate Whitt's old nemesis, Roy McKinnon.

So, they were back to Joplin, Buddy or Meredith. Elise hoped they were the only ones on her list but maybe not. What if the culprit was someone else? Perhaps someone from her past.

Some former potential employees she'd given an unfavorable report and who was now out for revenge?

She made a mental note to go through her old files and see if there was something she'd missed. Over the years, there had been a few people who'd gotten angry that she'd uncovered something unsavory about them, but no motive for murder immediately came to mind. And she was pretty sure she would have remembered something like that.

Colt checked the time. "The Ranger should be here within an hour or so. We'll work out the details of where you're going then."

Because she had so much on her mind, it took a moment for that to sink in. Those *details* with the Ranger likely wouldn't involve Colt staying with her. That should have pleased her. And it would have done just that twenty-four hours earlier.

Not now, though.

"You're uncomfortable around me because of the kiss," she admitted, even though she figured it was a subject Colt would want to avoid.

He did. The sudden tightening of his jaw confirmed that. "I'm uncomfortable around *me* because of the kiss. Because it shouldn't have happened." He cursed. "Us getting involved would be the worst idea in the history of bad ideas."

She couldn't argue with that. His father and brothers probably hated her, and she was the last person on earth they'd want around Colt. Plus, she didn't think it was her imagination that Colt was still holding a grudge for her leaving all those years ago.

Or not.

A grudge would have meant that he'd actually had feelings for her that went beyond a teenage crush. He certainly hadn't said a word to stop her when she'd brought up the subject of leaving Sweetwater Springs to go to college in Dallas instead of heading to the University of Texas where he was going.

Not. A. Word.

Okay, so maybe Colt wasn't the only one holding on to a grudge here. A grudge still mixed with attraction.

Yes, nothing could go wrong with that combination.

"We can just agree that the kiss was a mistake," she said, "and that it won't happen again."

Colt gave her a flat look. "If we're around each other, it'll happen again."

She returned the flat look. Or rather tried. "It won't happen again," she repeated, hoping if she said it enough, it would come true.

Or at least it might want her to make it come true.

"It'll happen," he argued. His gaze went from her mouth to her breasts. "And next time, it might not just stay a kiss."

Oh, that really didn't help. The look alone had caused her to go all warm and golden, and the thought of pushing this further took her well past the warmth stage and made her forget all sorts of things.

Like the grudge. And common sense.

At least for several moments.

Then Colt took the final turn for her place, and the house and barn came into view. He slowed the truck to a crawl and put his hand over his gun. Bracing for an attack. But Elise didn't see anything that would require him to pull his weapon.

Well, other than the obscene threat scrawled in red paint on the side of her barn. And there was no doubt about it, it was a threat.

Stay here and you die.

It was surrounded by other obscenities, all obviously meant to unnerve her.

Sadly, it was working.

"Don't get out yet," Colt insisted when he brought the truck to a stop.

Cursing, he used his phone to take several pictures, but Colt didn't get out until Reed had stopped directly behind him. "Help me keep an eye on Elise," he told his fellow deputy.

He walked toward the barn, his attention still firing all around them. Reed's, too. They drew their weapons, went to the barn opening and looked inside.

Colt glanced back at her and shook his head. "No one's here."

Elise wasn't exactly relieved about that. If Colt had managed to catch the person red-handed, literally, then the danger would be over, and she might be able to get on with her life.

"I'll check the house and make sure no one broke in," Reed offered.

The deputy walked toward her front porch. Elise got out of the truck and went to stand by Colt. He opened his mouth, maybe to tell her to get back in the truck, but they both knew she wasn't necessarily any safer there than she was by the barn. After all, bullets could go through glass.

When she made it to the doorway, Elise immediately saw the spilled can of red paint. Or rather what was left of it. The person who'd written that message had used most of what remained to put that garbage on the wall.

But who had done that?

"I don't suppose a handwriting expert can figure out who wrote it?" she asked.

He lifted his shoulder. "I'll send a photo of it to the crime lab, but graffiti's hard to match. Still, we might get some prints off the paint can and the brush."

That was a start, but if they did find Buddy's prints on it, he could claim they'd gotten there from the time he'd admitted to vandalizing her barn. That left Joplin and Meredith, and neither should have been inside her barn and near that paint can.

Of course, she hadn't seen paint on Meredith's white outfit, so it if had been the woman's doing, then she'd used gloves and had avoided any splatter. Still, she didn't seem the sort of woman who'd get her hands dirty.

Colt cursed again, and Elise followed his gaze to see what had gotten his attention. There, on the inside of the wall was yet more red paint. Unlike the other warning and profanity, this appeared to be just one word, but Elise couldn't make out what it was.

She stepped closer at the same moment that Colt did, and Elise felt something bump across the front of her leg. At first she thought it was twine from an old hay bale, but she saw the sunlight glint off it.

A wire.

"Move!" Colt yelled.

There was the groaning sound of the wood as the roof collapsed and fell right toward them.

COLT HOOKED HIS arm around Elise and snapped her backward. Away from the falling wood.

It wasn't a second too soon.

The roof of the rickety barn swooshed down, one of the thick beams glancing off the toe of Colt's boot, but he managed to get Elise out of the way. He pushed her into what was left of the doorway and then outside.

And he kept going with her in tow.

He dragged them behind the first thing he reached, an old watering trough, while the rest of the barn crashed to the ground. The dust, wood bits and debris kicked up all around them.

Elise's breath was already gusting, and her eyes were wide. "There was a wire," she managed to say.

"Yeah. I saw it a little too late." And that wire meant someone had rigged the roof to fall. Probably the same person who'd written the latest rounds of threats.

"Are you okay?" Reed called out. He came from the back of Elise's house, running toward them with his gun drawn.

Colt did a quick check to make sure Elise hadn't been hurt. She was visibly shaken, but thank heaven she didn't seem to have any new injuries. They'd gotten lucky—again—and Colt hated to rely on something like luck when it came to Elise's safety.

"Someone trip-wired it," Colt let his fellow deputy know.

Reed mumbled something under his breath when he saw the pile of rubble that'd once been the barn. "I'll get someone out here," he said, stopping to take out his phone.

Good. Because they'd need help. Maybe they would be able to get something to identify the sick SOB who'd done this. It was attempted murder. Not just Elise this time but Colt, too.

Elise looked at him, her bottom lip trembling. "What was the word written on the inside wall of the barn?"

Even though it wouldn't do anything to settle her nerves, Colt opened his mouth to tell her, but he heard something that stopped him. Some kind of movement on the other side of his truck. He looked up, didn't see anything.

Then he heard the shot.

"Get down!" he shouted to Reed, but the deputy was already doing just that.

Colt's heart jumped to his throat, and he shoved Elise lower so he could shield her with his body. Thankfully, Reed was still close enough to the house that he took cover by the side of the porch.

Just as another shot came their way.

The bullet went over their heads and into the barn debris. The trough that Colt was using was cast-iron but rusted through in spots. Definitely not enough protection from bullets, but it was too risky to try to move now. Especially when the shooter fired another shot.

Hindsight being twenty-twenty, Colt knew it'd been a huge mistake to bring Elise here to her ranch. A mistake that could cost them, big-time. All he could do now was stop this idiot and beat some answers out of him.

"I'm so sorry," Elise mumbled.

He wasn't looking for an apology, especially when this wasn't her fault, but Colt couldn't take the time to reassure her. Too much of a distraction. Instead, he focused on the angle of the shots. Whoever was trying to kill them was on the far side of his truck, probably behind some trees that rimmed the fence around Elise's property.

"You see him?" Colt shouted to Reed.

"Not yet. But backup's on the way."

Colt lifted his head just a fraction to see if he could get a glimpse of the guy, but Elise pulled him right back down. "Don't," she insisted. "He could kill you."

He wasn't especially fond of the idea of risking his life, either, but the shots couldn't go on like this. Even if one didn't hit them directly, there were too many things that could cause a bullet to ricochet.

The next shot came, and it was a lightbulb-over-the-head moment for Colt. Each of the shots was aimed at the same place. Not just nearby.

But in the exact spot in what was left of the barn.

If the shooter had actually been aiming at them, the bullets would have gone into the trough. Or into him when he'd lifted his head.

"I don't think he's trying to kill us," Colt mumbled. But that didn't mean that he could just jump out there and test the theory.

"Take out my phone," he told Elise, maneuvering toward her so she could do that. "Text Reed and tell him to circle around the back of your house so he can get a look at this guy."

Even though her hands were shaking as hard as the rest of her, Elise managed to get out his phone and send the text. The shots continued, spaced out about every five seconds. All still going into the same spot.

"If someone's trying to scare me," Elise whispered, "they're doing a good job of it."

Yeah. And maybe that was the only thing this nut job had in mind. If so, it could be Buddy or Joplin. Of course, Meredith might be getting plenty of pleasure from watching Elise being too terrified to go to her own home.

His phone buzzed. Elise still had it in a death grip, but Colt managed to see the screen and the message from Reed: Spotted a rifle in the trees by the fence. Can't tell who's shooting. Moving in closer.

Colt didn't have to remind Reed to be careful. Reed was a good deputy and would be. Still, if he spooked the shooter, the guy could send some of those shots Reed's way.

Another shot came, and Colt counted off the seconds in his head. Five, just like the others. And not a degree of variation on the angle of the shot. The recoil alone should cause most shooters to move their hands just a little to throw off the individual shots so that each bullet wouldn't land in the exact spot each time.

Hell.

"Text Reed to tell him that I think the rifle's rigged to a remote control," he said to Elise.

Elise looked back at him, her eyes widening again. While she texted, she glanced at the next bullet that bashed into the heap of wood. Each new shot confirmed Colt's theory. However, that didn't mean the shooter wasn't still out there, ready to gun them down if they stepped from cover.

The seconds crawled by. The shots continued.

Colt held his breath and hoped like the devil that Reed wasn't walking into some kind of trap. Or that the shooter wasn't closing in on Elise and him now that Reed didn't have their backs. Just in case, Colt kept watch all around them.

His phone buzzed again, and Reed's message popped up: You're right. Remote control. No shooter in sight.

But unless the remote control was on a timer, the shooter would have to be close enough to operate it.

Too close, and there were plenty of places for someone to hide.

I'm moving in, Reed texted.

Colt scrambled over Elise and to the end of the watering trough so he could try to provide some backup for his fellow deputy. He immediately spotted Reed darting from one tree to the other and directly toward the fence. It seemed to take an eternity, but Colt figured it was less than a minute before Reed made it to the rifle.

The shots stopped.

"Stay down," Colt warned Elise.

Even though the bullets were no longer a danger, they were far from being safe. He levered himself up and tried to pick through the surroundings to see if he could find who'd just set this all in motion.

Nothing.

No timer, Reed texted.

So, whoever had done this had to be close. Colt couldn't go after him because he couldn't leave Elise alone, but he watched, waited. While he kept his gun ready.

Finally, he heard something. A snap. As if someone had stepped on a twig. But it hadn't come from anywhere near the disarmed rifle and Reed. It'd come from behind Elise and him. On the other side of the barn.

Colt pivoted in that direction and saw the blur of motion. Someone moving behind an old storage shed. With just that brief glimpse, he couldn't tell if it was one of their suspects or someone else.

Maybe another hired gun.

But if it was a hired gun, why hadn't he just shot them? Why had the person instead rigged a gun on the remote control?

Maybe the plan was to pin them down and then come

in for the kill. Someone who wasn't so sure of their shot might do something like that.

Colt motioned to the shed. "Text Reed again," he said to Elise. "Tell him that's the location of the person who set all of this up."

She nodded but had barely gotten started when Colt heard another sound that he definitely didn't want to hear.

Someone running.

Whoever was out there was getting away.

Chapter Eight

"This is a really bad idea," Elise mumbled.

Not her first time to mumble it, either, since they'd driven away from her house. Elise had been saying it since Colt had told her that the gunman had gotten away.

And that he was taking her to his family's ranch.

She needed protection. The latest attack had proved that. But she wasn't sure that walking into the lion's den, aka the McKinnon ranch, was the best way to make that happen.

"You know your brothers and father don't want me there," she added.

"My brothers are at work, and my sister Rayanne and her husband are at a doctor's appointment in San Antonio."

That still left his father.

"Maybe the Rangers can find a different place to take me," she added.

Colt didn't say a word, but the glance he gave her said loads. She wasn't going anywhere with anybody until they got to the bottom of this.

Whatever *this* was.

Someone had rigged that barn to fall on them. Perhaps like the shots from the rifle being controlled remotely, it'd only been meant to scare her and get her running.

But why?

Did that mean her attacker hadn't wanted to kill her? Or maybe he hadn't wanted to get close enough to try to kill her with Colt around.

Part of her wanted to do just that—run. But the other part of her hated that someone was trying to force her out of her home. Maybe force her from testifying against Roy, too.

Which led Elise to repeat her mumble about this being a bad idea.

"Your father won't want me at the ranch," she reminded him. And she wouldn't blame him one bit. In this case, the truth wasn't going to set him free. Just the opposite. It didn't matter that she was in the middle of a fight for her life. Technically, Roy McKinnon was, too.

A muscle flickered in Colt's jaw. "You won't have to stay long. Just while I set up a safe house. I figured it was better to come here since it's closer than going back to the sheriff's office."

Where they could be attacked again on the drive over.

Of course, they could be attacked anywhere, including his family's ranch.

That was no doubt the reason Colt was keeping a vigilant watch all around them. Elise was, too, and she wondered just how long it would take her to stop looking over her shoulder.

A long time, especially if the attacks continued.

The only way they would stop was for them to find the person responsible and put him or her behind bars, but they seemed no closer to making that happen than when this had first started.

"Reed and Cooper will keep looking for the shooter," Colt continued. "And there might be some prints or something on the rifle and the stand. We might even be able to find the remote control he was using."

Elise knew that Colt's brother and Reed were good lawmen and would do their best, but their attacker had headed straight for the woods. Hard to find someone in there if they didn't want to be found. Besides, the guy probably had an escape plan in place before the attack even started.

"What about the barn?" she asked.

He paused a moment as if gathering his thoughts. "It wouldn't have been hard to set a trip wire to bring down an old barn like that. But the person would have needed some time to do it."

She shuddered because that likely meant someone had sneaked onto her land during the night or had done it while they were at the sheriff's office. And that led Elise to her next question.

"Would Buddy have had time when he went up in the hayloft to get that box?" she asked.

"Not really. He was only in there a couple of minutes, and it would have taken more time than that to brace those rafters to be brought down by a trip wire." He paused, groaned and wearily scrubbed his hand over his face.

"What is it?" she pressed.

"Buddy could have already had everything in place before he showed up. Maybe things he'd put in place on another visit. If so, he wouldn't have needed much time to string the wire onto whatever he'd rigged to bring down the roof."

She didn't have any idea of the mechanics of such a thing, but Buddy knew every inch of that barn. Of all their suspects, he would have known the best way to orchestrate this particular attack. He would have also had the easiest time sneaking onto the ranch since he no doubt knew the trails on the property.

It sickened her to think that Buddy would do something that could have killed them, but then he'd been nothing but hostile to her since her return. It didn't take much to believe that he could have escalated things with the booby trap and then the shots.

So, the culprit could have indeed been Buddy. In fact, as far as she was concerned, he was number one on their list of suspects.

"What was written on the wall?" she asked when Colt didn't continue.

She braced herself to hear yet another threat or warning for her to get out of town, but Colt's silence had her turning in the seat to face him. "What was it?" Elise pressed.

"It said 'For Roy.'"

It took her a moment to realize what that meant. Another moment for it to hit her like a punch to the stomach.

Elise pressed her fingers to her mouth. "Oh, God."

"It doesn't mean anything," Colt quickly said. "Buddy could have put it there to take suspicion off him. Meredith and Joplin, too."

He was right, of course, but it didn't make this easier to swallow, especially since they were so close to a meeting that she didn't want to have. Colt took the turn to his family's ranch where she would no doubt come face-to-face with Roy McKinnon, the very man that her testimony would implicate in a murder.

Of course, Roy's name on the wall implicated him in some way in the attacks against her. Or rather it implicated someone who wanted to protect him.

"This is a bad idea," she repeated—again.

"I called ahead. They know you're coming."

That didn't help, either. It also didn't help when Elise saw the woman standing on the porch.

Colt's sister Rosalie.

Once Elise and she had been childhood friends despite the three-year age difference between them, and while Rosalie had welcomed Elise's testimony so that it'd clear her mother's name, Elise still wasn't sure of the reception she'd get. From all accounts, Rosalie had reconciled with her father, so Elise braced herself for a frosty welcome.

That didn't happen.

Rosalie came down the porch steps when Elise got out of the truck, and immediately pulled her into her arms. "I'm so sorry. Are you both okay?" she asked, volleying glances between Elise and her brother.

Elise managed a nod and was feeling a little better about this visit. Until she spotted Roy in the doorway, that is.

"Dad," Colt greeted him. "You remember Elise."

"Of course." The corner of his weathered mouth lifted into what she thought might be a welcoming smile. "Sorry about the trouble you're having."

He sounded genuine enough, but Elise didn't expect to get the warm, fuzzy feeling that she'd just gotten from Rosalie.

Colt looped his arm around Elise's waist and got her moving up the steps. Good thing, too, because she no longer felt steady on her feet. "Elise just needs a place to rest and wait until I've made other arrangements."

His father nodded. "She's welcome here anytime. And for as long as she needs." His gaze came to hers. "I was sorry to hear of your grandmother's passing. She was a good woman."

Elise somehow got her mouth working and thanked him, and Roy stepped to the side, motioning for her to go in. She did, with Colt and Rosalie trailing right along behind her.

"The guest room's ready for you," Rosalie said, but she immediately stopped when she heard a baby fussing. "That's Sadie, my daughter, and she's obviously not happy with her lunch. I need to go and help Mary."

Elise didn't need an explanation as to who Mary was. She'd been a housekeeper at the McKinnon ranch for as long as Elise could remember. Yet someone else that she had fond memories of from childhood. Too bad all those memories didn't ease the discomfort she was feeling now.

"I'll be up to check on you later," Rosalie added. She hurried away, leaving Roy, Colt and her in an uneasy silence.

"You might have heard that Rosalie's getting married," Roy commented. "He's a good man. Rayanne's husband, too."

Thanks to the town gossips, Elise had caught up on the McKinnons. All of Colt's siblings were either married or engaged now and settling into a normal life. Well, as normal as life could be with their mother's murder trial hanging over their heads.

Even though the conversation was civil enough, Colt must have picked up on the fact that she was well past the awkward stage, because he took her by the arm. "This way," he said, glancing back at his dad. "Thanks."

Elise thanked him, too, and made her way up the stairs with Colt. She remembered this part of the house, had even done a sleepover with Rosalie when they were kids. Right before Whitt Braddock had gone missing and Rosalie's world had crashed down around her.

Colt's world, too.

After the scandal and rumors of her murdering her lover, his mother had left with his twin sisters and had started the bad blood that she could still feel twenty-three years later. It didn't matter that everyone had gotten on with their lives. Well, for a while, anyway. Until Jewell's arrest.

And Elise remembering the events of that tragic day.

Colt took her to the room at the end of the hall. Once this had been Jewell's sewing room, but now it was a guest bedroom decorated in dark browns and creams like the rest of the house. No trace of Jewell or the life that'd once gone on here.

"I'm sorry to put you through this," Colt mumbled.

"I'm sorry to put you through this," she repeated right back to him.

The corner of his mouth lifted, but the smile didn't make it to his eyes. Because he looked in worse shape than she felt, Elise reached out, pulled him to her. She felt his back muscles stiffen, and for a moment she thought he might pull away. But he didn't.

"Hugging is the last thing we should be doing," he reminded her. "That goes for touching, standing close to each other or even thinking about doing any of those things."

True. But that didn't stop her.

Being with him like this pushed aside the sound of those gunshots and the other attack. Somewhat of a miracle. But Elise knew it couldn't last. Still, she held on, needing this from him.

Colt must have needed it, too, because he put his arm around her, tugged her closer and closer until they were right against each other.

That helped distract her despite his warning that they shouldn't be doing this.

And so did the touch of his mouth when he brushed it over her lips. Very chaste. At first, anyway.

Colt made a groaning sound that rumbled deep in his chest, and he deepened the kiss. That really helped with the nightmarish images, and they faded fast, replaced by the instant heat that the kiss created.

Elise hooked her arms around his neck. Anchoring him against her. And she let that heat warm her in all the cold places. Soon, though, the warmth got much hotter when he pressed her against the door, closing it at the same time that he snapped her to him.

"Yes," she mumbled against his mouth.

But Colt certainly wasn't saying yes. She could feel the fight going on inside him. His muscles were corded. His heartbeat fast and wild. Like the kiss itself and the body contact.

Even though at least one of them should have had the good sense to back away, that didn't happen. Hard for good sense to prevail, though, when his kisses brought back the flood of emotions that she'd been trying to bury for the past decade.

Colt had had her hormonal number back then. And he still had it now.

The kiss raged on, but it didn't take long until it wasn't enough. Her body begged for more, and even though she didn't ask, Colt figured it out and gave her more. He aligned their bodies so that the front of his jeans was against hers.

"Yes," Elise repeated.

It was exactly what her body wanted. What she needed. But it was also something that shouldn't be happening. Not right now, anyway.

Did that stop them?

No.

But the knock on the door certainly did.

Groaning again, Colt moved away from her. "Yeah?" he managed to say, though his breath was gusting.

"Sorry to bother you," Rosalie said from the other side of the door. "But Elise has a visitor waiting on the front porch. It's Robert Joplin, and he's not alone. There's a man named Tim Sutcliff with him."

Colt looked at her, questioning whether she knew who that was. She didn't. But with the stunt that Joplin was trying with the mistrial, there was no telling who this other man could be.

"A couple of the ranch hands came to the porch when Joplin arrived," Rosalie went on. "They're armed and said you gave them orders to keep an eye out for him or anyone else who might show up while Elise was here."

Colt had indeed done that with a phone call he'd made on the drive out to the ranch.

"I'll be down in a few minutes," Colt answered. "Don't let Joplin in the house. Keep him on the porch with the ranch hands."

Rosalie paused, maybe waiting for an explanation, but finally said, "Okay."

Colt paused, too, his gaze combing over Elise, and then he cursed, shook his head. "We look like we just had sex."

Elise couldn't help it. She laughed. And because she thought they both could use it, she brushed a kiss on his cheek. A chaste one like Colt's that had started this whole kissing session.

"Well, for years I did dream about having sex with you," she admitted.

He'd already reached to open the door, but that stopped him. "You did?"

Elise nearly blurted out that she'd been attracted to Colt since the first moment she realized the difference between boys and girls. Before that, he'd been her friend. Yes, she'd had a thing for Colt McKinnon most of her life.

"You used to kill spiders for me in my tree house," she settled for saying. "Those kinds of heroics stay with a girl."

"Killing spiders, huh?" He shook his head. "That's what it took to be a hero in your eyes?"

"It's helped."

Despite their visitor, and their messy situation, they shared a smile. Too brief. Because then Colt opened the door, stepping in front of her.

"I don't want you near Joplin," he reminded her as they went downstairs. He was all lawman now. Ready to stomp on more spiders for her if necessary. "Stay in the foyer while I talk to him."

Elise didn't argue, mainly because she didn't especially want to see Joplin after the hellish day she'd had. However, she did want to know why he was there, so she stayed just inside the doorway when Colt opened the door.

Rosalie stepped next to her, standing shoulder to shoulder with her. That's when Elise realized Rosalie was holding a gun by her side. Obviously, she, too, thought there might be reason for concern. And maybe there was. After all, someone had attempted to hurt her twice in the past twenty-four hours.

"Colt," Joplin greeted, but there was no friendliness to it. The man hitched his thumb to the pair of ranch hands who were clearly guarding him from each side of the porch. "Is this necessary?"

"Yeah," Colt answered without hesitation. "We're a little tired of dodging bullets and falling barn roofs. How'd you even know Elise was here and what do you want?"

Those brusque questions didn't ease the tightness around Joplin's mouth. "When she wasn't at the sheriff's office, I figured you'd bring her here." He stepped to the side so that Colt and she would get a good look at the man he'd brought with him.

Tim Sutcliff was short and stocky with bushy brown hair. He gave his thick wool coat an adjustment so that it hugged the back of his neck. He was obviously cold, but Elise knew that wouldn't gain him or Joplin entry to the house.

"Mr. Sutcliff is a therapist," Joplin explained. "He's here to hypnotize Elise to see what else she remembers about that day she saw Roy in the Braddock cabin."

Elise wasn't sure who groaned louder. Colt or her.

"This can wait," Colt insisted.

"No, it can't. At the rate things are going, Elise might not live long enough to testify about what she saw."

Even though she wasn't standing directly in the gusting wind, that chilled her to the bone. Because it was true. And it might be true because of Joplin.

"Please tell me you didn't have anything to do with what's been happening to me," Elise said.

Oh, Joplin did not like that. But she didn't care. She wasn't especially fond of what had gone on, either, and right now, Joplin had a strong motive for the attacks against her.

"I wouldn't hurt you," Joplin snapped. "I'm trying to help you. Don't you want to remember that day?"

"Of course I do, but I'm not sure you have my best interests at heart." Something that'd taken her a while to figure out, but she certainly had it figured out now. Joplin's first and foremost concern was Jewell.

Elise's gaze shifted to the therapist. "Let me guess— you and Joplin are friends?"

The man opened his mouth, sputtering out a few frustrated sounds, before he answered, "That has nothing to do with your situation. Like Robert, I only want to help you."

"Robert," she repeated in a mumble. "I'd say that's the answer to my question, that you two are indeed friends."

Sutcliff shook his head. "Again, that has nothing to do with anything. I'm here to help you," he repeated.

"It has everything to do with this situation," Colt argued. "If Elise wants to see a hypnotist, then it should be someone she chooses. Someone who's not a friend of my mother's attorney."

Neither Joplin nor Sutcliff actually denied the friendship, but both look riled to the core. "Why would it make a difference if we happen to know each other?" Joplin challenged.

"I can think of a reason," Rosalie said before Colt or Elise could answer. "A dishonest or untrained therapist can plant false memories in a person while they're under hypnosis. Memories that you might use to clear your client."

Colt gave her an odd look, maybe because he was surprised that Rosalie wouldn't do anything and everything to clear her mother's name. "I only want to know the truth," Rosalie explained. "And I don't want Elise bullied into doing something she's not ready to do.

Especially by someone who might not even be quali-
fied to do it."

"Thank you," Elise told her and then turned back to
Joplin. "I'll make my own appointment to see a hypnotist, and no offense, Mr. Sutcliff, but it won't be with
you."

She didn't think it was her imagination that Sutcliff
seemed extremely uncomfortable about her decision.
Had Joplin pressured his old friend to do something illegal? Probably. Joplin was pulling out the stops when
it came to this trial.

"You don't trust me," Joplin said to her, his voice
low and filled with emotion. Well, one emotion, anyway. Anger.

"No, I don't," Elise readily admitted.

Joplin's nostrils actually flared. "This is a bad decision on your part. I'll petition the court to have you removed from Colt's protective custody."

"Good luck with that," Colt grumbled, obviously not
overly concerned about that happening.

Still, Joplin could make waves, and that was all the
more reason for her to get to a safe house where Joplin
couldn't just show up on a whim. Of course, that safe
house might come with a huge string attached.

Colt might not be there with her.

In fact, after that latest kiss—which he would see
as another lapse in judgment—he might try to distance
himself from her. Something that Elise figured was best
overall. But it certainly didn't feel best at the moment.

"I've also secured the Braddock cabin where Whitt
was killed," Joplin went on. "There's a guard with the
private investigators that I hired."

It took Elise a moment to realize why Joplin had said
that. Colt obviously got it right away because he huffed.

"My family and I have no intention of tampering with a crime scene," Colt informed him.

"Maybe not," Joplin said, speaking over his shoulder as he walked away. "But I'm removing the temptation just in case somebody puts something there that'd clear Roy's name at the expense of your mother."

Elise thought that part might be directed at her. Probably because she'd already admitted that she didn't trust Joplin, he might think that mistrust extended to Jewell. It didn't. She wanted to help the woman if she was indeed innocent.

"I don't think you've seen the last of him," Rosalie mumbled as they went back inside. All three of them stayed at the window to make sure Joplin and Sutcliff got in their car and drove away.

"It's true about someone being able to plant false memories?" Colt asked his sister.

Rosalie nodded. "It's especially easy to do with childhood memories. Some therapists have even convinced people they were molested and such when it didn't happen."

Mercy, and Joplin could have planned on doing that to her so that she believed Roy had been the one to kill Whitt Braddock.

And he might have been.

Even though her memories weren't crystal clear, Elise was certain about one thing. Roy had been at the cabin that day.

Rosalie gave her arm a gentle squeeze. "I know someone reputable who can do the hypnosis, and I can get you an appointment with her. But if you'd rather use someone else, I'll understand."

"No. Please make the appointment," Elise insisted. "If you trust her, then so do I."

Rosalie looked at Colt to see what he thought about it, and he nodded. "Thanks. For everything," he added.

"Yes," someone said.

Elise looked behind them and spotted Roy standing in the shadows of the adjoining family room. He came closer, his worn cowboy boots thudding on the hardwood floor, his hands jammed into his jeans' pockets.

"I don't know what you're going to remember while under hypnosis," he said. "But even if you saw something that leads to my arrest, I don't want you to hold back." His gaze drifted to Colt. "In fact, I don't want anything you remember to have any bearing on anything else."

Elise understood then. Roy could no doubt see the attraction simmering between Colt and her. Heck, it'd always been there, and it was getting stronger. Roy didn't want her feelings for Colt playing into her testimony.

And it wouldn't.

Still, she hated the thought of remembering something that might make all this worse for Roy, even if it made things better for Jewell.

"Who knows," Elise said, "I might remember someone else being in the cabin that day. Someone else who had a reason to harm Whitt Braddock."

There was no shortage of people who fell into that category. Even as a child, she'd known that Whitt wasn't a well-liked man, and his supposed affair with Jewell, a married woman, certainly hadn't helped his reputation any. Too bad all those people had airtight alibis, putting the blame squarely back on Jewell and Roy.

Colt drew in a long breath and made another check to ensure that Joplin had driven away. He had. And he took out his phone. "I'll check on the status of the safe house."

However, his phone buzzed before he could make a

call, and Elise saw Reed's name on the screen. Since the deputy was likely still at her place, she prayed that he'd found something to lead them to the identity of the person who'd launched the attacks on Colt and her.

Colt answered the call but didn't put it on speaker. Still, it didn't take Elise long to realize that something bad had happened. She groaned because she was tired of having this constant dose of bad news.

"Get in here, away from the windows," Colt insisted. He took her by the arm and hurried her into the family room.

That caused the skin to crawl on Elise's neck.

Mercy, what had gone wrong now?

Rosalie had a similar reaction. "My baby," she said on a rise of breath, and she raced off toward the back of the house.

"It's Buddy," Colt said the moment he finished the call with Reed. And he drew his gun. "He was just spotted on the road leading to the ranch."

Chapter Nine

"You should try to get some rest," Colt reminded Elise.

But it was a reminder that fell on deaf ears because Elise continued to pace back and forth across the family room while they waited for yet another call from Reed. Colt hoped this one would be to tell them that Buddy had been captured. Putting Buddy behind bars might not be the end of their problems, but at least he could question the man and find out why he was on the run.

Innocent men didn't usually run, and he was betting that Buddy had something to do with not only the barn falling but possibly the other attacks, as well.

"How long before your brothers get home?" Elise asked, glancing out the window again.

Well, glancing as much as she could, considering Colt had warned her to stay far away from the windows and doors. It was a necessity since shots from a long-range rifle could be fired at them from the woods across from the ranch. The ranch hands were all on alert, looking for anyone who might try to get close to launch an attack, but the ranch was huge and there was a lot of ground to cover.

"How long?" she repeated when he didn't answer.

He lifted his shoulder. "Don't worry. They won't come here. Cooper built a house in that clearing near the pond, and Tucker lives just up the road in my grand-daddy's old place. Besides, Tucker and his wife took their twins on a family vacation."

The only McKinnon sibling that Elise might have to face was his other sister, Rayanne, but Rosalie had already called Rayanne and asked that she and her husband stay in a hotel in San Antonio. With Rayanne being nearly six months pregnant, it was just too risky for her to return to the ranch.

Risky for Elise to be there, too, so Colt made yet another call so he could get an update about the safe house. The Ranger in charge didn't answer, and Colt left him a message. However, he'd no sooner done that when a text message popped onto his screen.

Colt cursed.

That definitely wasn't what he wanted to hear from Reed—that there was no sign of Buddy by the time the deputy had made it out to the road where the man had been spotted by a neighbor.

"Buddy got away," Elise concluded, and groaning, she dropped down on the sofa next to him.

"Yes," Colt confirmed. "For now, anyway. There are a lot of people looking for him, and the Appaloosa Pass Sheriff's Office has helped us set up a roadblock to help catch him. Buddy can't hide forever." He hoped. "Don't worry. The safe house should be ready soon."

But, of course, she'd worry. So would he. Every second felt like a time bomb clicking down to explosion.

And that wasn't just about the danger.

It was about all this heat sizzling and crackling between them. The timing for it sucked, not just because of her testimony, but also because attraction equaled a distraction, and something like that could get them killed. His family killed, too.

Another text message popped up, this one from Rosalie. "My sister scheduled you an appointment tomorrow morning with Suzanne Dawkins, the hypnotist."

Elise nodded. "Is it safe for me to go and see her?"

At this point Colt wasn't sure what was safe, but at least the appointment might give them some answers. Hopefully, one of those answers would help clear his father's name.

Colt went over Rosalie's text again. "According to what Rosalie's saying, the hypnotist will come to you, but since you'll be in the safe house by then, it's probably best if we go to the sheriff's office for the session. I want as few people as possible to know the location of the safe house."

She nodded again, stared at her hands. "You won't be staying there with me, will you?"

It was something Colt had gone over more than a dozen times in his mind, and he still didn't have an answer. He shouldn't stay with her, especially since he had a mountain of deputy work he should be doing. Also, he had obviously lost objectivity when it came to Elise, but he wasn't sure he was ready to turn her over to the Rangers.

Of course, the lost objectivity was coloring that last concern, too.

Another lawman could protect her, but he wasn't sure he wanted to give up that duty to someone else.

So, the argument inside him continued.

"We'll see," he settled for saying.

And he hated how unsure that sounded, but his final decision would come after he had a better idea of the arrangements the Rangers were making for her. If he felt that the safe house was truly the safest place to be, then he'd back off. No matter how hard it would be for him to do that.

"I'd like to go by my place and pick up some things before I go to the safe house," she said.

He shook his head. "I can have someone do that for you."

"I'd like to do it myself." And the color rose on her cheeks enough to get his full attention. His attention was enough to cause her to huff, though. "I don't want strangers going through my underwear drawer." She paused. "Plus, I need to get my meds."

Again, she got his attention. "Are you in pain?" he asked, glancing at the stitches still on her head. Now that she'd taken off the bandage, they were easy to see.

Another huff. "I need to get my birth control pills, all right?"

Oh. That. Colt kicked himself for not picking up on the fact she might need personal items that she didn't want to discuss with him. Then he kicked himself again for feeling that tug of jealousy that she'd need such a thing.

Hell.

What was wrong with him? Elise and he were on totally separate paths, and those paths would get significantly further apart if her testimony put his father behind bars. Plus, it was reasonable that an attractive woman like her would have a man in her life. A man who would require her to be on the pill.

Yet another pang of jealousy hit him before Colt could shove it away.

"There hasn't been anyone in a while," Elise said, no doubt reading his expression. "But I stay on them. Habit, I guess."

Colt didn't want to be relieved by that, but he was.

He quickly assured himself that it was because adding someone else—*anyone* else—into this mix would complicate things even more. It had nothing to do with those two scalding-hot kisses Elise and he had shared.

Okay, it did.

But Colt didn't intend to let those kisses play into this.

"I'd rather not ask someone to pick up my personal things," she added. "I'd like to go by my place for just a couple of minutes. Unless you think there might be other booby traps?"

"No. A couple of the deputies from Appaloosa Pass went over every inch of your place. If there were other trip wires or such, they would have found them."

"So we can go," she concluded.

His first instinct was still to say no, but the truth was, whoever was behind all this was just as likely to attack at the ranch as Elise's house. In fact, he probably should get her away from Rosalie and his niece—especially since Rosalie's fiancé was away on business and couldn't help protect her. It sickened him to think that this idiot might put a baby in danger to get to Elise.

Colt nodded, got to his feet. "I'll call Reed and have him meet us at your house, and one of the hands can follow us over there. Plus, the CSI team is still out there going through the barn rubble."

Maybe all that law enforcement around meant it was the last place Buddy or their attacker would show up. Ever. Because Colt was tired of Elise having to go through one nightmare after another.

"I can also have the Rangers meet us at your place so it cuts down on time you're out on the road," he added. "That way, they can take you straight from there to the safe house."

It took Colt a few minutes to make the arrangements

for what he hoped would be a short, safe trip, and then with Elise in tow, he went looking through the house for his father. He found him and Rosalie in the kitchen. His sister had a sleeping baby on her lap, so Colt made the goodbyes quiet and quick.

Elise certainly didn't object.

Despite the welcome that she'd gotten from Rosalie and Roy, it was clear she wasn't comfortable there.

Colt took Elise onto the porch, but he didn't move her to his truck until the ranch hand, Darnell Tate, had driven around the side of the house so he was in place to follow them.

"Stay low in the seat," Colt reminded her when they got in.

She did, but she kept her head just high enough so she could look around. The same thing Colt was doing. Even though Elise's place was only about fifteen minutes away, it would feel like a long drive.

Colt had barely made it off McKinnon land when his phone buzzed, and he saw Cooper's name on the caller ID.

"Did you find Buddy?" Colt asked his brother the moment he answered the call.

"Not yet. But one of those private investigators that Joplin hired did find something out at the creek near the Braddock cabin."

Colt certainly hadn't forgotten about the PIs, but he'd put that way on the back burner. "What?" he asked, but judging from his brother's hesitation, this was about to be yet another dose of bad news.

"A bone fragment," Cooper said. "It was only about twenty yards from the cabin."

Elise obviously heard that, and since she was trying to move closer to the phone, Colt put it on speaker.

"And?" Colt pressed when Cooper didn't continue.

"They're pretty sure it doesn't belong to an animal. It seems to be human."

Colt let that sink in a moment. "They think it belongs to Whitt Braddock?"

"Yeah. But it'll have to be tested, of course."

Of course. And if it did turn out to belong to Whitt, it was yet more proof of murder. Not that the prosecution needed more. There'd been enough blood found at the scene to indicate Whitt was dead, but without a body, there was always a question that somehow he'd managed to survive.

A bone fragment shot that question to Hades and back.

"Why did it take so long to find it?" Colt asked. "We've had CSIs out there, and the county sheriff's team went over it just a couple of months ago."

Heck, over the years he and his brothers had looked for anything that would prove their mother had murdered Whitt.

"It's a small piece," Cooper explained. "Easy to miss because of all the rocks."

Yeah, but the timing was suspicious for it to turn up now. Of course, maybe he felt that way because of all the other stuff happening. Colt couldn't see, though, how any of their suspects could use this to their advantage.

"I'll keep you posted," Cooper said, and he ended the call.

Colt dropped the phone on the seat between Elise and him, and in the process got a glimpse of her expression. "I'm sorry," she whispered.

So was he. And he groaned. "This could go against my dad."

She made a small sound of agreement. "Because a jury might think he helped Jewell move the body."

It wouldn't matter if Roy hadn't been the one to kill Whitt, but an accessory carried the same penalty as murder. Death.

"Has your mother ever talked about what happened that day?" Elise asked.

Colt automatically started to clam up. Something he usually did when anyone mentioned his mother and the murder. But Elise had just as much of a stake in this as he did. And his softened feelings toward her didn't help, either. Hard to play mute with someone he'd kissed like crazy.

"She's never talked to me about it," Colt answered. "And the only thing my dad has said was that he was drunk and doesn't remember much. Still, I think he'd remember dragging a body from the cabin to the creek."

Another sound of agreement. "And I certainly don't remember seeing anything like that." She paused. "What I do remember is that Whitt was a big man. So how does the DA think Jewell got his body out of the cabin?"

Colt lifted his shoulder. "There were drag marks leading out to where Whitt parked his truck when he used the cabin. People fueled with adrenaline can lift things they wouldn't be able to under normal circumstances."

But now there was a problem with that theory. If Jewell had managed somehow to get Whitt into the truck, then why hadn't she driven the body miles away? Why had she dumped him so close to the cabin that all these years later, a bone fragment would be found?

"Don't borrow trouble," Elise reminded him. "The bone isn't necessarily a game changer."

No, but Colt didn't like the fact that it could make this

situation turn even uglier for his father. Still, he couldn't see Joplin planting something like that, either, because it would still hurt Jewell in the long run.

His phone buzzed again. Not Cooper this time. Instead, he saw a message from the Texas Ranger on the screen.

Safe house is ready. On my way to Ms. Nichols's place now to pick her up.

He handed the phone to Elise so she could read it for herself. They'd both known this was coming, but it suddenly seemed as if it was happening way too fast for Colt. Judging from the way Elise pulled in her breath, it did to her, too.

"We'll find Buddy or whoever's behind this," Colt reminded her. "After that, you won't need a safe house."

Or him.

But that was a good thing, he reminded himself. Elise and he both needed to get on with their lives. And if they got together again for another kissing session, it sure as heck wouldn't be fueled by fear and adrenaline.

"You'll be at the sheriff's office for the hypnosis tomorrow?" she asked.

"Sure." However, Joplin might find some way to block him and his brothers from being with Elise during the actual session. Still, Joplin couldn't stop him from being in the building.

And then something occurred to him. Something bad.

"Do you think you could have blocked out…something more than what you saw?" he asked.

"I'm not sure." She answered so quickly that it was obvious she'd given it some thought. "I have wondered why it took me so long to remember seeing Roy. Twenty-three years," she mumbled. "I didn't remember any of it until I read about Jewell's arrest."

Yeah, and that bothered him, too. A lot. Not because he thought she was lying about the memory but because she could remember so much more. After all, people blocked out bad stuff all the time. Especially bad stuff.

"Why were you even by the creek that day?" Colt asked.

She glanced at him. "Because of you. Remember?"

No. He didn't.

Wait.

He did.

"You'd come to the ranch earlier with your grandmother. She was picking up a calf that she'd bought from Dad. I was talking to you, and my brothers started teasing me about liking you."

"And you got mad and said I was the last girl in Texas that you'd ever like," she finished for him.

Yes, he had said that, along with a few other not so nice things. "I'm sorry."

"You were nine years old," Elise reminded him. "Like killing spiders, being mean to girls came with the territory."

"But I clearly upset you. You went to the creek to blow off some steam?"

She smiled softly. "I went there to cry, and then I tried to think up some curse that I could put on you. Hey, I was nine, too," she added when he gave her a hard look. "I wanted a little payback."

Her smile vanished as quickly as it'd come. "But I didn't think payback would mean your family being torn apart."

He was about to tell her that she'd in no way been responsible for that. Nope, that was solely on his mother's shoulders because even if his father had been an accessory, Whitt wouldn't have died if Jewell hadn't gotten involved with him in the first place. However, before Colt could say anything, his phone buzzed again, and it was another call from his brother.

Maybe this time, it'd be good news.

"The CSI out at Elise's place just called," Cooper said.

"Please tell me they found prints to ID the person who rigged that booby trap," Colt grumbled.

"No. It's worse than that. They found a body."

Chapter Ten

Elise was back to pacing across the room again. This time it wasn't at the McKinnon ranch but in the kitchen of her own home. She was afraid to ask herself what else could go wrong because it was obvious that plenty could.

A body. On her land.

Yes, that was plenty bad.

She glanced out at the yellow crime-scene tape that now surrounded the very spot where she'd planned on building the new barn and stables. A fresh start for her return to Sweetwater Springs.

But it didn't feel so much like a fresh start now.

Along with Cooper, there was Reed and a trio of CSIs. All of them were focused on the small area where the forensic investigator was carefully digging. Both Cooper and Reed were on their phones, no doubt coordinating what would turn out to be yet another investigation—depending on what they were about to uncover.

And according to the CSIs, what they were about to uncover was a body.

"There's no need for you to watch that," Colt said to her.

He'd just finished his latest call—this one to tell the Ranger to delay picking her up for the safe house. Something that Elise had demanded that Colt do. She wasn't leaving until she'd learned whose body they were digging up.

He walked to her, gently taking hold of her arm and trying to urge her into the living room. But Elise stayed put.

"What if it's Whitt Braddock?" she said, repeating what had been going through her mind since she'd first heard the news. "What if my gran had some part in this? After all, she and Jewell were friends. She could have helped her."

"Don't," Colt insisted. "Remember when you told me not to borrow trouble? Well, now, I'm telling you the same thing. There's no immediate way of knowing how long that body's been out there. There are even some Indian burial grounds around here."

Elise wanted to believe that. Mercy, did she, but she kept going back to that bone fragment that'd just been found by the creek. Maybe Jewell had dumped the body and then moved it later.

But when would she have done that?

Colt's mother left town just days after Whitt's disappearance. Not much time to do something like this, and it didn't make sense that Jewell would move the body from the woods near the creek to a place on her gran's ranch where it could have been dug up at any time. Heck, it was only about twenty yards from the house, and in the very spot where her gran's rose garden had once been. Elise had played there too many times to count.

It sickened her to think that she might have been playing on top of a dead body that whole time.

"You're trembling," Colt pointed out. "And if you

don't come and sit down, I'll have to do something to distract you."

His gaze dropped to her mouth.

That surprised her. "Are you threatening me with a kiss?" she asked.

He lifted his shoulder. "Whatever works. The one thing that isn't going to work is you pacing and driving yourself nuts. Come on. Sit down."

His grip on her stayed gentle. Barely a touch. But it was enough to get her moving to the sofa. Part of her hated that Colt could so easily persuade her to do something, but she was thankful he was there.

Even if he'd used the kiss threat.

Something that wasn't actually a threat when she knew it would be a nice distraction that her body would appreciate.

Colt sat next to her, pulling her into the curve of his arm. All in all, a comforting place to be. Well, it was until her thoughts went back to what was going on just yards away.

"I wish they'd just hurry and dig it up," she mumbled. Not that it would help with the wild scenarios going through her head. Even if it didn't turn out to be Whitt, there was still someone's dead body out there.

"You can always wait at the safe house," he offered, "and I'll call you the second we know anything."

It wasn't the first time he'd made the offer, and Elise figured he'd continue to make it as long as she stayed put. And as long as she was as visibly shaken as she was now. "I haven't made up my mind if I want to go or not."

Colt didn't roll his eyes exactly, but it was close. "You can't possibly want to stay here."

"No. At least not until that body is gone. But I'm

not sure I want to go to a strange place with, well, a stranger."

Elise waited for him to try to convince her that the Ranger who would be guarding her wouldn't be a stranger for long. And that he would be someone she could trust. He didn't do either of those things. Colt only made a sound of agreement and pulled her deeper into his arms.

"We'll work it out," he said, brushing a kiss on her forehead.

And that's how his brother Cooper found them when he came in through the back door. Colt's mouth on her forehead. Her, snuggled in his arms. Colt and she immediately moved apart, but Cooper couldn't have missed the close contact between them.

Unlike Rosalie and Roy, there was no warm welcome from Cooper. In his divided family, Cooper was clearly on his father's side, and he saw her as a potential threat. Or maybe the look he was giving her was because he now saw her as someone connected to the body they'd just found.

Cooper was wearing his usual "uniform" of jeans, white shirt, a Stetson and boots, with his badge pinned to his belt beneath his buckskin jacket. His eyes and dark brown hair were a genetic copy of Colt's, and like Colt, Elise had no trouble seeing the fatigue and stress in his eyes.

"Anything yet?" Colt asked, getting to his feet. Elise did, too, and she tried to move away from Colt, but he held on, dropping his arm from her shoulders to her waist so he could anchor her in place.

"It'll be a while before the body's fully excavated. They're being careful because they don't want to disturb anything around it in case it might contain evidence.

But it's definitely not a Native American burial. There are clothing fragments on the remains. What appears to be denim."

So, it was someone wearing jeans. Someone like Whitt. That caused the knot in Elise's stomach to tighten even more.

"How did they even discover the body?' she asked. "Because I certainly didn't see any signs of it."

"The CSIs brought out a cadaver dog to go through the barn rubble. They wanted to make sure the person who set the trip wire hadn't been killed and buried in the process. The dog sensed something all right but not at the barn. The CSI dug around and found the body in a fairly shallow grave."

Just those two words, *shallow grave*, sent a cold shiver down her. "I swear I didn't know anything about this," she said to Cooper.

If he believed her, he made no indication whatsoever. Instead, his attention went to his brother. "I just got an update from the Appaloosa Pass deputy handling the roadblock. Still no sign of Buddy."

Great. The man had nine lives when it came to escaping, and until they caught him, Cooper or Colt couldn't question him about his involvement in all of this. However, no matter what Buddy said, he was still her top suspect for what'd happened in that barn.

"But there is some good news," Cooper went on. "The county DA isn't arresting Dad for these attacks. Not yet, anyway. And Joplin's request for a mistrial was denied."

It was indeed good news, even though that meant she'd be testifying, after all. She wasn't looking forward to that, but Elise was glad that Joplin hadn't managed to put a stop to the trial before it'd even started.

Colt and his family needed closure. Heck, so did she. Though she wasn't sure how any of them would feel if *closure* landed their father in jail.

"I'm sorry if all of this put your family in danger," Elise said.

Something flashed through Cooper's eyes. Anger, no doubt. But then those hard eyes softened a bit, and he scrubbed his hand over his face. "What time is she seeing the hypnotist tomorrow?" he asked Colt.

"Eight in the morning."

Cooper nodded. "Stay with her until then. I'm putting you back on protection detail."

The relief flooded through her. Too much relief, considering that she figured Colt might be ready to put some distance between them. But then she saw the quick glance that the brothers shared and knew there was more to this.

"What happened?" Colt asked.

Cooper pulled in a long breath, nodded. "The woman Elise investigated, Meredith Darrow, is making waves. She's filing a lawsuit against Elise for defamation of character, but I'm not as concerned about her as I am about her brother, Leo."

"Her brother?" Elise and Colt repeated in unison. "Why would he have any part in this?" Elise added.

"Because he's a small-time thug, that's why, and he came by the sheriff's office demanding to see you. I won't repeat the names he called you," Cooper said to Elise. "He didn't exactly threaten you, but it was close."

Oh, mercy. She so didn't need this on top of everything else. Colt's arm went back around her.

"Did you arrest him?" Colt asked, and judging from his tone, he was just as riled about this as she was upset.

Cooper shook his head. "No cause. *Yet*. But I did

issue him a few threats of my own and gave him a ticket for illegally parking outside the office. That didn't help his temper," Cooper added. "I checked, and Leo has a record for assault and a couple of restraining orders against him from former girlfriends and employers. He's obviously very protective of his sister, so he might cause some trouble. You'll need to be on the lookout for him, along with getting your own restraining order if he doesn't back off."

Great. Now, in addition to a dead body and the idiot trying to kill them, they also had to worry about a hot-head.

Except they might be one and the same.

"Leo could be behind the attacks," Elise concluded, and neither Colt nor Cooper disagreed with her. Any man who'd used violence in the past was probably in-clined to use it again.

"We'll be tied up here for a while yet," Cooper went on a moment later, "but the sheriff in Appaloosa Pass said he'd bring in Leo and question him for us. I figure it'll just rile Leo even more, but maybe he'll do some-thing stupid like take a swing at the sheriff, so they can arrest him and get him off the streets."

It was a testament to how crazy her life was that she actually hoped Leo did try to assault a lawman. They already had enough suspects out there without adding another one to the mix. Especially one who felt he had to avenge his sister and her illegal activity.

"There's more," Cooper went on, and she could tell from his expression that this was more bad news. "I just talked to the Rangers before I came in, and someone's trying to follow the sergeant who was coming out here to pick up Elise."

Yes, definitely bad. It meant someone had likely

learned that she was to be taken to a safe house. If their attacker discovered the location, it would make her an easy target. Again.

"The Ranger will try to get an ID on the person following him, but it's probably best if Elise stays put for a while. When I can, I'll escort you to the sheriff's office. You can stay there until we make sure it's safe to head to the new location."

Elise was afraid that might never happen. Hard to feel safe with her world crashing down around her.

"It's not much," Cooper went on, "but there's a small flop room just off the break area at the sheriff's office. It has a single bed and bathroom. It won't be comfortable, but it might work out better if you stayed there tonight so someone can help Colt guard you."

"Yes," she immediately agreed.

She was a trouble magnet these days, and with someone trying to follow the Ranger, the sheriff's office was better than going back to the McKinnon ranch where Colt's family could be hurt. Plus, Colt would have backup at the sheriff's office and maybe their attacker would be less likely to come after her there.

Maybe.

Cooper turned to leave but then stopped. "I'm sorry," he added as he walked out.

Coming from him that was practically a hug, but it was Colt who actually did it. He wrapped his arms around her and pulled her close.

"I'm sorry," Colt repeated.

That helped, too, but Elise felt if she stayed still, she might explode.

"I have to do something. *Anything.*" She glanced around at her already clean kitchen. For once she wasn't pleased about being a neat person.

"You should pack some things before we leave," Colt suggested.

Yes, and it would get her moving. Better than pacing and waiting by the window for them to pull the body out of the ground. Elise headed toward her bedroom.

Colt followed her, of course. With everything going on, he probably wasn't going to let her out of his sight—something she didn't mind.

Elise took an overnight bag from the shelf in her closet and stuffed it with a pair of jeans. She managed to pack some sweaters before the first tear spilled down her cheek.

Mercy, she was a wreck.

Colt made a soft sigh, and before the second tear came, he already had her in his arms again. Something he'd been doing way too much of lately, but like the other times, Elise didn't resist. However, she did try to stave off a full-fledged crying jag.

She failed at that, too.

"I hate crying," she mumbled.

"Seems to me that you've got a solid reason to cry. If it helps, I can lend you a shoulder or two."

"Your shoulders always help," she answered, her voice a choked whisper. "That's part of the problem." Elise pulled back, and even though she figured she looked pretty bad with her red eyes and puffy face, she still met his gaze. "What are we doing, Colt?"

Thankfully, she didn't have to explain that. She could see that he knew what she meant, and he sighed again. "To hell if I know. Seems as if we picked up where we left off as kids."

They had, but the situation wasn't nearly the same as it was back then. "Your brothers—"

But that was all she managed to get out before he

kissed her again. It was instantly one of those mind-numbing ones, and he was so good at it. Too good. It dried up her tears, fast, but it replaced her feeling of doom and gloom with more of that heat that she knew would only complicate things.

Still, that didn't stop her. Elise melted into the kiss, and let Colt's clever mouth ease her fears. Okay, it did more than ease them. That coil of heat went a long way to getting her mind on other things. Like more kissing.

More everything.

Colt and she had never gotten past the make-out stage, but her imagination was pretty good in that area. If this was how she felt just kissing him, then landing in bed would be an experience to remember.

Elise held on to that. Held on to him, too. And let his mouth work some magic on the rest of her body.

For a few seconds, anyway.

She pulled back even though that was the last thing she wanted to do. What she wanted was to test that landing-in-bed theory. Especially since the bed was just a few feet away.

Colt glanced at the bed. Then, at her. So not good. Because they were both thinking the very thing that could get them in trouble.

Thank goodness the only thing that saved them was that there was a team of lawmen just outside the window and any one of them could come walking in at any minute. Cooper had already caught them in a semi-intimate embrace. Best not to let him walk in on something that Colt and she shouldn't even be thinking about doing.

"I would say that won't happen again," Colt mumbled. "But I don't like lying to myself."

That made her smile, and Elise realized Colt was

probably the only person on earth who could make her do that right now. And that was a huge red flag.

Because she was falling hard for him.

Another *so not good*. It meant she was fast on her way to a broken heart, and Elise wasn't sure she was mentally strong enough to deal with that right now.

That didn't mean she couldn't put off a broken heart until later, though.

She heard the sound of the door opening in another part of the house. Colt moved ahead of her, and they hurried back into the kitchen just as Cooper was walking in.

"It's not Whitt," Cooper immediately said.

Elise released the breath that she'd just sucked in. Yes, there was still a body buried on her property, but at least her gran hadn't had anything to do with Whitt's murder.

"Any idea who it is?" Colt asked his brother.

"It's a woman by the name of Brandy Seaver, from San Antonio. Her wallet was in her jeans, and the driver's license matches the description of the body. Did you know her?" Cooper asked Elise.

She repeated the name, trying to figure out if it rang any bells. It didn't. So, Elise shook her head. "Who is she?"

"I made a quick call after we found the wallet and ID," Cooper went on. "Brandy Seaver had a long record of prostitution, mainly in San Antonio, and a missing person's report was filed on her nearly a year ago."

A year ago. When Elise had still been living in Dallas. She hated to think of something like that now, but at least it meant Cooper might believe she didn't have anything to do with putting the woman's body in the ground.

"How did this Brandy Seaver get out here to Sweetwater Springs?" Colt asked his brother.

"According to the report that SAPD just sent me, the girls who worked the streets with Brandy said she was last seen getting into a truck with a *customer*. None of them got the license-plate number, but several were able to describe the vehicle and the driver."

Cooper paused. "The description of the driver matches Buddy to a tee."

Chapter Eleven

Colt rolled over, the pain shooting through his shoulder and back, and he groaned out loud before he could stop himself. The groan immediately grabbed Elise's attention because she jackknifed to a sitting position. Her breath already gusting. Her eyes wide with concern.

And she looked down at him from the small twin bed. It was really more like a glorified cot in the break room at the sheriff's office.

"You're in pain," she said.

"Just not used to sleeping on the floor," Colt assured her. And a hard tile floor at that.

He worked his way out of the sleeping bag and would have gotten to his feet. If his feet hadn't both been asleep, that is. He had no choice but to drop onto the bed next to her.

The very place he'd been trying hard to avoid for the past eight hours.

Now, here he was. In bed, literally, with Elise. And despite the lack of sleep and mussed hair, she managed to look way past the hot stage. Of course, she always managed to look hot, so that was nothing new.

"I'm moving," he insisted.

But she took hold of his arm and scooted over so that she was pressed right against the wall. "We can control ourselves for at least a minute or two while you get the feeling back in your feet."

Colt tried to smile, failed. Because being this close to her was a special form of torture. "After the dream I had about you, I shouldn't be within a mile of you," he mumbled.

"I hope it was sexual." Her eyes widened again when he looked at her. "I mean better sexual than your wanting to wring my neck."

He leaned in, risked brushing a kiss on her cheek. "There are a lot of things I want to do to you, but wringing your neck's not on the list. Kissing it sounds like a good way to start the morning, though."

And a bad one, too. Because he hadn't been kidding about that dream. It had been a scorcher. Him and Elise butt naked, not on some tiny bed or floor, either. His bed. And they'd done things that he'd been thinking about doing with her for days.

Like kissing her.

Tasting every inch of her.

Sinking hard and deep into her.

Then, kissing her again.

So, that's exactly what he did. He kissed her, knowing that it was a dumber-than-dirt kind of thing to do. Despite the pain and numb feet, every other part of him was humming and aching for her.

"Bad idea?" she questioned, his mouth hovering over hers.

"Oh, yeah. The worst idea."

Somehow, that made the kiss even better. He'd never been into the whole forbidden-fruit fantasy, but in Elise's case, he'd make an exception. So, he upped the *worst idea* into a full-blown kiss. But he didn't go after her mouth this time. He went after her neck again so he could finish what he'd started.

Well, finish a little part of it, anyway.

He could do something about tasting her.

Oh, man. She was just as good as he'd imagined she would be.

Colt enjoyed the little shivering sound that Elise made when his mouth touched her throat. Enjoyed even more the kick he felt in his own body. The taste of her cruised right through him—all fire and heat—and one part of him in particular was urging him to go in for more.

Which would definitely lead to down-and-dirty morning sex.

Really not a good idea since they were just one wall away from the squad room where Cooper, Reed and heaven knew who else was already at work.

That didn't make pulling away from her easier, though, and Colt couldn't quite stop himself. He added yet another kiss several inches lower and heard another of those silky sounds of need from her.

Yet more fire and heat.

Too much for just kisses.

She eased back, her gaze connecting with his. Uh-oh. There wasn't a let's-stop-this-now kind of look in her eyes. It was pure need. And plenty of it. Probably the same amount mirrored in his, and Colt figured if he kissed her again, he was going to forget all about that one-wall barrier and go for broke.

And he'd regret it.

Maybe not while he was deep inside her. But later. The last thing Elise needed was a sex-clouded mind. Ditto for him. If he had any chance of protecting her, then he had to stay out of her bed.

Easier said than done. But Colt forced his mind back on what it should have been on in the first place.

He checked his watch. Cleared his throat. He didn't dare try to stand yet and seriously doubted he could walk.

"The hypnotist will be here soon," he reminded her. "Why don't you go ahead and grab a shower."

They'd both taken one when they'd gotten in around 10:00 p.m., but at least a shower would get them off the bed.

Maybe.

"You want me to shower alone?" she asked.

Colt groaned. That didn't help. "No, I'd rather be in there with you and your soap-slick body, but that would fall into the worst-idea category. Best if you shower alone."

His body protested that, of course.

Elise leaned in, kissed him. That didn't help, either. Then she groaned.

"The shower," she repeated, and he didn't think it was his imagination that she had to force herself to leave. Colt sure had to force himself to let her leave.

Once she was in the shower with the water running, Colt groaned again. What he should do was stick his head, and another part of him, in a bucket of ice water to cool him down and maybe regain his senses. He was playing with fire when it came to Elise, and he was pretty sure both of them would end up getting burned.

Or worse.

If he didn't keep his focus, the danger was going to come back to bite him in the butt, and in this case it could get her killed. That reminder helped even more than a bucket of cold water.

His phone buzzed, and Colt rifled through the sleeping bag to find it. He figured it was Cooper, calling to make sure it was okay to come to the flop room, but it wasn't a number that Colt recognized.

"It's me," the man said when Colt answered, and unlike the number, it was a voice he instantly recognized.

"Buddy," Colt *greeted*. "Where the hell are you?"

"Nowhere near you, so don't bother looking for me. Don't bother trying to trace this call, either, because I'm using one of those prepaid cell phones. I wanna talk to Elise now."

"She's busy." And Colt had no plans to unbusy her so she could take this call. "You can talk to me and not just over the phone. I want you down at the sheriff's office ASAP so we can chat face-to-face."

"Yeah, I'll bet you do so you can arrest me on the spot. Don't you think I know what in Sam Hill is going on? It's all over the news about the body that the cops dug up at Elise's place."

It didn't surprise Colt that the story had already made the news. Something like that couldn't be kept under wraps for long, especially since there was an APB out for Buddy's arrest.

"You need to turn yourself in," Colt insisted.

"Not gonna happen. I didn't kill that woman."

"But she got in the truck with you on the very night that she disappeared." Colt had read all the details in the report that SAPD had sent Cooper. "That makes you a prime suspect."

Buddy didn't jump to deny that, but he did hesitate. "Yeah, she was with me. So what? Doesn't mean nothing."

"Did you kill her?" Colt came right out and asked.

Again, Buddy hesitated. "No. She started whining about wanting more money for staying the whole night.

We got in an argument, I maybe sort of pushed her to stop her from slapping me, and she fell and hit her head on the kitchen counter. I didn't kill her."

It would be days or even weeks before a cause of death could be determined, but a fatal blow to the head should show some kind of trauma. Of course, it might not tell if it was accidental or intentional.

"If that's really what happened, then why didn't you just call Cooper and tell him there'd been an accident?" Colt pressed.

"Because I figured he wouldn't believe me, that's why." Buddy no longer sounded hesitant, and he cursed. "I also figured nobody would miss her. She was just a working girl. Lower than dirt. I probably gave her a better burial than she would have gotten on the street."

Even though Colt didn't know the dead woman, it turned his stomach to hear Buddy talk about her that way. Once he caught up with Buddy, he'd do whatever it took to make the man pay. Because even if this had been an accident—and Colt doubted that it was—the woman still deserved a whole lot better than being buried in a shallow grave.

"All of this is Elise's fault," Buddy continued at the exact moment that Elise came out of the bathroom.

She mouthed, "Who is it?"

Colt wasn't especially eager for her to hear what this dirtbag was saying, but he couldn't keep it from her, either. However, he did motion for her to keep quiet. No way did he want her in a shouting match with Buddy, and that's what would happen if she heard Buddy blaming her for everything.

"If Elise had just sold me the place like I wanted," Buddy went on, "then nobody would have ever found that girl."

"And you would have gotten away with murder," Colt promptly reminded him.

"I told you that it wasn't murder!" Buddy shouted. "It was an accident, and if I'd thought you and your brother would have given me a fair shake, I would have already told you about it."

The color drained from Elise's face. She likely already knew that Buddy had killed the woman, but it clearly hit her hard to hear it spelled out like that.

"So instead you decided to try to run Elise off her own land," Colt said. "When trashing the place, intimidation and graffiti didn't work, then you escalated things by rigging the barn so that it'd fall and kill us."

"What?" Buddy asked, sounding surprised.

Of course, the man could be faking that particular emotion. Murdering the prostitute wasn't personal, but an attack against Elise and him certainly was. Buddy had to know something like that would make Colt come after him and come after him hard.

"You heard me," Colt snapped. "You tried to kill us."

"I didn't." And Buddy repeated it several times. Not a shout, either, like before. He was mumbling like a confused man. Or a man pretending to be confused. "That barn was old. It probably just fell on its own."

"No. It had some help, and I don't think it's a coincidence that it happened shortly after you went to the barn and got that box. Did you set the booby trap then, or did you wait until nightfall?"

Buddy cursed. "I knew calling you was a mistake. Tell Elise what I said." And with that, he hung up.

Elise stood there, waiting for him to fill her in, but Colt took a deep breath first. "Buddy's blaming everyone but himself for the dead body. He said it was an accident, that the woman fell and hit her head."

"You believe him?"

"No." But Colt immediately had to rethink that. "Maybe, about that part, anyway."

Elise stayed quiet a moment, obviously giving it some thought, too, and she made a sound of agreement. "But if Buddy owned up to the woman's death and the vandalism, why wouldn't he also just admit he rigged the barn?"

Colt shrugged. "Maybe because he knew it'd make me come after him." However, Buddy had to know that Colt was already after him. "But if that's not the reason, I'll find out as soon as I talk to him."

That meant keeping the pressure on to find Buddy, and while a burner cell phone couldn't be traced, they might be able to locate the tower that'd been used for the call. If so, they could get a general idea of Buddy's location and find out if the man was still near Sweetwater Springs.

He made a quick call to Reed to tell him about the call so the deputy could get started on the trace. Colt would also need to write down everything the man said in case it was later needed for a trial. And unless Buddy made some kind of plea deal, it would be needed.

"Give me a minute to wash up," Colt told Elise. "And then I'll get to work so we can find some answers to all these questions."

Colt hurried because he was anxious to get started but also because Elise didn't look too steady on her feet. That caused him to curse. She wasn't getting many moments of peace and quiet these days, and Buddy's call certainly hadn't helped.

She was sitting at the foot of the bed, staring down at her hands when he came back into the room. "Don't let Buddy get to you," he said, but he already knew that the man had managed to do just that. "Now that he's confessed to burying the woman, we can arrest him. And it won't be hard to pin murder charges on him."

Elise nodded. "But I still have to get past the hypnosis."

He certainly hadn't forgotten that some big bad memories could be uncovered during that session.

"One step at a time," he reminded her. Reminded himself, too. "I'll call the diner and have them send over some breakfast."

But when Colt led her into the squad room, he saw that someone had already taken care of that. There were pastries and coffee—thank God. He poured a cup for each of them, but after seeing Cooper's expression, Colt wished he had a shot of something a little stronger.

"You weren't able to get the tower for Buddy's call," Colt concluded.

"Nothing on that yet," Cooper answered. "But I just got word Frank Wellerman's going to turn Elise's report over to SAPD so they can question Meredith about possible embezzlement activity at her last job. Let's just say Meredith's not too happy about that. She's called here twice already looking for Elise."

Colt definitely didn't like the sound of that. "Any chance Meredith will go out to our ranch looking for her?"

"Maybe. I've already alerted Dad and the ranch hands. We're locking down the place for a while."

"Oh, God," Elise mumbled. "I'm so sorry."

"No need to be," Cooper assured her. "This is on her, not you. In fact, none of this is on you. I've got Reed looking into both Meredith and her brother. Maybe something else will pop up that we can use to file our own charges against them."

Cooper's attention turned back to Colt. "Here's the second round of news that you probably don't want to hear before having coffee. Since Joplin's request for a mistrial was denied, he's trying a different angle. He's trying to have Elise declared a hostile witness so he can have her removed from our protective custody."

Colt should have seen this coming, but then he hadn't exactly had a lot of time to sit down and try to figure out what Joplin might do next. Obviously, the lawyer was doing everything he could to get Elise away from the McKinnons.

"Will Joplin succeed?" Elise asked, the worry dripping from her voice.

Cooper lifted his shoulder. "Joplin's claiming that you two are having an affair and that Colt is exerting undue influence over you that could in turn affect your testimony."

Hell. After all the dirty thoughts he'd had about Elise, it probably did look as if they were sleeping together, and Joplin had arrived at the ranch shortly after Elise and he had had a steamy kissing session.

Now it was Elise who cursed. "I'm sick and tired of that man. It's none of his business if Colt and I are having an affair. And since when would sex—even great sex—fry my brain to the point where I couldn't tell the truth under oath during a murder trial?"

She glanced around at Cooper, him and the other two deputies in the room. "Sorry," she mumbled, obviously a little embarrassed about that great-sex comment. But then the embarrassment faded, and she snapped back toward Cooper. "Can I get a restraining order against Joplin because this is harassment?"

Cooper didn't actually smile, but it was close. "I'll see what I can do." Thankfully, his brother didn't touch that great-sex comment, didn't address a possible affair between them, either, and he strolled in the direction of his office.

"No need to say you're sorry again," Colt said when Elise opened her mouth. And since she immediately closed it, he figured he'd pegged exactly what she'd been about to say to him. "Cooper's right. This isn't your fault."

She shook her head. "But it certainly feels that way."

Even though they weren't alone, Colt put his coffee aside and pulled her to him. "Try to eat something," he coaxed. "The hypnotist will be here soon. Since the session might take a while, you don't want to start it on an empty stomach."

However, the words had no sooner left his mouth when a car pulled into the parking lot of the sheriff's office. Elise probably wasn't mentally ready for the appointment. Colt wasn't sure he was, either. But whatever she might remember was just something they'd have to face.

Like all the other junk that'd been coming their way.

"Oh, no," Elise mumbled, her attention on the side window that faced the parking lot. "Not this. Not now."

Colt immediately saw what had caused that reaction, and while it was already too late to block the door, he did step in front of Elise in case this turned as ugly as he was afraid it might.

The door flew open.

Meredith tried to come in, but the hulk of a man next to her practically shoved her aside, and he stormed into the building first. Even though Colt had never met the man, he recognized him from the photo that'd come up during the background check.

Leo Darrow.

"Where the hell is Elise Nichols?" Leo snarled. "Because it's payback time for what she's trying to do to my sister."

Chapter Twelve

Elise hated having yet another confrontation, especially since the morning had already started out with that phone call from Buddy. But there was no way she would back down from this despite the fact that Leo was downright intimidating.

Ignoring Colt's warning for her to stay put, Elise stepped to his side and faced Leo and Meredith head-on. It was actually a good thing that her stitches were throbbing and that she hadn't dosed up with caffeine yet because that would help her give the pair as ornery a look as they were giving her.

Leo certainly looked menacing with his heavily muscled body and flattened nose. A sign that it'd been broken a few times—no doubt in bar fights. There were nicks and scars on his face, and along with the bulging veins on his neck, Elise figured his idea of *payback* was physical violence. Something he looked more than capable of doing.

Reed obviously thought so, too, because even though he was on the phone, he stood, moving closer to Colt and her. Still, Elise figured two armed lawmen weren't going to stop Leo and Meredith from speaking their piece.

Hopefully, speaking was all they would do.

Of course, if they did something violent, or just plain

stupid, then it would give Colt a reason to arrest them on the spot.

"Frank Wellerman's turning over your report to the cops," Meredith said, stepping to her brother's side, too.

Elise nodded. "I heard."

Meredith had to get her jaw unclenched before she could speak again. "The cops will think I did something wrong."

Good. Because she had. "Trust me, as bad as your day's been, I've got you beat. And if you're here to demand I pull the report that I wrote up on you, then you're wasting your time."

"Oh, you're pulling that report, all right," Leo insisted, and the step he took toward her had Colt taking a step of his own. Colt also put his hand over the gun in his holster.

"You'll want to take a moment," Colt warned him. "So you think about what you might or might not do in the next couple of seconds. If you're wanting to spend a lot of time in jail, then go ahead and come closer."

Leo stopped, all right. Well, he stopped moving, anyway, but the venomous look he aimed at Elise only got worse.

"If the cops believe your lies, my sister could go to jail," he said as if that excused his behavior.

"That's not my call," Elise answered. "I only reported the facts as I found them. I didn't tell Mr. Wellerman what to do with the information I gave him."

"Facts," Leo spat out. "Yeah, right. If you get your way, you'll have the cops looking at both of us for something we didn't do."

"If you're innocent, you'll be able to prove that in a court of law, won't you?" Colt argued. "But coming here like this darn sure won't help your case."

"To hell it won't," Leo argued right back. Except he turned to Elise. "You don't think I have friends? I can ruin any chance you have of continuing this line of so-called work you do."

"I'm sure you have friends," she answered before Colt could issue another threat. "I have them, too, and if I want to keep working, then I will."

"We'll see about that," Meredith snapped. "I'm going through with my defamation of character lawsuit, and—"

"Hold that thought," Reed interrupted, and while he finished his phone call, he lifted his index finger in a wait-a-section gesture. The moment he hung up, the deputy handed the notes that he'd been taking to Colt.

"What now?" Meredith snapped. "More lies and allegations about me?"

Elise didn't get a chance to read the note before Colt dropped it on his desk and shot a glare at Leo.

"Tell me about Simon Martinelli," Colt ordered, and there was no mistaking his tone. It was an order.

Meredith shook her head, maybe pretending not to recognize the name. But Elise certainly did. It was the now-dead hit man who'd run her off the road.

"What about him?" Leo countered. "He has nothing to do with this."

Colt shook his head. "Wrong answer, try again. You knew Martinelli."

Oh, mercy. This wasn't a connection she wanted. A thug paired with a hit man. And the timing of the attack could have meant that Leo had been the one to hire Martinelli.

Of course, Meredith could have done the hiring, too. And that meant this only complicated their investigation even more since Buddy, too, had known Martinelli, and Buddy had just as much motive as these two to hire a hit man.

"So?" Leo's chin came up a notch.

"So," Colt repeated. "Martinelli's dead."

Leo didn't seem the least bit surprised about that. Of course, it had been on the news, so he could have already heard. "I had nothing to do with that."

Elise had expected the denial. She certainly hadn't believed that Leo would confess to murder right here, right now. Though it would have made her life a whole lot easier, and safer, if he had.

"How about hiring Martinelli to come after Elise?" Colt countered. "Did you have something to do with that?"

"No!" he shouted at the same moment Meredith answered, "You're not dragging my brother into this. He's innocent, just trying to help me."

Elise doubted Leo was *innocent*, but she also doubted that just knowing a hit man was enough to arrest Leo.

Maybe Leo would throw a punch or something, after all.

"Call and put a freeze on their bank records," Colt told Reed, and the deputy immediately took out his phone to do that. "I want to see if either of these clowns have some suspicious payouts that could have gone to Martinelli."

"You can't do that," Meredith insisted.

"Let 'em," Leo disagreed. "They won't find anything."

Meredith made a sound of outrage that caused her mouth to tremble. "I've already had my privacy violated enough. Come on," she said, taking hold of her brother's arm.

Leo obviously didn't want to budge, but Meredith got

him moving. "This isn't over," Meredith warned them, and she hurried out the door with Leo in tow.

"Good catch," Colt told Reed the moment that the pair was out of earshot. "How'd you find the connection between Leo and Martinelli?"

Reed lifted his shoulder. "I didn't. It was a bluff. I figured a thug like him would probably know another thug."

It was a bluff that'd worked since Leo had indeed admitted an association with the hit man.

"Thanks," Colt told him, and he kept his attention pinned to Meredith and Leo, watching them drive away before he turned back to Elise. "After your appointment, I'll see what I can do about getting you out of here. I figure sooner or later Joplin will want to pay you a visit."

He would. "You're talking about taking me to the safe house with the Ranger?" she asked.

"You could use my place instead," Reed quickly offered. "It's not that far out of town, it has a security system with all the doors and windows wired. Plus, I have two dogs who bark at everything. You're welcome to it since I'll be pulling duty here tonight. I can even call a couple of your ranch hands if you like and have them stay over just to keep watch."

Elise liked that idea much better than being taken miles and miles away.

Colt made a sound of agreement. "Thanks. Call the Rangers and cancel the plans for a safe house."

He'd hardly finished telling Reed that, however, when he snapped toward the window, and she saw yet someone else making their way toward the sheriff's office. It was a short woman with auburn hair, and she was carrying a bulky briefcase.

"I'm Suzanne Dawkins," their visitor said the moment she stepped inside the building. Her attention went straight to Elise. "I'm here for your hypnosis appointment."

Elise had known this was about to happen. But she still dreaded it. "I'm ready." A lie, but then she was as ready as she'd ever be. "Would it be okay, though, if Colt stayed with me during the session?"

Suzanne nodded, sighed and glanced around, looking as uncomfortable as Elise felt. "I need to tell you up front, though, that if you recall anything during the session, I can't swear it'll stay between us. I'm not your physician or a psychiatrist, so it's possible I can be subpoenaed to testify about what you recall."

And Joplin would definitely do that if it helped clear Jewell's name.

"You'll probably remember everything you say while under hypnosis. That includes any bad things you might have witnessed. It could mean dealing with some, well, disturbing images. So, you still want to go through with it?" Suzanne asked.

Elise looked at Colt, and he finally nodded. Elise nodded, too, though she hoped this didn't turn out to be a mistake.

One that could send Colt's father straight to jail for murder.

COLT STOOD NEAR the door of the flop room and waited for the hypnotist to continue questioning Elise.

He was saying a few prayers, too.

Prayers for his father, and for what could be a whole boatload of nightmarish memories that Elise might have to relive.

He hated that she had go to through this.

Suzanne had already given Elise some kind of meds,

and her eyelids were drooping while she drifted in and out of consciousness. Something that the hypnotist had explained would happen. She'd also been adamant that Colt not say a word because it could interfere with whatever Elise might say.

"Elise, you're back by the creek next to the Braddock cabin," Suzanne said, her voice a soothing whisper. "You're nine years old. Remember?"

"Yes," Elise mumbled. "I'm mad at Colt."

Despite everything, he smiled. Then he frowned. He'd been a nine-year-old butthead to upset her like that.

"But Colt's not with you at the creek, now, is he?" Suzanne went on. "Are you alone?"

Elise nodded. "I'm stirring the water with a stick."

Maybe trying to put that curse on him she'd mentioned.

"Did you go near the cabin or look in the window before you went to the creek?" she asked.

"I'm not allowed to go near the cabin. Gran's rules. Mr. Braddock doesn't like kids playing around it. Even his own kids. They aren't allowed to go there."

"Okay," Suzanne answered. "Do you hear anything or see anyone while you're stirring the water with the stick?"

"No." But then Elise paused. "Yeah. I hear a door closing, I think, and someone walking. He's walking up from behind the cabin." Another pause. "It's Colt's dad. Hi, Mr. Roy." Elise's voice was small now, and she was no doubt deep into that childhood memory.

"Did Mr. Roy answer you?" Suzanne asked.

Another head shake. "He stumbled on the porch step of the cabin and said some bad words that I can't repeat. Gran'll wash my mouth out with soap if I do."

Colt pulled in his breath, praying it was his father's stumbling and nothing else that'd caused the profanity.

"Elise," Suzanne said, "don't repeat the bad words, but I need you to look at Mr. Roy. Did he actually come out of the cabin?"

"Maybe. I heard a door close."

"But you're not sure that Mr. Roy was the one who closed it?" Suzanne asked the very question that Colt wanted her to ask.

"No. Not sure."

Good. Yeah, it was only a little doubt, but it was far better than Elise having seen his father come out of the cabin.

"Is it windy?" Suzanne continued.

Even though her eyes were closed, he could see them moving behind her eyelids. "Yes. The leaves are rattling on the trees." She paused. "I guess the wind coulda blown the door shut."

Colt added another *good*. Of course, that didn't clear his father. From what Elise was recalling, the door had been open and that meant someone had opened it.

"Is Mr. Roy alone, and what's he wearing?" the therapist asked.

Elise's forehead bunched up, the expression a person would make when concentrating. "Nobody's with him. And he's got on jeans, boots, a brown shirt and his hat."

"You're sure he's alone?"

"I'm sure," Elise said after several moments. "I don't see or hear anybody else. If somebody was inside, I'd think they'd hear Mr. McKinnon cussing and come out. He's not being very quiet 'cause he's banging his fist on the front door right now."

That put a too-clear picture in Colt's mind of what his dad was going through. Drunk and furious that his wife was having an affair with a man he considered his enemy. His father had gone to the cabin no doubt to confront them.

But Jewell and Whitt hadn't been there.

Well, Whitt hadn't been there alive, anyway. It was possible while all of this was going on that Whitt's body was inside and that his mother was hiding.

"Mr. Roy's still banging on the door," Elise continued several moments later. "And he's yelling for Mr. Braddock and Miss Jewell to open up. But I don't think anybody's in there. The place was quiet before Mr. Roy got there. If I'd seen Mr. Braddock, I wouldn't have hung around the creek. Gran's rules."

It was a good rule, too. Whitt wasn't a friendly sort, and Colt had been on the receiving end of some of Whitt's yelling when he'd caught him playing too close to the cabin. Of course, in hindsight, Whitt might have done that because he'd been trying to conceal the fact that he had Jewell in there with him. Since his mother had stayed quiet about the subject, Colt had no idea how long the affair had been going on.

"Is there anything odd about Mr. Roy's clothes?" Suzanne pressed when Elise didn't continue. "Is there maybe mud…or something else on them?"

That question required Colt to hold his breath again, and it didn't help that it seemed to take Elise an eternity to answer. "No mud, but his hair's messed up bad, and he's stumbling again. Cussing, too. I think he's had too much to drink."

Yeah, he had. Drunk, which left a lot of gaps in his memory. Gaps that Elise could be about to fill.

"You're sure about the mud?" Suzanne asked. "Take a closer look. Is there anything on Mr. McKinnon's clothes, anything wet maybe?"

Again, Elise took her time thinking about that. "No." She paused. "But he's got something in his hand."

Oh, man. Not a knife or a gun. If so, it would put his father at the murder scene with a potential murder weapon.

"What's in Mr. Roy's hand?" Suzanne asked.

Yet another pause. Even longer than the others. "A bottle. Of whiskey, I think. He keeps drinking from it in between all the yelling."

Colt tried to make his breath of relief as silent as possible.

"That's good, Elise," Suzanne said, sounding a little relieved, too. "Is there anything else you notice about Mr. Roy or the cabin? Think hard."

"Nothing else," she said after several moments. "I have to go home now. Can I leave?"

"Of course. Elise, I'm going to count to three, and when I reach three, you'll open your eyes, and you'll be back in the Sweetwater Springs Sheriff's Office." Suzanne counted off the numbers, and just as she'd said, when she reached three, Elise opened her eyes.

Despite the obvious fatigue, Elise's gaze went straight to Colt. "I remember everything I saw. No blood," she mumbled. "Your father's innocent."

Colt was glad she remembered what she'd told them. Glad of the outcome, too.

Of course, this was just the beginning, and while it cleared his father, it didn't mean the danger was over for Elise. Just the opposite. Buddy was still missing, and it was obvious that Joplin, Meredith and her idiot brother, Leo, had the potential to cause plenty of trouble.

"Elise might be a little drowsy for a while," Suzanne said, standing and gathering up her things. "And someone should stay with her just in case she has any adverse reactions to the mild sedative that I gave her."

"I'm not leaving her," Colt assured her.

The moment Suzanne left, Elise sat up, touching her fingers to her head.

"Are you in pain?" Colt immediately asked.

"No." She took several deep breaths. "In fact, I feel better than I have in the past couple of days." And to prove it, she got to her feet.

Colt was right there to catch her, but she didn't so much as wobble. "Did Joplin or Meredith come back while I was under?"

He shook his head.

"But they will," she added. "What are the odds that we can get out of here before then? Maybe go to Reed's house? I don't think I'm up to another battle today."

Colt wasn't at all sure about moving Elise, especially so soon after Suzanne had given her that mild sedative, but he wasn't up to doing battle, either. With his arm looped around her, they went back into the squad room, ready to ask Reed for the keys to his place, but the deputy was already one step ahead of him. He handed Colt a key and a piece of paper with the code for the security system.

"Stay as long as you need," Reed offered, and he hitched his thumb to the other deputy, Pete Nichols, who was already getting to his feet. "Pete'll be driving out there with you, and I'll make that call to your ranch hands to have a couple of them meet you at my house. If anything goes wrong, I can be out there in ten minutes."

It all sounded like a good plan, except for Elise. She wobbled, giving Colt two choices. He could carry her back to the flop room and let her sleep off the medication, or he could take Reed up on his offer.

"Joplin called," Reed added as if reading Colt's mind. "He's at the jail with Jewell right now but said he's heading up here when he's done."

Elise groaned, and Colt knew he'd get her out of there. Part of him wanted to stay, to confront Joplin and see if he could get the lawyer to back off, but Elise would still be able to hear that confrontation even if she stayed out of sight. Plus, he doubted he could say anything to make Joplin change his mind.

"Did Joplin petition to have me removed from Colt's custody?" Elise asked.

Reed nodded. "And he just might get it approved. Yet even more reason you should get the heck out of here," he added to Colt. "When Joplin shows, I don't intend to tell him where you are."

Good. Because Elise needed at least a few hours of peace and quiet. Heck, so did he.

"I'll follow in my truck," Pete said, following them to the door. "It's parked right next to yours."

"Thanks," Colt told both his fellow deputies. When this was over, he owed them, big-time. His brother, too, since Cooper had made protecting Elise a top priority.

Colt put on his coat, helped Elise with hers and he paused in the doorway. He had a look around. Nothing seemed out of place, but still he hurried as much as he could. He used his keypad to unlock the truck, and reached for the passenger's-side door so he could get Elise inside fast.

But his hand froze on the handle when he saw what was on the driver's seat.

Hell.

"Get down!" Colt yelled.

Chapter Thirteen

Elise was woozy, everything swimming in and out of focus, but she still managed to see what had caused Colt's reaction.

A gun rigged with some kind of device.

Colt ran, dragging her along with him, and he pulled her to the rear of the nearest vehicle—one parked on the side of the street by the parking lot. Not a second too soon. He'd barely gotten them on the ground when the shots started.

That jolted away some of the wooziness, and her heart slammed against her chest. Mercy, not this, not now.

"The gun's activated by remote control," Colt said, drawing his own weapon and crawling on top of her to protect her.

"Get down!" he shouted again.

Elise couldn't see anyone other than Pete, the deputy, and he'd taken cover on the side of a truck. He, too, had his gun drawn and ready, and like Colt, his gaze was firing all around them.

It hit her then that the gun in Colt's truck could be some kind of ruse to draw their attention away from the person who'd launched this attack.

Elise lifted her head a fraction to look around. Or at least she tried, but Colt put her right back down.

The shots continued, and even though she could no longer see Colt's truck, she could hear the bullets ripping through the door. If this was like the remote-control gun at her ranch, then the shots would be hitting the same spot. She prayed that spot wasn't the sheriff's office or any of the other nearby buildings.

This monster might be after her, but he or she could end up killing an innocent bystander.

Colt reached up and tested the door handle of the vehicle they were using for cover, but he cursed when it was locked. Maybe the owner would realize what was happening and open it from wherever he or she was.

That created another slam of fear inside her.

"What if this car is rigged to blow up or something?" she asked, though she wasn't sure how Colt could understand her with her words slurred and her voice shaking as hard as the rest of her.

"Any of the vehicles could blow up," he reminded her. "But this car doesn't belong to the shooter. It belongs to Herman Vinton, and he'll be in the diner this time of the morning."

That was something at least, but it didn't mean the shooter hadn't managed to get into Herman's car, as well.

"See anything?" Colt shouted to Pete.

"No. He might be on one of the roofs."

Mercy, there were plenty of them, including the sheriff's office itself. With all the activity going on inside the building, it was possible that no one had noticed the person who'd broken into Colt's truck and left that remote-control gun. Worse, the gun could have been put there during the night when no one would have been likely to see what was going on.

"The gun should run out of bullets soon," Colt said to her over the deafening blasts.

Elise could hear the frantic shouts and cries from the people in the diner across the street. At this time of morning, it was possible there were even schoolchildren out and about. But until the shots stopped firing, Colt and she were literally pinned down and unable to help.

It was hard to tell exactly where the shots were going, but, thankfully, it wasn't toward them or the other deputy. Also, other than the initial sound from Colt's truck window, she didn't hear any breaking glass.

Maybe that meant the shots weren't going into any of the buildings.

"Tell Reed we need eyes on the roofs," Colt shouted to Pete, and the deputy took out his phone to make a call. He was no doubt calling for some kind of backup, too, since they would need to search the entire area.

Maybe this time they'd get lucky.

Of course, the person who'd set all of this up could be just another hired gun like Martinelli. That meant any of their suspects could be responsible.

"Joplin would know about the restraining order I filed against him," she said. And Elise figured that certainly hadn't made him happy.

Had it caused him to do something like this?

Of course, this was also right up Buddy's alley. Meredith's, too, since her scummy brother could have done the dirty work for her.

The shots stopped. Finally. But Colt didn't move. He stayed on top of her, keeping watch. Protecting her—again. She hated that his life and so many others' were in danger because of her.

"Reed's making calls," Pete relayed. "Cooper and your brother Tucker are on their way to set up a roadblock."

Good. That might stop this idiot from escaping. If the person was still around, that is. With the shots silenced, there didn't seem to be any sign of their attacker. Of course, he could be waiting for them to leave cover so he'd be able to gun them down.

"I'm sorry," she whispered. "I shouldn't have insisted we leave the sheriff's office."

"Don't," Colt warned her. "He would have just found another way to come after us."

Colt was right, but that tightened the knot in her stomach. This monster wasn't going to stop until he killed Colt and her.

Colt's phone buzzed, and without taking his attention off their surroundings, he handed Elise the device so that she could no doubt read the text message that popped up on the screen.

"It's from Reed," she relayed. "He's going out the back of the sheriff's office so he can get a better look at the roofs."

"Good. Ask him to call Herman and see if he has a way of unlocking his car from the diner," Colt instructed.

Elise fired off the text to Reed. And waited. Her body bracing itself for yet another attack. At least if they were in the car, that would give them some small measure of protection.

But that idea quickly went south.

"'Herman doesn't have a remote key to unlock the car,'" she read aloud when Reed answered.

It was an older-model car so that wasn't surprising. But that meant they were stuck. It was a good twenty-five feet to get back into the sheriff's office. About the same distance to get into the diner. That was a lot of space where they'd be out in the open and vulnerable to an attack.

"As soon as Reed gives us the all clear," Colt said, "we'll move."

That couldn't come soon enough. But the seconds crawled by, turning into minutes. Colt and she had on coats, but it didn't take long for the cold from the pavement to seep through her clothes. She started to shiver.

"He's on the roof of the diner!" Pete shouted.

That was the only warning they got before the blast ripped through the air. This time, there was the sound of shattering glass because the shot blew out the window just above their heads.

"Get under the car," Colt insisted, but he was already shoving her in that direction.

It wasn't fast enough. More shots came, one slamming into the tire just inches from them.

"Keep moving," Colt told her. "Get to the other side of the car."

She scrambled over the rough pavement, but there wasn't a lot of room between Herman's car and the curb. Still, Elise managed to squeeze in, and she reached for Colt to pull him to safety.

Just as the hail of bullets started.

She could no longer see Pete, but she prayed he'd managed to get out of the way in time. Reed, too.

"Stay here," Colt ordered the moment he was fully out from beneath the car. He crawled toward the rear of the car, and using it for cover, took aim.

And fired.

Elise couldn't tell if he hit the shooter, but at least the bullets stopped. For a few seconds, anyway. Then they picked back up, and she realized the shooter had moved. Probably because Colt had come close to taking him out.

"There," Colt said, motioning to someone behind him.

Elise spotted both Reed and Pete on the side of the sheriff's office. They, too, had their weapons aimed at the roof of the diner, and both fired.

Again, the shots stopped.

And this time, they didn't immediately start back up.

"Hell, he's getting away," Colt said, and judging from his body language, he'd been about to bolt. No doubt to go in pursuit. But then he must have remembered she was there.

"It could be a trick," he added. "To get you alone." Colt mouthed some profanity and looked in the direction of the other deputies. "Reed, is it safe for you to move?" he asked.

Reed looked around, nodded, and he told Pete to cover him. Reed raced toward Herman's car and dropped to the pavement next to Colt.

"Guard Elise," Colt told Reed.

The deputy didn't question Colt's order, but Elise certainly did. "It's not safe. This could be a trick to draw you out."

"I'm not letting him get away again," Colt insisted, and he gave her a look. A warning, actually, for her to stay put, and he took off.

"He'll be okay," Reed told her, and he held her in place when she tried to lever herself up. But Reed didn't sound totally convinced of that.

And for a good reason.

The shooter on the roof had a much better vantage point than any of them. He could gun Colt down before he even made it across the street.

Pete didn't stay put, either. As Reed had done, he hurried toward the car and took cover behind the back bumper where Colt had just been.

"Did you get a look at the shooter?" she asked.

Pete shook his head, but Reed nodded. "A guy, but I couldn't see his face. Don't think it's anyone we know, though."

Then maybe she'd been right about it being a hired gun. Elise wanted to yell out to the guy that it hadn't turned out so well for the last person who'd been hired to do her harm. He'd been blown to bits. But yelling would only give away their exact position—if by some miracle the shooter didn't already know that.

Of course, a distraction might stop him from trying to take a shot at Colt.

She pulled off her shoe and hurled it over the front end of the car. It worked. Well, sort of. The guy did indeed fire a shot, and it slammed into the hood.

Reed cursed and shoved her flat on the pavement again.

"Colt won't be happy about you doing that," Reed told her.

No, but at least it'd pinpointed the position of the shooter, and it'd gotten his attention off Colt. Hopefully long enough for Colt to make it to cover so he could go after this guy.

"He's still on the roof," Pete said when a second shot came their way.

Pete levered himself up and returned fire, the blast so close to Elise that the sound of his gun shot through her head. Not good. She was still a little woozy, and she wanted a clear mind in case they had to escape or help Colt.

"Colt's using the Dumpster to get onto the roof,"

Reed relayed to her. And he, too, sent a shot the gunman's way. No doubt to keep him distracted so he wouldn't hear Colt trying to sneak up on him.

Elise held her breath and prayed some more. As much as she wanted the bullets to stop, the silence was even more chilling when they did.

Did that mean the shooter was onto Colt? He could be walking right into another trap.

"Go help him, please," Elise whispered to Reed.

But Reed quickly shook his head. "Colt will have my hide if I leave you."

He would, but they had to do something, anything. "Fire some more shots at the gunman to distract him."

Another head shake from Reed. "I can't fire any more shots because Colt just got on the roof."

Oh, mercy.

Elise had to see what was happening. Without lifting her head—something Reed obviously wouldn't have allowed her to do, anyway—she angled her body and looked up, craning her neck so she got a glimpse of the roof.

She didn't see anyone.

But she certainly heard something.

A gunshot.

Then another.

She couldn't tell if they'd come from Colt's gun, the shooter's. Or both. It was possible they'd fired and shot each other.

With that horrible thought racing through her head, she had to fight to make herself stay put. The seconds crawled by, and because she was listening so carefully, the next gun blast caused her to jump.

So did Reed.

He got to his feet, automatically aiming his gun at the roof. But the deputy didn't fire.

Elise got just a glimpse of the man falling. Before he crashed with a thud onto the street below.

Chapter Fourteen

Colt hated the fear he saw in Elise's eyes. Hated that he hadn't been able to stop the latest attack. Hated even more that he might not be able to stop another one.

It'd been a hellish long day what with the shooting, the mop-up from it and Elise's hypnosis session. Colt was hoping for a much more peaceful night.

"The guy's name is Arnold Levinson," Reed said.

Even though Colt didn't have the call on speaker, Elise was close enough so she could clearly hear every word the deputy was saying to him.

"Who was he?" she asked.

"A lowlife with a long record, but among other things he's done work as a bouncer," Reed answered, obviously not having any problems hearing Elise, either. "No connection that I can find to any of our suspects. But I'll keep looking," Reed added before Colt could ask him to do just that.

"Another hired gun," Elise mumbled. That got her pacing across Reed's kitchen while she scrubbed her hands up and down her arms. She probably wasn't cold since the house was toasty warm, but it might be a while before the chill left her.

If ever.

"Call me if you find out anything from our suspects," Colt added.

Since Reed had already said that he was bringing in Joplin and Meredith for questioning, he might learn something new. And while Colt was wishing, he added that maybe someone would find Buddy and haul his butt in, as well.

"It could have been you falling off that roof," Elise said the moment he finished the call with Reed. "It could have been you with a bullet to the chest."

"But it wasn't." He went to her, knowing that she would resist when he pulled her into his arms. She did. She was too wound up to stay still, but Colt held her, anyway. "You heard what Reed said. The guy was a lowlife not a pro."

He could thank his lucky stars for that. If the idiot had been a better shot, they might all be dead. Instead, the would-be killer was the one who'd been killed.

The remote-control device would be sent for testing, of course, and his truck would be dusted for prints and any other evidence that could be found connected to the break-in. That and all the other things they had in motion might help them ID this sack of dirt before he or she did any more harm.

Elise made a shivery sound of frustration, and Colt pulled her even closer. Yeah, it was dumb and dangerous. There was already enough tension left over from the attack without adding a different kind of tension. The kind that came from holding Elise in his arms.

That didn't stop him.

Colt figured the sweet torture was worth it if it gave her any comfort whatsoever. Of course, what was comfort for her would be another torture session for him.

"At least we won't have to deal with any surprise visits while we're here," Colt reminded her.

The security system was on and armed. Darnell, the ranch hand, had a gun and was in the living room at the front of the house, where he'd stay for the night. Plus, Reed's two dogs, Sampson and Delilah, were on the glassed-in porch at the back of the house. They were barkers, Reed had told them, and would alert them to anything.

Colt was counting heavily on that.

Still, even with all those measures and the fact that Elise was continuing to fight the effects of the sedative from the hypnosis session, Colt figured this would be yet another restless night. That was okay. He'd take restless over danger.

"You should go to bed," he reminded her—again. Like his other reminders, she stayed put as if somehow staying awake would protect them.

"Alone," Colt added when her eyebrow came up.

"Alone," she repeated, leaning into him.

She probably hadn't meant for her body to land against his like that. But it did. And Colt's body noticed, all right.

He quickly told those noticing parts to knock it off.

"Come on," he added, giving her a nudge toward the bedroom. "I brought the sleeping bag with me, and I can crash on the floor again."

Maybe.

But he figured that he'd get about as much sleep as Darnell and Elise. Little to none. Between keeping watch and reining in his body, it was going to be a long night.

She finally moved when Colt gave her another nudge and got her walking in the direction of Reed's guest room. The walls were decorated like a nursery in pale yellow with baby-duck decals. No doubt leftover decor from Reed's ex-wife, who, from all accounts, had desperately wanted a baby but hadn't been able to have one. Even though Reed obviously hadn't gotten around to redecorating since the divorce, he'd added a bed that looked freshly made and ready for Elise.

Not for Colt, though.

With everything they'd been through, getting into bed with her would lead to trouble. Even though his back was already protesting the hard floor and another part of him was protesting because it wasn't going to get lucky. The floor was where he'd spend the night keeping watch.

She didn't change into the gown that she'd brought from her house. Good thing. Best if she stayed covered so he couldn't see what he was missing. Instead, Elise dropped onto the bed, staring up at the ceiling. Colt turned off the light and did the same. He got onto the sleeping bag that he'd already rolled out.

"If I just leave town, disappear," Elise added. "Then I could hire a bodyguard. I could give a deposition for my testimony, and you and your family would be safe."

"*You* still wouldn't be safe," he reminded her.

But it was a moot point, anyway. He wasn't letting her leave. Yeah, it was probably cocky to feel this way, but he'd do a better job protecting her than some bodyguard for hire.

"What if it's never safe?" she asked. She rolled to the edge of the bed and looked down at him.

Best to put a lighter spin on this since even though he couldn't see her eyes in the darkness, he figured the fear was creeping back into them. Or maybe it'd never left.

"You don't have much faith in my abilities as a lawman, do you?" He didn't wait for her to answer. "Well, you should. I've been a deputy for nearly nine years now, and I've always done a good job with protection detail. Only been shot once."

She made a sharp sound of surprise. "You were shot?"

Heck, he figured her grandmother had told her all about that. Apparently not. So much for his attempt to lighten things up. Talking about gunshot wounds would do anything but.

"Sue Morgan's ex shot me when I was trying to break up a fight between them," he said, and he automatically rubbed what was now a faint scar on his abdomen. "Nothing serious."

Well, he'd nearly died, but best to keep that to himself, too.

"Whatever happens," she said, "I don't want you to step in front of a bullet for me. I'm already on your family's bad side. I'd rather not add personal injury or attempted personal injury to it."

Colt couldn't help it. He chuckled. "You're soon to be on their good side. Well, my brothers' good sides, anyway. You cleared our dad's name."

"Yes, that was something at least. Still, stay out of the path of bullets. And don't go charging up on any other roofs to get bad guys."

"Uh, that's kind of my job description."

She stared down at him. Now that his eyes had adjusted to the dark room, he could see that her own eyes were narrowed a bit. Elise obviously wasn't happy that he would put himself in danger for her.

But he would.

"Okay," he said to placate her. And hopefully to get her to go to sleep. "No charging after bad guys."

Not until it was absolutely necessary, that is.

"Good." She mumbled something else that he didn't catch and dropped back down on the bed. "Here we are sleeping under the same roof again. You can bet Joplin will try to use this against me in some way."

Yeah, he would. "He might try," Colt settled for saying.

That brought her to the edge of the bed again, and he expected the conversation to continue. After all, Elise no doubt had plenty of fears and concerns that she needed calming.

Or not.

That wasn't exactly a soothe-me look she had in her eyes now.

Elise eased off the bed and landed next to him on the floor. "This can work two ways," she said. "I can throw myself at you, and you can crush me by saying no. Or—"

Colt didn't need to hear the other part of that. Because there was zero chance of his saying no. Even if that's exactly what he should be saying.

He slipped his hand around the back of her neck, pulled her to him and kissed her. This might not help their situation, but he figured it would help them. For a little while, anyway.

She slipped right into the kiss. Right against him, too, and put her arms around him to pull him even closer. Not that he wasn't already heading in that direction, anyway, but she closed the already narrow gap between their bodies.

Colt took things from there. He deepened the kiss. Felt that punch of heat that he knew would be there. Then felt it burn even hotter. It made him wonder how he'd been able to go so long resisting this. Resisting her.

"I should give you an out," he whispered.

"I don't want one." And she pulled him right back to her for yet another kiss.

It was just as good as the first kiss, but there was a big problem with kisses like that. They only caused the heat to rise higher and higher until soon kissing wasn't nearly enough.

Colt slid his hand beneath her sweater, unhooked her bra, and her breasts spilled into his hands. No way could he resist that, so he shoved up her top and moved the kisses from her mouth to her nipples.

Elise obviously liked that.

She made a silky sound of pleasure, threaded her fingers through his hair and let him feast on her. It was just as good as the kisses, too, but soon it wasn't enough, either.

Elise tried to do something about that. She went after his shirt and would have managed to shove it off if his shoulder holster hadn't gotten in the way. Colt had to stop the breast kisses to help her unhook it. The holster and gun went on the floor next to them, followed by his shirt.

Then, her sweater.

He got another punch of that burning need when her bare skin landed against his. He'd thought about being with her like this for years. Since they'd shared that first kiss way back when, and those years hadn't diminished the need one little bit. He still wanted her—bad.

"Let's finish this," she insisted.

He had no plans to argue with that, either.

Colt rid her of her jeans. It wasn't a pretty maneuver, and the need made them fumble, but they grappled enough to get his jeans off, too.

And then he remembered the stitches on her head.

Something he should have considered before he even started kissing her.

"I don't want to hurt you," he said.

She blinked, as if trying to figure out what that meant. Maybe she was thinking about all the emotional fallout they'd have from this.

"Your head," he added.

"Oh." She sounded relieved and kissed him again. "You won't hurt me."

Colt wasn't so sure of that at all, especially since that latest kiss upped the ante tenfold. So did stripping off her panties. Ditto for his touching her in the center of all that heat.

Oh, man.

She was hot, wet and ready.

And even though his mind kept telling him to slow down and be gentle, they were well past that stage.

Colt gathered her beneath him and sank into her.

The sound that Elise made was one of relief. Then, pure pleasure. It was a sound that slammed through him, and coupled with the feel of being inside her, there was no way Colt couldn't do what she'd demanded.

Finish this.

He moved inside her. Elise moved with him. It was perfect. But perfect meant this would all end a heck of a lot sooner than he wanted.

Still, Colt had no choice. His body was in control now, and it drove him to take her. To push her toward the only place either of them wanted to go.

It didn't take much. She was so ready that he felt that climax ripple through her. And in that moment, the moonlight landed on her face. So beautiful. As perfect as the moment.

That couldn't last.

Colt pushed into her one last time, releasing them both from the blazing fire.

ELISE HAD TO catch onto Colt to stop him from immediately moving off her.

"Your stitches," he reminded her again.

"Aren't bothering me in the least," she assured him.

It was somewhat of a miracle. She'd been in pain for two days, ever since the attack that'd resulted in the stitches, but sex with Colt seemed to be the cure for even the worst pain.

However, it obviously wasn't a cure for Colt.

He brushed one of those chaste kisses on her cheek and eased off her, dropping next to her on the sleeping bag. "I didn't use a condom," he murmured.

She was surprised that he could think of anything at the moment. Her brain was still a nice whirl of pleasure and other post-sex sensations. "I'm on the pill, remember?"

He no doubt did since she'd made such a big deal of personally getting them from her place.

But maybe this wasn't about the lack of condom. Maybe this was about the other thing that'd she been sure would surface.

"You're already regretting this," she said.

Colt stiffened and turned on his side so he could look at her. "No. That's the problem. I'm not regretting it at all, and I should be." He gave a heavy sigh. "It's best to keep a clear head in the middle of an attempted-murder investigation." He slipped his hand between them, touched her breast. "This doesn't equal clear head."

His touch gave her a nice little shiver of pleasure. Enough so that she wondered if she could coax him into another round. Well, maybe not if he was trying to keep a clear head.

"So, you're sure there are no regrets?" she clarified.

"Maybe one." He swiped his thumb over her nipple, causing another of those nice little waves of heat to race through her. "I should have made it last longer."

So, not the kind of regrets that she was worried about. Still, Elise didn't want him to feel hemmed in by what was essentially an old attraction.

But she rethought that.

Yes, it was an old one. But this didn't exactly feel old. Oh, no.

Not this. Not with Colt.

However, *this* was exactly what was happening.

She wasn't just falling for him. She was falling in love with him.

"Are you in pain?" he quickly asked, levering himself up. "You made a funny sound."

No way would she tell him that sound involved the *L*-word. That would send a man like Colt running.

Before tonight, it might have sent her running, too. She'd always worked so hard to create her own life. And not one that she'd necessarily been born into. That was the reason she'd steered away from serious relationships. That, and no man had ever quite lived up to the one she'd left behind.

Colt.

"I'm fine," she lied.

But she wasn't. This really put a crimp in the plans she had. Getting a ranch up and running would take plenty of time and hard work. Elise certainly hadn't factored in a complicated relationship.

And with Colt, it would be complicated.

Even though she could essentially clear his father's

name, that wouldn't put her in the good graces of Colt's sister Rayanne, who had no doubt hoped that Elise's testimony would put the blame on anyone but Jewell. Heaven knew how long it'd take to mend fences with her. And with Jewell herself.

"So, what's wrong?" Colt asked. "Because you're being even quieter than I am."

Elise was about to turn the tables on him and ask him about that quietness. However, the quietness disappeared in a flash.

The dogs started barking.

The sound echoed through the house. Through her. And it brought both of them to their feet. They immediately started scrambling to put on their clothes.

"It might be nothing," Colt reminded her. "Reed said the dogs will bark at anything."

But Elise figured with their luck, it wasn't just anything. It was *something*. Or worse—some*one*.

"Darnell, I'll be out there in a second," Colt called out to the ranch hand. He zipped his jeans and put on his shoulder holster and gun. "You see anything?"

"Not yet," Darnell answered.

The dogs didn't stop. In fact, their barking got even louder, and Elise could tell they were on the side of the porch that was farther from the bedroom.

The moment Colt finished dressing, he threw open the door. "Stay away from the windows," he reminded her. "And don't turn on the lights."

With his gun drawn and ready, he hurried to join the ranch hand.

Elise pulled on the rest of her clothes and stepped into the dark hallway. Listening. But the only things she could hear were the dogs and Colt and Darnell's mumbled conversation.

She eased closer, keeping her footsteps light so she wouldn't disturb them, and she found both men in the living room. Darnell was looking out the front window, and Colt, out the side one. They weren't standing directly in front of the glass but, rather, were peering around the window edges.

Elise held her breath. Waiting. Something she'd been doing a lot lately. For the past couple of days, her life had been filled with one attack after another.

Well, with the exception of making love with Colt.

That'd been a wonderful reprieve, but Colt would no doubt blame himself for that lapse in focus.

"I think I got something," Colt said, and that sent Darnell scurrying to the side window with Colt.

But Darnell shook his head when he had a look.

"In the pasture near the fence," Colt added.

Elise wasn't that familiar with Reed's ranch. She'd only gotten glimpses of it when they'd driven in because Colt had been so anxious to get her inside. However, she remembered the fenced side pasture that led to a small corral area and a barn. If someone was out there, they were already very close to the house.

And the dogs confirmed that.

Their barking became even more frantic, and it sounded as if they were trying to get out of the glassed-in porch so they could go after whoever was out there.

"Should I let the dogs out?" Darnell asked.

Colt shook his head. "No. If the person's armed, I don't want the dogs hurt. Besides, I'd rather them stay put in case there's an attempted break-in."

Oh, mercy. That really didn't help with her nerves. It was bad enough having someone so close, but she definitely didn't want another hired gun getting into the house. And it wasn't much of a stretch to believe the person behind the attacks would just hire someone to come after her since there were already two dead hit men who'd tried and failed.

"There," Colt said, pointing toward someone on the left side of the window. "Did you see it that time?"

Darnell didn't jump to answer. Then she saw the muscles in his body tense. "Yeah."

Elise didn't go closer, but she looked over their shoulders out into the night landscape. There was still a full moon, plenty light enough for her to see something she definitely didn't want to see.

A man.

Elise caught just a glimpse of him as he ducked behind the barn. But a glimpse was all she needed to see that the man was armed with a rifle.

Chapter Fifteen

"Elise, get down on the floor now," Colt ordered her.

She was already headed in that direction, which meant she had no doubt seen the latest threat outside the window. The armed guy less than twenty yards from the house. Hard to miss him with the moonlight glinting off the barrel of his rifle.

Darnell and Colt both took aim at the man, but since he was using the barn for cover, they didn't have a clean shot. But once they did, it was a shot that Colt would take. He doubted this was a neighborly visit at this hour, and with all the mess that Elise and he had been through, he didn't intend to take any more chances.

Colt fired off a text to Reed and his brother requesting backup ASAP and hoped Reed had been right about it not taking them long to get out there. With the gunman already in place, they didn't have much time.

The dogs continued to bark, and Colt wondered if that was the reason the guy was staying back. The Dobermans sounded ready to tear someone limb from limb, and probably would if they got the chance. It might just stop this idiot from trying to break in.

"Is it just one man?" Elise asked him.

"Yeah."

But Colt wasn't holding out hope that the guy had

come alone. If the person who wanted her dead was as desperate as Colt figured he was, there could be several hired guns out there hiding somewhere.

"Go to the kitchen and keep watch," he told Darnell just in case someone tried to sneak up on them from that direction. If that happened, hopefully the dogs would move to that side of the porch so they'd have some warning.

That thought had no sooner crossed his mind when the dogs did exactly that. He heard the Dobermans scramble to the other side. No longer focused just on the pasture, something else had obviously alerted them. Something on the very side where he'd just sent Darnell.

"I don't see anyone," Darnell called out.

Hell.

Colt hadn't meant to curse out loud because he didn't want to alarm Elise more than she already was. But she obviously heard his profanity and knew what it meant. That they might be right in the middle of an ambush, and if they couldn't even pinpoint their attackers, there was no way to prevent something bad from happening.

"I can keep watch out front," she said. "And I'll stay down and back from the windows."

Colt wanted to refuse, but the truth was, he needed her eyes and ears right now. Between Darnell and him, they had the sides and the back covered, but someone could use the road directly in front of the house to get to them.

"Cooper or Reed should arrive in the next five minutes," Colt told her.

She nodded, moved to the wall between the front door and a window.

"I've got a guy behind some trees," Darnell called out. "I'm pretty sure he's got a rifle, too."

Yes, that's what Colt figured, too. With rifles, the shooters wouldn't have to get too close to the house to do some serious damage.

But what were they waiting for?

With the dogs, they'd clearly lost any element of surprise, and they had to know that Colt and anyone else inside would be armed and ready. Colt immediately thought of a bad reason why they hadn't already started to shoot up the place.

Maybe they were waiting on even more firepower.

Until he'd realized that, Colt had been about to text Reed and tell him to make a quiet approach. So that perhaps they would stand a chance at catching these guys and could get information from them. But no way could that happen now. Colt wanted sirens blaring in an effort to scare off these idiots.

"The guy behind the tree isn't moving," Darnell said at the same time that Elise spoke up. "There's someone driving up the road toward us. It's an SUV, but the headlights are off."

"It is Reed or Cooper?" Colt asked.

Elise leaned in closer to the window, prompting Colt to order her to stay back. She did but then shook her head. "I don't think it's Reed or your brother. I don't recognize the vehicle."

Great. They were coming at them from all angles now, and Colt still didn't know how many were out there.

"There's a gun on the top of Reed's fridge," Colt told her. "Get it."

Even though he hated the thought of Elise being put in a position where she might have to pull the trigger. Still, he had to be reasonable here and give her a way to defend herself if the worst happened. Especially since plenty of *worst* had already happened to them.

Elise scurried into the kitchen, and it took her only a few seconds before she returned to the window. "The SUV stopped on the side of the road," she relayed. "No, wait. It's pulling off the road and into some bushes."

No doubt so it'd be out of sight. Maybe in place to ambush anyone who came to help. While Colt kept an eye on the guy by the barn, he sent a text to Reed to let him know what was going on.

"Reed's not far out," Colt relayed to Elise and Darnell as soon as he got a response from his fellow deputy.

The seconds crawled by, and Colt hoped that Reed's presence would be enough to send these guys scattering. Maybe then he could pick off one of them and arrest the sorry piece of dirt.

"The car door opened," Elise said. "Someone got out, but I can't see who. I think he's heading toward the guy behind the trees."

So, three of them. At least.

Finally, Colt heard a sound that he wanted to hear. Reed was obviously close by, and he had the sirens blaring at max volume.

Elise blew out what sounded to be a breath of relief, but Colt didn't do the same. That's because the guy behind the barn moved.

And not just moved.

The man leaned out and fired a shot directly at Colt.

THE BULLET CRASHED through the window, sending a spray of glass all over the room. And right at Colt.

"Get down!" Elise shouted, praying he wouldn't get hurt.

Colt didn't listen. However, he did bolt from the window and ran toward her. He hooked his arm around her waist and pulled her to the floor.

Not a second too soon.

Because another bullet blasted through what was left of the window. Unlike the shots that'd been rigged with the remote control, the angles were totally different on these, which meant they had a real shooter on their hands.

And it was obvious this guy was trying to kill them.

With his arm still around her, Colt crawled with her toward the kitchen. She spotted Darnell, not on the floor, but he'd taken aim at the window where he'd been keeping watch. However, before Colt and she could even reach him, a bullet tore through the kitchen window.

Then through the front door.

Sweet heaven.

All three gunmen were shooting at them, and they were trapped in the middle with no way out.

"If anyone opens a door or window, the alarm will sound," Colt reminded her.

It was good that they'd get a warning, but Elise figured it was possible for those bullets to damage the security system. Then, while they were busy defending themselves and dodging gunfire, one of the shooters could sneak into the house.

Colt pushed her to the side of the fridge door. Probably because it was as safe a place as they could manage right now. She reached to pull him down with her, but he went to the window, and both Darnell and he returned fire.

The dogs had worked themselves into a frenzy now, and she could hear them trying to claw their way out. Maybe the gunmen would stay away from there because it was too dangerous for someone to go back to the glassed-in porch to check on the animals.

Colt fired off another shot, pulled back, and this time the gunman's bullet tore into the wall just above her head.

"They're using cop killers," Colt told her.

Her heart was already bashing against her ribs, and that didn't help. "What?" she asked.

"Teflon-coated bullets," Colt answered while he volleyed his attention between the front door and the window. "They'll be able to go through the walls of this old house."

It didn't take long for her to realize just how true that was. The bullets coming through the front door were tearing through the half wall that separated the living room from the kitchen. With the shots coming from both sides of the house, it wouldn't be long before the place was ripped to pieces.

"Reed won't be able to get closer with all this gunfire," Darnell added.

Elise prayed that he didn't try, either. As much as she wanted help, she didn't want anyone else's life put at stake because of her, and Reed would definitely be in grave danger if he tried to get to them now.

More bullets came. Nonstop. And Colt and Darnell had no choice but to drop down on the floor next to her. They were literally pinned down and with no way to fight back. If they stood up to return fire, one of those cop-killer bullets could take them out.

"We have to move," Colt said, glancing all around him. "If we go out the back, they'll probably just gun us down."

That definitely was not an option that Elise wanted. But he was right, they had to move. At the rate those bullets were coming, soon there wouldn't be enough of the walls left to give them any cover.

Colt's attention landed on the small utility room that divided the kitchen from the porch where the dogs were closed off. Except he wasn't looking at the door that led to the porch. He was looking at the ceiling.

"Come on." Colt took hold of her hand. "There's an attic. If we can get up there, Darnell and I will have a better chance at picking these guys off."

An attic definitely sounded better to her than staying put, but bullets could go through the utility room as well as they could any other part of the house.

Colt didn't waste any time getting them moving. They stayed on the floor, crawling, and he didn't stand up until he'd made it all the way to the laundry room. He pulled down the wooden attic stairs and climbed up to have a look around.

Elise got a new slam of concern. What if someone was up there waiting? The security alarm hadn't gone off, but maybe one of the gunmen had managed to get on the roof and climb into the attic. She doubted the security system was armed for that part of the house.

"It's clear," Colt said.

Thank God. And he motioned for Darnell and her to follow him.

The steps were narrow and wobbly, but with Colt's help, Elise made it to the top and into the attic. However, once Darnell was there, Colt went back down, causing her adrenaline to spike again.

To release the dogs, she soon realized.

The moment he opened the door of the porch, the barking Dobermans charged through the house.

"Stay," Colt ordered, and Elise was surprised when they sat on the laundry room floor and obeyed. Maybe since they were now sitting down low enough, that would keep them out of the line of fire.

Colt came back up and then pulled up the stairs behind him. No doubt so if the shooters got into the house, they wouldn't be able to find them right away. Still, she wasn't sure it would fool a determined killer for long.

Darnell hurried to the small wooden ventilation window that was at the front of the attic, and he looked out. "I see one of them," he relayed to Colt a moment later. "And I think we're close enough to take the shot."

Good. Elise hated the thought of anyone being killed, but she didn't want the gunmen to have a chance to kill them. And that's exactly what would happen if they got the chance. The other attacks had proved that.

Darnell stepped to the side once Colt made it to the window, and Elise stayed back as Colt did a quick assessment of the situation. He bashed through the wooden slats with the butt of his gun, and without wasting even a second, he took aim.

And he fired.

The problem was that the shooter fired, too, and the shots blasted through the air at seemingly the same time. Colt ducked down, waited a few seconds and then had another look.

"Got him," Colt said. "One down, at least two to go." He moved to the other side of the window, no doubt looking for the shooter who'd been near the kitchen.

But the sound stopped him.

An alarm.

And Elise immediately knew what that meant. Someone had triggered the security system and was in the house.

Oh, mercy.

If the gunman came up the stairs, they could be in the middle of another shoot-out.

She heard something else. Maybe a door opening. And a moment later, the dogs bolted outside into the front yard. Still barking, they raced toward the SUV that was parked just up the road. Several moments later, both Dobermans disappeared into the trees.

Then, Elise heard something else she didn't want to hear. Something that caused her heart to skip a beat or two.

The dogs stopped barking.

There'd been no gunshots, so maybe the intruder had used some kind of Taser on them. She hoped that's all that had happened, anyway, especially since the dogs had saved their lives by alerting them of the first intruder. Without their warning, the gunman could have gotten close enough to do some serious damage while Colt and she were still in the guest bedroom.

"Stay back," Colt whispered to her.

He moved in front of her and lifted his head, obviously trying to pick through the clamor of the security alarm so he could try to pinpoint the location of their intruder.

But it didn't take long to hear something.

Footsteps.

And they were headed straight for the stairs below them.

Chapter Sixteen

Hell. Colt had hoped that by going up into the attic it would keep those bullets away from Elise.

Now the shooter could be coming for them.

It wouldn't take the intruder long to search the place, and once he realized they weren't in any of the rooms of the one-story house, then the attic would be the most obvious hiding place. Especially since they hadn't gone outside. Plus, these goons likely figured out that the shot Colt had fired had come from the attic.

If the shooter came up the stairs, they'd be trapped.

Colt couldn't move Elise to the sides or front of the attic because there might be gunmen in place ready to start firing at them. All he could do was stand in front of her and keep his gun ready. The moment the guy surfaced on the stairs, Colt would have to fire.

The seconds crawled by with each step the gunman took. Thanks to the creaky floors, Colt had no trouble hearing the guy even over the security alarm. However, he also heard something else.

His phone buzzed.

Not exactly a good time for a call, but it might be Reed or Cooper phoning to warn them of something.

"See who it is," Colt whispered to Elise, and he angled his body so that she could take his cell from his jeans pocket.

"It's Rosalie," Elise answered in a whisper as soon as she checked the phone screen.

His sister was the last person that Colt expected to be calling him, but since he didn't want Elise or himself distracted by the call, he let it go to voice mail. Maybe soon he'd get a chance to call Rosalie back—after he had Elise and Darnell safely out of this mess.

Downstairs, the sound of the footsteps stopped, and Colt braced himself for the attack that he was certain would follow. His heartbeat was already hammering in his ears. His muscles tightened and knotted. He was ready to finish this.

But the shooter didn't pull down the stairs so he could come into the attic.

In fact, it sounded as if this idiot was just standing still.

What the heck was he doing down there?

"Don't move," Colt warned both Elise and Darnell, keeping his voice as soundless as possible. "The guy might be listening for us so he can shoot through the ceiling."

If so, they had to be prepared to move and move fast.

The problem was, there weren't many places for them to go in the attic, especially since there was at least one other gunman outside the house. In hindsight, it'd been a mistake to bring Elise up here, but they hadn't exactly had a lot of options about that, either. If they'd stayed on the bottom floor of the house, one of them could have been shot.

Without warning, the security alarm stopped, plunging the house into an eerie quiet. Since Colt doubted it operated on a battery, that probably meant someone had managed to disable it either by cutting the connections or the phone line.

That was both good and bad.

Colt could better hear the shooter, but the shooter could better hear them, too. Also, without the alarm, Colt got a confirmation of something he'd already suspected.

The dogs were quiet.

It meant these goons could have neutralized them in some way. Or maybe, though, they'd made it safely to Reed. His fellow deputy had to be somewhere nearby, and the dogs would have picked up his scent. If so, Reed would have made sure they were safe.

Reed could also do something else.

He'd know the ins and outs of the grounds. Maybe he'd even be able to sneak up on the gunman outside.

But that still left Colt to deal with the one inside.

Why wasn't he moving?

Colt wasn't a patient man under normal circumstances, but this was wearing his nerves even thinner than they already were.

He mumbled some profanity when his phone buzzed again. This time, indicating that he had a text. Colt only hoped the shooter hadn't heard the buzzing sound so he could use it to zoom in on them.

"It's Rosalie again," Elise whispered. "She says it's urgent and that she needs to talk to you."

Well, his urgency trumped Rosalie's, but with everything else that'd been going on, Colt had no trouble filling in some blanks with worst-case scenarios. Maybe his sister was calling to say there'd been some kind of attack at the ranch.

If so, his family could be in serious danger.

"Text her back," Colt mouthed to Elise. "Ask her what's wrong."

Elise started to do that, but her hand froze when they heard the noise on the floor below them. It was hard to tell what it was exactly, but it sounded as if someone had dropped something metal.

Colt waited, listening for more, but that was it. Just that brief metallic sound. It took several moments for the footsteps to start again, but this time they weren't coming toward the attic stairs.

But rather toward the front of the house.

He motioned for Darnell to head back to the window, and the man cursed as soon as he looked out. Colt cursed, too, because he heard the front door open.

"The guy ran out," Darnell said, and he took aim and fired, the shot blasting through the attic.

Colt could tell from Darnell's body language that he'd missed, and the ranch hand fired again.

"I smell smoke," Elise said, lifting her head.

Colt didn't. Not at first, anyway. But then he caught a whiff of it making its way through the seam around the stairs.

Oh, man.

That metallic sound was likely some kind of incendiary device, and the reason the guy had run was because he'd just set the place on fire.

"We need to get out of here," Colt said, taking hold of Elise's arm. "Now."

ELISE SHOVED COLT'S phone into her jeans pocket so that it'd free up her hands in case she had to help shoot their way out of the house.

And that's almost certainly what would happen.

Unless their attackers meant to burn them alive.

Then this was probably a way to force them outside where the two remaining shooters would have an easier time picking them off. Of course, if they stayed put, the fire and smoke would kill them, too, so either way they were in grave danger.

Colt hurried across the attic and threw down the attic stairs. However, he didn't bolt down them. Instead, he looked around. Hard to see, though, with the thick white smoke already billowing through the house.

"Wait here a second," Colt told both of them.

Even though she hated that Colt was the one to go down the stairs first, Elise knew he wouldn't have it any other way. He was the lawman now. Fully in charge. And he would take any risk to try to protect her.

With his gun ready, Colt eased down several of the narrow steps, his gaze shifting all around. Almost immediately, he started to cough, and he had to cover his mouth with the sleeve of his shirt while he continued to make sure their attackers weren't still inside the house.

Elise and Darnell coughed, too, the smoke coming right at them. What she didn't feel was any kind of heat, though, so maybe that meant the place wasn't actually on fire. That metallic *plinging* sound she'd heard earlier could have perhaps been some kind of smoke bomb. If so, it would serve the same purpose as a full-fledged fire in getting them out of the house.

"Move fast," Colt said, motioning for them to come down the stairs.

Elise tried to do just that, but the stairs were wobbly, and her grip was shaking on the flimsy rope handrail. The coughing certainly didn't help, either. Still, she made it to the bottom with Darnell right behind her.

"This way," Colt added.

The moment they hit the floor, Colt got them running, not toward the back porch, which was closer. But toward the front of the house. Maybe because he figured that's the exit their attackers were least likely to use. It was also the place where Reed would be approaching.

They were all coughing now, and it got worse with each step. Elise's eyes and throat were burning, and she felt as if her lungs were on fire. It also didn't help that her heart was bashing against her ribs. Still, she kept moving.

Colt paused again when they reached the front door, and he eased it open. Elise held her breath, praying that someone didn't open fire on them.

No shots.

In fact, no sounds at all.

So, Colt opened the door a little farther.

Just the small crack of space brought in some fresh air. It helped with her breathing, but some of the smoke was also on the porch. It wasn't thick, just white wisps coiling around, but since someone had also knocked out the porch light, it was next to impossible to see beyond the steps that led into the front yard.

No doubt the way their attackers had planned it.

"We need a distraction," Colt said, glancing back at Darnell. "Fire a shot toward the back porch. It might get them focused there so we can make a run for it. Just as soon as you've pulled the trigger, we'll all run to the side of the porch and drop down into those shrubs."

Colt tipped his head to their right. To the side of the house where he'd already taken out the shooter. Of course, that didn't mean that the person who'd orchestrated this hadn't already put someone else in place, but it was still their best bet.

"Fire now," Colt told Darnell.

Because Darnell was so close to her, Elise covered

her ears for the brief second that it took him to get off the shot.

Then they moved.

Fast.

Colt took hold of her arm, and with Darnell right behind them, they bolted toward the side of the porch.

Just as the shot came their way.

The bullet slammed into the front of the house, but Colt didn't stop to return fire. He pulled her off the porch and into some Texas sage bush. The branches tore at her clothes and skin, but they all managed to get off the porch and into the meager cover before there were more shots.

Colt moved in front of her, of course.

He shoved her against the concrete slab and exterior wall. It was hard for her to see much of anything, what with the smoke and the darkness, but Elise thought the gunfire was coming from the front of the house. Maybe from the person who'd gotten out of that SUV parked just up the road?

However, that thought had no sooner crossed her mind when the angle of the shot changed.

The shooter was moving.

Coming for them.

Even over the thick blasts, she heard Colt's phone buzz again, and she fished it from her pocket so she could see the screen.

Rosalie again.

Something had to be seriously wrong for Colt's sister to keep calling and texting. Of course, Rosalie had no way of knowing that they were fighting for their lives right now.

Since Elise hadn't gotten to send the text when they were in the attic, she sent it now, asking Rosalie what she wanted. The moment she pressed the send button, Colt nudged her again.

"Start crawling toward the back," he told her, "but stay as close to the house as possible."

Thankfully, the line of Texas sage bush went all the way to the back porch, but Elise knew there wouldn't be any protection whatsoever against bullets. Still, the thick shrubs might keep the shooter from seeing them.

With Colt ahead of her and Darnell behind her, they started crawling. The ground was frozen and littered with small rocks and dried twigs that dug into her hands and knees. Still, Elise kept moving.

It seemed to take an eternity to go the ten yards or so, but once they reached the back porch, Colt stopped and looked around again. Just ahead was a storage shed, and he motioned toward it. At least she thought he was motioning, but then she realized he threw a handful of rocks at it.

Nothing.

No one came out with guns blazing, and even though the shooter was continuing to fire, those shots were going toward the front part of the house.

For now, anyway.

She figured that would soon change when he realized they'd moved. Or maybe when *she* realized they'd moved. After all, it was possible that Meredith was the one orchestrating this. If so, Elise hoped she got the chance to give the woman—or anyone else behind this—some payback.

First, though, Colt, Darnell and she had to survive.

Just as she'd known would happen, the angle of the shots changed again. The shooter was coming their way.

"We'll move to the left side of the shed," Colt said.

"Don't fire unless you have to, because we don't have a lot of ammo."

Mercy, she hadn't even considered that. These monsters had likely brought an arsenal with them, but Colt, Darnell and she only had the weapons in their hands. Not exactly an equal gunfight, especially since Elise wasn't even sure she could fire straight enough to help. Still, that wouldn't stop her from trying.

"Stay low and start moving to the shed," Colt instructed.

But almost immediately, he stopped and lifted his hand, a signal for them to stay put.

Elise followed his gaze to see what'd captured his attention. Colt was focused on a woodpile only about ten feet from the shed. She didn't see anything, but Colt obviously had, because even though the shooter was getting closer, he still didn't move.

Colt's phone buzzed again, indicating that someone had texted. Probably Rosalie, but Elise didn't want to look down to respond. Instead, both Darnell and she kept their guns lifted in case they had to fire.

"Hell," Colt said, his attention still on the woodpile.

Elise finally saw something. Some movement at the end of the pile nearest the shed.

Mercy, was it another gunman waiting there?

If so, he would have shot them before they could have made it out into the yard.

But the person didn't shoot. However, he did move again, because Elise got a glimpse of the sleeve of his jacket.

"Maybe it's Reed," Darnell said.

Judging from Colt's body language, it wasn't, but Elise couldn't tell who it was. Not until he moved again, that is.

The person ducked his head out from the woodpile for just a glimpse at them. But it was more than enough for Elise to get a glimpse of him.

What the devil was *he* doing here?

Chapter Seventeen

Buddy.

Colt had figured it was either Buddy, Meredith or Joplin behind these attacks, but he hadn't expected Elise's former tenant to actually take part in the shootings.

Especially since he had so many hired guns to do the job. From Colt's estimate there were still at least two of them out there somewhere.

"Don't shoot me," Buddy called out to them. "I'm here to help you."

Right. No way was Colt going to buy that.

After all, Buddy was wanted for murder, and he hated Elise for refusing to sell him the place where he'd buried the body. He no doubt blamed Elise for the trip he'd be making to jail, and that gave him plenty of motive for this attack.

"Somebody wanted me to kill Elise," Buddy went on. "I got a call. I couldn't make out who it was, but the caller said if I came here tonight, I could settle the score with Elise. I figured I was supposed to murder her, but that's not why I'm here. I never meant to kill that woman, and I don't want to kill Elise, either."

Colt glanced back at her to see if she was buying any of this. She wasn't. Elise had her gun aimed right at the woodpile where Buddy was hiding.

"You hear me, Colt?" Buddy asked.

Colt didn't answer because the sound of his voice would make it too easy to pinpoint their location. But there was some movement in the backyard on the other side of the shed.

Oh, man.

One of the shooters was no doubt moving closer. It was the same for the one at the front of the house. And that made it too risky to try to move Elise and Darnell to the shed.

"Get down as low as you can," Colt told her.

He positioned himself in front of her, but he knew he wouldn't be much protection if the bullets started coming at them from all directions.

"Colt?" someone called out. Not Buddy this time.

Reed.

Judging from the sound of Reed's voice, he was somewhere near the front of the house, too. Good. Maybe he'd be able to take out the shooter.

Or maybe he already had.

Colt realized it'd been a minute or so since anyone had fired a shot. Reed could have sneaked up on him and clubbed the guy. Colt hoped so, anyway, because he wanted to focus his attention on Buddy and on getting Elise to safety.

Wherever *safety* was.

"More help's on the way," Reed said. "Plenty of it."

Good. Colt wished he could bring in an army to stop these dirtbags.

"Text me your location," Reed added.

Just as another shot was fired.

That one went in Reed's direction.

"Text him," Colt whispered to Elise. "Tell him our location. The shooters. And Buddy's, too."

She gave a shaky nod and used his phone to fire off the text. Maybe Reed would be able to use the info to get himself in a better position to attack. Maybe, too, Reed would stay out of the line of fire.

Because it continued.

More shots came. Not just from the front but from the back side of the house. The shooter over there had obviously moved since they'd last spotted him from the kitchen window.

"I said don't shoot!" Buddy yelled, and he added a long string of raw profanity.

Buddy obviously thought Colt was doing the firing, or he wanted to make them believe he thought that. Colt still wasn't about to give away their position by answering him.

"Reed's going to try to get closer to the woodpile," Elise relayed when she got the text response from the deputy. "Cooper's at the end of the road, and he's going on the opposite side of the house from Reed."

Colt was more than thankful for the backup, but it meant Darnell or he wouldn't be able to fire any more random shots. He couldn't risk hitting Reed or his brother.

The shots continued to come, some of them aimed at the woodpile. Either this was another ploy to get them to trust Buddy, or these shooters wanted him dead, too.

Buddy cursed again, and he leaned out. That's when Colt saw the rifle, but Buddy didn't aim it at them. He pointed it in the area just past the shed, an area that was out of Colt's line of sight.

And Buddy fired.

Colt heard a sharp groan of pain, and it sounded as if someone collapsed onto the ground.

Hell. That could be his brother.

"Text Cooper now," Colt told Elise.

And Colt held his breath, waiting and praying. Thankfully, it only took a few seconds for Cooper to respond.

"Cooper's okay," Elise said, blowing out her own breath of relief. "Buddy shot one of the gunmen."

Good. But again it could be a ploy to get them to trust him and come out in the open. That wasn't going to happen.

"If Reed can neutralize Buddy, I can get you into the shed," Colt whispered to her.

Of course, if Reed took out Buddy, and Cooper got the guy who'd been at the front of the house, there would be no need for Elise to be in the shed. The danger would be over.

He hoped.

And that meant they needed to keep Buddy alive so they could get any other details of the attack. One way or another, Colt wanted to end the danger tonight.

His phone buzzed again, and Colt hoped it was a message with good news from Reed or Cooper. However, judging from the way Elise pulled in her breath, it wasn't.

"It's another message from your sister," she said, her voice a shaky whisper. "Your father's missing."

"Missing?" A dozen thoughts and emotions slammed through him. None good. Had their attacker managed to get to his dad?

But Colt didn't even get a chance to ask for more information. That's because the shots started again.

This time all being fired at Buddy.

Buddy leaned out to return fire. Something that Colt couldn't let him do since it could very well be Reed doing the shooting.

Colt took aim at Buddy and would have pulled the trigger.

If someone hadn't beaten him to it.

The bullet slammed into Buddy. His shoulder, from what Colt could tell. That didn't stop Buddy, though.

Still cursing, Buddy came out shooting.

ELISE HAD NO idea what was going on, but with the way Buddy was acting, maybe she'd been wrong about his being behind the attacks. Buddy fired some shots and took off running into the wooded area behind the storage shed.

The moment he disappeared from sight, the shots came at them again.

But that wasn't the only gunfire. She heard someone else shooting. Maybe Reed or Cooper. If so, perhaps they could get this situation under control so they could figure out what'd happened to Colt's father.

Missing, Rosalie had said.

And Elise doubted the man had just taken a late-night stroll. No. He was likely in as much danger as they were.

Maybe more.

She hated to think the worst, but Roy could be dead. Some kind of payback for whatever she'd done to make these monsters launch this attack against her. An attack that had now extended to Colt's family. And to Reed and Darnell.

"Hold your fire!" someone shouted.

Not Buddy this time, but it was a voice that Elise instantly recognized.

Meredith.

That caused the skin to crawl on the back of her neck. There was no good reason for her to be out here at Reed's place. But there was one especially bad reason.

Because maybe she was the one trying to kill them.

Of course, Buddy was out there, so maybe he was the one. Heaven forbid if they'd paired up to launch this attack together.

Despite the injury that Buddy had gotten in the gunfight, it could have all been staged to make everyone think he was innocent. Heck, Buddy could have set all this up as some kind of hoax to rescue them so he could in turn get a lighter sentence for the murder charges that would be filed against him.

"Text Reed again," Colt told her. "See if he knows why Meredith's here."

Elise did, and she got a quick response from Reed. "He doesn't know. Reed didn't even know Meredith was around until she just yelled out."

She'd barely relayed that to Colt when his phone buzzed again. Rosalie. And the message that Elise saw on the screen had her heart jumping to her throat.

Rosalie had found drops of blood on the back porch of the McKinnon home, and there appeared to have been some kind of struggle.

Mercy. What had happened?

"What is it?" Colt asked, glancing over his shoulder at her.

"We need to finish up here so we can find your father," Elise settled for saying. No need to worry Colt further when they were trapped.

But, of course, he was already worried. Colt took the phone from her, read the message for himself and mumbled some profanity. "Tell Cooper he needs to get back to the ranch and find out what's going on."

Elise sent the message, praying that Cooper would get there in time to stop whatever was happening with their father.

"I need help!" Meredith shouted. "Joplin hit me with a Taser, then tied me up and brought me here."

Great. If Joplin was indeed out here, then all their suspects were in one place. Now the problem would be to figure out which one was guilty.

No sign of Joplin, Reed immediately texted. I'm moving closer so cover me.

Elise relayed that to Colt, and he angled his body to give Reed the cover he'd requested. It didn't take long for her to see Reed dart out from some trees behind the woodpile. His gaze fired all around, and he must not have seen anyone, because Reed raced toward them and dropped down on the ground next to them.

"Is Buddy still out there?" Colt asked him.

Reed shook his head. "Didn't see him, but I did spot Meredith. She's on the other side of the house in those trees."

The spot where they'd seen a gunman earlier.

"Anyone with her?" Colt pressed.

"Not that I could tell."

That didn't meant Leo or Joplin wasn't out there hiding.

"What about the dogs?" Elise hoped nothing bad had happened to them.

"Someone Tasered them. They'll be fine, but whoever did it will have to answer to me."

Elise only hoped Reed got the chance to make that happen. Being Tasered was horrible, but at least the person hadn't killed the poor animals.

Reed tipped his head to the shed. "There's still too much smoke in the house. From a smoke bomb, I think.

But we can get Elise in through the back of the shed and wait for Cooper to have more men in place."

"Cooper had to go back to the ranch." Colt paused. "Dad's missing."

"What the hell else could go wrong tonight?" Reed said after he cursed.

Elise was afraid she didn't want to know the answer to that.

"I figure Cooper will send someone else out here," Colt went on. "But in the meantime, let's get Elise out of the line of fire."

No one argued with that. Except her. "I don't want to be tucked away someplace safe while you three are taking all the risks."

Colt shifted his gaze to her, and he looked ready to give her a huge argument about that. Instead, he dropped a kiss on her mouth. Surprising her. Probably surprising Reed and Darnell, too.

"Let's go," Colt told Reed a split second before they started running.

Elise braced herself for more shots to come their way.

But none did.

In fact, the only sounds were their footsteps, ragged breaths and Meredith yelling for someone to untie her. If she was indeed tied up, she was going to have to stay that way for a while. At least until they were certain all the gunmen had been captured or killed.

Once they reached the side of the shed, Colt stopped and peered around the corner. There were two doors, one on the side opposite the woodpile—where Meredith and the other gunmen likely were. The other door was at the rear, and that's obviously the one Colt planned to use. Probably because he thought it would give them the best chance of getting inside before they were gunned down.

It was much darker here than by the house because of the angle of the moon and the trees. Elise considered taking out Colt's phone and using it for illumination, but she didn't want to make themselves a spotlight for the gunman.

"Don't go in yet," Colt warned her when he pulled her behind the shed with him. "Wait here with Reed and Darnell."

Colt went closer, no doubt ready to open the door and check inside to make sure no one was hiding and about to attack. However, he only made it a few steps before he stumbled on something. Elise couldn't see what, but she knew from Colt's profanity that it wasn't good.

"What is it?" she asked, almost afraid to hear the answer.

Colt cursed again and reached down to touch something. "It's a dead body."

Chapter Eighteen

Elise tried to look over Colt's shoulder, but thankfully it was too dark for her to see anything. He hoped. He darn sure didn't want her seeing *this*.

"It's Buddy," he told her.

Her breath stalled in her throat. "He's really dead?"

Colt nodded.

"Oh, God," she whispered.

Colt repeated it under his breath. He'd known that Buddy had been shot, but he hadn't thought it was that serious, especially since Buddy had run from the scene. However, when Reed used his phone for illumination, that's when Colt saw the gunshot wound to the head.

Unfortunately, Elise saw it, too.

"That didn't happen when he was by the woodpile," she said, touching her fingers to her lips.

No, it hadn't. Of course, with all the bullets that'd been flying around, Buddy could have been shot at any time afterward. Still, Colt hadn't heard gunfire coming from this particular direction.

"He was shot at point-blank range," Reed said to him.

Yeah, Colt had noticed that, too. That meant the killer had either sneaked up on Buddy or else Elise's former tenant had trusted the person who'd pulled the trigger.

Colt took hold of her again to lead her away from

Buddy's body and into the shed, but the movement stopped him. It was the sound of footsteps. Not someone trying to sneak up on them, either. These footsteps belonged to someone who was running.

"You've got to help me!" Meredith shouted.

Judging from the sound of her voice, she was headed directly toward them.

"Don't shoot me," Meredith begged. "Please don't shoot."

Despite Colt's moving in front of her, he figured that Elise got a glimpse of the woman making her way across the backyard. She was indeed coming toward the shed.

And Meredith had a gun in her hand.

That got Colt, Reed and Darnell all aiming at her.

But something wasn't right.

Meredith's arms were stiff by her sides, the gun dangling from her hand on the outside of her thigh, and she was staggering, barely able to stay on her feet. Colt, Reed and Darnell obviously realized something was wrong, too, because they didn't fire.

"Joplin wants you to shoot me," she called out to them. "He wants me dead because I know the truth."

"Stop right there," Colt ordered.

Meredith did, but he gave an uneasy glance over his shoulder. "He'll kill me. He'll kill us all."

"You mean Joplin?" Colt challenged.

"Of course," she said, and she came even closer. "He put the duct tape around me and shoved me out from the trees so you'd kill me."

Meredith dropped onto the ground by the side of the shed. That's when Colt could see that there was indeed tape wrapped around her body.

"Why would Joplin want me to kill you?" Colt demanded.

"Because he's crazy, that's why. I overheard him talking on his phone after he left the sheriff's office. He was plotting to kill Elise so she can't testify and clear your father's name. Before I could tell you about what I heard, he had one of his hired thugs Taser me and he brought me here."

That didn't make sense. Unless Joplin had planned on setting up Meredith for all of this. Or maybe Joplin just wanted them to get rid of Meredith since she'd overheard him scheme to commit murder. That was definitely enough motive for Joplin to want Meredith dead—if it'd happened the way she said, that is.

"Help me get out of this tape," Meredith insisted.

No one moved to do that. In fact, Colt stayed in front of Elise, his gun aimed at Meredith while Darnell and Reed kept watch around them.

"Go ahead and check out the shed," Colt said to Reed. "Then get Elise inside it."

Reed opened the door and used his phone to light up the interior. It was a small space crammed with tack and other supplies, so he had to step in, no doubt to make sure no one was lurking in the shadows.

As soon as Reed was inside, the shot rang out.

Heck, not again. Colt was sick and tired of having bullets come their way.

Colt immediately pulled Elise to the ground with him. Darnell dropped down behind them, his gun still ready. Their attention all went to Reed.

Had he been shot?

But he was standing there. Unharmed.

The blast had been so sudden that it took Colt a moment to realize it hadn't come from inside the shed. Instead, it'd come from the direction of the house, and it was soon followed by a second shot.

Then another.

"He's trying to kill me!" Meredith yelled.

And that's exactly what seemed to be happening. Both shots slammed into the shed just above Meredith's head.

Colt still didn't move to help the woman, but he didn't stop Meredith when she scrambled behind the shed with them.

Another shot came their way, this one tearing through the shed. Reed cursed and dropped down.

"Are you hit?" Colt immediately asked him.

Reed shook his head. "I'm fine."

But the words had no sooner left Reed's mouth when there was more movement next to them.

From Meredith.

Before Colt could even turn his attention from Reed and back to Meredith, the woman brought up her gun and put it right to Elise's head.

Colt's stomach went to his knees.

The duct tape had been a ruse. Colt could see that now. The strip only stretched across the front of her body. She'd been free this whole time, and now she was free to try to kill them.

"Drop your gun," Meredith ordered Colt.

Colt shook his head. "You drop yours."

"I should probably clarify something." Meredith's voice was eerily calm. "I'm wired with a communicator, and my brother's on the other end of this line. If you don't drop your gun now, he'll act according to my orders."

"Orders," Colt spat out like profanity. "What orders?"

The corner of Meredith's mouth lifted, and she turned her gun on Colt. "I have your father. If you don't cooperate, he dies."

ELISE GLARED AT the monster holding the gun aimed at Colt.

If Meredith was lying about having Roy, then she was doing a convincing job of it. Of course, anyone who could put together a string of chaos like this was certainly capable of lying through her teeth.

"Why the hell would you take my father?" Colt snapped. He didn't move to put down his gun as Meredith had demanded.

"To make you cooperate, to make this plan work," Meredith readily answered.

Without shifting the gun away from Colt, Meredith motioned toward the back of the house. A moment later, the third gunman stepped out from the shadows and made a beeline toward her.

"If you shoot him, I shoot Colt," Meredith warned Darnell, Reed and her.

Elise's finger tightened on the trigger, but there was no way she could try to end this. Not with Meredith's gun on Colt. Hopefully, Reed and Darnell wouldn't fire, either. They could all get off a shot, but so could Meredith.

A shot that would indeed kill Colt.

The goon with the bulky shoulders came closer, and Elise saw that he had something in his left hand. A phone.

"Show them," Meredith told the man.

He turned the screen in their direction, and Elise had no trouble seeing a photo of Roy, tied up and gagged. He was on the floor, his feet bound as well, and he was glaring right at the person taking the photo.

Colt obviously saw the photo, too, because the muscles in his jaw turned to iron. "Let him go." He didn't shout, but there was definitely a dangerous edge to his tone.

"Not until you cooperate." Meredith glanced at Darnell and Reed. "Sorry that you two got caught up in this, but if you do what I tell you, neither of you will get hurt."

Judging from the sound that Reed made, he didn't believe her. Neither did Elise. Because she knew Meredith's plan included murder.

No way would she leave witnesses behind when she was so desperate to make this asinine plan work.

"Even if we're dead, you might still be brought up on criminal charges because of what's in my report," Elise said. "That is why you're doing this." And it wasn't a question.

"It is, and conversation won't distract me if that's what you're trying to do."

"I'm trying to figure out how you could have gone stark raving mad," Elise snapped.

Meredith didn't even react to that. She turned her attention back to Colt. "I have no intention of me and my brother going to jail for what Elise uncovered, and once you're out of the way, I'll make the report disappear, too."

"But Frank Wellerman's turning it over to the cops," Elise reminded her.

"He can't turn over what he doesn't have. Let's just say my computer skills are good enough to make things like that disappear. And if Wellerman doesn't cooperate, he'll find himself in just as much hot water as you are."

Elise sucked in her breath. "Sweet heaven. Are you going to kill him, too?"

"I'll do whatever it takes," Meredith snapped. "Because this isn't just about me. It's about Leo, too. He's already on probation, and a charge like this could put him away for a long time."

"You mean for life," Colt corrected. "Because the charges aren't just for embezzlement. It's murder. Leo's the one who killed Martinelli, isn't he? Or maybe he just helped you set that explosive. It doesn't matter. Either way, it's still murder."

That tightened Meredith's mouth, but she didn't address Colt, only Elise. "You understand what it's like to protect someone you love. Well, that's what I'm doing. I'm protecting my brother, who I love. I don't want him to spend a minute in jail for offing a lowlife like Martinelli."

Yes, definitely stark raving mad. But that only made Meredith even more dangerous.

"Martinelli tried to kill me when he ran me off the road," Elise said.

"Not kill you. He was supposed to bring you to me so I could get on with my plan to set up Roy. In addition to being a lowlife, Martinelli was an idiot."

Thank goodness. If he'd been more efficient at his job, Elise might already be dead.

"The gun," Meredith reminded Colt, and with a simple motion of her hand, the goon latched on to Colt and dragged him to his feet.

Meredith knocked the gun from Colt's hands while she aimed her own weapon at the rest of them. Since her hired muscle now had his gun trained on Colt, Elise had no choice but to drop her gun.

Reed and Darnell did the same.

Maybe at least one of them had some kind of backup weapon on them, and while Elise was hoping, she added that maybe Meredith wouldn't search for any other weapons before she took them wherever she was planning on taking them.

"How did you even know Colt and Elise were here?" Reed asked.

"I hired someone to watch the sheriff's office, and he used binoculars to look through the window. He saw you give them your keys."

So, Meredith had covered all the bases. Maybe. But Elise was hoping that the woman had missed something. Something that would keep them alive.

"Why not just kill us here?" Elise asked her.

Meredith made a sound to indicate the answer was obvious. "Because I need to be able to pin your death on Roy, and that means having you two at the same place at the same time. Colt and the others will be unfortunate accidents who got in the way when Roy and his hired gun came to kill you so you can't testify against him."

Elise shook her head. "But I did hypnosis and didn't remember anything incriminating against Roy."

"That doesn't matter. All that matters is that Roy will want to stop you from remembering anything that could come up in a future hypnosis session. The McKinnons haven't exactly been quiet about how much they're concerned about what you're going to say when you take the witness stand."

That sent a chill through Elise. She was already shivering from the cold, but that made it worse. "And then you'll kill Roy," she concluded.

"He'll commit suicide," Meredith said as casually as if discussing the weather. "Let's go. Once we have this contained," she added to her hired goon, "then you'll need to do cleanup here."

Elise didn't want to know what that entailed, but she figured Meredith would make sure there was no evidence left behind that could be traced back to her or anyone she'd hired.

"Move," Meredith's man ordered. With Colt in his meaty grip, he started walking, and dragged Colt right along with him.

Elise quickly followed because she wanted to be near Colt in case things turned worse than they already were. Or in case they were able to come up with some way to escape.

But how?

Anything they did right now would endanger Colt.

The hired gun started leading them away from the house, toward the spot where she'd seen the SUV pull off the road earlier.

"Don't count on your brothers or Deputy Pete coming out to help," Meredith told Colt. "They're all out trying to find your dad."

"And I'm sure you planted some false information to send them on a wild-goose chase," Colt mumbled.

Meredith didn't confirm it, but Elise figured that's exactly what the woman had done. However, she couldn't imagine all his family leaving Colt in the middle of a gunfight, so maybe Cooper had arranged for help from one of the deputies of a nearby town.

Elise listened for anyone who might be out there. Obviously, so did Meredith and her hired gun, and they approached the SUV with caution, both of them looking around to make sure they weren't about to be ambushed.

But no one was there.

Well, no one except a driver. Yet another hired thug, no doubt. And that meant Meredith had an extra gun and some muscle to make sure she led them to their deaths.

Colt's gaze met hers, and even though he didn't say a word, she knew he was trying to tell her not to get in the SUV. Once they were inside, Meredith would have even more control over them than she did now.

But what should she do?

She glanced back at Reed and Darnell, who were glancing around as well, no doubt trying to figure out their best way out of this.

Meredith threw open the back door to the SUV. "It'll be a tight squeeze, but I want Colt, Reed and Darnell in the back with Gordy here." She smiled when she looked at Elise. "You'll be up front with me. I think Colt will be less inclined to do something stupid if this gun's pointed at you."

He would be, and that's why they had to do something now.

Meredith took hold of her arm, to shove her onto the seat. But the sound stopped her.

A low, menacing growl.

One of the dogs.

"Get in now!" Meredith yelled, and she volleyed her attention between them and the direction of that growl.

Elise saw the movement from the corner of her eye. Then heard the sound of more movement.

Colt lunged at Meredith, and in the same motion, he pushed Elise out of the way. The hired goon, Gordy, reached for her. No doubt to pull her in front of him and use her as a shield to stop Darnell and Reed.

But it was too late for that.

One of the Dobermans came out of the bushes and went straight for Gordy. The dog knocked the man down, and his gun went flying. Before it even hit the ground, the second dog tore through the bushes to come at the man, too.

That didn't stop the thug behind the wheel, though.

He took aim at Reed and fired.

Reed got out of the way in the nick of time, but he didn't stay down. Darnell and he both went across the seat to grab the guy's gun.

With her heart going way too fast, Elise frantically searched the ground and finally spotted the thug's weapon. She snatched it up and took aim at Meredith. At least she tried, but Colt and the woman were too close. No way could she risk firing a shot because she might hit Colt.

The dogs continued to keep Gordy on the ground, and Reed and Darnell managed to wrestle the gun away from the man behind the wheel.

Then Elise heard another sound.

One that she didn't want to hear.

A shot blasted through the night.

Oh, God.

Meredith still had hold of her gun, and she'd managed to pull the trigger. For one heart-stopping moment, she thought that maybe Colt had been shot. And maybe he had. But she saw him move.

He was alive and still wrestling with Meredith to get that gun away from her.

Nothing could have stopped her at that point. Elise couldn't fire, but she brought back the gun, and with as much strength as she could muster, she bashed it against Meredith's shoulder. Then, the side of her head.

Meredith howled in pain, and even though she didn't move off Colt, it was enough to give Colt the edge. He knocked Meredith's gun from her hand, and in the same motion, he pinned Meredith to the ground. Colt didn't waste a second. He got to his feet and dragged Meredith to hers.

Thank God, it was over.

Elise handed Colt the gun, and Reed and Darnell

came out of the SUV. Reed had a firm grip on the hired gun. With just a low whistle, the dogs stopped their attack and backed away. However, Elise was pretty sure Gordy was too injured to do much fighting back.

Reed took some plastic cuffs from his pocket to restrain the guy, and he handed a pair to Colt to use on Meredith. "Let's get this trash to jail," Reed grumbled.

But Meredith laughed. "You think you've won but you haven't."

"What the hell does that mean?" Colt snarled, and he pushed Meredith into the backseat of the SUV.

"It means I have someone holding your father. Or did you forget?"

"I didn't forget," Colt assured her and caught onto the collar of her coat. "Where is he?"

Meredith laughed again. "If I can't get back at Elise, at least I have the pleasure of knowing that your father's dead. Or at least he will be soon if I don't make a call to save him."

"Where is he?" Colt repeated.

"There's only one way you can save him." Meredith paused, her oily smile aimed at Colt. "Let me go now, and your father gets to live. Once I'm out of the country, I'll call and tell you where to find him."

"Right." Colt added some profanity. "Like I'd trust you after everything you've done."

"You don't have a choice," Meredith insisted, staring him right in the eyes.

"I think I do." Colt caught onto Meredith and tossed her out of the SUV and onto the ground. "Watch them, and call my brothers," Colt told Reed. "I'm going after my dad."

Chapter Nineteen

Colt didn't want to risk taking his truck in case Meredith or one of her henchmen had managed to plant some explosives in it. So he jumped behind the wheel of the SUV. The problem was that Elise got in with him, as well.

"I'm going with you," she insisted, and he could tell from her tone and body language that it wouldn't do any good to argue with her.

And he wouldn't.

For one thing, he needed to get to his father ASAP and didn't want to waste even a second. For another, he wasn't sure that he wanted Elise at Reed's place, what with the dead bodies and the chaos. At least if she was with him, Colt could make sure she was all right. Of course, so far his track record at keeping her safe wasn't that good.

Something he'd kick himself for later.

Elise buckled up and looked at him. "I think your father's at my house. I think the photo was taken in my living room."

"Yeah." Colt had already come to that conclusion, too, and that's the direction he headed. "I figure Meredith would want to do the murders there. Maybe to make it look as if my father broke in to kill you so he could silence you."

Of course, that didn't explain what Meredith had planned to do with his, Darnell's and Reed's bodies. Maybe she'd planned on setting up his father for that, as well. Maybe Meredith could have made it look as if Roy had gone insane.

When it was Meredith who'd gone off the deep end.

The woman would pay for what she'd done, but Colt prayed his dad didn't become another casualty.

"Are you okay?" Colt asked her. He was almost afraid to take a closer look. With everything that'd gone on tonight, it was possible she had injuries he didn't even know about.

"I wasn't hurt," she said, her voice almost soundless. She cleared her throat, repeated it. "How about you?"

"We're both alive," he settled for saying. Though he figured the nightmares would be with him for a long time.

Other memories, too.

Ones that he didn't want to deal with right now, not until he was sure his father was safe.

His phone buzzed, and that's when he remembered that Elise still had it. She fished it from her pocket, and when she saw Cooper's name on the screen, she put the call on speaker.

"I just talked to Reed," Cooper greeted. "What the hell's going on?"

"Long story," Colt answered. "But Elise and I are on our way to her place now. We think that's where Meredith has someone holding Dad, and we're about ten minutes out."

Cooper cursed. "I'm not that far from there—less

than five minutes. Pete and one of the ranch hands are with me."

Colt wanted any and all help right now. "Elise is with me, and we're in a black SUV that Meredith brought to Reed's place. So, don't shoot when you see the strange vehicle."

"Thanks for the heads-up. The only reason we're out here is because we got a message saying Dad was being held at the old Saunders farm."

Colt had been right about Meredith's attempts to throw them off track. And, heck, maybe he was still wrong about the location, but he prayed he wasn't.

If he was wrong about this, it could cost his dad his life.

"Is everyone else okay at the ranch?" Colt asked. "Did Meredith hurt anyone?"

"Everyone's fine. What I want to know—was Meredith working alone?"

"Her brother's probably involved, and she hired some muscle. Two of them are dead at Reed's place, but I'm pretty sure she wasn't working with Buddy. He's dead, too," Colt added.

That caused Cooper to curse some more, and Colt heard the soft shudder that left Elise's mouth. He slid his hand over hers and wished he could do more to soothe those frayed nerves. Of course, it was going to take a lot more than hand-holding and hugging to do that.

"Well, Meredith wasn't working with Joplin," Cooper continued. "Joplin's at the sheriff's office right now. Apparently, Meredith tried to kidnap him first so she could set him up, but Joplin got away. That's when she went after Dad."

"Is Joplin okay?" Colt asked.

"He's shaken up, but he'll be fine. He's already talking about getting ready for the trial."

"Good," Elise and Colt said in unison. Despite how they felt about Joplin and Jewell's upcoming trial, they already had enough injured people and dead bodies without adding more.

"I shouldn't have slept with you," Colt mumbled.

Oh, man.

He definitely hadn't intended to say that aloud. Especially not with his brother still listening.

"Uh, I guess this is a good time for me to hang up," Cooper said. "I'll be at Elise's place in a couple of minutes. I'll see you there."

"Yeah," Colt assured him, and he hung up, glancing at Elise to give her a real apology instead of that ill-timed mumble.

"Don't you dare," she warned him before he could say a word. She sounded a whole lot stronger than she had just several moments earlier. "You can regret sleeping with me if you want, but for the record, I don't regret it one bit."

"Well, you should. If I hadn't been on that floor with you, I might have seen the gunman coming sooner."

"Really? Even though the dogs hadn't seen him yet?" She didn't wait for an answer. "Sex didn't cause the attack, and it didn't obligate you to anything, so I darn sure don't want an apology."

All right. She was clearly mad at him or something he'd said, but Colt wasn't sure why. Added to that, he really didn't have the time to figure it out. They were just a couple of miles from her place, and he needed to establish some ground rules before they arrived.

"We'll table the apology for now," he said. "But when we get to your house, I don't want you out of my sight until I know it's safe. You've already dodged enough bullets tonight."

"So have you." That was the same argumentative tone. And she gave a heavy sigh afterward. "Whatever you do, just stay safe."

Oh, he would, and he'd keep her safe, too. Even if Meredith had planned some surprises for them.

Turning off his headlights, Colt made the turn to her ranch and then slowed so he could check out their surroundings. He immediately spotted Cooper's truck.

Headlights off, too.

And it was parked a good twenty yards from the house, the truck hidden in some trees. He didn't see his brother right away and the men he'd brought with him, but Colt figured they were making their way to the house where they would find his father alive and well.

He refused to believe differently.

Colt pulled to a stop near his brother's truck and reached to open the door. But then he stopped. With the sick plans that Meredith had put in place, it was best not to risk leaving her alone in case Meredith had another goon standing by, ready to grab her.

The woman sure had done some stupid things to protect herself. And her brother. Meredith had also done those stupid things in the name of love.

Yeah, love could do that to a person sometimes.

Even though he'd meant that thought for Meredith, Colt couldn't help but realize that he wasn't immune to that, either. Maybe not love exactly…

Or maybe that was exactly what it was.

"What's wrong now?" Elise asked.

"Nothing." He got his thoughts back on track and tipped his head to the house. "Stay behind me when we get out, and once we're closer, I'll have Pete and the ranch hand stay with you."

She nodded, looking a little uncertain. Maybe because she didn't want to jump back in the path of danger. Or maybe it was because of his *nothing* answer. Once his father was safe, he needed to clear his head and figure out how to finish this conversation.

They got out, Elise following behind him as he'd ordered, and they made their way to Cooper's truck. His brother and the others weren't there, but he quickly located them thanks to the milky-white light spearing from the front window and into the darkness.

Pete was on the left side of the house. The ranch hand, Zeke Mercer, on the right. And Cooper was on the porch standing next to the door and peering into the window.

Cooper must have seen something inside because he motioned for Colt and the others to stay quiet. Colt did, and he hurried Elise to the house and put her on the side next to Pete so he could join his brother. One look in the window and Colt's heart went to his knees.

His father was on the floor, not moving.

Colt had to fight through the punch of fear and dread, but he finally saw why his dad wasn't moving. His hands and feet were tied. Trussed up like an animal with his mouth taped shut, and Leo was seated at Elise's table while he chowed down on a bag of fast food. Meredith's brother didn't appear to have any backup with him.

Probably because he'd trusted that his sister's plan would work.

Big mistake.

Colt kicked in the door and rushed inside, with Cooper right behind him. Leo reached for his gun.

"Go head," Colt warned him. "See how fast you die."

And he meant it. He was sick and tired of all these idiots Meredith had used to try to destroy their lives.

Leo thought about it. Colt could see the debate on his face, but he also glanced at the two guns pointed right at him. Cursing, Leo stood and lifted his hands in surrender.

Colt made a quick check of his father. He didn't appear to be harmed, so while Cooper dealt with Leo, Colt checked out the rest of the house. Room by room.

It was empty, thank God.

By the time Colt made it back into the living room, Cooper had handcuffed Leo, and Pete and Elise had rushed in to help untie his father.

Later, Colt would fuss at her for not staying back until he'd made sure the house was clear. But for now, he was just thankful to have Elise, his family and the others alive and safe.

He hugged his father. Cooper joined in. And his father surprised him a little by hooking his arm around Elise and drawing her into the family embrace.

"You got Meredith?" his father asked.

Colt nodded. "We got her."

Roy looked at Elise, pushing her hair from her face so he could examine the stitches on her forehead. A fresh bruise was just below it, and the sight of it turned Colt's stomach.

He'd come way too close to losing her tonight.

It was that reminder that had Colt pulling her into his arms when his father and Cooper stepped away. His brother didn't miss the close contact between Elise and him, and Colt only deepened the contact when he brushed a kiss on her cheek.

Cooper handed off the prisoner to Pete, and his

brother's eyebrow lifted. "That's the best you can do?" Cooper asked him.

Colt was sure he scowled. This was about that slip of the tongue he'd made to Elise while still on the phone with Cooper.

I shouldn't have slept with you.

Heck, how many times would Cooper use that to taunt him? Judging from the glimmer in his eye, often.

"Pete and I need to take this guy to jail," Cooper added, a hint of a smile bending his mouth. "Zeke can take Dad to the hospital—"

"Not a chance," Roy interrupted. "I'm fine, but Elise might need to go."

She shook her head. "I'm okay, really."

But she wasn't okay. Far from it. She was shaking so hard Colt pulled her deeper into his arms. That's when he realized she didn't even have a coat, so he pulled a throw blanket from the back of the sofa and wrapped it around her. He got her moving outside and toward the SUV so he could take her and his dad out of there.

"Talk to her," Cooper whispered to Colt as they headed down the steps. "Grovel if necessary. Just don't be an idiot and let her get away again."

Because it was a habit for him to disagree with his big brother, Colt opened his mouth to do that. Then he realized what a stupid mistake that would be.

"I was wrong," Colt said to Elise. She was in midstep but stopped and stared at him.

"Yes, you were. It wasn't a mistake to sleep with me."

Thankfully, his father and Zeke were wise enough to keep on walking toward the SUV so they'd have some privacy. Even Cooper cooperated. While on each side of their prisoner, they headed toward Cooper's truck.

Giving Colt some much-needed time to trip over whatever the heck he was about to say to make this right.

But Elise spoke before he could.

"I'm in love with you," she blurted out. "Now, I know that doesn't make things easier. Not for you, not for me. I still want to make a go of this place and turn it back into a working ranch. That means I'm not going anywhere, and you'll have to learn to live with it."

"You're right," Colt said, giving that some thought. "It doesn't make it easier. But it does make it better."

She blinked, but before she could say anything else, Colt decided to do what he did best. And it wasn't talking.

He hauled Elise to him and kissed her.

Colt didn't make it a quick peck, either. He kissed her long, hard and deep. Until she made a throaty sigh and melted against him. Then he kissed her again.

"That's better," she repeated.

"Yeah, I thought so." And despite the bad night, he found himself smiling.

Well, he smiled until Elise shook her head. She was no doubt about to launch into lots of things that were all minor now that he knew how things were between them.

And things between them were definitely *better*.

Colt wanted a whole lot more than that, though.

"You will make a go of this ranch," he assured her. "And I'll help you. It's a good thing you're not going anywhere because I'm head over heels in love with you."

Elise froze, pulling in her breath, before a slow smile formed on her mouth. "You actually said it. I didn't think you would."

"Well, obviously I'll have to say it a lot more often." And he did. "I love you, Elise. I really love you."

That earned him another smile. Another kiss, too,

and Elise was just as good at it as he was. They made a great team.

"You'll marry me?" he asked.

"Of course." She nipped his bottom lip with her teeth. "You'll share your bed with me tonight?"

Colt couldn't think of a better way to seal the deal. He scooped up Elise in his arms and kissed her.

* * * * *

USA TODAY *bestselling author Delores Fossen's*
SWEETWATER RANCH *miniseries continues*
next month with REINING IN JUSTICE.

"It's crazy to think that you'd be attracted to me."

"It is?" That green gaze was intense on her face and then it slid down her body.

"Of course it is," she said. "I'm so fat and unattractive…"

"You're pregnant," he said. "And you're beautiful."

She laughed. "I wasn't fishing for compliments. I know exactly what I look like—a whale."

"I would not be attracted to a whale."

"You're not attracted to me." She wished he was. But it wasn't possible. Even if she wasn't pregnant, she knew he would never go for a woman like her.

He stepped closer, his gaze still hot on her face and body. "I'm not?"

She shook her head. But he caught her chin and stopped it. Then he tipped up her chin and lowered his head. And his lips covered hers.

THE PREGNANT WITNESS

BY
LISA CHILDS

Published in Great Britain 2015
by Mills & Boon, an imprint of Harlequin (UK) Limited,
Eton House, 18-24 Paradise Road, Richmond, Surrey, TW9 1SR

© 2015 Lisa Childs

ISBN: 978-0-263-25298-9

46-0315

Harlequin (UK) Limited's policy is to use papers that are natural, renewable and recyclable products and made from wood grown in sustainable forests. The logging and manufacturing processes conform to the legal environmental regulations of the country of origin.

Printed and bound in Spain
by CPI, Barcelona

Lisa Childs writes paranormal and contemporary romance for Mills & Boon. She lives on thirty acres in Michigan with her two daughters, a talkative Siamese, and a long-haired Chihuahua who thinks she's a rottweiler. Lisa loves hearing from readers, who can contact her through her website, www.lisachilds.com, or snail-mail address, PO Box 139, Marne, MI 49435, USA.

To Kimberly Duffy—with great appreciation for all our years of friendship! You're the best!

Chapter One

Gunshots erupted like a bomb blast, nearly shaking the walls of the glass-and-metal building. Through the wide windows and clear doors, Special Agent Blaine Campbell could easily assess the situation from the parking lot. Five suspects, wearing zombie masks and long black trench coats, fired automatic weapons inside the bank. Customers and employees cowered on the floor—all except for the uniform-clad bank security officer.

Blaine had already reported the robbery in progress and had been advised to wait for backup. He wasn't a fool; he could see that he was easily outgunned since he carried only his Glock and an extra clip.

But he left the driver's door hanging open on his rental car and ran across the parking lot crowded with customers' cars. How many potential hostages were inside that bank? How many potential casualties were there, with the way the robbers were firing those automatic weapons? Blaine couldn't wait for help—not when so many innocent people were in danger.

Ducking low, he shoved open the doors and burst into the bank lobby. "FBI!" he called out to calm the fears of the screaming and crying people.

But his entrance incited the robbers. Glass shattered behind him, as bullets whizzed over his head and through the windows, falling like rain over the customers lying faces down on the tile floor. The interior walls, which were glass partitions separating the offices from the main lobby, shattered, as well.

More people screamed and sobbed.

Blaine took cover behind one of the cement-and-steel pillars that held up the high ceiling of the modern building. He held out his hand, advising the customers to stay down as he surveyed them. Except for some cuts from the flying glass, nobody looked mortally wounded. None of the shots had hit anyone. Yet.

"Campbell," the security guard called out from behind another pillar. "You picked the right time to show up." The older man, who was also a friend, had called him here with suspicions that the bank was going to be robbed. Obviously Blaine's former boot-camp drill instructor's instincts were as sharp as ever. He had been right—except about Blaine.

He was too late. The robbers already carried bags overflowing with cash. If only he'd arrived earlier, before they'd gotten what they wanted…

He couldn't arrest them all on his own.

"Stay down!" one of the robbers yelled, as he fired his automatic rifle again.

A woman cried out as another robber tangled a gloved hand in her dark hair and pulled her up from the floor. She was close to one of the wrecked offices, so maybe she worked for the bank or had been meeting with one of the bank officers. She turned toward Blaine, her eyes wide with fear as if beseeching him for help.

But before he could take aim on the robber holding her, the security guard, armed only with a small-caliber handgun, stepped from behind his pillar. "Let her go!" Daryl Williams shouted as he fired at them.

"Sarge, get down," Blaine shouted.

But his advice came too late as a bullet struck the security guard's chest and blood spread across his gray uniform. The woman shrieked—either in reaction to Sarge getting shot or because she was afraid she might be next.

Blaine cursed, stepped out from behind the pillar and fired frantically back. One of the mask-wearing bank robbers spun around, as if Blaine had struck him. But he probably wore a bulletproof vest because he didn't drop to the floor as the guard had. Instead the robber hurried toward the back of the bank with the other zombies. One of them dragged along that terrified young woman. But now she stared back at Sarge instead of Blaine, her gaze full of fear and concern for the fallen security guard. Blaine scrambled over to his friend's side. The man wore his iron-gray hair in a military cut. He may have retired from the service, but he was still a soldier. "Hang in there, Sarge."

"Assist…assist." Daryl Williams tried to speak through the blood gurgling out of his mouth.

"I already called it in when I pulled up and heard the shots. Help is coming," Blaine promised, even though they both knew it would be too late.

Williams weakly shook his head. "Assist…manager…"

"The hostage?"

Daryl nodded even as his eyes rolled back into his head. He was gone.

And so was the woman. Of course Sergeant Williams would want Blaine to rescue her—the civilian. Remembering the stark fear on her pale face, Blaine snapped into action and hurried toward the back of the bank. Alarms wailed and lights flashed as the security door stood open to an alley. If it closed, he wouldn't be able to open it again. That must have been why the robbers had taken their hostage out the back, so she could open the security door for them. But why not leave her? Why take her along?

Blaine caught the door before it swung shut and pointed his gun into the alley. Bullets chiseled chips off the brick around the door as the bank robbers fired at him. If they had a getaway car parked in the alley, they obviously hadn't driven it away yet. He couldn't let them leave with the hostage or else nobody would probably ever see the young woman again. He had barely seen her long enough to give a description beyond dark hair and eyes.

Blaine risked a glance through the crack of the door and more bullets pinged off the steel. But he caught a glimpse of white metal—a van—as the side door opened. Another door slammed. The driver's? He couldn't let them get the hostage inside the vehicle, so he threw the bank door all the way open and burst into the alley. A shot struck him in the chest, but he kept going despite the impact of the bullet hitting his vest.

After his honorable discharge from active duty, he had thought the last thing he would miss was the helmet. He had hated the weight and the heat of it. But he could actually use one now—to protect himself from a head shot. More bullets struck his vest.

He returned fire, his shots glancing off the side of the van before one shattered the glass of the driver's window. Hopefully he'd struck the son of a bitch. But he didn't wait to find out; instead, he reached out for the hostage that one of the damn zombie robbers was pulling through the open side door. He caught the young woman's arm and jerked her backward as he fired into the van. The engine revved, and the vehicle burst forward, tires squealing.

But just in case the occupants fired back at them, he pushed the hostage to the ground and covered the young woman with his body. And that was when he realized she wasn't just terrified for herself but probably also for the child she carried.

She was pregnant.

The van kept going, but someone fired out the open back doors of it. And more bullets struck him, stealing his breath.

MAGGIE JENKINS'S THROAT was raw and her voice hoarse from screaming, but even though the robbers—dressed in those horrible zombie costumes—were gone, she wanted to scream again. She didn't want to scream out of fear for herself but for the man who lay on top of her. His body had gone limp as the breath left it.

He had been shot so many times. But he'd kept coming to her rescue like a golden-haired superhero. And then he'd covered her body with his, taking more shots to his back.

He had to be dead. Why had he interrupted the robbery in progress and risked his own life? He had claimed to be an FBI agent, but why would he have been alone? Why wouldn't he have waited for more agents and for local backup before bursting into the bank?

"Please, please be alive," she murmured, her voice no louder than a whisper. She grasped his shoulders—his impossibly wide shoulders—and eased him back. Something cold and metallic hung from his neck and pressed against her chest. A badge.

So he really was a lawman. But how had he known the bank was being robbed? When the robbers rushed the bank, she hadn't had the time or the nerve to push the silent alarm beneath her desk before bullets had shattered the glass walls of her office.

Maybe one of the tellers or Mr. Hardy, the bank manager, had pushed an alarm. Whatever the FBI agent had driven to the bank hadn't had sirens or lights. She hadn't even known he was there until he pushed open the lobby doors. But, then again, she had hardly been able to hear anything over all of those gunshots. Her ears rang from the deafening noise.

But now she heard his gasp as he caught his breath again. He stared down at her, his face so close that she picked up on all the nuances in his eyes. They were a deep green with flecks of gold that made them glitter. His body, long and muscular, tensed against hers. He moved the hand that was not holding his weapon to the asphalt and pushed up, levering himself off her.

"I'm sorry," he said.

He was apologizing to her? For what? Saving her life? Maybe shock had settled in, or maybe his good looks and his concern had struck her dumb. Usually she wasn't silent; usually people complained that she talked too much.

"Are you all right?" he asked.

Her hands covered her stomach, and something shifted beneath her palm. She sighed with relief that her baby was moving, flailing his tiny fists and kicking his tiny feet as if trying to fight off his mother's attackers.

But it was too late. This man had already fought them off for her. Of course her baby shouldn't be fighting to protect her; it was Maggie's job to protect him or her…

"Are you all right?" the man asked again. He slid his gun into a holster beneath his arm, and then he lifted her from the ground as easily as if she were half her size.

"How are you alive?" she asked in wonder.

He reached for his shirt and tore the buttons loose. The blue cotton parted to reveal a black vest. The badge swung back against it.

She was no longer close enough to read all the smaller print, but she identified the big brass-colored letters. "You really are an FBI agent? I thought you just said that to scare the robbers."

And she'd thought he had been a little crazy to try that when the robbers had had bigger guns than his. But maybe announcing his presence had scared the robbers into leaving quickly because they'd worried that backup would come.

Where was it, though?

"I'm Special Agent Blaine Campbell," he introduced himself.

"How did you get here so quickly?" she asked, still not entirely convinced that he wasn't a superhero. "How did you know the bank was being robbed?"

He shook his head and turned back to the building. "I didn't know that it was being robbed today. Sarge—Daryl Williams—called me a few days ago with concerns."

She gasped as she relived the security guard getting shot, flinching at the sound of the shot, at the image of him falling. He hadn't been wearing a vest, but he'd stepped out from behind that pillar anyway—undoubtedly to save her. "Is Sarge okay?"

The agent shook his head again, but he didn't speak, as if too overwhelmed for words. He had called Mr. Williams *Sarge*, so he must have known him well. Maybe Mr. Williams had once been his drill instructor, as he had been her fiancé's six years ago. The older man worked only part-time at the bank for something to do since he retired from the military.

If only he hadn't been there today…

If only he hadn't tried to save her…

The tears that had been burning her eyes brimmed over and began to slide down her face. She had just lost her fiancé a few months ago, and now she had lost another connection to him because Sarge had really known him. Not only had he trained him, but he'd also kept in touch with Andy over the years. He'd worried about him. He'd known that Andy shouldn't have joined the Marines; he hadn't been strong enough—physically or emotionally—to handle it. He had barely survived his first two deployments, and he had died on the first day of his last one.

Sarge had come for Andy's funeral and never left— intent on taking care of Maggie and her unborn baby since Andy was now unable to.

Strong arms wrapped around her, offering comfort when she suspected he needed it himself. Blaine Campbell had lost a man he'd obviously respected and cared about. So she hugged him back, clinging to him—until tires squealed and the back door of the bank burst open to the alley.

Guns cocked and voices shouted, "Get down! Get down!"

Fear filled her that the robbers had returned. She squeezed her eyes shut. She couldn't look at them again, couldn't see those horrific zombie costumes again. When she and Andy had been in middle school, his older brother had sneaked them into an R-rated zombie movie, and she'd been terrified of them ever since, even to the point where she didn't go to Halloween parties and even hid in the dark so no trick-or-treaters would come to her door.

But they kept coming to her.

Had they returned to make certain she and the agent were dead?

Chapter Two

"Agent Campbell," Blaine identified himself to the state troopers who'd drawn their weapons on him.

While he respected local law enforcement, especially troopers since his oldest sister was one in Michigan, he had met some unqualified officers over the years. So the gun barrels pointing at him and the woman next to him made him nervous. But he refused to get down or allow the pregnant woman to drop to the pavement again, either.

She had already been roughed up enough; her light gray suit was smudged with grease and oil from the alley. Her legs were scraped from connecting with the asphalt earlier. Had he done that when he'd shoved her down? Had he hurt her?

She had also lost a shoe—either in the bank or maybe in the van from which Blaine had pulled her, so she was unsteady on her feet. Or maybe her trembling wasn't because her balance was off but because she was in shock. He kept a hand on her arm, so that she didn't stumble and fall. But she needed more help than a hand to steady her.

"The bank robbers have already left in a white panel van," he continued. "The driver's-side window is broken and the rear taillights have been shot out." He read off the license plate number he'd memorized, as well.

One of the officers pressed the radio on his lapel and called in an APB on the vehicle. "What else can you tell us about the suspects, Agent Campbell?"

Fighting back the grief that threatened to overwhelm him, he replied, "One of them shot the security guard."

"We already have paramedics inside the bank," another officer told him. "They're treating the wounded."

They were too late to help Sarge. The man had died in his arms—his final words urging Blaine to save the assistant bank manager.

"You should have them check out Mrs….?" He turned to the young woman, waiting for her to supply her name. She hadn't offered it when he'd introduced himself earlier.

"Miss," she corrected him, almost absentmindedly. Her dark eyes seemed unfocused, as if she were dazed. "Maggie Jenkins…"

She was single. Now he allowed himself to notice how pretty she was. Her brown hair was long and curly and tangled around her shoulders. Her eyes were wide and heavily lashed. She was unmarried, but she probably wasn't single—not with her being as pretty as she was.

"The paramedics need to check out Miss Jenkins," he told the troopers. "The bank robbers were trying to take her hostage. She could have been hurt." But he might have been the one who'd done it when he had knocked her onto the hard asphalt of the alley.

"She should probably be taken to the hospital," he added. For an ultrasound to check out the well-being of her unborn child, too. But he didn't want to say it out loud and frighten her. The young woman had already been through enough.

The officer pressed his radio again and asked paramedics to come around to the back of the bank. They arrived quickly, backing the ambulance down the alley. A female paramedic pushed a stretcher out the doors and rolled it toward them.

But Miss Jenkins shook her head, refusing treatment. "What about Mr. Williams?" she asked. "He needs your help more than I do."

The paramedic just stared at her.

"The security guard," Miss Jenkins said. "One of the robbers shot him." Her already rough voice squeaked with emotion. "Will he be all right?"

The paramedic hesitated before shaking her head.

Tears spilled from Miss Jenkins's eyes again, trailing down her smooth face. She had cared about Sarge. But Blaine didn't think they could have worked together that long. Sarge had retired from the military only a few short months ago.

Blaine wanted to hold her again, to comfort her as he had earlier. Or had she comforted him? Her arms had slid around him, her curves soft and warm against him. He resisted the urge to reach for her, and instead he released her arm.

"Go with the paramedic," he said. "Let her check you out."

Blaine had questions for the assistant bank manager—so many questions. But his questions would wait until she was physically well enough to answer them.

The troopers immediately began to question Blaine. He had to explain his presence and about Sarge—even while tears of loss stung his eyes. He blinked them back, knowing his former drill instructor would have kicked his butt if he showed any weakness. Sarge had taught all his recruits that a good marine—a strong marine—controlled his emotions. Blaine had already learned that before boot camp, though.

"Why did the security guard call you?" one of the troopers asked.

"I just transferred to the Chicago Bureau office to take over the investigation of the robbers who've been hitting banks in Illinois, Michigan and Indiana." Bank robberies were his specialty. He had a perfect record; no bank robbery he had investigated had gone unsolved, no bank robber unapprehended.

Of course, some robbers were sloppy and desperate and easily caught. Blaine already knew that this group of them—in their trench coats and zombie masks—were not sloppy or desperate. And, therefore, they would not be easily caught. But he would damn well catch them.

For Sarge...

"You think those robberies are related to this one?" the trooper asked.

"I can't make a determination yet." Because he hadn't had a chance to go to the office; his flight had landed only hours ago. But ever since Sarge's call, the urgency in the man's voice had haunted Blaine and made him come here first—with his suitcase in the trunk of a rental car. "I need more information."

And he didn't want to give up too much information to the troopers before he'd verified his facts. He needed to check in with the Bureau, but he couldn't leave the scene yet.

He couldn't leave Maggie Jenkins.

He turned back to where the paramedic had helped her into the back of the first-responder rig. A man in a suit was standing outside the doors, talking to her. He'd come through the back door of the bank, so the troopers must have cleared him.

Blaine recognized him as one of the people who'd been lying on the floor, cowering from the robbers. Instead of checking on her, the man appeared to be questioning her—the way Blaine wanted to. But he wasn't certain she had any more information than he did.

He just wanted to make sure she was all right—that his rescue hadn't done her more harm than being taken hostage had.

MAGGIE WAS FINALLY ALONE. Mr. Hardy, the bank manager, had gone back inside the damaged building to call the corporate headquarters, as she had told him to do. At thirty, he was young and inexperienced for his position, so he had no idea what to do or how to manage after a robbery.

Unfortunately, Maggie did.

She trembled—not with cold or even with fear. She hadn't felt that until the bullet had struck Sarge, and he had dropped to the floor. Before that, when the gunmen had burst into the lobby wearing those masks and trench coats, she had been too stunned to feel anything at all.

Usually just the sight of those gruesome masks would have filled her with terror, as they had ever since Andy and Mark had sneaked her into that violent horror movie. She'd had nightmares for years over it. But for the past few months she'd been having new nightmares. And while they'd still been about zombies, they hadn't been movie actors—they'd been about *these* zombies.

"I can't believe it," she murmured to herself. "I can't believe it happened. Again…"

And it was that disbelief that had overwhelmed her fear—until Sarge had been shot.

"Are you all right?" a deep voice asked.

Startled, she tensed. It wasn't one of the paramedics. Their voices were higher and less…commanding. Agent Campbell commanded attention and respect and control.

He had taken over the moment he'd burst into the bank with his weapon drawn. He had taken over and saved her from whatever the bank robbers had planned for her. And he'd taken over the investigation from the state troopers more easily.

She nodded. "I'm okay," she assured him, worried that he might think she was losing it. "I always talk to myself. My parents claim I came out talking and never shut up…" But as she chattered, her teeth began to chatter, too, snapping together as her jaw trembled.

The FBI agent lifted the blanket a paramedic had put around her and he wrapped it more tightly—as if he were swaddling a baby. She had taken a class and swaddled a doll, but she hadn't done it nearly as well as he had. Maybe he had children of his own. She glanced down at his hands—his big, strong hands—but they were bare of any rings. Not every married man wore one, though. Her face heated with embarrassment that she'd even looked. His marital status should have been the last thing on her mind.

"Thank you," she said. "I'm fine, really…" But it wasn't cold out. Why was she so deeply chilled that even her bones felt cold? "I can go back inside the bank and help Mr. Hardy—"

"The bank manager," he said.

She'd noticed that he had stopped Mr. Hardy before letting him back inside the bank. And he'd questioned him. She doubted the young manager had been able to provide many answers.

"Yes," she said. "I need to go back inside and help him close up the bank and take inventory for corporate. There's so much to do…" There always was, after a robbery.

"You need to go to the hospital and get checked out,"

Agent Campbell said as he waved over the paramedic.
"You should have already taken her."

"She wanted to talk to you first," the female paramedic replied. She'd told Maggie that she wouldn't mind
talking to the agent herself, and her male partner had
scoffed at her lack of professionalism.

Maggie hadn't intended to go to the hospital at all—
not when there was so much to do inside the bank. And
Sarge…

Was he still inside?

She shuddered, then shivered harder. And the baby
shifted inside her, kicking her ribs. She flinched and nodded. "Maybe I should get checked out…"

For the baby. She had to protect her baby. She had
nearly three months left of her pregnancy—three months
to keep her unborn child safe. She hadn't realized how
hard that might be.

"My questions can wait," the FBI agent told her, "until
you've been thoroughly checked out." He turned toward
the paramedics. "Which hospital will you take her to?"

"Med West," the woman paramedic replied. "You can
ride along and question her in the back of the rig."

Maggie stilled her trembling as she waited for his
reply. She wanted him to agree; she felt safer with him
close. She felt safe in his arms…

And after what had happened—again—she would
have doubted she would ever feel safe. Anywhere.

"Agent Campbell," one of the officers called out to
him. He didn't pull his gaze from her, his green eyes intense on her face. The officer continued anyway. "We
located the van."

That got the agent's attention; he turned away from
her. "And the robbers?"

The officer shrugged. "We don't know if there's anyone inside. Nobody's approached it yet."

Maggie struggled free of the blanket and grabbed the agent's arm—even though she knew she couldn't stop him. He was going.

"Be careful," she advised him.

She had told Andy the same thing when he had left her last, but he hadn't listened to her. She hoped Agent Campbell did. Or the next time the robbers' bullets might miss his vest and hit somewhere else instead.

Agent Campbell barely spared her a nod before heading off with the state troopers. He had been lucky during his first confrontation with the thieves, but Andy had been lucky, too, during his first two deployments.

Eventually, though, luck ran out...

HIS GUN STEADY in one hand, Blaine slid open the side door with the other. But the van was empty. The robbers had ditched it between Dumpsters at the end of an alley.

"This vehicle was reported stolen three days ago," one of the troopers informed him.

Either they'd stolen it themselves or picked it up from someone who dealt in stolen vehicles. It was a lead that Blaine could follow. Maybe someone had witnessed the theft.

They must have exchanged the van for another vehicle they had stashed close to the bank. They'd had to move quickly, though, so they hadn't taken time to wipe down the van.

They had left behind forensic evidence. Blaine could see some of it now. Fibers from their clothes. Hair—either from their masks or their own. And blood. It could have been fake; they'd had some on their gruesome disguises. But that hadn't looked like this.

This blood was smeared and drying already into dark pools.

"You hit one of them?" a trooper asked.

He hoped he'd hit the one who'd killed Sarge. "I fired at them, but I thought they were wearing vests."

"You must be a good shot," the trooper replied.

More likely he had gotten off a lucky shot. He was fortunate one of them hadn't done the same. If they hadn't been worried that he had backup coming, they probably would have killed him the way they had Sarge.

Blaine sighed. "But the suspect wasn't hurt so badly that he couldn't get away." As they had all gotten away. But at least one of them had not been unscathed.

"Put out an APB that one of the suspects might be seeking medical treatment for a gunshot wound," Blaine said, "at a hospital or doctor's office or med center. Hell, don't rule out a vet clinic. These guys will not want the wound getting reported." And doctors were legally obligated to report gunshot wounds.

So he wouldn't worry that he had sent Maggie Jenkins off to the hospital in the back of that ambulance. He wouldn't worry that one of the men who had tried to abduct her earlier might get a chance to try again.

Again...

What had she been muttering when he'd walked up to the ambulance? Her already soft voice had been strained from screaming, so he'd struggled to hear, let alone understand, her words. But she'd murmured something about not believing that it had happened. Again...

Had Maggie Jenkins been the victim of a bank robbery before?

The same bank robbers?

Hell, Blaine was worried now. Not just that she might be in danger but that he might have let the best lead to the robbers ride away. Had he let her big, dark eyes and her fear and vulnerability influence his opinion of her?

What if Maggie Jenkins hadn't been a hostage but a coconspirator?

Maybe Sarge hadn't been trying to tell him to rescue the assistant bank manager. Maybe he had been trying to tell Blaine to catch her.

Chapter Three

Maggie pressed her palms over the hospital gown covering her belly and tried to soothe the child moving inside her. He kept kicking, as though he was still fighting. "I'm sorry, baby," she said. "I know Mama's not doing a very good job of keeping you safe."

But she'd tried.

Why was it that danger kept finding her? She had already changed jobs, or at least locations, but she couldn't afford to quit. Maybe she should have married Andy one of the times he had suggested it. They had been together since middle school, and she'd loved him. But she hadn't been *in* love with him.

"I'm sorry," she said again. But this time she was talking to Andy.

She should have told him the truth, but he'd enlisted right out of high school and she hadn't wanted to be the heartless girlfriend who wrote the Dear John letter. And when he'd come home on leave, she had been so happy to see him—so happy to have her best friend back—that she hadn't wanted to risk losing that friendship.

But eventually she had lost him—to a roadside bomb in Afghanistan. Tears stung her eyes and tickled her nose, but she drew in a shaky breath and steadied herself. She had to be strong—for her baby. Since he had already lost his father, he needed her twice as much.

A hand drew back the curtain of Maggie's corner of the emergency department. The young physician's assistant who'd talked to her earlier smiled reassuringly. "I had a doctor and a radiologist review the ultrasound," the PA said, "and we all agree that your baby is fine."

Maggie released her breath as a sigh of relief. "That's great."

"You, on the other hand, have some bumps and bruises, and your blood pressure is a little high," the PA continued. "So you need to be careful and take better care of yourself."

She nodded in agreement. Not that she hadn't been trying. That had been the whole point of her new job—less stress. But Mr. Hardy wasn't as competent as the manager at the previous branch where she'd worked. And the zombie bank robbers had hit the new bank anyway.

Maybe she would have been safer had she stayed where she'd been. "I will take better care of myself and the baby," Maggie vowed. "Do you know what I'm having?" She had had an ultrasound earlier in her pregnancy, but it had been too soon to tell the gender.

The young woman shook her head. "I wasn't able to tell."

Or she probably would have pointed it out then.

"But maybe the radiologist had an idea." The young woman's face flushed as she glanced down at the notes. "I'm sorry," she said. "I hadn't realized that you'd been at the bank that was robbed and that paramedics had brought you from the scene."

"That's fine," Maggie said. "I should have told you myself." But she hadn't wanted to talk about it—to remember what it had been like to see those gruesome masks again and to watch as one of them killed Sarge. She shuddered.

"Of course your blood pressure would be elevated," the PA continued. "You must have been terrified."

She had been until the FBI agent had saved her. Where was he? He was supposed to come to the hospital to interview her. Hadn't Agent Campbell survived his second run-in with the bank robbers?

"I'll be okay," she assured the physician's assistant. She had survived. Again. Daryl Williams hadn't been as fortunate—because of her. Maybe Agent Campbell hadn't survived, either.

The young woman nodded. "Considering what you've been through, you're doing very well. But I would follow up with your obstetrician tomorrow and make sure your blood pressure goes down."

"I will do that," Maggie promised. She was taking no chances with her pregnancy. She had already lost the baby's father; she wouldn't lose his baby, too.

"You can get dressed now." The young woman passed over some papers. "Here is your release and an ultrasound picture. There isn't any way of telling his or her gender yet."

Maggie stared down at the photo. She had seen her baby on the ultrasound screen this time and the previous time she'd had one. But this was the first photo she'd been given to keep—probably because he looked like a baby now and not a peanut. He or she was curled up on his or her side, and the little mouth was open. She smiled as she remembered her mother claiming that Maggie's mouth had been open during every ultrasound. She'd been talking even before she'd been born.

"Thank you," she told the PA. But she didn't look up. She couldn't take her gaze from the amazing photo of her baby. The child had already survived so much: the loss of a parent and two bank robberies.

"Good luck, Ms. Jenkins," the young woman replied as she pulled the curtain closed again.

Maggie's smile slid off her lips. She was going to need luck to make it safely through her pregnancy and deliver a healthy baby. He was fine now. And she would do everything within her power to keep him that way.

She dressed quickly so that she could pick up and study the picture again. Maybe she should wait for the FBI agent—to make certain that he was all right. It wasn't as if she could leave anyway. Her purse was back at the bank, so she didn't have any money to pay for a cab. And with Mr. Hardy busy with corporate, the only other person she could have called at the bank to bring it to her was dead.

Sarge…

If only he hadn't stepped out from behind that pillar…

If only he hadn't tried to save her…

Tears blurred her vision, but she blinked them back to focus on the baby picture again. She needed to focus on him or her, needed to keep him or her healthy and safe. The baby was her priority.

She would have to find a phone she could use and call a friend to pick her up. But she didn't really know anyone here in this suburb of Chicago. She hadn't known anyone but Sarge. After the bank where she'd previously worked had been robbed, she had transferred to the branch where Sarge worked—thinking she would feel safer with him there. But the danger had followed her and claimed his life—cruelly cutting his retirement short. The tears threatened again, but she fought them. Sobbing would not help her blood pressure.

The curtain moved as a gloved hand pulled it back.

"I'm sorry," she said, feeling guilty for taking up the

area. "I realize you probably need the bed for someone else…" For someone who actually needed medical attention. "I'm all ready to leave." She just needed someone to pick her up. "I can wait in the lobby."

Nobody said anything, though. But she could feel them standing there, watching her. So then she looked up, and her heart began to pound frantically as she stared into the creepy face of one of those horrible zombie masks. It was her nightmare come to life again.

She would have screamed but for the gun barrel pointing directly at her. She already knew that these people had no compunction about killing. They had already killed once and that had been because Sarge had been trying to save her. She couldn't scream and risk someone else getting hurt again. The only reason they would have tracked her down at the hospital was to kill again.

To kill *her*…

BLAINE CURSED HIMSELF as he flipped screens on his tablet. The Bureau had forwarded him the case file for the bank robberies.

Now he knew exactly what Maggie had been muttering in the back of the ambulance—because it had happened again. A different bank. A different city. But the same witness.

Maggie Jenkins had been robbed before—a couple of months ago—at another bank where she'd been working as an assistant manager. What were the odds that the same robbers, wearing zombie masks and black trench coats, would track her down at another bank in another city? Maybe it was a coincidence, but in his years with the Bureau, Blaine had found few true coincidences.

It was more likely that they knew her. And if they knew her, she knew them. He'd had a lot of questions for

Maggie Jenkins before; now he had even more. And he wouldn't let her tear-damp dark eyes or her sweet vulnerability distract him again.

He dropped the tablet onto the passenger seat and threw open the driver's door. After clicking the locks, he hurried across the parking lot to the hospital. He sidestepped through the automatic doors before they were fully open and flashed his badge at the security guard standing inside the doors. "I'm looking for a witness who was brought here from a bank-robbery scene. Maggie Jenkins."

After waving him through the blinking, beeping metal detector, the guard pointed toward the emergency-department desk. Blaine showed his badge to the receptionist. "I need to talk to Maggie Jenkins—from the bank robbery."

The older woman stared at his badge before nodding. "Nyla can show you where she is."

A young nurse stepped from behind the desk and pushed open swinging doors. "Ms. Jenkins is behind the last curtain on the left."

He followed the woman's directions, past a long row of pulled curtains, and he pulled aside the very last curtain on the left. The bed was empty but for a black-and-white photo. Maggie was gone. He picked up the photo and recognized it as an ultrasound picture. His older sisters had shown him a few over the past ten years. He'd thought they looked like Rorschach tests. They had all prized them.

No matter what her involvement was in the robberies, Maggie Jenkins wouldn't have willingly left that photo behind. He reached for his holster and whirled around to the nurse who'd followed him. "She's gone."

Unconcerned, the young woman shrugged. "She was cleared to get dressed and leave."

"She came by ambulance and didn't have her purse," he said. "She couldn't have left on her own." Not with no car and no money for a cab. At the very least, she would have had to call someone to pick her up. But then, why wouldn't she have taken the ultrasound photo with her? "Did you see anyone come back here?"

Metal scraped against metal as another curtain was tugged back, its rings scraping along the rod. A little girl, propped against pillows in a bed, peered out at Blaine. "The monster came for her."

His skin chilled as dread chased over him. "What monster?"

An older woman, probably the little girl's mother, was sitting in a chair next to the bed. With a slight smile, she shook her head. "It wasn't a monster. Just someone wearing a silly Halloween mask."

"But it's not Halloween," the little girl said, as if she suspected her mother was lying and that the monster was very real.

Blaine was worried that the monster was real, too. "Was it a zombie mask that the person was wearing?"

The woman shrugged. "I don't know."

But the little girl's already pale face grew even paler with fear as she slowly nodded. "It was a really creepy zombie. He was wearing a long black coat."

Blaine's dread spread the chill throughout him. He bit back a curse. One of the robbers had tracked her down at the hospital?

The woman shrugged again. "He put his fingers to his lips, so that we wouldn't say anything. He was just playing a joke."

Apparently the woman hadn't seen any of the news coverage about the zombie robbers.

The nurse shook her head in vigorous denial of the

little girl's claim. "I didn't see anyone dressed like that in this area, and the security guard wouldn't have let him through the front doors."

"What about the back doors?" he asked. "Could someone have come in another way?"

"Only employees can," the nurse replied.

He doubted that employees had to go through a metal detector the way visitors had to. "Show me."

The nurse stepped around the curtain to show Blaine another set of double doors on that end of the emergency department—just a few feet from where Maggie had been. If the robber had come through those doors, no one would have seen him but Maggie and apparently the little girl next to her. He wouldn't have gone through security if he'd come in the employee entrance. The nurse had to swipe her ID card to open those doors. They swung into an empty corridor.

"How would someone get to the parking lot from here?" he asked.

With a sigh of exasperation, as if he was wasting her time, she turned left and continued down the corridor to a couple of single doors. "The locker rooms have doors to a back hallway that leads to the employee parking lot," she said in anticipation of his next questions. "But it's too soon for a shift change, so nobody's back here now."

But a noise emanated from behind one of the doors. A thump. And then a scream pierced the air. Blaine grabbed the nurse's ID badge and swiped it through the lock. As he pushed open the door, shots rang out. A bullet struck him—in the vest over his heart. The force of it knocked him against the door and forced the breath from his lungs.

The nurse cried and ran back down the corridor. Then another scream rang out—from Maggie Jenkins. She had fallen to her knees. But the bank robber had a gloved hand in her hair, trying to pull her up—trying to drag her to that door at the back of the locker room—the door that would lead to the employee parking lot.

How did he know where to take her? How did he have the access badge to do it? He must either be an employee of the hospital or he knew an employee very well.

Ignoring the pain she must have been in from that hand in her hair, Maggie wriggled and reached as she continued to scream for help. But she didn't wait for Blaine's help. She tried to help herself. She grabbed at the benches between the rows of lockers and at the lockers, too, as she tried to prevent the robber from dragging her off. She flailed her arms and kicked, too, desperately trying to fight off her attacker. But then the gun barrel swung toward her face and she froze.

Was the robber just trying to scare her into cooperating? Or did he intend to kill her right here, in front of Blaine?

Chapter Four

Maggie couldn't breathe; she couldn't move. She couldn't do anything but stare down the barrel of the gun that had been shoved in her face.

Agent Campbell had stepped inside the room, but then a shot had slammed him back against the door. Wasn't he wearing his vest anymore? Was he hurt?

Or worse?

She wanted to look, but she was frozen with fear. Because she was about to be *worse*, too. With the barrel so close to her face, there was no way the bullet could miss her head. She was about to die.

In her peripheral vision, she was aware of the gloved finger pressing on the trigger. And she heard the shot. It exploded in the room, shattering the silence and deafening her. But she felt no pain. Neither did she fall. She still couldn't move. Apparently she couldn't feel, either.

But the gun moved away from her face. With a dull thud, it dropped to the floor. And the robber fell, too, backward over one of the benches in what appeared to be the employee locker room.

The robber had forced her to be quiet while they'd been in Emergency—because he'd kept the barrel of the gun tight against her belly. He would have killed her baby if she'd called out for help. But when he'd brought her to this locker room, he'd had to move the gun away to swipe the badge. And so, as the doors were closing behind them, she'd risked calling out.

But she hadn't expected Agent Campbell to come to her aid again. He must have recovered from the shot that had knocked him back because now he started forward again, toward the robber. But he stopped to kick away the gun, and the robber vaulted to his feet. He picked up one of the benches and hurled it at the FBI agent. It knocked Blaine Campbell back—into Maggie.

She fell against the lockers, the back of her head striking the metal so hard that spots danced before her eyes. Her vision blurred. Then her legs, already shaking with her fear, folded under her, and she slid down to the floor.

While the bench had knocked over the agent, he hadn't lost his grip on his gun. And he fired it again at the robber. The man flinched at the impact of the bullet. But like the agent, he must have worn a vest because the shot didn't stop him. But he didn't fight anymore. Instead he turned and ran.

"Stop!" the agent yelled.

But the man in the zombie mask didn't listen, or at least he didn't heed the command in Agent Campbell's voice as everyone else had. He pushed open the back door with such force that metal clanged as it struck the outside wall. Then the man ran through that open door.

Campbell jumped up, but instead of heading off in pursuit of the robber, he turned back to her and asked, "Are you all right?"

The gunfire echoed in her ears yet, so his deep voice sounded far away. She couldn't focus on it; she couldn't focus on him, either.

But his handsome face came closer as he dropped to

his knees in front of her. His green eyes full of concern and intensity, he asked, "Maggie, are you all right?"

No. She couldn't speak, and she was usually never at a loss for words. Her heart kept racing even though the robber and his gun were no longer threatening her. In fact, the more she stared into the agent's eyes, the faster her heart beat. The green was so vibrant—like the first leaves on a tree in spring. Just as she had been unable to look anywhere but the barrel of the gun in her face, she couldn't look away from the agent's beautiful eyes.

"Maggie..." Fingers skimmed along her cheek. "Are you all right?"

She opened her mouth, but no words slipped out. Her pulse quickened, and her breath grew shallower— so shallow that she couldn't get any air. And then she couldn't see Agent Campbell any longer as her vision blurred and then blackened.

BLAINE SHOULD HAVE been in hot pursuit of the robber. He should have been firing shots and taking him down in the parking lot. Instead he was standing over a pregnant woman, waiting for her to regain consciousness. And as he waited, he drew in some deep breaths—hoping to ease the tightness in his chest.

The intern, who had come running, along with the security guards, when Blaine had yelled for medical help, assured him that she was fine. She and her baby were fine. She must have just hyperventilated. And with someone shooting at her, it was understandable—or so the intern had thought.

Blaine wasn't sure what to think. Had she really passed out? Or had she only staged a diversion so the robber could get away from him and those guards that nurse Nyla had called to the locker room?

But then, if Maggie was an accomplice, why had she fought the man so hard? Why had she looked so terrified?

His older sisters had pulled off drama well in their teens. They'd worked their parents to get what they wanted, so he'd seen some pretty good actresses work their manipulations up close and personal. But if Maggie Jenkins had been acting in the locker room, she surpassed his sisters.

"Who are you really, Maggie Jenkins?" he wondered aloud. Innocent victim or criminal mastermind?

Her thick, dark lashes fluttered against her cheeks, as if she'd heard him and his words had roused her to consciousness. She blinked and stared up at him, looking as dazed and shocked as she had when she'd fallen against the lockers.

When he'd inadvertently knocked her against them. A pang of guilt had him flinching, and he fisted his hands to keep them from reaching for her belly to check on the baby. It had been real to him even before he'd seen the picture, but now it was even more real.

"The doctor said you and your baby are not hurt," he assured her. And himself.

"Are you okay?" she asked, and her brown eyes softened with concern.

He shrugged off her worry. "I'm fine."

He would probably have a bruise where the bench had clipped his shoulder, but his physical well-being was the least of his concerns right now.

She stared up at him, her smooth brow furrowing slightly, as if she doubted his words. "Really?"

No. He was upset about Sarge. And he was frustrated as hell that he'd lost one of the leads to Sarge's killer—or maybe the actual killer himself—when the robber had run out the employee exit to the parking lot. But Blaine had another lead—one he didn't intend to let out of his sight.

"I'm worried about you," he admitted. For so many reasons...

She tensed and protectively splayed her hands over her belly. "You said the baby isn't hurt."

"The baby is fine," he assured her. "And so are you."

She stared up at him again, this time full of doubt.

So he added, "For now."

Despite the blanket covering her, she shivered at his foreboding tone.

"You're obviously in danger," he said, "since one of the robbers risked coming here to abduct you from the ER." Or had she called him? Had she wanted to be picked up before Blaine could question her further?

He needed to take her down to the Bureau, or at least the closest police department for an interrogation. But if he started treating her like a suspect, she might react like one and clam up or lawyer up. Maybe it was better if he let her continue to play the victim...

But her eyes—those big, dark eyes—didn't fill with tears this time. Instead her gaze hardened and she clenched her delicate jaw. Angrily she asked, "Why won't they leave me alone?"

"I'm not sure why you were tracked down at the hospital today," he replied.

Could it have been another coincidence? Could the robber have been here to get treatment for the gunshot wound Blaine had inflicted and then stumbled upon her?

But the robber hadn't seemed injured—especially since he'd had the strength to hurl the bench with such force at Blaine. And he'd been fighting with Maggie before that. Maybe he wasn't the injured robber, but had been bringing that one for treatment...

But where was that person?

He'd already lost so much blood in the van.

"Why did one of them come here?" she asked—the same question Blaine had been asking himself. "What do they want with *me*?"

That was another question Blaine had been asking himself. "Maybe you saw or heard something back at the bank," he suggested, "something that might give away the identity of one of them?"

She shook her head. "I couldn't see any of their faces. They wore those horrible masks…" And she shuddered.

"What about their voices?"

"Only one of them spoke at the bank," she said, "and I didn't recognize his voice."

Did the others not speak because she would have recognized one of their voices? And now he wondered about the father of her baby…

But wouldn't she have recognized him despite the disguise? Wouldn't she have recognized his build, his walk, any of his mannerisms? Or maybe she had but wasn't about to implicate him and possibly herself.

Blaine waited, hoping that she would voluntarily admit to having been robbed before. But if she'd been about to confess to anything, she was interrupted when the hospital security chief approached.

The chief was a woman—probably in her fifties, with short gray hair and a no-nonsense attitude. Blaine had been impressed when he'd spoken with her earlier when she'd joined her security guards in the locker room. She was furious that someone had brought a gun into the hospital and nearly abducted one of the patients.

"Agent Campbell," Mrs. Wright said. "As you requested, I have all the footage pulled up from the security cameras."

"Thank you," he said. "That was fast." Hopefully one of those cameras had caught the robber without his hideous disguise. But Blaine hesitated again.

"The security room is this way," Mrs. Wright said, making a gesture for him to follow her from the emergency department.

But he didn't want to leave Maggie Jenkins alone and unprotected. "Do you have a guard that you can post here with Ms. Jenkins?"

Mrs. Wright nodded. "Of course. The police are here now, too. Sergeant Torreson is waiting in the security room to meet with you."

He needed Sergeant Torreson posted by Maggie Jenkins's bed, so that nobody could get to her. And so that she couldn't get away before she finally and truthfully answered all his questions. "Is he the only officer?"

Because he really didn't want to use one of the security guards—not when the zombie robber had to either be an employee or be close friends with an employee. He couldn't trust anyone who worked for the hospital. Not a doctor, nurse or even a security guard...

Mrs. Wright gestured to where a young policeman stood near the nurse who'd brought Blaine back to the employee locker room. He wasn't sure if the man was interrogating or flirting with her, so he waved him over to Maggie's bedside. "I'm Agent Campbell."

"Yes, sir," the young man replied. "We're aware you're the FBI special agent in charge of the investigation into the bank robberies."

Blaine studied the kid's face, looking for the familiar signs of resentment from local law enforcement. But he detected nothing but respect. The tightness in his chest eased slightly. He had backup, and given how relentless the bank robbers were, he needed it.

Of course, he could have called in more agents. Immediately after the robbery, he'd checked in, and the Bureau chief had offered him more FBI resources. But

Blaine had thought the bank robbers gone—the immediate threat over—until he'd come to the hospital and nearly lost the witness. But was Maggie a witness or an accomplice?

"Officer, this is Maggie Jenkins, the woman who was nearly abducted," he introduced them. "I need you posted here to protect her until I come back."

"I'll be fine," Maggie said. "I'll be safe." But her hands trembled as she splayed them across her belly again. She was either afraid or nervous. "I'll be safe," she repeated, as if trying to convince herself.

"We can't be certain of that," Blaine said. After all, the robbers kept returning...for her.

She slowly nodded in agreement, and tears welled now in her dark eyes. The tightness returned to his chest. But, growing up with three older and very dramatic sisters, he should have been immune to tears—especially since Maggie actually looked more frustrated than sad. But something about the young woman affected him and brought out his protective instincts.

But maybe the person he needed to protect when it came to Maggie Jenkins was himself.

"Be vigilant," Blaine advised the young officer. "For some reason these guys keep coming after her." And he intended to find out that reason. But he suspected he could learn more from the footage than he could Maggie Jenkins. She obviously wasn't being forthcoming with him.

So he headed to the surveillance room. But his mind wasn't on the footage he watched or on the police sergeant's questions, either. The hospital was a busy one—with so many people coming and going that it wouldn't be easy to determine which one might have walked in as himself and emerged as a zombie robber.

That was the only footage in which he could positively identify the person—as he burst through the back door and ran across the employee parking lot. But he kept the disguise on even as he jumped into an idling vehicle.

The sergeant cursed. "These guys—with those damn silly Halloween masks—have hit two banks in my jurisdiction."

As the vehicle, another van, turned, the driver came into view of the camera. But they must have known that camera would be there because the driver wore one of those damn masks, too.

"I want you to review your employees," Blaine told the hospital security chief. "Find out who wasn't working today."

"The hospital has hundreds of full- and part-time employees," Mrs. Wright said. "That'll take some time."

"*Your* employees," Blaine said. "I want you to focus on the security staff." He was really glad that he hadn't left Maggie Jenkins in the protection of one of the hospital guards.

"You think it's one of my people?" Mrs. Wright asked—with all the resentment he usually confronted with local law enforcement.

He pointed toward the masked men. "They knew where the cameras are—they knew how to get a gun in and out. They were familiar with employee-only areas of the hospital."

"But…" The woman's argument sputtered out as she grimly accepted that he was right.

Blaine turned toward the police officer. "I'd like you to bring in more officers, Sergeant. And check out anyone on that footage who walked in carrying a bag or a suitcase—anything big enough to carry that disguise and a weapon."

The woman sighed. "There is a metal detector at the front door."

Blaine was well aware of that—since he'd had to have a security guard wave him through it. But he'd wanted the security chief to come on her own to the same realization that he had. It had to be one of her people. But that didn't mean another robber hadn't come through the front door—an injured one.

"It'll still take me some time," she said. "We have three shifts, and since we have some trouble with gangs in this area, we have several guards on staff."

"Check out ex-staff, too," Blaine suggested.

"I'll help you," the sergeant offered.

He wanted the robbers, as well. But he didn't want them as badly as Blaine did. One of them had killed his friend and former mentor. Blaine couldn't let them get away with that—with ending what should have been Sarge's golden years way too soon.

"I have one of your officers helping me now," Blaine told the sergeant. "He's guarding the hostage for me."

The sergeant winced. "That kid's a trainee and easily distracted."

Blaine cursed and rushed out of the security room. He had wasted too much time on footage that had revealed no clues when he should have been interrogating his only concrete lead. But when he returned to the emergency department, he found the young officer flirting with the nurse once again.

And he found the bed where he'd left Maggie Jenkins empty. She was gone. Either she'd been grabbed again, or she'd escaped…

Chapter Five

Even though they had left the hospital a while ago, Special Agent Campbell had yet to speak to her. He only spared her a glare as he drove. The man was furious with her. A muscle twitched along his jaw, and his gaze was hot and hard. Maggie found his anger nearly as intimidating as his devastating good looks. But she couldn't understand why he was mad at her. Unless...

His stare moved off her to focus on the road again. He hadn't said where he was taking her. She had foolishly just assumed it would be to her apartment. Now she wasn't so certain...

Her wrists were bare; he hadn't cuffed her. She sat in the passenger's seat next to him—not in the back. But was he arresting her?

"Do you think I'm involved in the robberies?" she asked. "Is that why you were so upset when you couldn't find me at the hospital?"

That muscle twitched in his cheek again. "When you were gone, I assumed the worst."

The worst to her would have been one of the robbers in the creepy zombie mask returning. But she wasn't convinced that Agent Campbell thought the same.

"Is that really what you thought?" she asked. "That

one of them had come back for me? Or had you thought that I'd taken off on my own?"

"I thought you were gone," he said, which didn't really answer her question. "And I had left that young officer to protect you…"

"I was only using the restroom," she reminded him. "And he couldn't go into the ladies' with me." She had stepped out of the room to raised voices in the ER. For a moment she'd feared that one of the robbers had returned… until she'd recognized the voices.

At first she had been touched that Agent Campbell had been concerned about her. But he hadn't been relieved that she was okay; he had stayed angry. Even after checking her out of the hospital and seeing her safely to his vehicle, he was still angry.

"You do suspect that I'm involved in the robberies," she said, answering her own question.

"Robberies?" he queried, his tone guarded. But then, everything about Special Agent Blaine Campbell was guarded and hard to read—except for the grief he'd felt over Sarge's death. It had been easy to see his pain.

"They've robbed more than one bank," she said. "But you know that…" Or the FBI wouldn't have taken over the case. She suspected he was also aware of something else, too. "You probably know that they robbed the other branch of this bank where I previously worked."

"And then they followed you to the bank where you're working now…" His tone was less guarded now and more suspicious.

Of her?

Her stomach pitched. She hadn't had morning sickness even in her first trimester, so that wasn't the problem. It was nerves. He obviously did suspect that she was involved in the robberies.

"They have robbed a lot of other banks that I haven't worked at," she pointed out.

"How do you know that?" he asked, as if she had somehow slipped up and implicated herself. "How do you know how many other banks have been robbed?"

"From the news," she said. "They've even made national broadcasts. And our corporate headquarters sends out email warnings about robberies at other branches or other banks in the area. So it was just a coincidence that they hit both banks where I've worked."

A horrible coincidence—that was what she'd been trying to tell herself since the robbers, in those grotesque disguises, had burst through the doors of the bank earlier that afternoon.

"They have robbed other banks," he agreed. "But you're the only hostage they've tried taking. They didn't abduct anyone from any other bank."

She shuddered. "That was just today…" They hadn't tried to take her last time; they'd only had her open the security door to the alley. Then they'd left.

"So what was different about today?" he asked.

"You." He was the first thing that came to mind. Actually, since he'd saved her from being kidnapped the first time, Special Agent Blaine Campbell—with his golden-blond hair and intense green eyes—hadn't left her mind. Then he'd saved her a second time…

That muscle twitched again in his cheek, which was beginning to grow dark with stubble a few shades darker than his blond hair. "I wasn't the only thing different about today."

She uttered a ragged sigh and blinked back the tears that threatened as she remembered what else had been different. "They killed Sarge."

"Until today they hadn't killed anyone," he said. "Do you know what that means?"

She shook her head. She didn't know how a person could take another life for any reason. That was why she hadn't been able to understand Andy's insistence on joining the military. He had always been so sensitive. He had never even hunted and had been inconsolable when he'd accidentally struck and killed a deer with his truck.

Agent Campbell answered his own question, his voice threatening. "It means that whoever has been helping them will face murder charges, as well."

So he didn't think she was only a thief; he thought she was a killer, too. Anger coursed through her. She was the one who was mad now.

"Sarge was my friend," she said. "And what today means to me is that I lost a friend. I thought it meant the same to you. I thought you knew him and cared about him."

His teeth sank into his lower lip and he nodded. "That's why I want to find out who killed him and bring them to justice. All of them."

Her anger cooled as she realized she had no right to it. Agent Campbell was only doing his job, and not just because it was his job but because he'd cared about Sarge. And if she were him, she might have suspected her, too. She had been at the scene of two robberies.

She reached across the console and touched his hand. But it tensed beneath hers, tightening around the steering wheel. "I'm sorry," she said. "I understand that you have to question me. I just wish I could be more help for your investigation. I really don't have any idea who the robbers are."

He tugged his hand from beneath hers and reached

for the shifter, putting the car in Park after pulling into a space in the parking lot of her apartment complex.

She breathed a soft sigh of relief. He hadn't arrested her after all. He had actually brought her home. But she wasn't foolish enough to think that he no longer suspected her of being involved.

WAS HE BEING a fool? Blaine silently asked himself. Probably.

He should have taken her down to the Bureau or a local police department for questioning. But she was already trembling with exhaustion and dark circles rimmed her dark eyes. He wasn't heartless, but he hoped she wasn't playing him.

Maggie Jenkins had a sincerity and vulnerability that made him want to believe her and to believe that she was just an innocent victim.

Like Sarge…

He flinched over the loss of his friend. Instead of dealing with that death, he'd been busy trying to prevent another—to make sure that Maggie Jenkins stayed safe. He'd believed that was what Sarge had wanted. But what if his old friend had been trying to tell him something else about the assistant bank manager?

That she wasn't just involved in the robberies but maybe that she'd plotted them?

Her fingers trembled as she fumbled with the seat belt. Was she exhausted or was she nervous that he was questioning her? Or nervous that he'd brought her here?

He turned off the car, opened his door and hurried around the car to open hers. She was still having trouble with the seat belt, so he reached across her, brushed her fingers aside and undid the clasp. But now he was too close to her, too close to the curly hair that tumbled around her shoulders, to the big brown eyes staring up at him—to the full breasts that pushed against the thin material of her blouse. He'd never considered a pregnant woman sexy…until now. Until Maggie Jenkins…

Something shifted beneath his arm, which was pressed to her belly, as if her baby was kicking him for the thoughts he was entertaining. He jerked back and stepped away from the car. She slid her legs out first. Since she'd lost her shoe earlier, she wore slippers from the hospital. But she didn't need to wear heels for her legs to look long and sexy.

Remembering how his sisters had struggled to get out of cars while they were pregnant, he reached out to help her. She clutched his hand but barely applied any pressure to pull herself up. And then she was standing right in front of him, so close that her breasts nearly brushed against his chest.

She tugged her hand free of his, and a bright pink color flushed her face. "I—I don't have my purse," she said. "I don't have my keys to get inside."

"You live alone?"

"Now I do," she replied. "But I can get an extra key from my super." She glanced up to the darkening sky. "If he's still awake…"

"You don't live with the baby's father anymore?" He told himself he was asking only because of the case, but he really wanted to know for himself.

She shook her head. "I never did…" And there was something in her voice and her expressive eyes…an odd combination of guilt and grief.

Blaine wanted to ask more questions but Maggie was walking away from him. His skin chilled. It could have been because of the cool wind that was kicking up as night began to fall. It could have been because he had an odd sense of foreboding—the same sense he'd had as he'd driven up to the bank during a robbery in progress.

He glanced around the parking lot. The complex was big—an L-shaped, four-story redbrick building, so there were a lot of vehicles parked in the lot. Quite a few of them were vans. Could one of them have been from the hospital? Could the robbers have followed them here?

He hurried and closed the distance between them, keeping his body between hers and the exposure to the parking lot. His hand was also on his holster, ready to pull his weapon should he need it.

Maggie rapped her knuckles hard against the door of a first-floor apartment. "My super's a little hard of hearing," she explained.

It took a couple more knocks before the door opened. A gray-haired man grinned at her. "Hey, Miss Maggie, what can I help you with?"

"Hi, Mr. Simmons. I left my purse at work," she said but spared him the details of why. "I'm so forgetful these days." She'd actually had other matters on her mind, but again she didn't share those with the older man. "So I need the extra key to my apartment, please."

His gray-haired head bobbed in a quick nod. "Of course I'll get that for you. Who's your friend?" His cloudy blue eyes narrowed as he studied Blaine. Apparently Blaine wasn't the only one in whom Maggie brought out protectiveness.

"Blaine Campbell. He's an old friend," she said, easily uttering the lie.

What else had she lied about?

The older man nodded again, accepting her explanation. "I'll be right back with the key."

After he disappeared, she turned toward Blaine and explained. "I didn't want to worry him. He knows the bank I worked at in Sturgis was robbed, so I told him I left the banking business."

"What does he think you do now?" he wondered.

"He thinks I work in an insurance office," she said, "which isn't really a lie since the bank does offer insurance policies."

Keys jangled as the old man returned to the doorway. "Have you checked on that renter's policy for me yet, Maggie?" he asked.

"Yes," she replied. "I'll bring that quote home tomorrow." She held out her hand for the key, but the gray-haired janitor glanced at Blaine again.

"You're an old friend of hers?" he asked with curiosity instead of doubt.

Blaine just nodded.

"Then you must've known her Andy?"

Andy? Was that the father of her baby? Blaine just nodded again.

"Thought you looked like you might've been a marine, too," the old guy said with another bob of his head.

"I was, sir," Blaine replied, and the admission reminded him of the man who had made him a marine. Sarge… "I served two tours."

"That's how you knew Sarge," Maggie said, softly enough that the older man probably didn't even hear her. "He was your drill sergeant?"

Blaine nodded. As a drill instructor, Sarge had been tough but fair. And he'd been a good and loyal friend.

"Glad you made it home, boy," Mr. Simmons said and reached out to pat Blaine's shoulder. "Too bad her fiancé didn't…"

"Andy," Blaine murmured, and the older man nodded again. Shocked and full of sympathy for her, Blaine turned toward Maggie. Earlier she'd told him that she was single, but she hadn't told him why. She hadn't said that her fiancé died before they could marry.

Her lashes fluttered furiously as she fought back tears over the loss of her baby's father. The hand she held out for the key began to tremble slightly. "Thank you for letting me use your spare, Mr. Simmons."

Finally the old man handed over the key she'd been waiting for. The second she closed her fingers around it, she rushed off toward the other end of the complex.

With a nod at the older man, Blaine hurried after her, careful to keep looking around to make sure nobody had followed them—the way someone must have followed the ambulance to the hospital.

But why?

If Maggie really had no idea who the robbers were, why had they wanted to kidnap her so desperately that they hadn't tried just once but twice?

Blaine stopped at the door where Maggie had stopped, her hand with the key outstretched toward the lock. She gasped. Hearing the fear in her voice, Blaine reached for his gun and pulled it from the holster.

Then he closed his free hand around Maggie's shoulder. She tensed and gasped again. Peering around her, he saw what she had—that the door to her apartment stood ajar. Since Maggie had said she lived alone now, someone must have broken in.

A thud emanated from the crack in the door. Whoever had broken in was still there. Waiting for Maggie…

Chapter Six

Like a rowboat riding on high waves, Maggie's stomach pitched as fear and nerves overwhelmed her. It was bad enough that the zombie robbers had tracked her down at the new bank branch where she worked and at the hospital where she'd been treated after the robbery. But had they now found out where she lived?

"Someone's inside," she whispered in horror.

But Blaine Campbell had already figured that out since he held his gun, the barrel pointing toward that crack in the door. He stood between her and her apartment. Between her and danger. "Go back to Mr. Simmons's apartment," he told her. "And stay there until I come for you."

She would have asked where he was going. But she knew. He had already walked into one robbery in progress today. So why wouldn't he walk into another?

Because he could get killed. Her hand automatically reached out with the impulse to hold him back—to protect him. But he was already pushing open the door a little farther and turning sideways as if to squeeze through. He turned back to her, his green gaze intense. "Go back to Mr. Simmons and call the police."

"Call them now," she urged him. "Don't go in there alone." As he had earlier…

He'd been lucky that the robbers hadn't killed him. If they hadn't been intent on getting away, they may have killed him just the way they had killed poor Sarge. If they'd kept shooting at him, they would have hit him where the vest wouldn't have protected him.

Dismissing her concern, he replied, "I'll be fine."

That was probably what Sarge had thought, too, when he showed up for work that morning. That he would be fine. But he hadn't. And she worried that neither would Agent Campbell.

"I'll be fine as long as you get out of here," he continued. "Now."

She had noticed and admired his commanding presence earlier. Now that it was directed at her, she resented it a bit. And she resented even more that she hurried to obey his command, turning away to head back to Mr. Simmons's apartment.

The minute the nearly deaf super let her inside, she would call the police. But they wouldn't arrive in time to help Agent Campbell. He was already stepping inside her apartment, already facing down danger.

Alone.

As Maggie lifted her hand to knock on the super's door, she heard the scream. It was high-pitched and full of fear.

THE WOMAN'S SCREAM caught Blaine off guard. He'd expected a masked robber. Or at least an armed threat. Instead he walked inside to find a woman—dressed like Maggie in a dark suit—rifling through the drawers of the dresser in what must have been Maggie's bedroom. Instead of being a peaceful oasis, it was full of color—oranges and greens and yellows. It was lively and vibrant, like her personality, except for those times when she'd been too scared to speak. It was also messy, but that might have been because of this woman rifling through Maggie's things.

"Who are you?" he asked, even though the blond-haired woman looked vaguely familiar. Where had he seen her before? The security footage from the hospital?

Could it have been a woman who had tried to abduct Maggie earlier? He doubted that a woman could have hurled the locker room bench with enough force to knock him down, but maybe that was just his ego talking. At the bank there had been one robber smaller than the others. He hadn't given it any thought then, because it could have been a short man. But it could have been a woman.

She just stared at him—her eyes wide with fear and guilt. She didn't hold a gun this time, though. Instead she held a velvet jewelry case in her hand.

"Who are you?" he repeated.

"It's Susan Iverson," another woman answered for her.

Wearing those damn slippers had made Maggie's footsteps silent—so silent that she would have been able to get the jump on him had she been one of the robbers. Hell, he had only her word that she wasn't one of them.

"Susan works at the bank, too. She's a teller," Maggie said, explaining how she knew the woman. "What are you doing here?"

"You left your purse at the bank," Susan replied. "I was bringing it back for you."

"And going through my stuff?"

Maggie was asking the questions he should have been asking. But her sudden nearness had distracted him—not so much that he had lowered the gun, though. He kept it trained on the obvious intruder.

"You used Ms. Jenkins's key to let yourself inside her

apartment?" he asked now. "That's still breaking and entering, you know."

"I used to live with her," Susan replied. She stared up at Blaine through her lashes, as if trying to flirt with him. "You're the FBI agent who rescued us this afternoon from those awful robbers."

"Yes, and you haven't answered the question." She hadn't answered any of the questions—neither had she dropped that little jewelry box.

He'd thought the robbers must have had an inside man. And maybe that thought had been right. Thinking Maggie was their accomplice was what had been wrong.

"You don't live with me anymore," Maggie said. "So you had no right to let yourself into my place." Her voice, usually so soft and sweet, was now sharp with anger and dislike.

"I brought your purse to you," Susan said again, as if she'd been doing Maggie a favor.

"You could have left it with the super," Blaine pointed out, "instead of letting yourself inside. What are you doing here, Ms. Iverson?"

At the moment she was trying to flirt with him—as if that could distract him from what she'd done now and what she might have done earlier. He'd never let a pretty face distract him…before Maggie.

The blonde smiled. "I was searching for clues," she said. "This is the second bank Maggie's worked at that's been robbed. Don't you think that's suspicious, Agent Campbell?"

A hiss accompanied the quick release of Maggie's breath—as if she'd been punched in the stomach. Maybe the baby had kicked her. Or maybe this woman casting suspicions her way had shocked her.

He had come up with suspicions about Maggie on his

own, but he wasn't about to admit it to this woman. At the moment she had become the better suspect. "I think your behavior is questionable right now, Ms. Iverson."

"You caught me——" she fluttered her lashes again "——playing amateur sleuth. I was only trying to help the bank recover the money that was stolen."

He wasn't charmed in the least by her coy attitude. "And you think hundreds of thousands of dollars are in that small jewelry case?"

She glanced down at it, as if just realizing it was in her hand. And she shook her head. Blond hair skimmed along her jaw with the movement. "I——I just found it as I was looking for the money."

Or was that what she'd been looking for? With the hand not holding his gun, he reached for the jewelry case. She held it tightly, but he tugged it from her grasping fingers. He popped open the case and a big square diamond glistened in the dim light of the nearly dark apartment.

Maggie reached out and snapped the case shut, as if she couldn't bear to look at the ring.

"Your engagement ring?" he asked her.

Her beautiful face tense, she nodded.

"I'm sorry," he said. It must have been hard for her to see the ring her dead fiancé had given her—especially after all she'd been through that day.

"Sorry?" the other woman asked with a disparaging snort. "She never even wore that ring. She probably wouldn't have noticed it missing…"

"So you did intend to steal it?" Blaine asked. He needed to grab his phone and call in this attempted robbery, but when he tried to hand the ring case over to Maggie, she drew back as if she couldn't touch it, either. So he shoved it into his pants pocket to reach for his cell. "I'm going to call the local authorities to book you, Ms. Iverson."

"No," Maggie said, reaching out now to grab his arm and stop him from calling. "I don't want to press charges."

"Why not?" he asked. He was furious with this woman, and he wasn't the one she'd been trying to rob.

Maggie just shook her head, and the blonde breathed a sigh of relief.

But Blaine ignored them both. "This needs to be reported and Ms. Iverson needs to be questioned about her involvement in the robberies."

"What involvement?" the woman asked, her already high voice squeaking with outrage. "I have no involvement."

"I'm not so sure about that…" She could have taken advantage of Maggie leaving her purse behind to try to steal the ring. Or she could have been here waiting for Maggie—to abduct her for the others.

"You think I was stealing the ring," the woman said. "Why would I need to pawn that for money if I was helping rob banks for millions of dollars?"

It wasn't quite millions. Not yet. But he worried that it would be if the robbers weren't stopped. And he worried that more people would die. The robbers had killed once, so it would be easier for them to kill again.

Was that what they'd intended to do with Maggie? Kill her? Why? To keep her quiet? And if they needed to keep her quiet, she had something to say—something she hadn't shared with him yet.

But then, there was a lot she hadn't shared with him. Maybe Susan Iverson wasn't the only one who needed to be brought in for questioning…

MAGGIE WAS SO exhausted that all she wanted to do was put on her comfy pajamas, crawl into her bed and sleep for days. But she was still wearing the skirt and blouse from her suit. And this wasn't her bed. It wasn't soft and comfortable. It was hard and cold—kind of like she was beginning to believe Agent Blaine Campbell might be.

Despite her protest, he'd had Susan arrested for breaking and entering, and attempted theft. He should have just let her take the ring.

Susan was right that Maggie had never worn it. She couldn't even look at it without remembering what Andy had sacrificed to buy her that ring. He'd bought it with the bonus for re-upping and volunteering for that last deployment—the one that had taken his life.

And she had never wanted the ring. She should have told him—should have made it clear that she didn't love him the way he had deserved to be loved. Andy had been a wonderful man, and he'd been taken too soon.

Like Sarge.

Could Susan have been involved in the robbery that had claimed his life? If she was, Maggie was certain that Agent Campbell would find out. With just a look he made Maggie want to confess all. But she had nothing to confess.

He didn't look as though he believed her, though. Was he cynical because of his FBI job and all he'd seen on it? Or was being a marine the reason he didn't trust easily?

Of course he had no reason to trust Maggie. He didn't know her.

If he knew her, he would have just let her stay in her apartment. But he'd insisted that she would be in danger in her own home. Susan knew she lived there, and if she were involved with the robberies, some of the others might try to kidnap her again—as they had at the hospital. So he'd had her brought here—to some sort of "safe" house.

But even with an officer standing outside the motel room door, Maggie didn't feel safe.

She had felt safe only with Agent Campbell. But he'd had Maggie brought here, and he'd gone down to the local police station with Susan.

Maggie was surprised that he hadn't taken her to the station, too. She knew he considered her every bit as much a suspect in the robberies as he did Susan. So maybe that officer wasn't posted outside the door for her protection. Maybe he was posted outside the door to keep her inside—to keep her from escaping.

But where would Maggie go?

She had already tried to escape once—when she'd moved from Sturgis to the Chicago suburb where she lived now. But the robbers had followed her.

Was it only the coincidence she wanted to believe it was? After all, the bank she'd worked at before and the one she worked at now weren't the only ones that had been robbed.

But that danger wasn't the only thing Maggie hadn't been able to leave in her past. When she'd let Susan stay with her, the woman had pried into her life. She'd learned about Andy. That was how Mr. Simmons had heard Maggie's sad story. Susan had used it when she'd been late with her part of the rent.

So Maggie hadn't been able to escape her guilt and loss, either. It had followed her, or maybe she was carrying it with her. She clasped her hands over the baby. She didn't want to escape him or her, though. She wanted to protect her baby—the way she hadn't been able to protect Andy. She'd thought that she was saving him from pain by keeping the truth of her feelings from him.

Maybe there was no escape from her past. But what about the danger? Was she really safe here?

Moments later she had her answer as gunfire erupted outside the motel room. She wasn't safe. The robbers had come for her again.

And this time Agent Campbell wouldn't arrive in time to save her...

Chapter Seven

In the dark Blaine fumbled around the top of the door-jamb for the key his friend had left for him. "I found it," he told Ash through the cell phone pressed to his ear. "I can't believe it's still here."

If he'd left a key outside his apartment in Detroit, it wouldn't have been there long; neither would any of the stuff in his apartment. He wouldn't have thought a Chicago suburb would be much safer—especially after he'd found an intruder in Maggie Jenkins's apartment.

Of course, that intruder had been someone she knew. Apparently she hadn't known her that well, though, if she'd ever trusted the treacherous woman. Not only had Susan tried to steal Maggie's engagement ring, but when Blaine searched her purse, he found that she'd helped her-self to Maggie's credit and debit cards, as well.

Blaine blindly slid the key into the lock and quietly opened the door. Ignoring Ash's voice in his ear, he lis-tened carefully for any sounds within the small bunga-low. It was the only dark house on the street; that was how Ash had told him to find it.

At this hour everyone else was home—probably watch-ing TV after dinner. What was Maggie Jenkins doing right now?

Eating?

Sleeping?

She'd looked exhausted. Maybe he should have insisted that she stay at the hospital for observation. But then, she hadn't been safe there, either.

"I told the neighbors to expect a tall blond guy to show up at my door within the next couple of days," Ash said.

This was the kind of neighborhood where people watched out their windows, aware of their surroundings and strangers. Because of Ash's warning, they gave Blaine only a cursory glance before their curtains and blinds snapped back into place and they returned to their television shows.

Blaine pushed open the door to a dark and empty house. "Thanks for giving them the heads-up," he said. "And thanks for letting me crash here."

Ash Stryker was also an FBI special agent but with the antiterrorism division, so he traveled more than Blaine did. Right now he was in DC or New York; Blaine couldn't remember which city. Hell, maybe it was neither. Since he specialized in homegrown terrorism, he could have been off in the woods somewhere. Blaine knew better than to ask. Ash was rarely at liberty to say.

"Thanks for calling me about Sarge," his friend replied, his voice gruff with emotion.

Blaine stopped in midreach for the light switch. While he dealt with his emotions over losing Sarge, he would rather stay in the dark, but he hadn't wanted to leave Ash there. He'd had to tell him about their loss. He and Ash went back before the Bureau. They had been marines together, too.

"I'm sorry," Blaine said. "So damn sorry…"

If only he could have done something.

If only he could have stopped Sarge from stepping out from behind that damn pillar.

But Sarge had reacted instinctively to Maggie's scream and had come to her rescue. If the former military man had actually thought she'd been involved in the robberies, he probably wouldn't have tried so hard to save her. But maybe he still would have done it—out of loyalty to her dead fiancé. He suspected Sarge had been Andy's drill instructor, as well.

"I'm going to try to make it home for his funeral," Ash promised. "Let me know when it is."

"Sure thing," Blaine replied. He knew his friend hated going to funerals as much as he did because they had attended way too many. They'd had so many friends who hadn't made it home—like Maggie's fiancé. "I'll tell you as soon as I find out when the arrangements are."

"Thanks," Ash said. "And feel free to make yourself at home."

"I won't be here long enough," Blaine said. He was more determined than ever to catch these bank robbers. He flipped on the switch and an overhead light flickered on, illuminating the sparsely furnished living room.

"I'm not there much, either." Ash stated the obvious. "If my uncle hadn't left me the place, I would probably just rent an apartment or a hotel room for when I'm in the city."

Blaine had wondered why his friend owned a house. Ash was a confirmed bachelor. The only commitment he'd ever made was to their country and the Bureau. "Like me," Blaine murmured.

Ash chuckled. "Well, you have sisters you can crash with when you have the urge to feel domestic."

Blaine groaned as he thought of the noise and chaos of his sisters' households. Kids crying. Throwing toys. His sisters yelling at their husbands. "Staying with them and their families reminds me why I'm single."

But then he thought of Maggie Jenkins and the baby that had moved beneath his touch. Maggie, with her friendly chatter, would fit in well with his family. Hell, she would fit in better than he ever had.

"So I'm warning you," Ash said, "that the fridge and cupboards are probably bare. There are take-out menus in the cupboard drawer by the fridge, though."

Blaine didn't feel like eating. Ever since that bullet had struck Sarge's chest, he had felt sick. Maggie Jenkins hadn't made him feel any better. He'd had local authorities take her into protective custody at a nearby motel. She would be safe.

He didn't need to worry about her. But he was worried. Did the single mom-to-be have anyone she could trust? Even her former roommate had been trying to steal from her. After interrogating Susan Iverson, Blaine believed that was probably the woman's only crime. He didn't think she was smart enough to be able to hide it if she were involved in the bank robberies.

"It's not your fault," Ash assured him. "You know Sarge. He would have never backed down from a fight—not even when he was outgunned."

Blaine sighed. "I know, especially since he was determined to protect the bank's assistant manager." He'd given up his life for hers and the baby's.

A large part of Ash's job was picking up subtext in recorded conversations. That was how he found threats to security. He easily picked up on Blaine's subtext, too. "Sounds like Sarge might not have been the only one wanting to protect this…*woman*?"

"Yes," Blaine admitted. "She's female. She's also young and pregnant." Too young to have already lost her fiancé, her baby's father…

"Married?" Ash inquired.

"No, her fiancé died in Afghanistan." And she must miss him so much that she couldn't even bear to look at the engagement ring he had given her. Blaine patted his pocket, but the ring was gone. He'd handed it over to the local authorities as evidence in Susan Iverson's attempted robbery—along with Maggie's credit and debit cards. He would make sure that Maggie got back the cards and the ring.

But he couldn't bring back what she probably wanted most. Her fiancé…

While Blaine had dated over the years, he'd gotten over the breakups easily enough to know that he had never been in love. He couldn't relate to Maggie's pain, losing the man with whom she'd intended to spend the rest of her life. It had been hard enough losing the friends he'd lost over the years and now losing Sarge.

"Was her fiancé one of Sarge's former drills?"

He sighed. "I think so." It would explain why, after retiring from the military, Sarge had taken a part-time job in a bank. Maybe he'd heard about Maggie getting robbed at the first bank, and he'd intended to protect her. Or maybe she had switched to the bank where Sarge was working because she'd obviously known him. Sarge had always stayed in touch with his former drills.

"Then the old man would have been happy he died saving her," Ash said.

Blaine hadn't expected his cynical friend to come up with such a romantic notion. He blinked hard as his eyes began to burn. "Yeah, he would have been…" He sighed. "But the threat isn't over for Maggie Jenkins. One of the robbers tried grabbing her from the ER where the paramedics took her after the robbery."

"You stopped him, though." Ash just assumed.

"This time."

"You'll keep Maggie safe for Sarge."

Blaine wasn't so sure about that. He had that feeling again—that chill racing up and down his spine—that told him all was not well. The thought had no more than crossed his mind when his phone beeped with an incoming call.

"I have to go, Ash." He didn't waste time with good-byes, just clicked over the phone to take the next call. "Agent Campbell."

"Agent, this is Officer Montgomery," a man identified himself. He then continued, "We have a report of shots fired at the motel where we took the bank-robbery witness."

He cursed, and his stomach knotted with dread. The motel was nearby, but probably still too far for him to get there in time to save her.

MAGGIE STARED AT the locked bathroom door, waiting for somebody to kick it down or riddle it with bullets. But as she listened, an eerie silence had fallen where only moments before gunfire had deafened her.

She'd wanted to press her hands over her ears and hide under the covers in the dark motel room. But this wasn't a nightmare from which she could hide. So she had forced herself to jump out of the bed and run into the bathroom. Once in there she had locked the door and barricaded it shut by wedging the vanity chair beneath the knob. As a barricade, it was flimsy; it wouldn't take someone much to kick open the door and drag her out.

But she wasn't worried just about herself or about her baby. Had the officer who'd been stationed outside the door of her room been hurt or worse? Her stomach lurched with dread because she suspected the worst. If he was fine, wouldn't he have checked on her? Wouldn't he have at least knocked on the bathroom door and assured her it was safe to come out?

But Maggie wasn't even safe in a safe house.

Blaine Campbell was right. Even though she had no idea what it was, she must have seen or heard *something* that could identify at least one of the robbers. Why else would they so desperately want her dead?

Unable to stare at the door any longer, she squeezed her eyes shut. And she prayed. She prayed for that young officer who had only been doing his job. Like Sarge, trying to protect her.

And she prayed for her baby. Her hands trembled as she splayed them across her belly. Nothing shifted or kicked beneath her palms. For once the child slept— blissfully unaware of the danger he and his mother faced.

Was this all Maggie's fault?

Maybe karma didn't think she deserved the baby because she hadn't loved the baby's father the way she should have. Andy had been such a sweet guy; he hadn't deserved to die. And neither did his baby.

Maggie had to keep him or her safe. But there was no window in the bathroom, no way of escaping except through the door she had barricaded. But the shooting had been out front. Whoever had been shooting at the young police officer could already be inside the motel room, just waiting for her to leave the bathroom.

But the gruesomely masked gunman hadn't waited for her to leave the hospital. He had walked right into the emergency department and dragged her from her bed.

If one of those masked gunmen were inside the motel room, he wouldn't wait long for her to come out. He would break down the door to get to her.

To kill her? What else could they want with her?

She had no money to offer them. But after all the

banks they had robbed, they shouldn't need any more money. Some people, however, never thought they had enough. So maybe they wanted to keep robbing banks and for some reason thought she had the knowledge to stop them…

So they wanted to stop her from talking. They wanted to kill her.

As if her fearful thoughts had conjured up one of the men, the door rattled as someone tried to turn the knob. The chair legs squeaked against the vinyl floor, moving as someone wrenched harder on the knob—determined to get to her.

Could she convince them that she knew nothing? That she had no idea who they were?

It was the only chance she had. But she would be able to pull it off only if they still wore the masks. What if they didn't? Then she couldn't look at them—because they would kill her for sure.

The door rattled harder—metal hinges creaking, wood cracking. In case they came in firing, she climbed into the bathtub. She put her face down on her knees and wrapped her arms around the back of her head. Her stance wouldn't protect her or the baby from bullets. But she had no other way to protect herself…

The chair toppled over against the sink, and the door flew open with such force that the wood cracked against the side of the bathtub. Someone must have kicked it in.

But she didn't dare look up. She didn't want to be able to identify any of the robbers. She wanted the danger to end. She actually wanted Blaine Campbell and his protection. But he was too far away to protect her.

"Please leave me alone," she begged. "You don't have to hurt me. I don't know anything about the robberies. And I don't care…"

All she cared about was her baby. She actually hadn't been thrilled when she'd found out she was pregnant. But then Andy had died and she'd been relieved that she hadn't lost him completely.

But now she wasn't just going to lose that last piece of Andy—she was going to lose her own life, too.

Chapter Eight

Guilt had Blaine's shoulder slumping slightly. Or maybe he'd hurt it when he had broken down the bathroom door. "Maggie, it's me," he said.

But she kept her arms locked around her head, her body trembling inside the bathtub. Curled up the way she was, she looked so small—so fragile—so frightened.

He hadn't dared to say who he was as he broke down the door...because he hadn't known what he would find inside. Maggie might not have been alone. One of the gunmen might have gotten to her and barricaded them both inside the bathroom when he'd arrived. Or it might have only been one of the gunmen inside the bathroom and Maggie might have already been gone.

Blaine hadn't arrived quite in time. The officer outside the door had been shot. Maybe mortally...

Sirens wailed outside the motel as more emergency vehicles careened into the lot. Hopefully an ambulance was among them—with help for the young cop and for Maggie.

Maybe she needed medical attention, too. Had any of the shots fired at the officer struck her? Blaine looked into the tub again, but he noticed no blood on the white porcelain—only Maggie's dark curls spread across the cold surface.

"Maggie!" He reached out for her.

But she swung her hands then, striking out at him. "Leave me alone! Leave me alone!"

He caught her wrists and then lifted her wriggling body from the tub and into his arms. "Maggie! It's me— it's Blaine!"

Finally she looked up, her dark eyes wide as she stared at him in wonder. "Blaine!" Then she threw her arms around his neck and clung to him.

And his guilt increased. He never should have left her to the protection of anyone else. The young officer had been shot, and Maggie might have been taken if he hadn't gotten there in time. The wounded officer had held off the gunmen until Blaine had arrived.

Then Blaine had fired on them, too. He didn't think that he'd hit any of them, though. And tires had squealed as a van had sped out of the parking lot.

For a long, horrible moment he'd thought that Maggie might have been in that van. That he had been too late to save her. Then he had found the bathroom door locked inside the room, and he'd hoped that she'd hidden away. But Blaine had been doing this job too long to be optimistic. So he had expected the worst—that one of the gunmen had been left behind and barricaded himself alone or, worse yet, inside the bathroom with Maggie.

In a ragged sigh of relief, her breath shuddered out against his throat. She had undoubtedly expected the worst when he'd broken open the door.

He wrapped his arms tightly around Maggie, holding her close. She trembled against him—as if she couldn't stop shaking. She was probably in shock.

"I'm sorry," he said.

But he had to pull away and leave her again—only because he had to make sure that help had arrived for the young officer and for Maggie. He wanted a doctor to check her out again.

He wanted to make sure that she was all right.

How much fear could she and her baby handle?

There was only one way that Blaine would truly be able to protect her, the way Sarge had wanted and died trying to do. And that was to find out who was so determined to grab her or kill her.

Who were the bank robbers?

ONE OF THE paramedics assured Maggie and Agent Campbell that she was fine. Apparently she couldn't die from fear.

What about embarrassment?

She had embarrassed herself when she cried out his name and clung to him. She had acted like a girlfriend when he considered her a robbery suspect.

Or had he changed his mind about that?

Then he took her to his home—although *home* was stretching it. The bungalow obviously belonged to a single man. There were no pictures on the walls. No knickknacks on the built-in shelves. Not even a book or a magazine.

The living room held a couch and a chair while the dining room contained a desk instead of a table. The table was in the kitchen, but it had only two chairs at it. There was a bed in each of the two bedrooms.

Blaine showed her to one while taking the other for himself. Maybe she slept. Maggie wasn't sure. She drifted in and out, occasionally hearing Blaine's voice. She doubted he slept at all. He had been on his cell phone instead.

The house was quiet now. But Maggie knew he hadn't left because she smelled food. Bacon. And coffee. Her stomach grumbled, but she stayed in bed, not eager to face him. Her face heated even now, as she thought of how she'd acted.

Like a girlfriend...

But Blaine Campbell was just an FBI agent doing his job. He probably had a girlfriend somewhere, because a man that handsome was unlikely to be single. Unless Blaine's only commitment was his career...

She had to stop thinking of him as Blaine and remember that he was Special Agent Campbell. That was all he was and all he would ever be to her.

The baby kicked. Apparently they both wanted food. So she tossed back the covers and kicked her legs over the side of the bed. The T-shirt Blaine had loaned her as a nightgown had ridden up, revealing her high-cut briefs. She reached to tug down the hem of the shirt just as someone cleared his throat.

"Sorry," Blaine said, as he had the night before when he'd peeled her off him.

She was the one who should be apologizing—for inconveniencing him as she had. For costing him a friend like Sarge. For making his job harder. But for once she, who usually couldn't stop talking, couldn't find words to express herself and her gratefulness for his saving her over and over again.

"I was just coming up to see if you were awake," he said. "I had some groceries delivered and made breakfast."

The man could cook? He really was perfect.

But perfect wasn't for Maggie—not with the mess her life had become. She pulled the T-shirt down, but it was still short enough that it left her legs bare. And, in her mind, Blaine's gaze skimmed down her legs like a caress.

But that could only be in her mind—her imagination.

The FBI agent couldn't really be interested in her. Not for anything but information...

He proved that a short while later when he picked her empty plate up from the table and started asking questions. "You're sure that you didn't recognize anyone from the robberies?"

"I'm sure," she said. "I only recognized those horrible masks from the robbery at the Sturgis branch where I used to work." She shuddered as she thought of the grotesque masks. They could have come right from that R-rated zombie movie she'd gone to so long ago. "With the masks and the trench coats, I couldn't see any facial features or even body types of the robbers."

"You're not protecting anyone?"

She shook her head. But her hands automatically covered her belly. The baby had stopped moving. Maybe the food had satiated him. The cheesy scrambled eggs, crisp bacon and wheat toast had been delicious—so delicious that Maggie had probably eaten more than she should have.

But then, she could barely remember the last time she'd eaten. Some crackers at the hospital? Before that a breakfast she'd made herself—lumpy oatmeal with too much brown sugar. She would have to learn to be a better cook for the baby. If she lived long enough to cook for him...

"I want to protect my baby," she said. But she feared that she was going to fail, just as she had failed Andy. "That's the only person I'm protecting. So if I knew anything about the robbers, I would tell you."

"You haven't noticed anyone hanging around the bank, casing the place?" he asked.

She shook her head again. "I don't know what casing a place looks like. So I can't say that someone hasn't done it." Obviously they had or they wouldn't have pulled off the robbery so easily—until Blaine had arrived. If only he could have saved Sarge...

Blaine hadn't eaten nearly as much as she had. Most of his food was on his plate yet, forgotten, as he asked his questions. "Nobody came around both of the banks?"

Once again, she shook her head. "The branches are far enough away that they had different customers. I knew most of the clients from Sturgis since I'd worked at that branch since I graduated, but I'm just getting to know the people at this branch." Should she bother? Or should she move on again to another branch, another city?

How would she work there without remembering those robbers bursting in? That was why she'd left Sturgis. Because of the memories. But there were worse ones here; there was Sarge getting shot and dying.

"What about workers?" Blaine asked. "Did Susan work at both branches, too?"

"No," she said. "I'm the only one who worked at both branches." Which was why he had suspected she was involved, and she couldn't blame him for his suspicions. "But I really have nothing to do with the robberies."

He didn't look at her the way he had before, as if he doubted her.

Hope fluttered in her chest like her baby fluttered in her belly, waking up from his or her short nap. "Do you believe me?" she asked.

He uttered a heavy sigh of resignation. "I believe that you're not consciously involved."

She should have been happy that he didn't think she was a criminal mastermind, but his comment dented her pride. He clearly thought she was an idiot instead. "I'm not *unconsciously* involved, either."

"You haven't told anyone about your job?" he asked.

"Most people know that I work at a bank," she said, "except for Mr. Simmons."

"Because you don't want to worry him," he said with a slight smile, as if amused or moved.

She sighed. "That was all for nothing after you called the cops on Susan. He probably knows now. But that's all anyone knows about me—that I work there."

"You haven't told anyone any details that might make it easier for them to hold up the bank," he persisted, "to know which days you'd have the most cash on hand?"

"No," she replied, pride stinging at how stupid he thought her. He wasn't the only one who'd thought that. Because she talked a lot, people sometimes thought she was flighty. But her grades in school and college had proved them all wrong. She talked a lot because she really didn't like silence. It made her uncomfortable, so she generally tended to fill it with chatter.

"You don't talk to your family about your job?" he asked skeptically. "You wouldn't share any details with them?"

So now he thought her family members were criminal masterminds? She corrected that misassumption. "For his job, my dad and mom moved to Hong Kong a couple of years ago."

And since Andy's death, all they talked about was the weather—asking about hers, telling about theirs. Their conversations didn't get any deeper; they were probably afraid that they might make her cry if they brought up something that would remind her of Andy. Or maybe it would make them cry because they'd loved him like a son.

"You don't have any brothers or sisters?" he asked.

"No." And because she was sick of being the only one

answering questions, she started asking some of her own. "What about you?"

"I have three older sisters," he replied, and his lips curved into a slight smile as his green eyes crinkled a little at the corners.

Growing up, she had wanted sisters. But her father had been busy with his career, and her mom hadn't wanted to raise more than one child alone. Maggie would really be raising her baby alone.

She shook off the self-pity before she could wallow and asked, "Any brothers?"

"Just in arms," he replied.

Fellow marines. Andy had called them brothers, too. She sighed.

"Do you have any *friends* that you're really close to?" he asked. "Anyone that you would talk to without realizing that you might have let some information slip?"

He really thought she was an idiot. But maybe she had been—because she had told someone more than she should have.

Since he watched her closely, he must have caught her reaction as her realization dawned. "There is someone," he concluded. "Who?"

"It doesn't make a difference now," she said.

"Who is it?" he asked, his voice sharp as if he thought she was protecting someone.

"Andy," she said. "I told Andy everything…" Since they were kids, he had been her best friend, her confidant.

His blond head bobbed in a sharp nod. "Of course…"

But then she realized that she'd lied to the agent. She hadn't told Andy everything, or she would have told him the truth—that she didn't love him as anything more than her best friend. Maybe she'd told him so much about the bank because, as with her parents just discussing the weather, she had preferred to talk to Andy about her job than about her feelings or their future. She hadn't seen one for them, but not because she'd thought he was going to die.

"But Andy's gone," she said. "So there's no way he could have had anything to do with the bank robberies."

"Can I ask…how did he die?"

For once she was short with her words. "He drove a supply truck. An IED took out the whole convoy."

He flinched. "I'm sorry."

She nodded. It was her automatic reaction to everyone's condolences. Condolences she didn't feel she really deserved, just the way she felt she hadn't deserved Andy.

"Would Andy have told anyone what you told him?" Blaine asked.

"Why?" While he had listened to her, Andy really hadn't cared about her job. He'd been proud that she'd gone to college, that she'd gotten her degree in finance, but he'd thought that she would quit working once they got married and started having kids.

Andy really hadn't known her at all. Or he would have guessed that, while she loved him, she wasn't in love with him. So if Andy hadn't known her that well, maybe she hadn't known him, either.

"I can think of hundreds of thousands of reasons why he might have told someone," Blaine replied.

Maggie defended her friend. "Andy didn't care about money."

"But that was quite a ring he bought you…"

He hadn't just paid for that ring with money; he'd paid for it with his life, too. "He used his bonus—for re-upping and for his last deployment…"

Blaine nodded as if she'd answered another question—

one that he hadn't actually asked. "Maybe he didn't realize that he was revealing anything."

She hadn't realized that something she'd said could have led to those robberies, to Sarge's death. She hoped Blaine was wrong because she already had too much guilt to live with; she didn't need any more.

Chapter Nine

Maggie insisted on going to the bank, and Blaine agreed. The bank wasn't open for business, though. Not yet. Repairmen were working on replacing the broken windows and fixing the damaged walls and furniture. So Blaine took her around the back, through the security door that the robbers had dragged her out.

That was hard enough—watching her face drain of color as she relived those moments. She probably hadn't thought she was going to get away from the robbers. And for a few moments Blaine hadn't thought he was going to get her away from them—then or later at the hospital or the motel.

He relived all those moments and found his arm coming around her thin shoulders. "Maybe this was a bad idea," he murmured.

"I need to go to my office," she said. "And make sure I didn't leave anything out yesterday."

"The manager closed up the bank yesterday," he assured her. "I'm sure he locked up whatever paperwork you might have had out."

He did not want her going to her office. Since her walls were glass, it had also been damaged from the gunfire. And in the lobby was the outline where Sarge's body had been. She didn't need to see that, and neither did he.

Maggie shook her head. "No, Mr. Hardy wouldn't have done it himself. He probably let Susan do it and that's how she got hold of my purse."

Blaine hadn't been that impressed with the manager—especially when the guy had been firing questions at her while the paramedics were trying to assess her condition. It was obvious that most of the day-to-day administration had fallen on Maggie's slim shoulders. "She got your purse, your keys and your credit cards."

She sighed. "I should cancel my credit cards."

"She already used a couple of them," he said. While Maggie had been at the hospital, the greedy woman had used her cards. "Why did you ever have her as your roommate?"

Maggie shrugged hard enough to dislodge his arm and stepped away from his side. Maybe he had offended her by implying that she wasn't the greatest judge of character. "She was really nice to me when I first started working here," she said in defense of their relationship, "so I agreed to let her move in when her boyfriend kicked her out and she had nobody else to stay with."

He wondered if that had been a ruse. Maybe he had underestimated Susan Iverson's intelligence. He would take another look at her. But first he wanted Maggie to look at something; that was why he had agreed to bring her down to the bank.

He had also wanted to get out of Ash's small house before he lost all objectivity where Maggie Jenkins was concerned. She was too damn beautiful for his peace of mind. He couldn't lose the image of her hair tangled from sleep, her body all soft and warm and sexy. When she'd tossed back the blankets and revealed her bare legs and the shapely curve of her hips, he had been tempted to crawl into bed with her.

She sighed again. "But I learned quickly why her boyfriend had kicked her out."

"The woman can't be trusted." Blaine wondered if this one could. He wanted to trust Maggie Jenkins; he wanted to believe she was every bit as sweet and innocent as she seemed.

But he couldn't rule out any possible suspects yet. And she was a possible one—even after the attempts on her life. Or maybe because of them. Her coconspirators could be trying to prevent her from giving them up.

He led Maggie to a back office, near the rear exit, where he had had the bank security footage set up across six small monitors. He pressed a remote and started it rolling.

"What is all this?" she asked.

"Security footage." Sarge's security footage. "I want you to watch it."

"All of it?" She sounded overwhelmed. The six monitors probably were a bit daunting.

Blaine was used to it, as he often watched days, sometimes weeks or even months, of security footage when he was investigating bank robberies. But this time while they watched the monitors, he saw only Maggie—her full breasts and belly pushing against his old T-shirt. Those long, bare legs…

How would they feel wrapped around him? How would she feel when he buried himself inside her?

He shook his head, shaking off the thoughts. *They* would never happen. She wasn't just pregnant with another man's child; she was still in love with that man. It didn't matter that Andy was dead. A love like theirs—where she had told him *everything*—was deep and enduring.

Blaine had never had anyone in his life to whom he'd told *everything*. He had learned at a young age that if he told his sisters anything they would tell *everyone*. So he'd been keeping his own counsel for a long time— which was good because he had no intention of sharing his thoughts about Maggie with anyone else. In fact, he wanted to forget all about them.

So he focused on the video screens playing out on the monitors in Sarge's office. It might have been hard to be there, if Sarge hadn't been like Blaine and Ash—too nomadic to personalize any space. It wasn't as if they would be there long enough to put down roots anyway. If Ash hadn't inherited that house in the Chicago burbs, he would have just had an apartment like Blaine had in Detroit—something devoid of decoration and sparsely furnished.

Days of security footage passed before his eyes in a blur—slow enough to pick out faces but fast enough that hours passed in minutes. His head began to pound— maybe more from his mostly sleepless night than from watching the footage.

If staring at those monitors had affected him, he worried how it was affecting Maggie. "Are you okay?" he asked her.

Maggie nodded. "I'm fine." But her fingers touched her temple and she closed her eyes.

"We can take a break," he offered.

"I don't understand why we're watching *these* videos," she said as she gestured at the screens. "All of this happened a week or more ago."

Had she expected him to show her the footage of the robbery? That would have been too much for her—to relive those terrifying moments, to relive Sarge getting killed...

He may have already told her. So much had happened

that he couldn't remember exactly, so he asked, "Do you know why I showed up when I did yesterday?"

"Because you're working those bank robberies."

That was what he'd told the state troopers in the alley. "Sarge called me," Blaine said. "He told me that he thought the bank was going to be hit."

She gasped in surprise. "He knew?"

"Yeah, he must have realized that someone was casing the place." And hopefully that someone had been picked up on the security footage.

She shrugged. "But *I* don't know how to tell who's casing the place."

"I do," he said. While he'd worked his way up in the Bureau through other divisions, he specialized in bank robberies now. To date, his record was perfect; he always caught the thieves.

Always...

And this time he had even more incentive than his record and his career. He had Sarge. And Maggie...

"So what am *I* looking for?" she asked.

"Someone you know."

She laughed as if he'd said something ridiculous. "I know a lot of these people."

He could tell. Even though she hadn't been at this branch that long, she often stepped out of her office to talk to bank clients, her face breathtakingly beautiful as she smiled welcomingly at them. They all smiled back, charmed by her friendly personality.

But he stopped the footage on one monitor as he noticed that one man smiled bigger than the others. And he hadn't left his greeting at a smile. He had gone in for a hug—a big one that had physically lifted Maggie off her feet. She hadn't looked happy, though; she had looked uncomfortable.

"Who's that?" he asked.

She stared at the screen, her eyes wide and face pale as if she'd seen a ghost. "I always forget how much he looks like Andy..."

"Who is he?"

She released a shaky breath. "Mark—that's Andy's older brother, Mark."

"Does he have accounts at the bank?"

She shook her head. "No, he just came by to see me. To check on me."

Blaine's senses tingled as he recognized a viable lead. "Did he use to come by the other branch you worked at?"

"Sometimes."

He nodded.

"It's not what you think," she assured him.

She had no idea what he was thinking. People rarely did. He wasn't even thinking of the case. He was thinking that the man wasn't just looking at her with concern or familial affection. He was looking at her with attraction. The way Blaine looked at her...

But in the footage she wasn't looking at the man at all. Like the ring, it was as if she couldn't bear to look at him. Because he looked so much like her dead fiancé?

He was a good-looking man. With their frequently inappropriate comments, his sisters would've gone on and on about his dark hair and light-colored eyes. And Andy had looked like that?

A weird emotion surged through Blaine—anger or resentment? Jealousy?

He was jealous of a dead man...

"WHAT AM I THINKING?" Blaine was asking her, his voice gruff with a challenge as if he doubted she could read him.

Few people probably could. The man was incredibly

guarded. But he'd let that guard down, briefly, to mourn the loss of his friend and former drill instructor. So Maggie felt as if she had found a tiny hole in his armor.

"You're thinking that Mark is involved in the robberies," she replied. "And that's ridiculous."

Blaine turned back to the monitor and studied the frozen frame of Mark lifting her off her feet. That muscle twitched in his cheek—almost as if it bothered him that another man was holding her.

But her thought was even more ridiculous than his thinking that Mark Doremire was a robber. Blaine Campbell was not jealous of another man touching her. Blaine had no interest in her beyond helping him figure out who the robbers were.

"Why is it ridiculous?" Blaine asked.

"Because he's Andy's brother."

A blond brow arched, as if that made Mark guiltier. Because of what she'd told Andy? If only she'd kept her mouth shut…

Maybe her mother had been right—she talked too much. Or, in this case, she'd written too much.

Once again, she defended her best friend. "Andy was the most honest person I've ever known."

Blaine didn't challenge her opinion of Andy. He just pointed out, "That doesn't mean that his brother is honest, too."

"I understand their personalities being different. But not their fundamental beliefs. They were raised by the same parents—raised the same way," she said. "How could they be that different?"

"You are obviously an only child." He laughed. "I have three sisters, and they are very different from each other."

"How?" she asked. She had always wished she'd had siblings. But her dad's career was demanding, and he hadn't been around that much to help her mother. So Mom had won the argument to have only one child.

He laughed again. "Sarah is a car salesperson—with that over-the-top bubbly personality. Erica is a librarian—quiet and introspective. And Buster…"

"Buster?" She'd thought he'd said they were all sisters.

"Becky is her real name," he explained. "She's in law enforcement, too. She's a county deputy. So my sisters are absolutely nothing alike."

"Maybe not personality-wise," she said. Mark and Andy hadn't been that much alike, either. Mark had liked to tease and joke around, and Andy had always been so sensitive and serious. "But morality and ethics…"

"Sarah sells cars," he repeated. "I'm not so sure about the ethics…"

She laughed now. From the twinkle in his green eyes, it was obvious how much he loved all of his sisters—even the car salesperson.

"Mark has been coming around *because* of his ethics," she said, "because he made a promise to Andy—the last time Andy left for a deployment—that he would take care of me if something happened to him."

That blond brow lifted again with a question and suspicion. "How is he taking care of you?"

If he was asking what she thought he was…

She shuddered in revulsion. "Not like *that*. Mark is like my brother, too. We all grew up together."

Blaine clicked the remote and unfroze Mark's image. Andy's brother kept smiling at her…before Susan walked up and started flirting with him. "What about with her?" he asked. "Is he brotherly with Susan Iverson?"

She hoped not. "Mark is married. He's not interested in Susan." But as she watched the footage, she wondered. "Maybe he's just a flirt…" Sometimes it felt as if he was flirting with her, which always made her extremely uncomfortable. Because she really thought of Mark as a big brother and only a big brother.

"I need to talk to Mark," Blaine said. "Where can I get hold of him?"

"I think I have his address somewhere in my office. He and his wife invited me to dinner before." But she had politely declined because it was so hard to see him. "I can call him…"

She would really prefer calling him to seeing him.

But Blaine shook his head. "I'll get his address from your office. Then I'll put you back into protective custody."

"Because that worked out so well last time?" she asked. "How is that young officer?" Before they had left the little bungalow for the bank, Blaine had called the hospital to check on him, but all he'd told her was that the young man had made it through surgery.

"He's still in critical condition," he said.

"Then just let me call Mark," she urged, her heart beating fast with panic at the thought of being separated from Blaine again. "You can talk to him—you'll know that he had nothing to do with the robberies."

But Blaine shook his head in refusal. "No, I have to see him face-to-face."

So he had to leave her again.

And every time he left her, there was another attempt to grab her. One of these times the attempt was destined to be successful.

Would this be the time?

Chapter Ten

Every time Blaine left her alone or in someone else's protection, Maggie Jenkins was in danger. He didn't want to risk it again. It was better that she stayed with him. So she sat in the passenger seat of the FBI-issued SUV that had replaced his rental sedan as he drove to her almost brother-in-law's address.

But now was he the one putting her in danger?

He shouldn't have brought her along with him. But he couldn't risk a phone call that might have tipped off Mark Doremire to his suspicions. If the man was one of the robbers, he certainly had enough money to escape the country—to one where there was no extradition.

Hell, he was probably already gone.

But then, who kept trying to grab Maggie or kill her? And why? If she could identify them, wouldn't it be easier to escape now than to stick around to try to kill her?

"This trip is a waste of time," she remarked from the passenger's seat. "Mark won't be able to help you, either— just like I couldn't help you this morning at the bank."

She had helped him. He'd found a possible suspect. She just didn't want to see that her dead fiancé's brother could be a suspect.

"I watched all that footage and I didn't notice anyone *casing* the bank," she said, her soft voice husky with frustration. "I didn't notice anything out of the ordinary. And I didn't at the first bank that was robbed."

He should have brought up that footage, too. But she'd already admitted that Mark Doremire had been at that bank. Both banks had been robbed—it was a coincidence that was worth checking out.

But he should have checked it out alone. "You really shouldn't be along with me," he said regretfully.

"No," she agreed, even though it had been her comments that had talked him out of risking her safety to someone else's responsibility. "I don't want to see Mark. And I really don't want to see one of those zombie robbers again." She shuddered with revulsion. "Maybe I should go stay with my parents in Hong Kong."

His pulse leaped in reaction to her comment, to the thought of her going away where he couldn't protect her, where he couldn't see her. "You can't leave the country."

"Why?" she asked, her voice sharp with anger. "Am I still a suspect?"

He wasn't sure what she was. Entirely too distracting. Entirely too attractive…

He couldn't let her leave. "Right now you're a material witness."

"Some witness," she said disparagingly. "I can't help you at all. I didn't see anything on that footage. And during the robberies I only saw what everyone else saw— trench coats and zombie masks." She shuddered again at mention of the disguises.

She obviously hated those gruesome masks.

"You heard one of them speak," he reminded her.

She shrugged. "But I didn't recognize his voice."

So it hadn't been Mark Doremire who'd spoken. But it could have been someone he knew—a friend of his. "You might if you were to hear it again."

She sighed with resignation. "That's true. I doubt I'll forget him announcing the robbery the minute they walked into the bank."

Like the guns and disguises hadn't given away their intentions.

Announcing a robbery made them seem more like rookies than professionals. But then, they hadn't been robbing banks that long. Less than a year—barely half a year, actually. Blaine would catch them before they went any longer. If he had his way, the last bank they robbed would be the one at which Sarge had died.

"Which house is it?" he asked as he turned the black SUV onto the street on which Mark Doremire lived. The SUV would probably give away Blaine's identity, but he tucked his badge inside his shirt.

"I don't know," Maggie replied. "I haven't been here before." She leaned forward and peered at the numbers on the houses. "That one…"

This neighborhood wasn't like Ash's. Nobody looked out the windows. They probably looked the other way. The houses were in ill repair, with missing shingles and paint peeling off. If Mark had stolen any of the money, he hadn't spent it yet—at least not on his house.

"I'll stay in the car," she offered.

Blaine turned toward her. Her face was pale, as if she'd already seen a ghost. "I can't leave you in the car."

"Why not?"

"Someone could have followed us."

She glanced around fearfully. "Did someone?"

He doubted it; he had been too careful. "I don't know. But I don't want you out of my sight."

He didn't want her walking into the line of fire, either. So he handed her his cell phone. "Call him."

"But we're already here…"

If she tipped Mark off now and he ran, Blaine was close enough to catch him. He'd also radioed in his intentions to speak to a possible suspect. So other agents and the local authorities knew where he was and there was a deputy in the vicinity.

"Call him."

She sighed but looked down at the piece of paper that had Mark's address and cell phone. Then she punched in a number. "It didn't even ring. It went straight to his voice mail. Do you want— Oh, his voice mail is full." With another sigh, of relief, she hung up the phone.

Straight to voice mail? That wasn't a good sign— especially since the house looked deserted. Maybe he had already left. Just then an older car, with rust around the wheel wells and on the hood, pulled up across from them and parked at the curb in front of the house.

"That's his wife," Maggie said as a red-haired woman stepped from the car.

Nobody else was inside the vehicle, so seeing no threat to Maggie's safety, Blaine opened his door. "Mrs. Doremire."

She jumped as if startled. But then, in a neighborhood like this, it probably was strange for someone to call out her name. It was probably strange for anyone to even know her name. She slowly turned around and stared at him. "Yes?"

"Tammy," Maggie called out to her.

The woman peered around him and noticed Maggie inside the SUV. She smiled and waved. "Hi, there. Mark will be thrilled that you finally came over to visit."

"Is he here?" Blaine asked.

Tammy turned her attention back to him, and her brow furrowed with confusion. "I'm sorry…"

"Blaine." He introduced himself with his first name

only. If the press had mentioned him in any reports about the bank robbery, it would have been as Special Agent Campbell. "I'm a friend of Maggie's."

And, really, friendship was all he could expect from her—even though he wanted so much more. He wanted *her*.

"I'm sorry," Tammy Doremire said again, as she crossed the street to the SUV. "Mark isn't here right now."

"Where is he?"

She sighed. "He's at one of his folks'—probably his dad's."

"Dad's?" Maggie asked. "Mr. and Mrs. Doremire aren't together anymore?"

"They split up after Andy died," she said. "It was too much for them. So Mark keeps checking on them, like he checks on you, Maggie. He's trying so hard to take care of everybody since Andy's gone."

Maggie's voice cracked as she apologized now. "I'm sorry…"

It wasn't her fault that Andy had died. It was whoever had set the damn IED where the convoy would hit it. But Mark's wife didn't absolve her of guilt. She only shrugged.

"Sometimes he'll stay the night at his dad's," she said, "so you'll probably want to come back tomorrow."

Maggie nodded in agreement. But Blaine had other plans.

"It was nice meeting you, Mrs. Doremire," he said as he slid back behind the wheel.

She nodded, but her brow was furrowed again—as if she'd realized she hadn't really met him. He had only told her his first name.

"We'll come back tomorrow, then," he lied.

"Why?" Maggie asked after he'd closed his door. "You can tell Mark has nothing to do with the robberies. He's too busy taking care of everyone."

"Where does Andy's dad live?" he asked.

She shook her head.

"You don't know?"

"I didn't even know they had gotten divorced," she pointed out, and that guilt was in her voice again, as if she considered herself responsible, "so how would I know where either of them is living now?"

"One of them might have kept the house where they lived before Andy died," he said. "You know where that is."

He felt a flash of guilt that it might have been the house where Andy had grown up—a house where she and Andy had shared memories. It would be hard for her to go back to that.

"I know," she admitted and then confirmed his thoughts when she added, "but I don't want to go there."

He wished he didn't have to take her there. But he had to find Mark before his wife had a chance to warn him that a man, a friend of Maggie's, was looking for him. Because then the man would run for sure…

BLAINE CAMPBELL CARED only about his job. He didn't care about her or he wouldn't have made her give him directions to Andy's childhood home in southwestern Michigan. He wouldn't have kept her in the car to go with him. He wouldn't have made her keep revisiting her past and her guilt.

Everything had fallen apart since Andy's death. And that was all her fault. If she had told him the truth earlier, he wouldn't have reenlisted. He wouldn't have needed the money for the damn ring she had never wanted.

Blaine Campbell had taken it as evidence against Susan Iverson. She hoped he never returned it.

Maggie stared out the windshield at the highway that wound around the Lake Michigan shoreline. She had always liked this drive—until she had traveled it up for Andy's funeral. Then she had vowed to never use it again.

She hadn't wanted to go back. It wasn't home without her best friend. She had to make a new home for herself and for her baby. But she was afraid that she hadn't found one yet—at least, not one where they would be safe.

"Andy's been gone awhile," Blaine remarked.

"Nearly six months," she said. But sometimes it hadn't sunk in yet. Sometimes she still looked for his letters in her mailbox or an email in her in-box or a call…

"Did you even know that you were pregnant when you learned that he'd died?"

She nodded. Since her cycle had always been so regular, she'd taken a test on her first missed day. She hadn't been happy with those test results because she'd known that Andy would insist on marrying her. He had always been so old-fashioned and so honorable. But now he was dead…

Blaine's gaze was on the road, so he must have missed her nod. She cleared her throat and replied, "Yes, I had just found out."

"You're strong," he said.

She nearly laughed. Had he already forgotten how she'd screamed her head off that first day they'd met? She wasn't nearly as strong as she'd like to be. If she was, she might have saved Sarge. "Why do you say that?"

"Some women might have lost the baby," he explained, "because of the stress."

"I was fine." She hadn't had any problems then; she hadn't even had morning sickness. She was more afraid of losing the child now.

As if he'd heard her unspoken thoughts, he reached across the console and squeezed her hand. "I'll keep you safe," he promised. "I'll keep you both safe."

Andy had made promises, too. He'd promised that he would return from his last deployment. So Maggie knew that some promises couldn't be kept. She suspected that the promise Blaine had just made was one of them.

He didn't believe that, though. He thought it was a promise he could keep and his green eyes were full of sincerity as he shared a glance with her. Then he turned his attention back to the road and to the rearview mirror. His hand tensed on hers before he released it and gripped the wheel.

"Hold on!" he warned her as he pressed harder on the accelerator.

Maggie instinctively reached out for the dashboard, bracing her hands against it, just as the SUV shot forward. "What's going on? Why are you driving so fast?"

She had felt safe with him earlier. But not now.

"Just hold on," Blaine said again, as he sped up some more.

Tires squealed as he careened around a curve.

"What are you doing?" she asked again—with alarm.

But then more tires squealed and metal crunched as another vehicle slammed hard into the rear bumper of the SUV. The SUV fishtailed, spinning out of control toward where the shoulder of the road dropped off to the rocky lakeshore below. Nobody had ever broken a promise to her as fast as Blaine just had.

Maggie screamed in fear as the SUV teetered on two tires, about to roll over and plummet to that rocky shore.

Chapter Eleven

Blaine cursed and jerked the wheel, steering the SUV away from the shoulder. Gravel spewed from the tires as the SUV fishtailed, the back end sliding toward that steep drop-off to the rocky shore below. He needed all four tires on the pavement before he could accelerate. But before he could regain complete control, the van struck again. Metal crunched on the rear door of the passenger's side.

Too close to Maggie and her baby.

He had just promised that he would protect them. It was a promise that he'd had no business making. As a marine, he knew that there were promises that couldn't be kept—the way all his fallen friends had promised their families they would come home again. It was a promise that Maggie's fiancé had probably made to her when he'd given her that ring.

Blaine was not about to break his promise. At least not yet.

He pressed on the accelerator, taking the curve at such a high speed that a couple of the tires might have left the asphalt again. The black cargo van skidded around the corner behind him, its tires slipping off the pavement onto the gravel shoulder. So close to that dangerous edge, the van slowed down, and Blaine increased the distance between them.

He had grown up driving on roads like this—roads that curved sharply around lakes. But there had been mountains to maneuver, too, in New Hampshire. So he wasn't fazed. But neither was the driver of the van as he regained control and closed the distance between them again.

Blaine wanted to reach for his gun; he wanted to shoot out the van's tires and windshield. He wanted to do anything he could to stop the van from slamming into them again. But he needed both hands on the wheel to keep the SUV from plummeting over the rocky shoulder, and he didn't want Maggie trying to use his weapon.

He didn't want Maggie doing anything but hanging on—especially as the van made contact with them again. But the SUV absorbed the impact better than the van did.

In the rearview mirror, Blaine caught sight of a dark cloud as smoke began to billow from beneath the hood of the vehicle behind them. The rear bumper of the SUV was probably mangled, but so were the front bumper and the grille of the van.

If the radiator was ruined, it wasn't going to get far. He could just wait for it to stop running and try to apprehend the driver and whoever else was riding with him. But Blaine had no idea how many people were inside the van or how much firepower they had.

Even if he hadn't just made that promise to protect them, he couldn't risk the safety of Maggie and the baby. So he accelerated again and took the curves at breakneck speed. Maggie's hands were still pressed against the dashboard as she braced herself and her baby for another hit.

But the van didn't catch up again.

Blaine slowed down and, using his cell, called in the attempt to run them off the road. He described the van and then he asked for the nearest hospital.

"Do you think one of them was hurt?" Maggie asked as she peered behind them. But the van was no longer in view.

It might be where Blaine had left it smoking. Or the driver might have turned it around and tried to get somewhere they could hide it—the way they had tried to hide the getaway van between those Dumpsters in the alley.

He doubted blood would be found inside this van. He hadn't been able to take any shots at them. So he explained, "I'm taking *you* to the hospital."

She shook her head. "I'm fine."

Her face was eerily pale, and he could see the frantic beat of her pulse pounding in her throat.

"No, you're not fine," he argued, as he followed the directions the local dispatcher had given him to the hospital.

If there was something wrong with her or the baby, it was his fault. He should not have brought her along with him. He hadn't been any better at protecting her than the young officer the night before. Even with the van chasing them, he should have driven more carefully.

He slowed down on his way to the hospital. But he wanted her checked out. He wanted to make sure that she and the baby were fine.

Before he left them…

BLAINE HAD INTENDED to leave as soon as a doctor had taken Maggie into the ER to be checked out. But before he could cross the waiting room to the exit doors, another FBI agent, badge dangling down the front of a black leather jacket, showed up at the hospital.

"Agent Dalton Reyes," the dark-haired man introduced himself, hand outstretched. He didn't look much like the proverbial men in black since he wore a jacket and jeans instead of a dark suit.

But Blaine wasn't wearing a suit, either—just black pants and shirt. Since interrupting the robbery in progress, he hadn't had an opportunity to even take his suits out of their dry-cleaning bags.

"Reyes?" Ash had mentioned the young agent before. The Bureau had recruited him from an undercover gang task force with the Chicago PD. "You work organized crime?"

The dark head bobbed in a quick nod. "Yeah. Right now I'm working on a car-theft ring. The black cargo van that just tried running you off the road was recovered. It's one these thieves grabbed yesterday. This ring is very organized and very professional. You put in a request, and they'll steal the vehicle you want."

Blaine had put out a request himself—for information on a ring just like this. "Thanks for getting back to me about this, but you could have just called…"

Reyes grinned. "I could've, but then I wouldn't have gotten a chance to meet the infamous Blaine Campbell."

"Infamous?" Blaine asked. He didn't think that adjective had ever been used for him before.

"You've got quite a reputation."

He groaned. "What has Ash told you?"

Dalton laughed. "Ash doesn't talk. But he's damn good at getting other people to talk."

He was new to the Chicago Bureau, so people were bound to talk about him. To wonder what his story was, to worry that he might move up ahead of agents who had been there longer. He didn't care to move into management; he just wanted to take criminals off the street. He had never wanted to put anyone away more than these suspects. They'd already killed Sarge and were determined to kill Maggie, too.

"How about you?" Blaine asked, turning the conversation back to what he really cared about: the case. "Can you get these car thieves to tell you who's been putting in the requests for these vans?"

"I've got an inside man," Dalton said. "So I've got confirmation that the bank robbers have been paying—and paying big—to get disposable vehicles for the bank heists."

"Who?" he asked. "Who the hell are these robbers?"

Dalton shrugged. "My guys aren't the kind who care about names. In fact, they would probably rather *not* know. The only thing they care about is cash."

Blaine cursed as frustration overwhelmed him. He needed a lead and some hard evidence. "Does your inside man at least have a description of the guy ordering the vans?"

"Good-looking guy with dark hair and light eyes," Dalton replied with a chuckle. "My inside man is actually a woman."

That description matched the man from the security footage—the man who'd lifted Maggie into his arms. "I'll send you a picture to see if she can confirm it's my guy."

Blaine would forward him a screen shot from the security cameras as well as Mark Doremire's DMV picture. If he was the man, Blaine could link him to the vans and therefore the robberies. Maggie would have to accept his involvement.

But then it would probably be like losing Andy again—to lose another piece of him when she realized his brother wasn't the man she'd thought he was.

He hadn't been checking up on her as his brother had requested. He'd been casing the banks where she worked.

Dalton nodded. "Send me the photo. I'll get it to my informant right away. Whatever you need to get these guys, let me know. I'm happy to help."

He obviously knew about Sarge. Blaine sighed. "Ash must've talked some."

Reyes nodded again. "Yeah. He said this one's personal for you both."

It was, but not just because of Sarge. It was personal because of Maggie, too.

"He thinks it might be extra personal for you, though," Reyes continued, "because of the witness."

He glanced toward the ER, where Blaine kept looking, wondering how Maggie and the baby were.

"Ash talks too damn much," he said.

Reyes chuckled. "He's worried about you. He thought I should tell you about another agent who works out of the Chicago Bureau, Special Agent Bell. He works serial killers."

"Maggie's not a serial killer," Blaine said. She was not a criminal at all. "She's a victim."

"Yeah, Bell got too *personally* involved with a victim's sister," Reyes said. "It's the case he never solved. The serial killer he never caught."

Would these suspects be the ones that Blaine never caught—because he cared too much?

"You can't go!" Maggie exclaimed as she clutched at Blaine's arm, panicking at the thought of being separated from him. Since the first moment she'd met him, she'd thought him a golden-haired superhero, and every time he saved her life he proved that he was her hero.

"There are local authorities here," he said, gesturing with his free arm to where two police officers stood near the nurses' station. "You'll be safe."

She shook her head in protest. He couldn't pass her off to someone else again. He couldn't leave her. She was afraid that she wouldn't be able to protect her baby without him. "I'm not safe anywhere. Except with you."

"Not even with me."

"You kept me safe," she said. "They were trying to run us off the road. We would have been killed if you hadn't driven the way you had."

His voice gruff, he brushed off her gratitude. "But I could have hurt you…"

"The doctor said that the baby and I are both fine," she reminded him. "I can leave now. They don't need to keep me for observation." Blaine was the only one who wanted her to stay in the hospital with the local deputies guarding her. "I can leave with you now."

He wouldn't meet her gaze, just shook his head. "I don't think that's a good idea."

"Why not?" she asked. "Where are you going? Have they found the van?" She'd seen the smoke from under the hood. It probably hadn't gotten very far.

"The van has already been recovered," he said. "Empty. And it had been stolen."

"So you're not going there," she said. "So where are you going?" That he didn't want her along. Had he found another lead he was pursuing? Was he going to put himself in danger?

The thought of that scared her as much as being without his protection. She didn't want anything happening to Blaine. Maybe it was just the danger and the fear that had her so attached to him, but she had never felt like this before. She had never been as drawn to another person.

"I'm going to Andy's dad's house," he said. "I confirmed that he is still living in the house where Andy grew up."

She hadn't wanted to go back there, now that Andy was gone. "I thought you wanted me to go along."

"I was wrong to even consider taking you there," he said. "It's too dangerous."

"It's Andy's dad—"

"And maybe his brother."

If they believed Tammy...

Maggie wasn't so sure that they should. While Mark had always been caring and friendly, sometimes too friendly, Tammy had always seemed cold to her—even at Andy's funeral. Maybe that was just because Mark had been too friendly.

But Tammy wasn't at the dad's house. "They're not going to hurt me," she said. "I've known his dad for years." But, truthfully, she hadn't known Andy's parents that well. They had usually hung out at her house or around town more than at Andy's.

"Maybe his dad wouldn't hurt you," Blaine said. "But you're wrong about his brother. The description of the guy who ordered the stolen vans matches Mark's description."

"Dark hair? Blue eyes?" She shrugged. "A lot of guys look like that." Except for Blaine. She had never seen a man as attractive as he was, but it wasn't just his looks. It was his protectiveness and his courage and his intelligence that she found even more compelling than his physical appearance.

"I sent someone a picture of Mark for a positive ID," he said.

"It won't be," Maggie said. She refused to accept that Andy's big brother could be robbing banks. "Mark wouldn't hurt me." He had promised Andy that he would take care of her. He would never break his promise to his brother.

Blaine sighed as if exasperated with her. Maybe that was why he wanted to leave her at the hospital. He was tired of her. "Don't you think it's strange that we were run off the road shortly after leaving his house?"

Her heart—that had finally slowed from a frantic beat—started pounding hard again. "No…" She really didn't want Mark involved. "That van could have followed us from the bank."

"I doubt it," Blaine replied. "I was too careful. I didn't see anyone following us. I think Mark was either in that house or his wife called him and told him where we were heading."

"But you didn't say where," she reminded him. "You said that we would come back to their house the next day. If they were involved, wouldn't they have just waited for us to come back?"

"Or they'll make damn sure they're gone before tomorrow." He pushed a hand through his disheveled blond hair. "Hell, they could be gone now. I have to go."

She didn't release his arm. "You can't go without me." She hadn't wanted to go back to Andy's house, hadn't wanted to relive the past. But now she was more afraid of the future. She didn't want to be separated from Blaine and she wasn't sure it was just because she was scared.

"I can't put you in danger again," he said.

"I won't be in any danger," she said. "This is Andy's family. I'm carrying Andy's baby. They're not going to hurt me." They wouldn't want to lose that last piece of Andy any more than she did.

His mouth curved into a slight grin. "What about me?"

"They're not bad people," she said. "They won't hurt you, either."

"That wasn't what I meant." He stared at her, his green

gaze tumultuous with regret. "I'm worried that I'm going to hurt you."

"You've saved my life again and again," she reminded him. She would never forget how he had protected her and her baby. Maybe gratefulness was the feeling overwhelming her and making her panic at the thought of him leaving her. But it didn't feel like just gratitude. "You're not going to hurt me."

Physically—he wouldn't. She knew that he would protect her from physical harm. He had proved that over and over again.

But he was only doing his job. And she had to remember that. She had to remember that, when he caught the robbers, Blaine would move on to his next assignment, and he would leave her.

For good.

So he probably would hurt her. Emotionally. If she let herself fall for him…

But she wouldn't do that. She wouldn't risk her heart on anyone right now. She was going to save all her love for her baby.

Chapter Twelve

Maggie was getting to him in a way that no one had ever gotten to Blaine before. He couldn't even draw a deep breath for the panic pressing on his chest.

What had he been thinking to bring her along? He shook his head in self-disgust.

"What?" she asked from the passenger seat of the battered SUV.

"I shouldn't have brought you…"

"I told you that I won't be in any danger."

Maybe she wouldn't be. But he was worried that *he* was in danger. He was in danger of falling for her. And that would be the biggest mistake he'd ever made.

It wasn't that he still believed she was involved in the robberies. But he would be a fool to totally rule out the possibility. Even though there were attempts being made on her life, it could be to silence her, so that she wouldn't reveal her coconspirators. But he doubted that. If she actually knew anything about the robbers, she would have told him by now; she was too scared to keep secrets any longer.

The reason it would be a mistake for him to fall for Maggie Jenkins was because she was in love with another man. He suspected she would forever love her dead fiancé.

That was why she had insisted on coming along with him. To protect Andy's family from him.

"I really don't believe they're involved," she insisted. And he wondered now if she was trying to convince herself or him.

"Andy could have told them what you had shared with him about the bank," he said. "What did you share with him?" And how did it tie in to the robberies?

"I rambled on," she said, "like I usually do since I talk so much. I complained about working harder than the manager. I told him what my duties were—how I handled the money deliveries and pickups—how I knew the security code for the back door and the vault."

That information had definitely been used in the robberies. Even at the other banks, the robbers had threatened the assistant managers and never questioned the managers.

"It sounds like Andy shared that information with his brother." And Mark had used it to rob all the banks.

She shook her head, tumbling her brown curls around her shoulders. "Andy wouldn't talk to anyone about my job."

"Why not?" he asked, and he wondered about her dismissive tone.

She shrugged. "It's not very interesting."

"It's not?"

"Most of the time it's very boring," she said.

Had Andy thought her job boring and uninteresting? "But you told him about it anyway?"

"I wrote about it," she said. "I guess my letters to him were kind of like writing in a journal. I complained about stupid policies and procedures."

"You wrote him letters?"

"Yes," she said. "Didn't I tell you that before?"

"Not about the letters—just that Andy was the only person you'd told about your job," he said. Because she told Andy everything. He'd thought that had been in person, though. "Where are the letters now? Did you get them back?"

She shook her head. "No. I don't know what would have happened to them after he...after he..." She trailed off, unable to talk of his death. Of her loss...

"His personal effects would have been returned to his family," Blaine said. He was definitely right about Andy's family; they had to be involved in the robberies.

Maggie sucked in a breath, as if she had just realized it, too. "But they wouldn't have read his personal letters..."

"If they miss him as much as you do," he pointed out, "they might have."

"But those are letters that *I* wrote to him," she said, her voice cracking with emotion. "They're not the letters he wrote to me. They're not about Andy and his life."

"I'm sorry," he said. She had every right to be angry. "Those letters should have been returned to you. They're your personal thoughts and feelings. Hell, you were his fiancée. You should have gotten everything."

She shook her head in denial. "We weren't married. So his personal effects should have gone to his family."

"You're family—you and his baby," Blaine said. "His parents and brother should have at least given you those letters."

"Maybe they just didn't have time..." She kept defending them.

Maybe she was naive. Maybe she just tried to see the best in everyone. But that was how she had wound up with Susan Iverson as a roommate. She didn't need protection just now; she needed it every day. She needed protection from her own sweetness and generosity.

"His brother's been checking on you," he said. The image from the security footage of him hugging her hadn't left his mind. "He could have brought the letters to you then. He's had six months to get them to you." Unless he had been using them for something else—to help him plan the bank robberies.

"We're here," she said with a sigh of relief as he pulled the battered SUV to the curb across the street from the brick Cape Cod.

He could have sworn earlier today that she hadn't wanted to come back here. Of course, she thought she was going to prove to him that Andy's family wasn't involved. But with every new thing he learned, his suspicions about them grew. He didn't even need confirmation from Dalton Reyes that Mark Doremire was the one ordering those stolen vans.

He was so convinced that Doremire was involved that he'd had a local officer watching the house before they arrived. The car was parked a little way down the street. Too far down the street if Doremire and his father were armed. The other men from the bank could be there, too.

Maggie reached for her door handle, but Blaine caught her arm and held her back from opening the door. With his other hand, he grabbed his cell and checked in with the officer.

"Nobody's come or gone, Agent Campbell," the officer assured him.

So what did that mean? That they had holed up in the house with weapons? At least the driver of the van, and whoever else might have been riding inside, couldn't have joined them. They wouldn't have had time to ditch the van for another vehicle and drive up without the officer seeing them.

Blaine clicked off the cell and turned back to Maggie. "I want you to stay here until I check out the inside of the house."

"Mr. Doremire may not let you in unless he sees me," she warned him. "Andy's parents kind of kept to themselves when we were growing up. They didn't socialize much. So he's not going to open his door to a stranger."

Blaine tugged his badge out of his shirt. He wasn't hiding it this time. "This will get him to open the door," he said. Or he would knock down the damn thing. "You need to stay here until I determine if it's safe or not."

He waited until she reluctantly nodded in agreement before he stepped out the driver's side. But moments later Mr. Doremire proved her right. When Blaine knocked on the door, a raspy voice angrily called out, "Go away!"

"I am Special Agent Campbell with the FBI," Blaine identified himself. "I need you to open up this door, sir. I need to talk to you about your son."

"It's too late for that!"

That was what Blaine was afraid of. That Mark was already gone—that he'd taken off to some country from which he couldn't be extradited. But then, who had tried running them off the road on the way here? Only Mark would have known they had stopped at his house looking for him. Only Mark would have known where they'd been heading.

"Go away!" the older man yelled again.

"Let me try," a soft voice suggested as Maggie joined him at the solid wood door to the Cape Cod. It was painted black—like the shingles on the roof. And there was no welcome mat.

"I told you to stay in the vehicle," he reminded her.

Even with the squad car not far away, she wasn't safe; someone could have taken a shot at her as she had crossed the street.

Ignoring him, she knocked on the door. "Mr. Doremire, it's me—it's Maggie. Please let us in…"

Inside the house, something crashed and then heavy footfalls approached the door. It was wrenched open, and a gray-haired man stared at them from bloodshot eyes.

Blaine could smell the alcohol even before the man spoke. "Have you heard from him?" he demanded to know.

"Mark has been by to see me," she said. "At the bank. Is he here?"

"Mark?" the older man repeated, as if he didn't even recognize the name of his eldest son. "I'm not talking about Mark."

Did the man have other boys? Maybe there were more Doremires involved than Blaine had realized. Maybe they made up the entire gang.

But Maggie's brow furrowed with confusion, and she asked, "Who are you talking about?"

"Andy," Mr. Doremire replied, as if she was stupid. "Have you heard from Andy yet?"

She reached out and clasped the older man's arm and led him back inside the house. "I'm sorry, Mr. Doremire," she said as she guided him back into his easy chair. A bottle of whiskey lay broken next to the chair. But no liquor had spilled onto the hardwood floor. He'd already emptied it.

She crouched down next to the old man's chair and very gently told him, "Andy's dead. He died in Afghanistan."

"No!" the gray-haired man shouted hotly in denial.

"He didn't die. That's just what he made it look like. He's alive."

She shook her head, and her brown eyes filled with sympathy and sadness. "No…"

"I've seen him," the man insisted. "He's alive!"

"No," she said again. "That's not possible. His whole convoy died that day. There's no way he survived." And her voice cracked with emotion and regret.

Mr. Doremire shook his head in denial and disgust. "That boy wasn't strong enough for the Marines," he said. "He had no business joining up. He got scared. He took off. He wasn't part of that convoy."

Why was Andy's father making up such a story? Just because he couldn't handle his son being dead?

"They wouldn't have reported that he was dead if they hadn't been certain," Maggie continued, patiently. "They wouldn't have put us through that and neither would Andy."

"None of the remains recovered have actually been identified, so there is no way of proving that he was part of the convoy," the older man insisted. "They never even recovered his dog tags."

"They are still working on DNA," Maggie said with a slight shudder. "But they know that Andy's gone…" And from the dismal sound of her voice, she knew it, too.

Blaine hated that she was reliving Andy's last moments. Or had those actually been his last moments? Was Andy's father right? Was Maggie's fiancé still alive? Mr. Doremire had claimed that he'd seen him.

If so, Blaine had another suspect for the robberies—one who had definitely read her letters and knew about the bank's policies and procedures, and the duties and responsibilities of the assistant manager.

"Will you be okay in here?" Blaine asked Maggie.

She nodded. "Of course."

But she stared up at him with a question in her eyes as if wondering where he was going...

"I have to make a call," he said.

From his years as a marine, he had connections, people he could call to verify if Andy Doremire had been identified among the convoy casualties. Maybe they hadn't identified the remains immediately after the explosion, but in the past six months they would have. And he couldn't trust that Mr. Doremire's drunken claims were valid. Or was Andy alive and robbing banks?

MAGGIE BIT HER bottom lip to stop herself from calling out for Blaine. She didn't want to be left alone with Andy's dad and his outrageous story. He was drunk, though. That had to be why he was talking such nonsense.

"He's calling someone in the military," Dustin Doremire said. "He's going to talk to some marines."

Blaine had been a marine. He would know whom to talk to.

"Probably," she agreed. "He's wasting his time, though." Andy was dead. Therefore, he was not robbing banks—as Blaine probably now suspected.

"They're not going to tell him anything," Mr. Doremire said with a derisive snort. "It's a cover-up."

So he was drunk and paranoid. "What are they covering up?" she asked. She wasn't even sure who "they" were supposed to be. First Andy had faked his death and now someone else was covering it up?

"You know what they're covering up," he accused her, suddenly turning angrily on her.

She edged back from his chair, not wanting to be so close to him. "I don't know what you're talking about." That was definitely the truth.

"Andy told you everything," he said. "You know..."

But now she wondered. Had Andy told her everything? He had never mentioned his father drinking so much. Maybe it had started only after his death. But now she wondered—because she hadn't come over to Andy's house very often. He had always come to hers. And if his car was broken down and she had to pick him up, he met her on the street.

Maybe she hadn't been the only reason Andy had joined the Marines. Maybe he hadn't done it just to support her, the way he had old-fashionedly claimed he'd wanted to do. Maybe he had also joined to escape his father.

"That boy loved you so much," Mr. Doremire continued. "He was crazy about you."

Andy had loved her. If only she could have loved him the same way...

The older man uttered a bitter laugh. "The boy was such a fool that he couldn't see you didn't feel the same way about him."

"I cared about Andy," she insisted. "He was my best friend." And she would forever miss him and she would regret that his son or daughter would never know him— would never know what a sweet guy he'd been.

"But you didn't love him," the older man accused her, as if she'd committed some crime. "It's your fault, girl. It's all your fault."

"What's my fault?" she asked.

"It's your fault he joined the Marines, trying to prove he was man enough for you." Mr. Doremire shook his head. "He wasted his time, too. You never looked at him like you're looking at that man..." He gestured toward where Blaine had gone out the open front door.

"That man is an FBI agent," she said. "He's investigating the robberies at the banks where I've worked." He had to have heard about the robberies; they'd made the national news.

But the older man just stared bleary-eyed at her. Had he even known she worked at a bank?

"I don't care who the hell he is," Mr. Doremire replied. "He's not going to be raising *my* grandchild."

She hoped Blaine had stepped far enough away from the open door that he hadn't overheard that. But her face heated with embarrassment that he might have. She assured the older man, "Agent Campbell is not going to be raising my child."

She knew that once the robbers were caught he would move on to his next case. She was nothing more than a witness and possible suspect to him.

"That's Andy's child!" Mr. Doremire lurched out of the chair and reached for her as if he intended to rip the baby from her belly.

She jerked back to protect her baby. She didn't even want his hands on her belly, didn't want him hurting her child—before he or she was born or after—the way he must have hurt Andy had he ever spoken to him the way he'd spoken of him.

"Mr. Doremire," she said, "please calm down." *And sober up.*

"Andy won't be letting some other man raise his kid," he ominously warned her. "You'll see. He'll show himself to you, just like he's shown himself to me."

She wondered how many bottles of whiskey it had taken for Andy to show himself. She suspected quite a few.

"Andy is gone, Mr. Doremire," she said. "He's dead."

His hand swung quickly, striking her cheek before

she could duck. Tears stung her eyes as pain radiated from the slap.

"That's what you want," Mr. Doremire said. "You want him dead. But he's not! He's not dead!"

"Okay, okay," she said, trying to humor the drunk or deranged man. "He's alive, then. He's alive."

He had no idea how much she really wished that Andy was alive. Then she wouldn't have lost her best friend. She wouldn't feel so alone that she was clinging to an FBI agent who was only trying to do his job.

Maybe she was as crazy as Andy's dad to think that Blaine could have any interest in her beyond her connection to the bank robberies.

The older man started crying horrible wrenching sobs. "If he's dead, it's your fault," he said again. "It's all your fault!"

She nodded miserably in agreement. Maybe it was...

If he hadn't wanted to buy her that damn ring...

If he hadn't wanted to take care of her...

"You're the one who should be dead!" He swung his arm again.

And, realizing that the man wasn't just drunk but crazy, too, she cried out in fear that he might actually kill her.

Chapter Thirteen

Maggie's scream chilled Blaine's blood. He dropped his phone and ran back into the house—afraid of what he might find.

Why the hell had he left her alone? He hadn't even checked the house. Mark Doremire could have been hiding somewhere, waiting for his next chance to grab Maggie.

But when he burst into the living room, he found only the older Doremire and Maggie. She was backing up, though, and ducking the blows of the man's meaty fists.

Blaine jumped forward and caught the man's swinging arms. He jerked them behind his back. "Dustin Doremire, I am placing you under arrest for assault."

"No," Maggie said. "You don't need to arrest him." But her cheek bore a red imprint from the older man's hand.

Blaine jerked Doremire's arms higher behind his back, wanting to hurt him the way he had hurt Maggie. The old drunk only grunted. After all that whiskey, he was probably beyond the point of feeling any pain. Only inflicting it…

"He hurt you," he said. And Blaine blamed himself for leaving her alone with Andy's drunken father.

"He's hurting," she said, making excuses for the man's abuse. "He misses his son."

Blaine had placed a few calls. But nobody had really answered his questions about Andy Doremire. In fact, they'd thought he was crazy to even ask. Of course the man was dead. His family wouldn't have been notified if his death hadn't been confirmed.

Otherwise, he would have been listed as missing. Blaine knew that. But for some reason he had wanted to think the worst of Andy Doremire. He'd wanted proof that her dead fiancé wasn't the saint that Maggie thought he was—he wasn't a man worth loving for the rest of her life.

But he was a better man than Blaine was. Andy wouldn't have willingly left her alone and in danger.

"Are you all right?" he asked her. "How badly did he hurt you?"

She brushed her fingertips across her cheek and dismissed the injury. "It's nothing. I'm fine."

She wasn't fine. He could hear the pain in her voice. But he wasn't sure whether it was physical or emotional pain. He suspected more emotional. She hadn't wanted to come here—to Andy's childhood home. And now he understood why.

"He needs to be brought in," he said. "I need to arrest him." Actually he only intended to hand him over to the officer outside to make the arrest and process Mr. Doremire.

"Please don't," she beseeched him, her big brown eyes pleading with him, too.

"You never want me to arrest anyone," he said. "You make it hard for me to do my job." He had ignored her and arrested Susan Iverson anyway. He was tempted to do the same with Mr. Doremire. "I need to question him."

"Let *me* question him," she said.

He settled the older man back into his chair. The guy collapsed against the worn cushions. The chair was one of the only pieces of furniture left in the nearly empty house. In fact, the Cape Cod made Ash's little bungalow look almost homey.

Blaine had no intention of letting Maggie question him. But before he could ask, she already was. "When did you see Mark last?"

"Mark?" The older man blinked his bloodshot eyes, as if he had no idea whom she was talking about.

"Mark is your oldest son," she prodded him. "His wife, Tammy, said he was here—visiting you."

He shook his head in denial. "I haven't seen that boy for months. He's not like Andy. Andy keeps coming around to check on me."

Did he have his sons confused? Even Maggie thought they looked a lot alike. He shared a significant glance with her as they both came to the same realization.

"When was Andy here last?" she asked. "When did he come see you?"

Doremire's eyes momentarily cleared of the drunken bleariness, and he stared at her with pure hatred. "You have no right to say his name."

The old man would have reached out again; he would have swung his arm if Blaine hadn't squeezed his shoulder and held him down onto the chair.

"She has every right to say his name," Blaine insisted. "They were engaged."

The older man shook his head. "She never would've married him. She didn't care about him…"

"That's not true," Maggie said, but her voice was so soft she nearly whispered the words.

"She loved him," Blaine said. "You know that. You have the letters she wrote to your son. Where are they?"

The drunk blinked in confusion, the way he had when she'd asked about Mark. "Letters?"

"*My* letters," she said. "The ones I wrote to Andy when he was overseas. Do you have them?"

He shook his head. "His mother probably took them— like she took everything else when she left."

Blaine could see that she had taken most everything. And he could see why she had left, too, if the man had been like this with her. If he had been abusive…

"Where did Mrs. Doremire go?" Maggie asked.

"She took all Andy's life-insurance money and bought herself a condo."

That money should have gone to Andy's fiancée and his unborn child, but Andy must not have listed her as his beneficiary yet. Knowing she was carrying Andy's child, his family should have given her the money, though. It would have been the right thing to do.

But this family obviously didn't care about what was right. Or honorable. Or legal.

He had to find Mark Doremire—had to catch him before he got beyond Blaine's reach.

"Where is her condo?" Maggie asked.

Andy's father named some complex that had her nodding as if she knew where it was. "It's not that far from here," she said. "We can go there now."

Blaine had no intention of taking her anywhere but to a bed. To rest…

But the thought of a bed reminded him of that morning, of her flicking back the covers to reveal all her voluptuous curves. The woman was so damn sexy.

"Tell that witch that she didn't break me," Mr. Doremire said. "Tell her that I'm fine…"

He was anything but fine. The former Mrs. Doremire was probably well aware of that, though.

"I hope you will be," Maggie said. After how the man had treated her, how could she wish the best for him?

Blaine had met few women as sweet and genuine as Maggie Jenkins.

But the old man stared up at her again with stark hatred. "I hope you get what you deserve."

It wasn't so much what he said but the venomous tone with which he said it that had Blaine protesting, "Mr. Doremire—"

"And you, Mr. Agent, I hope the same for you. Maybe you two deserve each other…"

Blaine knew that wasn't true. Maggie deserved a better man. He should have protected her better than he had. So, finally, he guided her toward the door.

"But don't go thinking you're going to be raising that baby together," Mr. Doremire yelled after them. "Andy's going to take that baby. He's going to raise his son himself."

Maggie sighed. "Andy's gone…"

"He's not dead," the older man drunkenly insisted. "You're going to see when he comes for his baby boy. You're going to see that he's not dead."

Maybe he wasn't dead—in his father's alcohol-saturated mind or in Maggie's heart. Blaine wished he was man enough to deserve her love. But he suspected she had none left to give anyway.

ONCE BLAINE SAID it was too late to see Mrs. Doremire, Maggie feigned falling asleep in the SUV. She didn't want to talk. She didn't want to even look at Blaine. Her face was too hot, and not from Mr. Doremire's slap but with embarrassment over all the horrible things that old drunk had said in front of Blaine.

Maybe he hadn't heard everything; maybe he'd been outside during the worst of it. But he had come running back when she'd screamed. He had saved her—as he always did.

Mr. Doremire hadn't been wrong about how she looked at the FBI agent. Despite not wanting to fall for him, she was falling. She had more love to give than she'd realized. But Blaine wouldn't want her love—or anything else to do with her, for that matter—once the bank robbers were caught.

The SUV drew to a stop. Then the engine cut out. A door opened and then another. Hers.

Blaine slid one arm under her legs and another around her back, as if he intended to lift her up the way he would a sleeping child. She jerked back.

"Sorry," he said. "I didn't mean to scare you. I just didn't want to wake you up."

"I'm up," she said.

But he didn't step back; he didn't give her any room to step out of the SUV. He was too close, his green gaze too intense on her face.

Her skin heated and flushed. She wished he wouldn't look at her. She lifted her hand to her face.

But he beat her to it, bringing his hand up to cup her cheek. "I don't think it'll bruise," he said.

She shrugged. She couldn't have cared less about her face. The man's words had hurt far more than his slap. "It's fine."

"I'm sorry," he said.

"You're sorry?"

"I shouldn't have left you alone with him." Blaine pushed a hand through his disheveled hair. "I knew he was drunk. I never should have stepped outside."

"You called someone about Andy," she said. It wasn't a question because she knew that he'd done it. She had watched the new suspicions grow in his green gaze. "To make sure that he's really dead."

Finally he stepped back and helped her from the SUV. Then he escorted her from the street up to the little bungalow where they had spent the night before. He hadn't taken her back to the hospital or to a hotel.

Her chest eased a little with relief.

"Are you going to ask me what I found out?" he asked, opening the door.

She shook her head as she passed him and entered the living room. "No."

"So, you're sure he's dead?"

"I know it." Even before Mark had called her, she'd known. She'd seen the news of the explosion—of the casualties—and she had known Andy was among them.

"But they didn't even recover his dog tags," Blaine said.

She shrugged. "I don't know what was recovered or not. I don't know if my letters were even sent back. You should have let me talk to Mrs. Doremire."

"It's been a long day for you already," Blaine reminded her as he flipped on the light switch. "We went back to the bank and watched all that footage. Then we saw Mark's wife and nearly got run off the road."

She shuddered at the reminder of those harrowing moments when she had thought the SUV was going to flip over and crash onto the rocky shoreline.

"And if that wasn't already too much for you," he said, "then you were assaulted by a crazy drunk."

"He is crazy," she agreed. "Thinking that Andy's alive…"

"That makes sense, actually," Blaine said, "that he doesn't want to let his son go."

She sighed. "I guess that is his way of dealing with his grief—denial and alcohol."

"How about you?" he asked.

She stared up at him in confusion. She had dealt with her grief months ago and neither alcohol nor denial had been involved. "What do you mean?"

"Are you going to be able to let Andy go?"

"I don't think he's alive," she assured him. "I'm not seeing him anywhere." She didn't see ghosts. Regrettably, she did keep seeing zombies—in person and in her nightmares. She would probably rather see ghosts.

"That's not what I meant," he said.

"What did you mean?" she wondered.

Instead of explaining himself, he just shook his head. "It doesn't matter."

She thought that it might, though—to her. Did he want her to let Andy go? Or was he like her almost father-in-law and not entirely convinced that Andy was dead?

"What did the people that you called tell you?" she asked. She already knew, but she didn't want to leave him yet. As tired as she was, she didn't want to climb the stairs and go to bed. Alone.

"They said that Andy's dad's claims were crazy," he replied. "They're not covering up anything…"

"Mr. Doremire said a lot of crazy stuff," she said. Hoping to dispel her embarrassment, she continued, "Like that nonsense about us…"

"Nonsense?"

Her skin heated again and not just on her face; she was warm all over. "Of course. All his drunken comments about you and me. That was just craziness…"

"What was so crazy about it?" he asked.

She drew in a deep breath to brace herself for honesty. "It's crazy to think that you'd be attracted to me."

"It is?" That green gaze was intense on her face and then it slid down her body.

Now her warm skin tingled. "Of course it is," she said. "I'm so fat and unattractive…" And he was the most beautiful man she'd ever met.

"You're pregnant," he said. "And you're beautiful."

She laughed at his ridiculous claims; they were as outrageous as Mr. Doremire's. "I wasn't fishing for compliments. Really. I know exactly what I look like—a whale."

He laughed now as if she were trying to be funny. She had just been honest. He was not being the same as he replied, "I would not be attracted to a whale."

"You're not attracted to me." She wished he was. But it wasn't possible. Even if she wasn't pregnant, she knew he would never go for a woman like her—a woman who talked too much and didn't think before she let people get close to her.

He stepped closer to her, his gaze still hot on her face and body. "I'm not?"

She shook her head. But he caught her chin and stopped it. Then he tipped up her chin and lowered his head. And his lips covered hers.

Maybe he had intended the kiss as a compliment or maybe it was just out of pity. But it quickly became something more as passion ignited—at least in Maggie—and she kissed him back.

She locked her arms around his neck and held his head down for the kiss. Her lips moved over his before opening for his tongue. He plunged it into her mouth, deepening the kiss and stirring her passion even more.

Making her want more than just a kiss…

Chapter Fourteen

It had just been a kiss. But even though it had happened hours ago, Blaine still couldn't get it out of his mind. Probably because it hadn't been just a kiss. It had been an experience almost profound in its intensity.

And he hadn't wanted to stop at just a kiss. He had wanted to carry her upstairs to one of the bedrooms and make love to her all night long.

But he'd summoned all of his control and pulled back. His cell had also been ringing with a summons from the Bureau chief to come into the office for an update on the case.

"You've lost your objectivity," the chief was saying, drawing Blaine from his thoughts of Maggie.

"What? Why?"

"The witness," Chief Special Agent Lynch said.

Blaine glanced at the clock on the conference room wall. He had left her alone too long. Of course, he hadn't actually left her alone. He had left her with two agents guarding Ash's house—one patrolling the perimeter and one parked in a chair outside her bedroom door. They were good men, men for whom both Ash and Dalton Reyes had vouched. They weren't special agents yet; they were barely more than recruits. But Truman Jackson had been a navy SEAL and Octavio Hernandez had worked in the gang task force with Reyes.

She should be safe…

But he had thought that when he'd left the local authorities to protect her.

"The witness is in danger," he said. "That was proven today—" he glanced at the clock again and corrected himself "—*yesterday* when someone tried running us off the road."

"The van was processed."

"Any evidence?"

"Not like in the first one," the chief replied. "No blood."

"Have you gotten a DNA match yet?"

The chief shook his head. "We'll check some other databases—see if we can find at least a close match."

"Good—that's good."

"What leads have you come up with?" the chief asked. "Or have you been too busy protecting the *witness*?"

"She is the best lead," Blaine insisted.

"You checked to see if her fiancé is really dead," the chief said. "She's leading you to a dead man as a suspect?"

"She didn't think he was alive. It was the man's father who raised some questions…"

"You think her fiancé's family is involved in the robberies."

He sighed. "Her fiancé's brother is a viable suspect. Reyes even confirmed him as having bought the van recovered after the robbery. The one in which the blood was found." Someone else had ordered the black cargo van. Why? Was Mark already gone?

"Where is he?" the chief asked, as if he had read

Blaine's mind. "Why haven't you brought Mark Doremire in for questioning?"

"We haven't found him yet."

"We?" the chief asked. "You're having the witness help you do your job?"

"I have an APB out on him," he said. "The witness is helping me figure out places where the man could be hiding. We checked out his dad's house."

The chief studied him through narrowed, dark eyes. "So you're only using her to lead you to a suspect?"

Blaine tensed as anger surged through him. "I'm not using her. I'm trying to keep her and her baby from getting killed."

"Is it the pregnant thing that's getting to you?" the chief asked.

If this was the way this chief ran this Bureau, Blaine wasn't sure he would want to stay in Chicago after all. And he'd considered staying here, putting down roots. Chicago wasn't that many miles from his sister Buster, who had settled in west Michigan.

"What?" he asked, offended that his professionalism was being questioned.

"I've read your history. I know you have a few sisters. Is that it?" the chief persisted.

He didn't feel at all brotherly toward Maggie Jenkins. And he suspected that neither did Mark Doremire. "The robbers keep trying to grab her. One of these times that they're trying, we'll be able to catch them."

"So you're using her as bait."

He tensed again. Furious and offended. "You may have read my file, but you don't know me."

"Ash Stryker does," the chief said. "He vouched for you. Says you're the best."

Although Blaine appreciated his friend's endorsement, he added, "My record says that."

"I'm still worried about the witness."

So was Blaine.

"You no longer think she's personally involved in the robberies?" the chief asked, as if he wasn't as convinced.

"She didn't plan the robberies." Blaine was certain of it. "She didn't recruit the other robbers."

"What evidence do you have of that?" Chief Lynch asked. "Her word?"

"The attempts on her life," he replied.

"Coconspirators have never tried killing each other?" The chief snorted. "You've been doing this job long enough to know better than that."

"No honor among thieves," Blaine murmured.

"Or loyalty."

"If that were true, she would have given them up," Blaine pointed out. "If she knew who they were, the fastest way to stop them would be to tell me who they are."

"You really believe that she doesn't know?"

He nodded. "But the robbers don't realize she doesn't. They must think that she can identify them somehow. That's why she's our best lead to them. It's also why she's in so much danger."

"But guarding her isn't the best use of *your* time or talents," the chief said. "We'll put other agents on her protection duty. We can keep Jackson and Hernandez on her."

Blaine was used to butting heads with local authorities trying to run his investigation. Usually the Bureau respected his handling of a case. But maybe the chief was right. Maybe he had lost all perspective where Maggie Jenkins was involved.

Maybe it would be better for him to trust her protection to someone else…because he couldn't trust himself where Maggie Jenkins was concerned.

BLAINE HAD BEEN gone so long—all night and all morning—that Maggie doubted he was ever coming back. And she felt sick to her stomach because of it. Maybe that was why the baby was restless; maybe it was because he missed him, too.

Him? Andy's dad had called him a boy. Sometimes she thought her baby was, too. But she didn't care if she had a boy or girl; she just wanted a healthy baby. That was all she wanted.

She didn't want Blaine Campbell. *Liar,* she chastised herself. She had wanted him, the night before, when he'd kissed her senseless. But when he'd pulled back, and her senses had returned, she'd recognized his kiss for what it was. A balm for her battered ego. Pity…

So she didn't want Blaine Campbell anymore. All she wanted was a healthy baby. And she couldn't have that with someone trying to kill her. So she gathered her courage and picked up the phone one of the agents had let her borrow. She dialed a number she had looked up online. Andy's mom was listed.

"Hello?" a friendly female voice answered on the first ring.

"Mrs. Doremire?"

"Maggie? Is that you?" the older woman asked. "Is everything all right? Is the baby all right?"

"Yes." For now…

"Oh, thank God." The woman released a sigh of relief that rattled the phone. "What can I help you with, honey?"

Honey. She didn't hate her like Andy's dad did? "I stopped by your old home yesterday…"

The woman drew in a sharp breath. "I'm sorry that you did that. Was it…unpleasant?"

Maggie's cheek hadn't bruised, but it was still sensitive to the touch. "I understand that he's very upset about Andy's death."

"What death?" she asked.

And that sick feeling churned harder in Maggie's stomach. Was Andy's entire family crazy?

"My ex-husband refuses to accept that Andy's dead," Janet Doremire continued.

"Is that why he's drinking so much?"

"It's his new excuse to drink," Janet replied. "But he always had one."

Why had Andy never told her what he'd gone through at home? They had been best friends. But apparently neither of them had really told each other everything.

"I'm sorry…"

"He refuses to accept Andy's death because then he'll have to admit his blame for it."

"Blame?" Someone besides her blamed himself for Andy's death?

"He's the reason Andy joined the Marines," Janet explained. "Dustin told him that it would make a man of him."

But Maggie and Sarge had been right. Andy hadn't had the temperament for it. He wasn't like Blaine Campbell, who hadn't hesitated over firing his weapon or risking his life.

Mrs. Doremire sighed again. "Instead it killed him."

Was that why Andy's mom had left his dad? Because she blamed him, too? Or was it over the drinking? Maggie didn't want to pry.

But Mrs. Doremire willingly divulged, "Andy's death showed me that life's too short to waste. I wasted too many years with my ex. I didn't want to spend another minute in that unhappy marriage. Andy would have wanted me to be happy."

"Yes, he would have," Maggie agreed. He had loved his mother very much. But now she realized he had never said that much about his father.

"Andy would have wanted you to be happy, too," Janet Doremire continued.

Tears stung Maggie's eyes, but she blinked hard, fighting them back. He would have wanted her to be happy because that was the kind of man he'd been.

"I know you're carrying his baby, but you need to move on, Maggie," Janet Doremire continued. "You and Andy only ever dated each other. You got too serious way too young—like me and Andy's father had. You should get out there." The woman chuckled. "Well, once the baby's born."

"Mrs. Doremire, I can't—" Maggie couldn't have this discussion with Andy's mother. She couldn't talk about dating someone else. "That's not why I called you…"

"I'm sorry, honey," Mrs. Doremire said. "Why did you call me?"

"I was wondering if you had the letters I wrote to Andy—if they'd been returned in his personal effects…?"

"I don't know," Mrs. Doremire said. "I never looked through his stuff."

"Do you have it?"

"No. I left it and the rest of my past at the old house. I don't want to wallow in it. You shouldn't, either," Mrs. Doremire said. "You don't need those letters, honey. Let them and Andy go."

The baby shifted inside Maggie, kicking, as if in protest. Would Mrs. Doremire even want anything to do with her grandchild once he or she was born? Or was she determined to forget everything about Andy?

That was obviously her way of dealing with her grief. And Andy's dad chose to wallow in alcohol. Since his ex hadn't taken everything, as he'd claimed, he must have either broken it or sold it. What had he done with her letters?

"Thank you, Mrs. Doremire..." But she spoke only to a dial tone. The older woman had already hung up. "But I really do need those letters..."

"We just need to know who has them," a deep voice remarked.

She turned to find Blaine standing in her bedroom doorway. She hadn't even heard him open the door. How long had he been there?

"She says her ex-husband," Maggie replied with a sigh. "I don't want to go back there, but I really want those letters."

"I'll send an agent with a warrant for Andy's personal effects," he said. "We'll get them."

Her face heated with embarrassment. "I wish nobody had to see those letters."

"Nobody cares about the personal parts," Blaine said. "Just the parts that relate to the bank procedures."

"That's what I worry about someone reading," she admitted. "I was such a fool to share those details with anyone. I'll probably get fired when it gets out that it's all my fault."

"We don't know that it is," Blaine said. "Maybe nobody read those letters. And as you've pointed out, other banks were robbed."

"Other banks that probably follow the same procedures we do," she said with a sigh. "I'll get fired and be unable to get a job anywhere else." And then how would she support herself and her baby?

"Don't panic," Blaine said. "We'll figure this out."

No, he would. And once he figured it out, he would be gone.

"Where have you been?" she asked. Then her face grew hotter as she realized she sounded like his wife or girlfriend, like someone who actually had a right to ask him where he'd been.

"Bureau chief wanted an update on my progress," he replied easily, as if he felt she had a right to ask.

"You were gone a long time," she said. "You must've had a lot to tell him." He had probably told the chief about her letters and Andy's brother and dad.

"He had a lot to say, too," Blaine said with a sigh. "He thinks that I'm losing my objectivity where you're concerned."

"Because he thinks you should still consider me a suspect?" Maybe Blaine did; he had never really said that he no longer had any suspicions about her.

"Chief Lynch thinks that I shouldn't be the one protecting you," he said.

That explained the other agents who'd guarded her last night and today. But the thought of losing Blaine's protection panicked her. She wasn't just frightened for the baby's safety or hers; she was panicked at the thought of no longer seeing Blaine. "I don't understand. You've saved me. You've kept me safe."

"He's right," Blaine said. "I should not be protecting you. I have lost my focus."

"So you're going to send me away—to one of those *safe* houses again?" She was losing him already. She had been right to not fall for him. But despite her best intentions, she was afraid that it was already too late.

"Not yet," he said. And he stepped inside the room and closed the door behind himself. "Not tonight…"

"Blaine…?"

"This is why I shouldn't be the man protecting you," he said, "because I want you. Because I'm attracted to you, and when I'm around you, I can barely think, let alone keep you safe."

She must have fallen asleep; she must have been dreaming—because he couldn't be saying what she was hearing. Testing her reality, she reached out and touched his face. His skin was stubbly and sexy beneath her palm, making her fingers tingle.

"You're attracted to me?"

"I showed you last night," he reminded her, "with that kiss."

"I thought that was pity."

He laughed. "That wasn't pity."

"Then why did you stop?" She'd lain awake all night—wanting him. Needing him…

"I thought I was taking advantage of you," he said, "of your vulnerability."

She shook her head. "You weren't…"

"I want to," he said. "I want you…"

She wanted him, too, so she tugged him down onto the bed with her. And she kissed him with all the desire he had awakened in her the night before—all the desire she had never felt before. It coursed through her again as their lips met.

He kissed her back. And it was definitely not with pity but with desire. He touched her, too, his hands moving gently over her body.

Her pulse pounded madly. She wanted him to rip off her clothes, but he removed them carefully, slowly, as if giving her time to change her mind.

She had never wanted anything—anyone—more. She didn't take off his clothes slowly; she nearly tore buttons and snaps in her haste to get him naked. When all his golden skin was bare, she gasped in wonder at his masculine beauty. His body was so sleek but yet so muscular, too.

He made love to her reverently, moving his lips all over her body. He kissed her mouth, her cheek, her neck before moving lower. He nibbled on her breasts, tugging gently on her nipples.

She moaned in ecstasy, her body already pulsing with passion. She pushed him back on the bed and he pulled her on top of him, gently guiding his erection inside her.

"This is all right?" he asked, his hands holding her hips—holding her up before she took him all the way inside her. "For the baby?"

She bit her lip and nodded. Even though she had told her doctor it wouldn't be an issue, the female obstetrician had assured Maggie that sex wouldn't jeopardize her pregnancy at all. "It's fine."

He pulled her down until he filled her. And she moaned again.

"Are you okay?" he asked.

"Not yet," she said, as she began to move again—rocking back and forth—trying to relieve the inexplicable pressure building inside her. "But I will be…"

He helped, guiding her up and down—teasing her breasts with his lips and gently with his teeth—until ecstasy shattered her and she screamed his name. Then he thrust and called out as he joined her in ecstasy.

She collapsed on top of him, their bodies still joined. He clasped her to him, holding her tightly in his arms. His heart beat heavily beneath her head, and his lungs panted for breath. Finally his heart slowed and his breathing evened out, and she realized he'd fallen asleep beneath her.

She would have been offended if she wasn't aware that he'd had no sleep the past two nights. And maybe even more nights before that. She hadn't had much more sleep, so she began to drift off, too.

Until her eyes began to burn and her lungs…

At first she blamed guilt. But Mrs. Doremire was right. Andy would have wanted her to be happy, so she couldn't use him as an excuse. But as it became harder for her to breathe, she realized what the real problem was.

Smoke. Someone had set the house on fire.

Chapter Fifteen

"Blaine!"

The sound of his name—uttered with such fear and urgency—jerked him awake as effectively as if she'd screamed. He coughed and sputtered as smoke burned his throat and lungs.

Soft hands gripped his shoulders, shaking him. "The house is on fire! We have to get out!"

They pulled on clothes in the dark and Blaine grabbed up his holster and his gun. He couldn't believe that he hadn't awakened earlier. The fire must have been burning for a while because there was a lot of smoke—so much that it was hard to breathe. Hard to see. But there wasn't much heat.

Maybe the smoke was just a ruse to get them out of the house—where Maggie could be grabbed. Or shot. But the smoke, growing denser and denser, could kill her, too.

She coughed and sputtered. But she didn't speak. She must have been too scared.

So was Blaine. He was scared that he had failed her and the baby—that he had broken his promise to her that he would keep them safe. He shouldn't have let his desire for her distract him. He shouldn't have crossed the line with a material witness.

"We have to stay low," he said as he helped her down

to the floor. He reached forward and touched the door, his palm against the wood. It wasn't warm—at least, not as warm as the floor beneath his knees.

Maggie must have felt it, too, because she gasped and started to rise. But Blaine caught her arm and pulled her back down as she began to cough.

Getting out wouldn't be easy, especially if the whole first floor was engulfed as he suspected. But he didn't have time to devise a plan. He had to act now—before the floor gave way beneath them.

So he opened the door to the hall. The smoke was even thicker than in the bedroom. He crossed it quickly to the bathroom, grabbed towels from a shelf and soaked them under the tub faucet. Maggie was still in the hall as if she hadn't been able to see where to go. He wrapped Maggie's face and body in the wet towels, and then he picked her up in his arms.

"Blaine…"

He coughed, and his eyes teared up from the smoke. But there was no time. And maybe there was no escape. He couldn't jump out a second-story window—not without hurting Maggie and her baby. So he ran toward the stairs. The bottom floor was aglow from the flames, but none licked up the steps. So he ran down them—wood weakening and splintering beneath them from the heat and the fire.

The house creaked and groaned as the flames consumed it. And the smoke overwhelmed him, blinding him to any exits. But he remembered where the front door was.

But had it been barricaded? Or were those gunmen waiting outside it to make sure they didn't escape?

As he headed toward it, the door burst open, and men in masks hurried into the house. These weren't those horrible zombie masks. These masks had oxygen pumping into them and were attached to hats. Firemen had arrived. Of course one of Ash's neighbors would have called the police. They would have noticed the flames—unlike Blaine.

He shouldn't have sent the other agents away. But he had wanted one last night alone with Maggie. That night might have cost her life or her baby's life. Her body was going limp in his arms.

One of the firemen took Maggie from him and carried her out. Blaine should have fought the man. He should have made certain that he really was a fireman. What if it was one of the robbers in another disguise?

Blaine hurried after him, but the smoke was so thick in his lungs now that he couldn't draw a breath deep enough. He couldn't breathe. And before he could hurry after Maggie, the house shuddered as the second story began to fall into the first…

MAGGIE'S THROAT BURNED. From the smoke and from screaming. Over the fireman's shoulder, she had seen the roof collapse and the house fold in on itself…and on Blaine. She'd pounded on the fireman's shoulders, but he hadn't released her.

And for a moment, she had stared up in fear that the mask wasn't any more real than the zombie masks had been. She'd worried that it had just been a disguise.

And she'd reached for it. But she'd been too weak to pull it off. Too weak to fight off the man as he carried her away. He put her into the back of a vehicle, and it sped away with her locked inside. Sirens wailed and lights flashed, but she still did not trust where it would take her. She didn't trust the oxygen either that a young woman gave her in the back of that van.

What if it was a drug or a gas? What if it knocked her out? She tried to fight it, but she didn't have the strength to pull off the mask. And then it began to make her feel better, stronger.

So when the doors opened again, she was strong enough to fight. To run. But the doors opened to a hospital Emergency entrance. She pulled off the oxygen mask and asked, "Where's Blaine?"

The paramedic stared down at her as she pushed the stretcher through the sliding doors of the ER entrance. "Who?"

"Agent Campbell," she said. "He was in the house…" She coughed and sputtered, but she wasn't choking on the smoke. She was choking on emotion. "He was in the house…when the roof caved in…"

The paramedic shrugged. "I don't know…"

"Do you know if anybody else got out?"

Blaine hadn't been the only one inside; there had been other firemen, too. Real firemen, she realized they were. They would have saved him. Right? They would have made certain Blaine got out alive.

"I don't know, miss," the female paramedic replied. "We were told to get you to the hospital right away because of the baby."

Maggie had one hand splayed across her belly, feeling for movement. Was he okay? She hoped the smoke hadn't hurt him. She was scared to think of what it might have done to his heart. His brain…

"That's good," she agreed. "We need to check out the baby."

"And you, too," the paramedic said. She leaned back as doctors ran up.

But Maggie grabbed the young woman's arm. "Was

there another ambulance there?" Was there someone who could help Blaine?

Because after seeing the roof collapse, she had no doubt that all of the people still inside would need medical help. Maggie was glad that she and her baby had been brought to the hospital so quickly. But she also wished they would have waited for Blaine—to bring him in with her.

Then she would know how badly he'd been hurt. Or if he had survived at all...

The young paramedic didn't have a chance to answer her question before doctors and nurses whisked Maggie's stretcher into a treatment area. They hooked her to another oxygen machine and an IV. There was also a heart monitor for the baby and an ultrasound.

She breathed a sigh of relief when she heard the fast but steady beat. "He's alive..."

"His heart sounds good," a doctor agreed.

"And his lungs?"

"Did you ever lose consciousness?" someone asked. "Did you pass out from the smoke?"

Maggie shook her head.

"We'll administer some prenatal steroids to help the development of his lungs," the doctor said, "to make sure everything's fine..."

But everything wouldn't be fine until she learned if Blaine had made it out of the burning house.

"He's active," the doctor said as he watched the ultrasound screen.

He. The picture on the ultrasound confirmed what Maggie had previously only suspected. She was carrying a baby boy. She wanted to share that news with her best friend. But he was gone. She wanted to share that news with the man she loved. But Blaine was gone, too.

Maybe the IV contained a sedative because she must have drifted off despite her worry. She didn't know how much time had passed, but when she awoke, she was no longer in the emergency department. She was alone in a room but for the man—tall and broad-shouldered—who stood in the doorway.

Hope burgeoned in her heart. "Blaine?"

The man stepped forward…into the light that glowed dimly from another doorway, perhaps to the bathroom. The man's hair was dark and his eyes were light, not gold and green like Blaine's. Disappointment made her heart feel heavy in her chest. "You're not Blaine."

But the man who had purchased those stolen vans had been described as dark haired with light eyes. This man matched that description as much as Mark Doremire had.

Could he be one of the robbers? And if he'd forgone the zombie mask, then he had no intention of letting her live.

"Who are you?" she asked. She didn't recognize him. She would have had no way of identifying him as one of the suspects in the robbery.

"I'm not Blaine Campbell," he agreed with a short chuckle. "My name is Ash Stryker. I'm also an FBI agent and a friend of Blaine's."

"Is he okay?" she asked. "Is he here?" She struggled to sit up, ready to jump out of bed and go to him.

Ash shook his head. "No. He's not here. That's why he asked me to stay with you."

"But is he okay?" she asked, and her panic grew. Had Blaine asking Ash to stay with her been his deathbed request? Was that why he wasn't there?

Because he was gone? Dead and gone?

Ash nodded, but he had that same telltale signal of stress that Blaine did. A muscle twitched in his cheek.

Maybe that twitch wasn't just betraying his stress but his lie—like a gambler's tell in a poker game.

"No," she said, her voice cracking as hysteria threatened. "I don't believe you. I saw the roof collapse. He couldn't have gotten out of there without some injuries."

Serious injuries.

Fatal injuries.

The man flinched as if he'd felt Blaine's pain. "He has some bumps and scratches," he admitted. "And a couple of small burns. But he's fine. Or I wouldn't be here."

Even though Blaine had asked him? But then, he would have been too distraught over the loss of his friend to worry about her.

Maybe Blaine wasn't gone.

The dark-haired man sighed. "Of course, I have no place to go right now…"

"It was your house he was staying at," she realized. And that Blaine had let her stay at, as well. He should have taken her to a motel. It might not have protected her, but it would have protected Ash Stryker's house. "I'm sorry…"

"It wasn't your fault," he assured her.

"But whoever set the fire is after *me*," she said. "So I feel responsible." She felt responsible for the house and for those injuries Blaine had suffered. How badly had he really been hurt?

Agent Stryker moved closer to the bed and assured her, "You're not responsible for any of this."

"I wish that was true," she said. "I shouldn't have stayed at your house. I shouldn't have stayed with Blaine." Or made love and fallen in love with Blaine.

He chuckled. "Blaine was right…"

"What was he right about?"

"He said that you couldn't possibly have anything to

do with the robberies," Ash said. "He said that you're too good a person to be consciously involved."

He thought she was a good person?

"I figured Blaine was only thinking that because he grew up with sisters and has this whole chivalry thing going on," Ash said.

She nodded. "He is very chivalrous and protective." The man was a hero like she had never known.

"I also guessed that you're pretty," he said.

She didn't feel pretty now. She felt bedraggled from the smoke. Maybe it was good that Blaine wasn't there. He would have regretted sleeping with her.

Maybe he did regret it. Maybe that was why he wasn't here—with her. Had he even checked on her?

"Where is Blaine?" she asked.

Ash sighed. "He's determined to end this," he said. "He wants these guys caught."

"He wants to avenge Sarge's death," she said. "Sarge is—"

"I knew Sarge, too," Ash said with a grimace of regret and loss. "He was also my drill instructor."

"I'm sorry."

"Stop apologizing," he said. "None of this is your fault. Blaine is going to prove that. He's going to find out who the hell is responsible and bring them to justice."

She breathed a small sigh of relief. He had to be okay, then. He had to be strong enough to want revenge. But her breath caught again as she realized that he was putting himself in more danger.

"You should be with him," she said. "You should make sure he's really all right. The doctors wanted to keep me here because they're worried about my lungs having a delayed reaction to all that smoke. I think it's called hypoxia." That was why they were keeping her on oxygen.

Blaine wouldn't have oxygen with him. He wouldn't have anyone to help him if hypoxia kicked in, depriving his body of oxygen. He could die.

He wasn't just in danger from whoever was trying to kill them. He was in danger from his own body shutting down on him.

That muscle twitched in Ash's cheek again. He was worried, too. Blaine must have checked himself out against doctor's orders.

"Have you heard from him?" she asked.

He shook his head.

Maybe it was already too late to help Blaine.

Chapter Sixteen

Maggie was okay. So was her baby. Blaine hadn't left the hospital until he'd learned that. He hadn't left the hospital until Ash had shown up. He wouldn't have trusted anyone else to protect her. He probably shouldn't have trusted Hernandez and Jackson since he wasn't sure how the robbers had discovered where Maggie was staying.

He'd been so careful to avoid being followed—to avoid anyone discovering where he had hidden her. But he hadn't kept her safe. Ash would. Or at least he would try…the way Sarge had tried.

Maggie was in too much danger. She and her baby had survived this time. But eventually their luck would run out.

Blaine had to focus on finding the robbers. He couldn't think about her—or what they'd done right before the fire started. He couldn't think about anything but suspects.

He was determined to find the one who had so far eluded him. So he went back to Mark Doremire's house.

His wife opened the door and stared at him through eyes wide with surprise. At first he thought it might have been because of the hour; it was barely dawn. But she was looking at him instead of the sky.

"Are you all right?" she asked.

He felt as if a roof had fallen on him. But then, it had.

He'd been fortunate to come out with only a few scrapes and light burns. The firemen had used their own bodies to protect him. His lungs burned, though, from all the smoke he'd inhaled. The doctor hadn't authorized him to leave the hospital. He'd wanted to keep Blaine for observation—something about a delayed reaction to smoke inhalation.

But Blaine felt time running out since each attack on Maggie had been harder for her and for him to survive. So he had refused to stay and checked himself out against the doctor's orders.

"No, I'm not fine," he admitted. "I'm about to arrest you for obstruction of justice if you don't tell me where your husband is hiding."

She shrugged but continued to block the doorway to the kitchen the best she could with her thin frame. "I can't tell you what I don't know."

He could have pushed her aside and searched her house. But he'd had someone watching it—someone with thermal imaging who'd detected only one person inside the house. Mark really wasn't there. "You don't know where your husband is?"

She shook her head. "I figured he was following Maggie around like his brother used to. But it seems as though you're doing that now."

"I'm just doing my job," he said. But it was a lie. Protecting Maggie had less to do with his job than with his heart. He had fallen for her.

And just as Dalton Reyes and his boss had warned him, he'd gotten distracted. Because of that, he had nearly lost his life and hers, as well. He had to put aside his feelings for her and focus only on the case. He wasn't going to be like Special Agent Bell and leave this case unsolved.

The younger Mrs. Doremire snorted derisively as she recognized his lie. "So you've let sweet Maggie get to you, too," she said. "Something about her makes a man feel more important, more manly. That's what killed Andy. That dumb kid actually thought he could be a soldier—for her."

"That was Andy," Blaine said. "What about his brother? He's *your* husband." He wanted to goad her—to piss her off at Mark—so that she would give up his whereabouts.

"But I don't need him like dear sweet Maggie does," Tammy replied. "It doesn't help that before Andy left for his last deployment he asked Mark to watch out for her. Why do you think we moved here?"

Blaine shrugged even though he could have guessed. The robberies...

"Because she moved here," Tammy said. "I left behind my friends and family for Maggie."

"You hate her."

She laughed. "That's the thing about Maggie. You can't hate her. She's too sweet. But she's also manipulative as hell. She'll suck you in and ruin your life."

"Has she ruined yours?" he asked, wondering why the woman resented her so much.

"She ruined my marriage. I haven't seen Mark in days," she said. So she blamed Maggie for all the problems in her marriage instead of blaming her husband. "I have no idea where he is. So if you want—arrest me. Take me in for questioning. Drug me with truth serum. I'm not going to be able to tell you what I don't know."

"Who would know where he is?" Blaine wondered.

Tammy sighed and leaned wearily against the doorjamb. Her red hair was tousled, and she wore a robe. But somehow he doubted she'd had any more sleep than he had. "Like me," she said, "Mark left his friends behind in Michigan. Maybe his mom or dad would know where he's gone."

"His dad only talks about Andy," Blaine admitted.

"Everybody loved Andy. He was sweet—like Maggie," she said. "But genuinely sweet. He was a good man who died too soon."

"What about Mark?" he asked. "Is he a good man?"

She shrugged again.

"Could he be involved in the bank robberies?"

She gasped in surprise.

He narrowed his eyes skeptically at her surprise. "You didn't figure out that's why I'm looking for him?"

"I had no idea why you're looking for him," she said. "I thought you were just a friend of Maggie's."

He was so much more than just friends with her.

"I'm a special agent with the FBI," he said. "And I'm working the bank robberies—the one where the suspects wear zombie disguises."

She sighed. "Mark wouldn't have gotten involved in the robberies on his own." She laughed now. "God knows he's no criminal mastermind. He would have only gotten involved because someone asked him—or manipulated him—into getting involved."

He suspected what she would say next, on whom she would place the blame, but still he had to ask, "Who?"

"Maggie, of course."

"You think she's a criminal mastermind?" He could have laughed, too, at that thought. Not that Maggie wasn't smart. She was. She was also too honest and open to take anything from anyone.

She hadn't even been willing to take a compliment from him. But then she'd taken his desire—his passion. She'd made love with him, too.

"I think she's a desperate single woman who's about

to be raising a baby alone," Tammy Doremire said. "She just might be desperate enough to start stealing."

He doubted Maggie Jenkins was a bank robber.

And Mrs. Doremire must have seen that doubt because she added, "She's not above stealing, Agent. Even you think she probably stole my husband."

He doubted that, too. She thought of Mark as an older brother. But maybe Mark didn't think of her as a little sister. Maybe he saw her for the sweet, desirable woman that Blaine did.

He pressed his business card into the woman's hand. "If you see your husband, give me a call. I need to talk to him."

"If anyone knows where he is," she said, "it'll be Maggie. You should ask her where he is."

"If Maggie knew where he was, I wouldn't be here," he said with certainty. He had wasted his time talking to her.

Tammy Doremire glanced down at the card he'd handed her, then called after him when he started walking toward his SUV, "Be careful, Agent Campbell. The most danger you're in is from Maggie Jenkins."

He couldn't argue with her because he suspected she was right. Maggie was dangerous to him—to his heart. But somebody else was a danger to her, and Blaine wouldn't be able to leave her until he found out who and stopped that person.

"IF YOU DON'T find him, I will," Maggie threatened as she struggled to escape her bed. But the oxygen line tugged at her nose and face. And the IV held her like a manacle.

Ash stretched out his hands, as if trying to hold her back. "Maggie, you have to stay here for observation."

"*You* don't," she said. "Go find him."

"I'm here for observation, too," Ash said. "I'm here to observe you."

"I don't need observation," she said. "I need to know that Blaine is really all right. And if you won't find out for me, I will find out myself." She struggled to sit up again.

"Blaine will kill me if I leave you," Ash said. "I promised him I'd watch out for you."

"Have someone else stand outside the door," she suggested. "A deputy or another agent."

"I'll send one of them to look for him."

She shook her head, rejecting his offer. A stranger wouldn't know where to look for Blaine. "You're his friend. You care about him. I trust you and only you to find him and make sure he's okay."

Ash replied, "I am his friend. And that's why he trusted me to protect you."

"You're not protecting me," she said. "I'm not supposed to get upset because of my blood pressure." She had been warned that she had to watch it, that she had to make sure that it didn't stay high. "And not knowing if Blaine is all right is upsetting me."

"Maggie…"

"Please, go find him," she urged his friend. "That's what you can do to protect me." Because not knowing whether or not Blaine had really survived the fire was the greatest risk to her health.

Ash sighed in resignation. "Damn it, if he's okay, he's going to kill me for leaving you. But I'll make sure the man who replaces me on protection duty can be trusted."

She wasn't worried about herself right now. She wasn't even that worried about the baby. The doctors had assured her that he was fine. Now she needed assurance that Blaine was, too.

Just knowing that Ash was looking for him eased her mind some—enough that she eventually drifted off to sleep. And Blaine popped vividly into her mind.

Naked, his golden skin stretched taut over hard muscles. He had made her feel emotions she had never felt before: lust, passion and love.

She hadn't wanted to fall in love with him. But it was too late. She had lost her heart to Special Agent Blaine Campbell. And now she may have lost him.

He should have stayed in the hospital—stayed where they could give him oxygen and monitor him to make sure he had no serious aftereffects from the fire. But he'd gone off on his own to track down killers.

Those zombie-masked men had been dangerous enough when Blaine was in full superhero mode. But in his weakened state, with his injuries…

She shuddered to think of what might have happened to him. But she clung to hope the way she clung to the memories of their lovemaking. With her eyes closed, she relived every kiss, every caress.

Her skin grew hot. But not with passion. She smelled the smoke again and felt the heat of the flames. And in her mind those flames began to consume Blaine…

She jerked awake with a scream on her lips. But a hand covered her mouth, holding that cry inside her. So that she couldn't alert anyone to his presence?

With the lights out, even the bathroom one, she saw only a big, broad-shouldered shadow looming over her. This couldn't be whoever Ash had asked to take his place protecting her. An agent or a deputy—a real one—wouldn't have been standing over her in the dark.

Who was this person?

What were his intentions? To smother her with a pillow? Or simply with his big hand?

She reached up, trying to fight him off. And she smelled the smoke again. This time it wasn't just a vivid memory. This person had been at the fire, too.

Chapter Seventeen

"I'm sorry," Blaine said, his voice gruff from the smoke that still burned in his throat and saturated his hair and clothes. "I didn't mean to scare you." He slid his hand from her lips. But he wanted to cover her mouth again—with his. He wanted to kiss her.

Maggie sat up and threw her arms around his neck. "You did scare me—so badly," she said as she trembled against him. "I thought you didn't make it out of Ash's house."

"Where is Ash?" he asked, furious that his friend hadn't been the one guarding her door. Dalton Reyes had been standing outside, and while Blaine admired what he'd done with the Bureau, he wasn't sure he could trust him, even though Ash obviously did.

"I begged him to look for you," she said.

Begged or manipulated? He shook off the thought, angry with himself for letting Tammy Doremire get to him. She was probably the real manipulator. "Why?" he asked.

"I wanted to make sure that you hadn't had aftereffects from the smoke," she said.

"I'm fine." But he wasn't. He was in even more danger than her almost sister-in-law had warned him about. He was in love with his witness.

"Then where were you all this time?" she asked, her eyes glistening in the darkness as she stared up at him.

Guilt and regret tugged at him for leaving her alone. After the fire, she had to have been terrified. But apparently she'd been more concerned about his safety than hers or she wouldn't have sent her protection away. She wouldn't have sent Ash out to find him.

Anger at Ash flashed through him, but then, he couldn't blame the man for letting her get to him. She had gotten to Blaine, too.

"I was working the case," he said. "Trying to track down a suspect."

"Mark?" she asked. From her tone it was obvious that she was still reluctant to believe Andy's brother could have anything to do with the robberies.

"I went to see Tammy Doremire to see if she'd heard from her husband yet." Mark was definitely one of the robbers—probably the mastermind, no matter that his wife thought he was an idiot.

"Has she heard from him?" she asked with more concern than suspicion.

He shook his head.

"He's her husband," she said. "How can she not know where he is?"

"I don't think their marriage is that great," Blaine said. His sisters would have killed their husbands if they'd gone hours, let alone days, without checking in with them. Hell, Buster probably knew where her husband was every minute of every day.

"Is he seeing someone else?" Maggie wondered.

"Maybe." He was thinking of Susan Iverson, but he added, "She thinks *you* know where he is."

She gasped. "I don't."

"She thinks you two may have been involved." He

could believe that Mark had been interested in Maggie. But he believed that she thought of the man only as an older brother—maybe as a link to her dead fiancé.

She gasped. "That's crazy." And she drew back from him. "Do you think that, too?"

"No." He trusted her. He believed her.

But then he worried that maybe he was being a fool. Maybe she had manipulated him just as Tammy had warned. Maybe Maggie had manipulated Blaine into falling in love with her. Or maybe he was just scared that for the first time in his life he'd fallen in love and he worried that she would never be able to fully love him back. Not when her heart still belonged to her dead fiancé.

BLAINE WAS STANDING there right in front of her, right beside her hospital bed, but Maggie felt him pulling away from her. Whatever Tammy had said must have gotten to him—must have gotten him doubting her.

She felt like a suspect again.

"If I knew where he was, I would tell you," she said. Not because she thought Mark was guilty of anything, but to prove his innocence. Then Blaine would be able to focus on who was really involved in the robberies.

"His wife thinks you know…"

"His wife is paranoid," she said. Tammy had never been nice to her; she was the kind of woman who couldn't be friends with other women. "She's delusional, too, if she thinks I'm having an affair with her husband."

"Maybe there's another reason you might know where Mark is," Blaine said. "Maybe he's hiding someplace that Andy might have gone. Did he have an apartment or a house of his own?"

Everything kept coming back to Andy and those damn

letters she'd written him. If only she'd had something to tell him about other than her job.

If only she'd had the guts to tell him about her feelings, her true feelings…

She shook her head. "No, it would have been crazy for him to have a house or apartment when he was hardly ever home. Andy stayed with his parents whenever he was home on leave—which hadn't been that often since he joined the Marines after high school."

"He wasn't home much?"

After seeing how mean a drunk his father was, she understood why he hadn't come home a lot. "No."

Then she remembered that he hadn't always come home. "He did sometimes stay somewhere else…" She should have thought of it earlier, but it was a place she'd wanted to forget.

That muscle twitched in Blaine's soot-streaked cheek. "Your place?"

"No." As much as she had missed her best friend when he'd gone so long, she hadn't wanted him to stay with her. She hadn't wanted him to think they were more than they were. She should have said no when he asked her to marry him; she should have refused that ring.

"Then where else had he stayed?" Blaine asked.

"The Doremires have a cabin near Lake Michigan— at least, they had it before Andy died," she said. "I'm not sure if they kept it after they divorced. I can call Mrs. Doremire and ask…"

He shook his head. "No. Let me check it out. I don't want anyone tipping off Mark before I can track him down."

"I'm not so sure his mother would call him." Especially since she hadn't seemed to want anything to do with her life before Andy's death.

Janet Doremire was right—that life was too short to waste. The fire had proved that to Maggie. She was lucky that she hadn't lost her baby and Blaine.

"I don't want to take that risk. Where is the cabin?" he asked.

"It's north of where they live," she said. "Close to Pentwater. But I don't know the name of the actual road. I would need to show you where it is."

He shook his head. "I can't take you along with me. I'll be able to find it. I know that area."

"But you sound like you're from out East," she said.

"New Hampshire," he said. "But my sister lives near Pentwater."

"Which sister?"

"Buster."

She wanted to meet all of his sisters, but most of all Buster because he talked about her with the most affection and exasperation.

"It's good you have family within a four-hour drive." Her family was too far away to offer much support. "So maybe you will stay here even after you find these robbers?"

He shrugged. "I can't think about that until I finish up this case."

Probably because he would be moving on to the next case.

"I need to find that cabin," he said.

"It's really remote and hard to find," she warned him. Even if she could talk Blaine into taking her along, she wasn't certain that she would be able to find the cabin again. She had gone there only a couple of times with Andy—one summer during high school and most recently when he had proposed to her. She shouldn't have gone then. She should have known what he was going to ask her.

"It sounds like the perfect place to hide," Blaine murmured. "He has to be there."

Maybe he was. "But just finding Mark won't prove him guilty of the robberies."

"I'm hoping to find more than Mark. I'm hoping to find the guns, the cash. Hell, if it's so remote, it might be their hideout."

And that meant that he might find not just Mark there, but the other robbers—if Mark really was involved.

"You can't go alone," she warned him. "Not if there's any chance that it's their hideout…"

Because they weren't going to want to be found. Blaine hadn't died in the fire, but that didn't mean that he was safe—especially since he kept willingly risking his life.

BLAINE COULDN'T TAKE her along for so many reasons, but he missed Maggie when she wasn't with him. He worried about her. The doctors had assured them that she was fine. They had even released her.

In his opinion, that had been too soon. But then, keeping her in the hospital wouldn't have ensured her safety. Someone had nearly abducted her from an ER. Had nearly burned her up in the home of an FBI agent.

Maggie wasn't safe anywhere.

Hell, he couldn't even trust her safety to a friend like Ash. She'd gotten to him. So he'd left her in the protection of the one person he knew who could not be sweet-talked or manipulated.

Maggie would be safe.

But as his SUV bounced over the ruts of the two-lane road leading to the cabin, he wondered about his own safety. The place wasn't just remote. It was isolated. He had seen nothing but trees for a long while. This was the kind of place where serial killers would bring their victims, so nobody could hear their screams for help.

Blaine shuddered with foreboding. But maybe he was just overreacting, as Maggie kept insisting. Maybe Mark wasn't involved. Maybe he was just taking a time-out from his jealous wife and his drunken father and the loss of his brother...

Maybe the guy really had nothing to do with the robberies, and Dalton Reyes's informant had identified the wrong guy. As Maggie had pointed out, a lot of guys looked like Mark Doremire. Andy had. Hell, even Ash did.

Even though he would have to start all over looking for suspects, Blaine almost hoped Mark had nothing to do with the robberies. If he didn't, Blaine could just check in with him and make sure that everything was all right with the man.

Then he could return to Maggie and ease her worries about her letters to Andy inspiring the robberies. She already took on too much responsibility for everything that had happened. Maybe that was his fault, too—for being so suspicious of her. Maybe he should have told her that he trusted her.

Instead he had pulled away from her. Physically and emotionally. He needed distance. He needed perspective. Hell, maybe if Mark wasn't at the cabin, Blaine would hang out for a while. He would try to regain his lost perspective.

But he worried that time and distance wouldn't change his feelings for Maggie. He would probably always love her. And she would probably always love Andy.

Finally some of the trees gave way on one side of the two-track road, making a small space for a little log cabin. Blaine couldn't see any vehicles. Only a small space of the dense woods had been cleared for the cabin, so he doubted there were any vehicles parked around the back.

Maybe Maggie had been right. Mark wasn't here. Coming here had probably been a waste of Blaine's time. Because no matter how much distance he gained, he was unlikely to gain any new insights.

Still, he shut off the SUV and stepped out of it. He would take some more time to enjoy the silence.

To clear his head.

But the silence shattered as gunfire erupted. And Blaine worried that he was more likely to lose his head than clear it.

Chapter Eighteen

Maggie had wanted to meet Buster, but not like this—not riding along in the Michigan state trooper's police cruiser. At least Buster had let her ride in the passenger's seat and not the back.

The woman had pulled off into a parking lot, and now she studied Maggie through narrowed eyes that were the same bright green as her brother's. She was blonde, too, but most of her hair was tucked up under a brown, broad-brimmed trooper hat, so it wasn't possible to tell if it was golden, like his, or lighter.

She was older than he was but not more than a few years. And she was even less approachable. Maggie, who usually had no problem making conversation, had no idea what to say to the woman, so an awkward silence had fallen between them—broken only by an occasional squawk of the police radio.

Finally Buster cleared her throat and remarked, "Blaine has never asked me to guard anybody for him."

"I'm sorry for being such an inconvenience," Maggie said. "I know you're too busy for babysitting."

"I have four hyper kids and an idiot husband," Buster shared, "so I'm used to babysitting."

The heat of embarrassment rushed to Maggie's face. She hated feeling so helpless and dependent.

But then Buster continued, "*This* isn't babysitting. Nobody is trying to kill my kids or my husband—except for me when they piss me off too much. You're in real danger."

Maggie felt safe, though, with Blaine's older sister. She had an authority about her—the same authority that had Blaine easily taking over the bank investigation and her protection duty.

"Blaine is the one in danger now," Maggie said, as nerves fluttered in her belly with the baby's kicks. "He's trying so hard to track down those robbers."

"That's his job," Buster said. "He's been doing it for a while. And he's been doing it well."

Maybe he was right about Mark, then. Maggie hadn't wanted to believe Andy's brother capable of violence, but she was on edge and it had less to do with how Buster was studying her and more to do with the danger she felt Blaine was facing. "I'm still worried about him."

"I see that…"

With the way she had been staring at Maggie, she had probably seen a lot. More than Maggie was comfortable with her seeing.

Buster continued, "I see that you love him."

Maggie's breath shuddered out in a ragged sigh. She could have lied—although she sucked at it—and said Buster was mistaken. But she wasn't a liar. And maybe it would relieve some of the pressure on her chest—and her heart—if she admitted to her feelings. "Yes…"

"You could have denied it," Buster said.

"Why?"

"Because you haven't told him yet," his sister replied. "And he's the one you should have told first."

Maggie shook her head. "I can't tell him at all." Ever.

"Why not?"

"Because he doesn't have the same feelings for me that I do for him," Maggie said. "And I would just embarrass him." The way she had at the hospital when she'd clung to him, refusing to let him leave without her.

"Blaine doesn't embarrass easily," Buster said. "Trust me. I've tried." She chuckled. "He has three older sisters. He may not get embarrassed at all anymore."

Maggie laughed, too, as she imagined a young Blaine enduring his siblings' teasing and tormenting. He had probably handled it as stoically then as he handled everything now. Her laughter faded. "It may not embarrass him, but it would make it awkward for him. He's only doing his job—"

"He has never asked me to protect anyone for him before," Buster repeated as if that was monumental.

As if it meant something.

Could he return her feelings?

Maggie shook her head. "That's because I'm in a lot of danger," she said. "People have been trying to kidnap and kill me."

"People?"

"He thinks the brother of my…" She didn't know what to call Andy. While she had accepted his proposal, she'd done it only to avoid hurting him, not because she'd ever intended to actually marry him.

"Baby daddy?" Buster supplied the title for her.

Maggie laughed again. But Andy would have been appalled at that title, especially since he'd been trying so long to get her to marry him. He'd wanted to marry right out of high school, but she'd told him she wanted to go to college first. And then when she'd graduated, he had suggested they get married. But she'd put him off, saying that she wanted to get her career established first.

Poor Andy…

Buster reached across the console and squeezed her hand. "You cared about him."

"We were friends since sixth grade, when my family and I moved to town. He was the first person who was nice to the new girl in class." Because he had been nice to her, she had latched on to him, declaring them best friends. But Andy hadn't wanted to be just a friend.

Buster nodded as if Maggie's words had given her sudden understanding. "So he's the only boy you ever dated?"

"Yes," Maggie replied.

"It must have been hard losing him and finding yourself alone," Buster said, "with a baby on the way."

Did Buster think that Maggie was afraid to be alone? That that was why she'd fallen in love with Blaine? Because he'd been nice to her? Maggie knew that he was only doing his job, though. He didn't want more than friendship from her; he probably didn't even want friendship.

"But that's not why I…" she began defensively, "…why I have feelings for your brother." She couldn't say it—couldn't express those feelings.

"That's not why you've fallen for my brother," Buster said, as if she didn't doubt her.

"He might not believe that, though," Maggie said. "Or he might think I'm just grateful for all the times he has saved my life and the baby's."

"May I?" Buster asked, as she moved her hand from Maggie's arm to her stomach. She smiled as the baby kicked beneath her palm. "You should tell Blaine how you feel about him. That's the only way you're going to know what he thinks and how he feels about you."

Was it possible that he could return her feelings? He had made love with her. He'd wanted her…

"My brother has never been an easy man to read," Buster said. "Hell, he wasn't even easy to read when he was a little boy. It's always been hard to tell what Blaine is thinking or feeling. So don't assume that you know."

Maggie had been making assumptions. But it wasn't based so much on what she thought of Blaine but more on what she thought of herself. She didn't believe that she, especially pregnant, could ever attract a man like Blaine Campbell. The gorgeous FBI special agent was more of a superhero than a regular man. "But—"

"Do you want any more regrets?" Buster interrupted. "It seems like you already have a few."

About Andy. About never telling him the truth…

"I don't regret my baby," Maggie said, anger rushing over her.

"I know," Buster said. "And I am a firm believer in everything happening for a reason. So stop beating yourself up about the baby's daddy."

Apparently Maggie wasn't very hard to read at all.

Buster patted Maggie's belly. "Remember—everything happens for a reason."

Because she carried his child, Maggie would always have a piece of Andy with her. She hadn't completely lost her best friend.

"You're right," Maggie agreed.

But she didn't have a chance to tell Buster exactly what she was right about because the police radio squawked again—interrupting them. "Shots fired during FBI raid on cabin. Possible casualties…"

She grabbed Buster's hand and clutched it. Possible casualties? Was one of them Blaine? Had he been shot?

"WE DIDN'T FIND the shooters," Trooper Littlefield reported to Blaine. He was one of Buster's coworkers.

He had provided backup—along with a couple of FBI agents—in case the cabin had been the robbers' hideout. But they had arrived early and hidden in the woods so that it would look as though Blaine had come alone.

Blaine had even felt alone in the middle of the woods. These law-enforcement officers were so good that he hadn't seen a single one of them—until the gunfire had erupted. Then they'd stepped out of their hiding spots and returned fire—giving him cover so that none of the shots had actually struck him.

"They had a vehicle parked on a two-track gravel road that led to another cabin, and before we could block them in, they'd gotten away," the trooper said regretfully.

Blaine sighed. They had eluded him so many times that he wasn't surprised. "In a van?"

The trooper nodded.

Dalton Reyes stepped up to him. "Another stolen one," he confirmed with a curse. "The guy who ordered this one isn't the one that my informant ID'd, though. She claims she hasn't seen him again."

Blaine had a bad feeling that Mark Doremire was already gone. But still he held out hope. "You sure you can trust your informant?" he asked. Mark was a flirt; maybe he'd turned the woman to his side.

"I don't really trust anyone." Reyes shrugged. "Maybe she's been lying to me."

"Do you think any of the guys you're after could be involved in the robberies?" Blaine asked. "There were five guys at the bank." But more could have been involved.

He had no idea how many had been shooting at him in the woods.

Dalton shrugged again. "I'm not sure. I didn't get a look at any of the shooters."

"And the guy inside the cabin?" Blaine asked, as he

walked back into the run-down log structure. He'd already been inside but Agent Reyes hadn't. He hoped Dalton recognized the corpse because Blaine was afraid that he did.

Dalton checked out the scene and cursed. The guy was slumped over in a wooden chair, a pool of blood dried beneath him. His clothes—a camo shirt and pants—were also saturated and hard with dried blood. Bloody bandages were strewn across the table in front of him.

But those weren't the only things on the table. A pile of envelopes, bound with a big rubber band, sat atop the scarred wooden surface, too.

Maggie's letters…written to her fiancé. Blaine hadn't looked at them; he probably wouldn't be able to look at them. But he knew they were hers.

"What the hell happened to him?" Dalton asked.

"I think I killed him."

Dalton snorted. "This guy has been dead for days. You didn't do this."

"I think I did. During the bank robbery," he said. "That first van that was recovered had blood inside, and I did get off some shots during the robbery."

Ash stepped into the cabin behind Dalton. "Is he the one?"

Blaine nodded. "Yeah, I'm pretty sure this is the guy who shot Sarge."

Ash patted his shoulder. "You got him!"

"I wasn't sure I hit him. They were wearing vests…"

This guy's vest was lying on the floor near his chair along with the zombie mask and the trench coat. He had definitely been one of the robbers. Was he the one who'd killed Sarge?

When Blaine had fired back, he'd thought that he shot the one who'd hit Sarge.

"He must not have had his vest tight on the sides," Dalton said as he leaned over to inspect it. "Looks like it was too small for him—probably left a gap."

So Blaine had gotten a lucky shot into the guy's side. "There was a smaller robber—maybe their vests got mixed up…"

"I don't care what happened," Ash said. "I just care that you got him—for Sarge."

But who was he? Blaine stepped closer to the body, intent on tipping back the guy's head to get a better look. But then a glint of metal caught his eye, and he saw the dog tags dangling from the chain around the corpse's neck.

He picked up the tags and read, "'Sergeant Andrew Doremire…'"

"Who the hell is that?" Ash asked.

"A dead man," Blaine replied. He tipped up the face— he looked like the man on the security footage from the bank. Maggie had said that Andy and Mark looked eerily similar.

Dalton snorted. "Obviously…"

"No, he's Maggie's dead fiancé."

Dalton Reyes cursed. "Do you think she knows he didn't really die in Afghanistan?" Of course he would ask that; he'd already said he didn't trust anyone.

"No way," Blaine said with absolute certainty. Maggie carried too much guilt over his death, probably because she hadn't been able to talk him out of joining the Marines. But she hadn't been to blame for Andy's death.

Blaine was.

Apparently Dustin Doremire hadn't just been a delusional drunk. He'd been right. Andy wasn't dead—or, at least, he hadn't been until Blaine had shot him.

"He was one of Sarge's drills," Ash said. "He must

have been worried that Sarge had recognized him. That's why he killed him."

Or because Sarge had been trying to kill *him*...

Blaine pushed a hand through his hair. "That must have been why they were trying to take Maggie along with them—they probably thought she recognized him, too."

But she hadn't. She had refused to accept that even the brother of her childhood sweetheart could have had anything to do with criminal activities. She would never believe that Andy had.

So who were the other robbers? Definitely Andy's brother—unless the informant had mistaken Mark's picture for his younger brother. But if his brother hadn't been involved, where the hell was he?

Maybe even Andy's father was involved. That could have been why he'd been drinking so heavily when they'd gone to see him—because he'd known that Andy wasn't going to survive this time.

Blaine had killed him. Would Maggie be able to forgive him? Would she be able to forgive herself?

Chapter Nineteen

He was alive!

Blaine was alive.

Her heart leaped for joy the moment she saw him walk through the door of his sister's sprawling ranch house. When he'd asked Buster to protect her, he hadn't wanted her to take Maggie to her home—he hadn't wanted her to put her family at risk. Neither had Maggie.

But when they had been waiting to hear about Blaine, Buster had insisted on bringing Maggie home with her. In case the news was bad, Buster had probably wanted to be close to her family.

Her kids had gathered around them. She had three boys and one little girl—the opposite of Buster and her siblings. The boys had lost interest in Maggie quickly and gone back to playing with trucks in the living room while Maggie and Buster waited in the big country kitchen. Although shy, the little blonde girl had crept close to Maggie and pressed pudgy little fingers against her belly.

"Baby?" she had asked, though she was little more than a baby herself.

"Yes," Maggie had replied. And she had even managed a laugh when the baby kicked and the little girl had jumped away in surprise.

But fear for Blaine's safety had pressed heavily on

Maggie until he walked through the door. His bruises and scrapes were from the night before—from the fire. Otherwise he was unscathed from the shooting. Maggie had never been happier to see anyone in her life.

But she didn't dare launch herself into his arms the way she wanted to. He had that wall around him—that wall he'd put up back at the hospital. Something was wrong. Maybe it was just that he'd realized he had lost perspective with her, and he was trying to be more professional.

Buster pulled Blaine into a tight hug. "Thank God, you're all right. We were going crazy worrying about you."

"Why?"

"We heard the call on the radio," Buster said, "about the shooting and a possible casualty."

The little girl tugged on her mama's leg. "What's a castle tea?"

Buster pulled back from her brother and picked up her daughter. "It's nothing…"

But it wasn't. Maggie saw the look of regret on Blaine's face. Then he leaned forward and kissed his niece's cheek. "Hey, beautiful girl…"

"Hey, Unca Bane…"

Buster chuckled.

The boys abandoned their trucks and rushed into the kitchen, launching themselves at Blaine the way Maggie wished she had. She wanted his arms around her like they were around his nephews and niece.

"They're so many of you," he murmured. "You have your own Brady Bunch, Buster."

"There are only four—five counting Carl," she said. "But he had to go to work."

"Is that why you came home?"

She bit her lip and shook her head.

"It's because of what you heard on the radio?" He glanced at his niece. "About the castle tea?"

Buster nodded.

"I'm fine," he said. "I had no idea you would have heard…" He stopped himself. "That's right—there was a trooper along for backup."

"Since you're fine, us troopers must be good for something, huh, Mr. Special Agent?" Her green eyes twinkled as she teased him.

He shrugged. "I had a couple other special agents along," he said. "That's why I'm fine."

She gently punched his shoulder. Then she turned to where Maggie sat on the kitchen chair, watching them and wishing she was part of their loving family. Buster must have seen that longing because she reached out for Maggie's hand and tugged her up from the chair. Buster sighed and remarked, "You are so beautiful pregnant. If I'd looked like you, instead of a beached whale, I might have had a couple more."

"God help us," Blaine muttered.

He already had as far as Maggie was concerned, since he'd brought Blaine safely back to his family. And her…

But he wasn't hers. He had yet to even look at her. Maybe he was mad that she was at his sister's home—endangering his sister's beautiful family.

"I'm sorry," she said. "I know you didn't want me here. We can leave now."

Buster stared at her with wide eyes, urging her to tell Blaine her feelings. But Maggie shook her head. It was obvious to her that he didn't want her love. Why couldn't his sister see the emotional distance he'd put between himself and Maggie?

"We'll leave in a little while," he said, finally speaking

directly to her. But still, he wouldn't look at her. Instead he turned back to Buster. "Can we have a few minutes alone? Maybe in the sunroom?"

Buster nodded. "Of course."

He took Maggie's arm and drew her from the kitchen through a set of French doors off the family room. He pulled the doors closed behind him, shutting them alone in a solarium of windows. But the sun had already dropped, so the room was growing dark and cold.

Maggie shivered.

"If you're cold—"

"No, I'm fine," she said. "Why do you want to talk to me privately?" Did he want to yell at her for endangering his family? "I told Buster it was a bad idea to bring me back here."

"Buster rarely listens to anyone but herself," he replied. "Poor Carl…"

She suspected that Carl was a very lucky man, and that he was smart enough to know it. No matter how much she joked about her husband, it was obvious that Buster loved him very much.

The way Maggie loved Blaine…

"Why did you want me alone?" she asked again. She tamped down the hope that threatened to burgeon—the hope that he wanted to tell her his feelings.

But that hope deflated when he finally replied, "I have to show you something."

Instinctively she knew it wasn't something she would want to see. He didn't even *want* to show it to her. He *had* to…and even without his choice of words, she would have picked up on his reluctance from the gruffness of his voice.

"Did you find the letters?" she asked. If they'd been at the cabin and if it had been used as a hideout, then the robberies were her fault. She shouldn't have talked so much about the bank. Her mother was right; she had always talked too much. Even though she hadn't given out security passwords or anything, she'd talked too much about her duties as the assistant manager. And it wasn't as if Andy had actually been interested; she'd just rambled.

"Yes, I found your letters," he replied. But he didn't hold them out for her to look at; he held out a photograph instead.

She didn't look at it. First she had to know, "What's this?"

"You tell me," he said as he lifted it toward her face. "Is it Andy?"

Her heart leaped again. Was it possible that Andy was alive? But then she looked at the picture. The man in it wasn't alive. And he wasn't Andy, either.

"Why would you think that was Andy?" She'd thought he had realized that Mr. Doremire had been drunk and delusional when he'd made those wild claims about Andy faking his death and the Marines covering it up.

"He had on Andy's dog tags."

The dog tags that his father claimed had never been found. No wonder Blaine had thought it was Andy. She shook her head.

"He must have been mistaken," she said. And with as much as he drank, it would be understandable.

"The dog tags must have been in his personal effects along with the letters," she explained. "His brother must have taken them when he took the letters."

"Now you think Mark took the dog tags?" he asked.

She pointed at the photo. "That's Mark, so he must have, since he was wearing them when he died."

"You're sure that's Mark?"

"I'm sure," she said. "I'm surprised you didn't recognize him from the security footage." But he did look different dead. He didn't look like the smiling man on the television monitor.

Blaine released a ragged breath as if he had been holding it for a while, maybe since he'd found the body and had thought it was Andy. "I think he's the robber I shot at the bank."

Shock and regret had her gasping. She remembered that horrific moment—remembered Blaine firing back at the man who'd shot the security guard. "You think he's the one who killed Sarge?"

Mark had been like her big brother, too. He had always seemed as sweet and easygoing as Andy had been, and he had adored his younger brother. How could he have killed a man that Andy had loved? A man she had loved, as well?

Sarge had been so kind and supportive after Andy's death. He had kept checking on her. Maybe he had made a promise to Andy. Mark must not have. Or, if he had, it was a promise he'd broken.

Blaine nodded. "He was wearing a vest that was too small for him. I got a shot into his side. He bled out from the wound."

"Nobody got him help?" she asked, horrified that his coconspirators would have just let him bleed to death.

Blaine shook his head. "No. They got him to the cabin, but they couldn't stop the bleeding."

"He wasn't the one who tried grabbing me at the hospital, then," she said. "That man was healthy and strong." It gave her some relief that Mark hadn't been trying to hurt her. "He couldn't have been behind any of those other attempts on our lives."

"No," Blaine agreed. "It must've been whoever he was working with."

There had been five of them. So four other men were still out there, apparently still determined to kill her and Special Agent Blaine Campbell.

BLAINE HUSTLED HER quickly out of his sister's house. It was less for his family's safety and more for hers. He wanted to protect her. He also wanted to comfort her because he had seen the fear on her face when she'd realized that she was still in danger.

"We'll be safe here," he said, as he locked the motel room door behind them. He could have driven her back to Chicago. But night had already fallen, and she was obviously exhausted. She trembled with it and maybe with cold. He turned up the thermostat as she shivered.

"I thought you weren't going to protect me anymore," she said. "Didn't your boss tell you that you shouldn't?"

He nodded. "And he's right."

"You said that last night…"

Before he had made love to her. What the hell had he been thinking to take advantage of her that way?

"I'm sorry," he said. "About last night…"

"You didn't start the fire," she said.

"But I should have been awake. I should have been alert," he said. "My boss was right. You will be safer with someone else protecting you."

"I feel safe with you," she said, and she turned back to him and stared up at him with those chocolaty brown eyes.

There was such an overall glow about her. Maybe it was the pregnancy. But he suspected it was just her— just Maggie's warm personality. She had even won over Buster and that was never easy to do.

"Maggie, I have to focus on the case," he said. He hoped she would understand that he couldn't let her distract him any longer. "I have to dig deeper into Mark's life and find all of his associates."

"I can help you," she said.

"You know his friends?"

She shook her head. "He was older than me and Andy, so I don't know who he hung out with." She nibbled her lower lip. "I guess I can't help you."

"You need to focus on yourself and your baby," he said. "Stay healthy. Stay well."

She touched her belly with trembling hands. "Yes…"

"I will find them all," Blaine promised. "I'll stop them." He just hoped he could stop them before they tried to kill her again. They obviously cared little for human life since they had let one of their own die instead of getting him help. To save themselves…

So, even dead, Mark could lead him to the others. That must have been the reason they hadn't sought out medical attention or wanted his body found.

"Thank you," she said.

"I haven't done anything yet," he said.

"You've saved my life," she reminded him. "Many times. Thank you for that."

He shrugged off her gratitude. "I was just doing my job." But it was so much more than that, and they both knew it.

"And thank you for last night," she said, "for making me feel desirable. Wanted…"

He wanted her again. But he kept his hands at his sides. He wouldn't reach for her again.

But she reached for him. Sliding her arms around him, she pressed her voluptuous body close to his. And the tenuous hold he'd had on his control snapped. He couldn't resist her sweetness, her passion.

She rose up on tiptoe and pressed her lips to his, sliding them across his mouth—arousing his desire. He kissed her back.

She eased away from him but only to ease her hands between them and undo the buttons of his shirt. He helped her take off his holster. And his jeans…

She gasped, as she so often did, as she stared at his nakedness. "You are the most beautiful man."

Maggie's words filled him with heat and pride.

She touched him, her fingers caressing his skin. "You were hurt last night."

He had some scrapes, a couple of first-degree burns. "It's nothing."

She shuddered. "When that roof caved in, I thought you were gone. And then when we heard that radio call…"

"About the castle tea?" he teased.

But she didn't laugh. In fact, her eyes glistened with tears. "I was so scared."

He drew her against him and held her close. "I hate that you were scared."

But he was scared, too. He was scared that he'd irrevocably fallen for her.

"Make me forget my fears," she challenged him. "Make me forget about everything but you. Make love to me…"

He couldn't refuse her wishes. He helped her off with her clothes and then helped her into bed. Joining her, he kissed and stroked every inch of her silky skin. And with every kiss and every caress, she gasped or moaned and squirmed beneath him. Then she caressed him back, running her soft hands over his back and his hips and lower. She encircled him with those hands. He nearly lost his mind, but he fought for control. He wanted to give her pleasure.

So he made love to her with his mouth. She cried out. But this was a cry he loved to hear from her—a cry of pleasure as she found release. Then, carefully, he joined their bodies. He tried to move slowly and gently.

But she arched and thrust up her hips. And her inner muscles clenched around him, tugging him deeper inside until he didn't know where she ended and he began. They were one. And as one, they reached ecstasy—shouting each other's name.

He held her close as they both panted for breath. He held her and waited—for the next attempt on their lives. He didn't know if it would be another fire or more shooting. He didn't know what it would be; he just knew that it would happen. As if on some level he had known that he would fall for Maggie Jenkins.

She had taken his heart. Now he just had to hold on to his life…

Chapter Twenty

Maybe it had been only days. But it felt like weeks since Maggie had last seen Blaine. She knew he was busy working the case. He had explained that he had to hand off her protection to someone else so that he could focus.

Had she distracted him?

She was working again, too. But she was preoccupied by thoughts of Blaine. It wouldn't matter how long she went without seeing him; she knew she would never *not* think of Special Agent Blaine Campbell.

A noise at her office door startled her, and she jumped.

"Sorry," the bank manager said. "I didn't mean to frighten you."

"It's not your fault," she assured him. Even though no attempts had been made to kidnap or kill her the past few days, she was still on edge. Still waiting for the robbers in their hideous masks to burst through the bank doors or into her apartment with their guns drawn.

"Has everything been all right?" he asked.

She nodded instead of uttering a lie. Because everything was not all right—not without Blaine. She ached for him.

"Things are back to normal now," Mr. Hardy said with a sigh of relief as he gazed around at the bank. The glass had all been repaired. Everything was back in its place as if the robbery had never happened. "And with one of the robbers found dead, maybe the others have gone into hiding."

"Agent Campbell will catch them," she said with unshakable confidence.

"Hopefully," he said, but he sounded doubtful. "I understand that the robber that was found dead was related to you."

"No," she said.

"Well," he said again, his voice rising with a slight whine, "he would've been had your fiancé not died."

She wouldn't have married Andy, though—even after finding out she carried his child. She hadn't wanted friendship love in her marriage; she'd wanted passionate love. She had wanted to be in love, not just to love someone. She had finally found that with Blaine, but he didn't want the instant family he would have with her. He probably didn't even want a relationship. He was totally focused on his career—so much so that she hadn't even heard from him.

Mr. Hardy was looking at her strangely. Then Maggie recognized the suspicion. "I was not involved in the robberies," she said. "I had nothing to do with them."

Except for those damn letters she'd written. Did he know about those, too?

He nodded. "Of course you didn't…"

But she heard the doubt in his voice. "I need this job, Mr. Hardy. I wouldn't have done anything to jeopardize it."

"Susan Iverson thinks you may have been involved with that man."

"Susan may have been," Maggie said. "But I wasn't. He's just someone I used to know." And apparently she hadn't known him nearly as well as she'd thought she had. "Like Susan, he proved to be someone I couldn't trust."

"She claims that the agent totally misread the situation when he found her in your apartment—"

"Stealing my engagement ring," she said.

"She assured me she wasn't stealing it," he defended the blonde bank teller. "That she was only looking for evidence that you were involved in the robberies."

Maggie shook her head. She'd had enough of people lying and scamming her. "She used my credit cards," she said. "She can't explain that away."

"You owed her rent money."

Anger surged through her, and she stood up. "That's a lie. And if you choose to believe her lies over me, maybe I don't need this job as much as I thought."

He held out his hands. "Calm down, Maggie. I know this is an emotional time for you. Susan needs her job, too, and if you drop the charges against her, I think you could work together again."

Blaine had caught the woman in the act of stealing. It wasn't up to Maggie whether or not charges were pressed. But she didn't bother explaining that.

"Why are you defending her?" she wondered. And then, as color flooded his face, she realized why. He was involved with the young teller. "Oh…"

"I don't know what you're thinking," he said fearfully, as if he actually did know, "but you're wrong."

"No, *you're* wrong." Especially if he had betrayed his wife with the blonde opportunist. "There actually is evidence against her, and she will be prosecuted. I couldn't drop the charges even if I wanted to."

Maybe Susan had been involved in the robberies, too. Maggie wouldn't put anything past the woman. She was a user. Mr. Hardy would figure that out soon enough.

Disgusted with him, she grabbed her purse and said, "I'm going home."

"Yes, get some rest and think about it," he suggested.

Maybe Maggie needed to return to the branch where she had previously worked. She couldn't work for Mr. Hardy anymore. She couldn't work with Susan Iverson. Maybe she needed to join her parents in Hong Kong. It wasn't as if Blaine would miss her. He had gone days with no contact.

As she headed out the door, her new protector followed her. The burly young man, Truman Jackson, was something with the Bureau—maybe a new recruit. Since there had been no recent attempts to grab her, she doubted they would have wasted a special agent on babysitting duty. She had been lucky to have Blaine as long as she had.

"Are you all right, Miss Jenkins?" the young man asked as he helped her into his unmarked vehicle.

"Maggie," she corrected him as she had the past few days. "And I'm fine."

"But you're leaving early…"

She hadn't done that the past couple of days. In fact, she had worked late, trying to catch up from the time the bank had been closed for repairs.

"I'm tired," she said. And that was no lie. She was exhausted. From looking over her shoulder. From worrying.

From missing Blaine.

"So you want to go right back to your apartment?" Truman asked.

"Yes, please," she said, and happy that he was driving, she closed her eyes and relaxed as much as she could.

"Do you think I'll need protection much longer?" she asked. If no more attempts were made on her life…

"I couldn't say, Maggie."

"Do you know if Special Agent Campbell has gotten any closer to apprehending the other bank robbers?" She wanted to know what was going on with the case, but most of all she wanted to know what was going on with Blaine.

Was he okay? Had he recovered completely from the fire? Had anyone tried to kill him again?

Truman shrugged his broad shoulders; one of them nudged hers. "I don't know," he replied. "Do you have his number? Could you call and ask?"

No. She hadn't been given his number. He had barely looked at her as he'd passed off her protection to someone else.

"I don't want to bother him," she said. And that was true. She didn't want to distract him anymore. He had a job to do, and she had only been part of that job to him.

Truman had lost interest in their conversation, his attention on her apartment door as he pulled into the parking lot. He reached for his holster. "Who is that?"

A woman stood outside the door. She wore dark glasses that obscured most of her face, but Maggie recognized the bright glow of her red hair.

"It's my..." almost sister-in-law? "...friend." But Tammy had never really been her friend—not even when they were younger. Like Maggie and Andy, Tammy and Mark had dated all during high school. Tammy had actually been there when Mark had sneaked her and Andy into that horror movie. She had thought Maggie's fear funny—as Mark had. And recently Tammy had been suspicious and resentful of Maggie. She had even suspected her of cheating with Mark.

Was that why she'd come here? To lash out some more in her grief? Maggie wasn't certain how much more she could take today.

BLAINE GRABBED AT his tie, struggling to loosen the knot. He felt suffocated within the walls of his new office, and he felt buried beneath the files atop his new desk. He would rather be out in the field, physically tracking down solid leads instead of fumbling through piles of paper.

He would actually rather be with Maggie, making certain that she was safe. There had been no new attempts on her life. But he was not a fool enough to think that it was over, not with so many of Mark's associates out there yet. Blaine was only a fool for Maggie—for falling for her.

As he'd had to so many times over the past few days, he pushed thoughts of Maggie from his mind and focused on the case again. He grabbed a file from the stack and read over the names of Mark Doremire's friends and family. Was old man Doremire one of the robbers?

Hell, was Andy? Maybe the guy wasn't really dead.

Blaine shook his head. He was losing it. Andy was gone. But another name on his list looked familiar. He shuffled through the other folders for the report from the security chief at the hospital, and he pulled out her list of employees. One of the names matched.

Mark Doremire's brother-in-law worked security at the hospital. Hadn't Tammy Doremire told him she had no friends or family in the area? Why had she lied to Blaine?

Had she been trying to protect her brother since she must already have known that she'd lost her husband? If her brother had been in on the thefts, she would have known that Mark had been hurt.

Maybe she had even been along for the robberies. Blaine touched his tablet and played some of the security footage from the holdup. There had been a robber who was smaller than the others. It was the one who'd dragged Maggie to the back door of the bank, the one who'd pulled her into the van.

Tammy Doremire wasn't just related to a couple of the robbers. She was one of them.

He just had to find the other two. They might be associates of her brother's. Or…

His phone rang, drawing his attention from all those files. He clicked the talk button. "Campbell."

"Special Agent Campbell?"

"Yes."

"This is Truman Jackson," a male voice said.

"You're the guard on Maggie." Blaine's heart slammed against his ribs as fear overwhelmed him. Before letting Truman protect her again, he had made certain that the man had not been compromised—that he could be trusted. Ash Stryker had vouched for him, so Truman had been chosen as her new protector. Had he failed his duty?

"Is she okay?" Blaine anxiously asked. "Has there been another attempt on her life?"

"No, no," the man quickly assured Blaine. But there was concern in his voice.

That concern had Blaine grabbing his keys and rushing out of his office. But even outside the confining walls, he couldn't breathe. Now panic and concern suffocated him.

"What's going on?" he asked. What had compelled the man to call him?

"I brought Maggie home from the bank," Truman relayed, "and there was a woman waiting at her apartment door."

At least she had been at the door and hadn't let herself inside the way Susan Iverson had. But maybe Susan had learned her lesson about doing that.

"Who was she?" Blaine asked.

"Maggie," he said, "told me that the woman was a friend but…"

"But what?"

"I don't know," the man replied. "But I didn't pick up the friendship vibe from her. Maggie insisted on speaking alone with the woman, though, so I left them together in Maggie's apartment."

Blaine clicked the lock on his SUV and jumped behind the wheel. "Did you check the woman for a weapon before you left them alone?"

"Of course," the man replied, as if offended. "She wasn't armed. And she's too thin to do any physical harm to Maggie."

That didn't ease Blaine's fears any. "Who is she?"

"A red-haired woman," Truman replied. "I checked her license."

Blaine didn't even need her name for confirmation. He knew who was with Maggie.

"Tammy Doremire…"

The robber from the bank—the one who had tried bringing Maggie along. Probably the only one who really wanted her dead…

Chapter Twenty-One

Maggie handed Tammy a cup of tea. Brewing it had bought her some time to gather her thoughts since she had no idea what to say to the new widow.

But Tammy must not have wanted the tea because she set the cup on the coffee table in front of her. Maggie kept hers in her hands, hoping the heat of the mug would warm her. But she still shivered—maybe more with nerves than cold.

"You still have a bodyguard," the other woman said.

It hadn't been a question, but Maggie nodded in reply. Truman had searched Tammy to make sure she carried no weapon, so of course she would have realized he was a bodyguard.

"But there haven't been any attempts lately," Tammy said. "It seems like the FBI wouldn't want to waste manpower."

"I don't know," Maggie replied. She had no idea why Tammy cared about the bodyguard or the FBI, let alone how she would have known about the attempts on Maggie's life.

Unless…

No, she refused to suspect the worst of everyone; she refused to be as cynical as Blaine had been. But Blaine had been right about Mark…

"Having protection for you is probably Agent Campbell's idea," the woman continued, her voice sharp with bitterness as she said his name. "I'm surprised that he's not still personally protecting you."

"He's busy," Maggie said. At least that was what she was telling herself to salve her wounded heart.

Tammy sighed. "It doesn't matter."

But it did matter to Maggie that she hadn't heard from Blaine—that she didn't know exactly what he was doing. Or feeling.

Since the mug was beginning to cool, Maggie set it beside Tammy's on the coffee table. But she didn't join her on the couch or settle onto one of the chairs across from her. Maggie didn't feel comfortable enough with this woman to sit down with her.

But she should have gone to see her earlier out of respect. "I'm glad you came over," Maggie said.

"You are?" Tammy asked skeptically.

"Of course. I've been wanting to talk to you, wanting to tell you how sorry I am about Mark." Of course she hadn't known how to express sympathy for a man dying in the commission of a crime—of a murder. If only Mark hadn't been involved in the robberies...

Both he and Sarge would be alive. How could Maggie express sympathy for that?

The woman ignored her remarks and pointed out a box that sat on the end of the coffee table. Wrapping paper with little rubber ducks covered the box, and a bright yellow bow topped it. "What's that?"

"I don't know," Maggie said. She hadn't noticed it earlier. Tammy hadn't had it with her when Truman had searched her body and her purse. He would have found the brightly wrapped package. "It wasn't here this morning."

"Maybe it was delivered today," Tammy suggested.

Maggie shook her head. "Then it would have been left outside the door." Not on her coffee table.

"Maybe your elderly janitor brought it inside for you."

Maggie's skin chilled as she realized that Tammy wasn't offering a possible explanation but a fact. She knew because she had given it to Mr. Simmons to bring inside for her. Why?

"This is yours?" Maggie asked. "You brought this for me?" Despite what she'd told Truman, they weren't friends. Why would the woman have brought her a baby gift?

"Yes," Tammy replied. "But let me open it for you." She tore the ribbon and easily slipped the top off the box. Then she smiled and lifted a gun out. "Now tell me how sorry you are about Mark."

Fear slammed into Maggie as she stared down the barrel of that gun. She covered her belly with her palms—even though she knew there was no way to protect her baby from a bullet. "What are you doing?"

"I'm going to do what we should have done at the first bank so you wouldn't have time to figure out it was us and report us to the FBI," Tammy said. "I'm going to kill you."

"But the guard is just outside the door," Maggie reminded her. "Truman is going to hear the shot. You won't get away with this. He might even shoot you."

"You think I have anything to live for?" Tammy asked, her face contorting into a mask of pain and hatred nearly as grotesque as those zombie masks. Tammy must have chosen them; she had found it funniest that Maggie had been so afraid during that movie. "Mark's dead because of you."

"I didn't shoot him," Maggie said.

"No, your FBI agent shot him," Tammy said. "I had

hoped that he was the one protecting you. That he would be here, so that I could kill you both."

"You've got your wish," a deep voice murmured as the apartment door opened with a slight creak of the hinges. "I'm here."

Maggie had spent the past few days missing Blaine and longing to see his handsome face again. But not now. She would rather have never seen him again than to have him die with her.

BLAINE HAD EXPECTED the gun because he'd met Mr. Simmons at the door. The older gentleman had wanted to make certain that Maggie got the baby gift that he'd put in her apartment for the red-haired woman. He'd thought the box was heavy for a baby-shower gift.

Of course it held no gift for Maggie or her baby. It had held the gun.

Tammy was clever—so clever that she had probably been the one who had actually plotted the bank robberies. She had probably been the one who'd read Maggie's letters.

"This is perfect," the widow said with a smile of delight as she stood up with the gun clutched in her hands. At least the barrel was pointed at him instead of Maggie, who stood trembling on the other side of the coffee table from the deranged woman.

"This is stupid," Blaine corrected her. "There's nothing specifically linking you to the robberies. No evidence that you were aware of the crimes your husband and your brother were committing. You could have gotten away with it all."

Her smile vanished off her thin lips. "My brother?"

The woman obviously didn't care about herself right now—not when she planned to shoot two people with another federal agent posted right outside the door. But maybe she cared about her sibling.

"He was the one who tried abducting Maggie from Emergency," Blaine said. "He's a security guard at the hospital."

Tammy shook her head in denial. "The fact that he works there doesn't prove anything."

"His security badge will prove he was the one who opened the back door of the employees' locker room when he tried to kidnap Maggie." At least Blaine hoped it would. He needed evidence—not just suspicion—linking the man to the crimes.

"No…" But the conviction was gone from Tammy Doremire's voice as it began to quaver. "You can't tie him to the robberies…"

Maybe he wouldn't be able to, but he wasn't going to let her think that. "I have a team working on it right now. They're getting search warrants. They're digging into all of his financials. They're checking all his properties for any evidence linking him to the robberies. I'm pretty sure they'll find something. Aren't you?"

Her thin face tightened with dread and hatred. She knew that her brother wouldn't have gotten rid of all the evidence—or at least not the money. He could see she was torn, tempted to call and warn her brother about the warrants.

So he stepped closer, prepared to grab her weapon from her hands. Her eyes widened with alarm as she noticed that he'd closed some distance between them.

"Get back!" she yelled. "I'm going to kill her. You're not going to stop me this time."

"Why do you want her dead?" he asked. "If you hadn't sent your brother to the hospital after her, I wouldn't have linked him to the crimes." He was sure that her brother had acted on her orders; all the men probably had.

"It's all her fault!" Tammy yelled, as if she thought that saying it loud enough would make it true. "If she hadn't written those damn letters to Andy…"

A noise emanated from Maggie, but she'd muffled it with a hand over her mouth. She had already held herself responsible for the robberies; she didn't need this crazed woman compounding her guilt.

But making her feel guilty wasn't enough torment for Tammy Doremire. She intended to kill her, too.

"Who read them?" Blaine asked, stalling for time—hoping to distract the woman enough for Maggie to escape. He had left the apartment door open. Maybe Truman could get off a shot.

"I—I did," Tammy admitted.

As he'd suspected, she was the mastermind behind the robberies. He acted shocked, though, as he edged closer to her and that damn gun she gripped so tightly. "You read her personal correspondence to her fiancé?"

She snorted. "Personal? There hadn't been anything very personal about them. They were not *love* letters—not like I would have written to Mark—" her voice cracked with emotion, with loss "—if he'd been in a war zone."

She had loved her husband. The grief and pain contorted her face.

"Why didn't you take Mark to a hospital when he was hurt?" he asked. "Why did you drive him instead to that cabin in Michigan?"

"He—he wanted to go there," she said. "He knew he was dying—because of you. Because you shot him!" She pointed the gun at Blaine's chest.

And he was glad; it wasn't anywhere near Maggie

now. Maybe she could escape. Instead, she gasped in fear for him.

And her gasp drew Tammy's rage back to her. She whirled the gun in Maggie's direction. "But we wouldn't have been there if it wasn't for her. Mark just couldn't stay away from poor, sweet Maggie. She caused his death— just like she caused Andy's."

"That's bull." Blaine called her on her craziness. "I killed Mark—not Maggie. I pulled the trigger. Not Maggie."

She swung the gun back to him, and her eyes were wild with rage and grief. "It was your fault!"

"I shot him, but the vest should have protected him," Blaine said. "But he wasn't wearing *his* vest. He was wearing *yours*."

Tears began to streak down the woman's face as her own guilt overwhelmed her. She knew why her husband had died. But she couldn't accept her own part in his death. It was easier for her to blame him and Maggie.

She sniffled back her tears. And as she tried to clear her vision, he edged closer yet. "No…" she cried in protest of her guilt more than his nearness. "He shouldn't have died…"

He was counting on her not noticing how close he was to her. But she wasn't looking at him anymore; she had swung the gun back toward Maggie.

"Mark killed an innocent man," Maggie said in defense of Blaine shooting him. Of course she would defend him as she did everyone. "Why? Why would you two resort to stealing and killing?"

"Mark and I needed that money," Tammy said, desperately trying to justify their crimes. "We needed it to start our family."

"Hundreds of thousands of dollars?" Blaine scoffed.

He wanted to irritate her, wanted her to shoot at him instead of Maggie. He wore a vest. Maggie was completely unprotected.

"I—I couldn't get pregnant. I need—needed—fertility treatments. Or in vitro. All that's so expensive, and Mark lost his job." Now she wasn't just pointing the gun at Maggie but at her belly, and jealousy twisted the woman's face into a mask nearly as grotesque as the zombie one. "But this one—she easily gets pregnant."

Maggie held her hands over her belly, trying to protect her unborn baby. But her hands would prove no protection from a bullet.

"You don't want to hurt the baby," Blaine said, as horror gripped him. Maggie's baby was a part of her, and because he loved Maggie, he loved her baby, too. He couldn't lose either of them.

"She doesn't deserve that baby," Tammy said. "She never wanted it. She never wanted Andy. She didn't love him like I loved Mark. It's not fair."

"Life's not fair," Blaine commiserated.

But the woman didn't hear or see him anymore. It didn't matter that he was the one who'd fired the shot that had killed Mark. She hated Maggie more—she hated that the woman had what Tammy had wanted most. A baby…

And she intended to take that baby from Maggie before she took her life. He had to protect them. So Blaine did two things—he kicked the coffee table into the woman's legs and he grabbed for the gun.

But it went off. And a scream rang out. Maggie's scream.

Chapter Twenty-Two

Pain ripped through Maggie; she felt as if she were being torn in two. She patted her belly, but she felt no stickiness from blood, just an incredible tightness. She hadn't been shot. She'd gone into labor.

Blaine dropped to the ground beside her. "Where are you hit?"

She shook her head. "No…"

His hands replaced hers on her belly, and his green eyes widened. "You're in labor?"

"It's too soon," she said, as tears of pain and fear streamed down her face. "It's too soon. You have to stop it. I can't have the baby now."

Or Tammy Doremire would get her wish. Maggie wouldn't have the baby the woman didn't think she deserved. Maybe she was right.

Maggie probably didn't deserve her baby. But she wanted him. With all her heart she wanted him.

"We're going to get you to the hospital," Blaine said. "We're going to get you help." But his hand shook as he dialed 911, and his voice shook as he demanded an ambulance.

He was worried, too. Somehow Maggie found that reassuring, as if it proved he cared. If not about her, at least he cared about her baby. He showed he cared when he climbed into the ambulance with her and let Truman take Tammy Doremire into custody.

He took Maggie's hand, clasping it in both of his. "Everything's going to be okay," he promised. "Everything's going to be okay."

"Thank you," she managed between pants for breath. "Thank you."

His forehead furrowed and he asked, "For what?"

"You saved my life again," she said. And she hoped that he had saved the baby's, too.

But when they got to the hospital, it was too late. The doctors couldn't stop the labor. Her little boy was coming. "It's too early…"

"He'll be fine," Blaine assured her. "He's tough— like his mama."

Was she tough? Maggie had never felt as helpless and weak as she did at that moment. She couldn't stop her labor; she couldn't stop him from coming.

"Push," a nurse told her.

"I can't…" She shouldn't. But the urge was there—the urge to push him out. A contraction gripped her, tearing her apart again. There had been no time for them to administer an epidural. No time for them to ease her pain. She didn't care, though. She cared only about her baby. "It's too soon…"

"We'll take care of him," the doctor promised. "Push…"

Blaine touched her chin, tipping up her face so that she met his gaze. "You need to do this, Maggie. You've taken care of him as long as you could. Let the doctors take care of him now."

So she pushed, and her baby boy entered the world with a weak cry of protest.

"He's crying—that's good," Blaine assured her. "He's going to be okay."

But the doctors whisked him away, working on him. Were his lungs okay? Were they developed enough? Maggie had so many questions. But she didn't want to distract the doctors from her son, so she didn't ask any of them.

Blaine stroked his fingers along her cheek. "He'll be okay. He'll be okay. He's tough—just like you are."

Even though he'd repeated his assurance, Maggie couldn't accept it. She didn't feel tough. She felt shattered. Devastated. And Blaine must have seen that she was about to fall apart because he pulled her into his arms. And he held her. He held her together.

And not just then but over the next few days. He stayed with her at the hospital, making sure that she and the baby were all right. Maggie fell so far in love with him that she knew she would never get over him.

She didn't want to get over him. She wanted to be with him always. She wanted to be his wife—wanted her son to be his son, too.

The doctors already thought he was the little boy's father. They called him Dad, and Blaine never corrected them. But it wasn't his name on little Drew's birth certificate—it was Andy's as the father. He deserved that honor. He deserved to be with his son.

Andy was gone. Maggie had accepted that, but she wanted to honor him by giving his son his name. Blaine was with Maggie when the nurse brought in the baby from the neonatal unit. "He's breathing on his own, Mom," she said. "No more machines. He can stay in here with you."

"He's so tiny," Blaine said with wonder as he stared down at the sleeping infant.

"Drew's going to be a big boy," the nurse assured them. "He's doing very well for a preemie." She handed the baby to Maggie before leaving the room.

Her heart swelled with love as he automatically snuggled against her, as if he recognized her even though she hadn't carried him as long as she was supposed to.

"He's so tiny," Blaine repeated, still in awe.

"He's doing well, though," Maggie assured him.

"Drew?" Blaine asked.

Maybe she should have run the name past him first. But he had never indicated that he wanted a future with her and her son. So she hadn't wanted to presume.

She nodded.

"That's good. It's a good name," he said, his green gaze on the baby in her arms.

"I'm glad you think so," she said. She wanted him to be part of their lives. But even as she contemplated asking, he started pulling away.

He stood up. "Now that you're both okay, I need to get back to work on the case," he said. "I need to find the other robbers and make sure they don't try to go after you or Drew."

She shivered, and the baby awakened. But not with a cry. He opened his eyes just a little and stared calmly up at her. She had been in danger for too much of her pregnancy. She appreciated that Blaine wanted to make sure that they would finally be safe. But she wasn't sure that was really the reason he was leaving.

Or if he just wanted to get away from her. Maybe he didn't like that everyone had assumed he was the baby's father. Maybe he didn't want to be an instant daddy.

Before he left, he leaned over the bed, and he pressed a kiss to her lips and another to the baby's forehead. "I have a guard posted at the door. Truman will protect you. You'll be safe," he assured her.

"What about you?" she asked.

He grinned. "I'll be fine."

She couldn't help but remember that Andy had promised the same thing when he'd left for his last deployment. Would Blaine not return, as well?

BLAINE WOULDN'T PUT it past Tammy Doremire to set a trap for him. He interviewed her at the jail. In exchange for a lesser sentence, she gave him an address—not just for her brother but for the two coworkers who'd helped them pull off the robberies. He doubted she actually cared how much time she spent behind bars; she just wanted to make sure that Blaine was dead—like her husband.

"What did Maggie have?" she asked, as if she actually cared.

His blood chilled with a sense of foreboding. But he had guards posted at the hospital. They weren't hospital guards, either. Once he'd realized a hospital security guard had been involved in the robberies, he hadn't trusted any of them. Truman was inside Maggie's room, personally protecting her and Drew. He felt so bad about Tammy getting her alone that he would give up his life before he would let anyone hurt her or her baby again.

"A boy," he said.

"Of course," she said, as if she should have known. "Boys run in the Doremire family."

"She named him Drew," he said.

She shrugged, and her red hair brushed the shoulders of her orange jumpsuit. She looked nearly as bad as she had in the zombie mask. "Maybe she loved Andy more than I thought."

Maggie had loved her fiancé. He saw it in her face whenever she talked about him. She missed him.

Could Blaine fill the void Andy had left in her? He loved her so much that he wanted to try. But did he love her enough for both of them?

He had no idea how she actually felt about him. She had turned to him for protection—for comfort. But who else had she had now that Andy was gone?

Who else could she trust now that the family that had almost been hers had turned on her?

"That's too bad for you, huh?" Tammy remarked. "Since you love her…"

Blaine hadn't told Maggie his feelings; he wasn't about to tell this woman. He stood up and gestured toward a deputy to take Tammy back to holding. As they led her away, she turned back and smiled a sly smile.

She had definitely set a trap for him. So he was ready. He took Ash Stryker and Dalton Reyes with him as backup, along with some Michigan troopers. According to Tammy, her brother and his friends had gone back to the cabin. Supposedly she and Mark had stashed the money there. After finding the body, the dog tags and Maggie's letters, Blaine hadn't taken the time to search the entire area. Maybe the money was hidden there.

But Blaine suspected he wouldn't find just the money. Or the robbers.

"We could have called in more troopers," Ash remarked as he pulled his weapon from his holster.

But if Blaine had requested more, he might have had to use his sister, and he didn't want to put her in danger, too. He wanted her to be there to help Maggie and the baby in case he couldn't. He wanted Maggie to have a friend she could trust—unlike Susan Iverson or Tammy.

"You face down terrorists every day," Dalton Reyes teased him. "You're afraid of a few zombie bank robbers?"

"Some of the worst terrorists I've dealt with have been the homegrown kind, holed up in remote spots just like this one," Ash warned them. "They could have an arsenal in there."

Blaine sighed. "Oh, I'm sure that they do…"

He had no more than voiced the thought when gunfire erupted. It echoed throughout the woods, shattering the windows of the cabin and the windows of the vehicles he and the other agents had driven up.

He gestured at the others, indicating for them to go around the back as he headed straight toward the cabin. He was the one that they wanted—the one that Tammy Doremire wanted—dead.

Maggie had already lost one man who loved her. She shouldn't lose another—especially when Blaine had yet to tell her that he loved her. He should have told her…

He was afraid now that he might never have the chance. The gunfire continued. They had to have automatic weapons—maybe even armor-piercing bullets. The vest probably wouldn't help him—neither would the SWAT helmet he and the other agents wore.

Ignoring the risk, he returned fire. He had to take out these threats to Maggie and the baby. He had to make sure that they couldn't hurt her or Drew ever again. One man, wearing the zombie mask and trench-coat disguise, stepped out of the cabin. Blaine hit him, taking him down, but as the man fell, his automatic weapon continued to fire.

And Blaine felt the fiery sting as a bullet hit him. He ignored the pain as another robber exited the cabin, aiming straight for him. Even as his arm began to go numb, he kept squeezing the trigger. The zombie fell, but so did Blaine. He struck the ground hard.

His ears ringing from the gunshots, he could barely hear the others calling out for him. "Blaine! Blaine!"

"Are you hit?" Reyes asked.

"Where are you hit?" Ash asked.

He didn't even know—because what hurt the most

was his heart—at the thought that he might never see Maggie again. "Tell her…"

But he didn't have the strength to finish his request. Like Mark Doremire, he was afraid that he was about to bleed out in the woods.

All he managed to utter was her name. "Maggie…"

Chapter Twenty-Three

Maggie had suspected the worst even before Ash Stryker and another man walked into her hospital room. Their faces were pale with stress, and their clothes were smeared with blood that wasn't theirs. They looked unharmed but yet devastated.

"No…"

He couldn't be dead. Blaine couldn't have died without learning how much she loved him. How much she needed him…

He had always been there when she had needed him. Why hadn't she been there when he had needed her?

She was already out of bed, standing over Drew's clear bassinet. She stepped away from it, so that she wouldn't startle the sleeping baby. But her legs trembled, nearly giving way beneath her. Truman grabbed her, steadying her with a hand on her arm.

Ash shook his head. "He's not dead, Maggie," he said. "He's not dead."

"But he's hurt." They wouldn't look the way they did if he wasn't. "How badly?"

Ash shook his head again. "I don't know."

"Where was he shot?" she asked. "How many times?"

"What the hell happened?" Truman asked the question before she could add it to her others.

"We went back to that cabin," the other agent replied. "The woman told us the others were there getting the money she and her husband stashed somewhere on the property."

Maggie gasped. "Tammy wouldn't have helped Blaine. She wanted him dead."

"It was an ambush," the agent confirmed.

"But Blaine was expecting it," Ash said. "We got them all. It's over, Maggie."

But so might Blaine's life be over. "Where was he shot?" she asked again. "How many times?"

"Just once," the other agent replied. But from Mark's and Sarge's deaths, she knew once was enough to kill. "The bullet grazed the side of his neck."

"It nicked an artery," Ash said. "He lost a lot of blood."

"But he's alive," she said, clinging to hope.

Ash nodded but repeated, "He lost a lot of blood, though."

"The doctors aren't sure he's going to make it," the other man added. "After they stabilized him, they flew him here."

"Why?" There were hospitals closer to the cabin. Good ones.

"The last thing he said was your name," Ash told her.

So they'd thought he wanted to be with her? He had probably only been worried that Tammy had set a trap for her as well as him. She'd wanted them both dead.

But Maggie didn't care why they had brought Blaine here. She had to see him. She turned to Truman. "Can you keep an eye on Drew while I go see Blaine?"

"Of course," the big man replied, but he looked nervously at the tiny baby as if afraid that he might awaken.

"This way," Ash said, as he guided her down the hall

to an elevator. They took it to the ground floor and the intensive care unit.

"Only one person at a time," the nurse at the desk warned them.

Ash waved her forward, so she followed the nurse to Blaine's bedside. Her golden-haired superhero looked so vulnerable and pale lying there. An IV dripped fluids—maybe plasma—into him, probably replacing the blood he'd lost. A bandage covered the wound on his neck. The injury had been treated.

Now he just had to fight.

"Please," she implored him as she grasped his hand. "Please don't leave me." Tears overflowed her eyes, trailing down her face to drop onto his arm. "I can't lose you. You have to fight. You have to live."

Panic had her heart beating frantically, desperately. What could she do to help him fight? How could she lend him some of her strength, as he had always given her his? She wouldn't have survived without him. Even with all the robbers dead or in jail, she wasn't sure that she could survive now without him.

"Please," she implored him again, "please don't leave me."

His hand moved inside hers, his fingers entwining with hers. He squeezed. She glanced up at his face and found his green-eyed gaze focused on her. He was conscious!

Embarrassed that he'd caught her crying all over him, she felt heat flood her face. "I'm sorry," she said.

"Sorry?" he asked, his voice a husky rasp.

"I—I'm crying all over you," she pointed out. "And I'm making assumptions."

"Assumptions?"

"I shouldn't have assumed that you're with me," she

said. "I know that you've just been protecting me—that you've just been doing your job—"

He tugged his hand from hers and pressed his fingers over her lips. "Shh…"

The man was exhausted, and here she was, rambling away. She had always talked too much.

"I'm sorry," she murmured again—against his fingers.

He shook his head—weakly. "You're wrong…"

Before he could tell her what she was wrong about, the nurse stepped back into the area. "He's awake? Mr. Campbell, you're conscious!" She leaned over and flashed a light in his eyes.

Blaine squinted and cursed. "Yes, I'm conscious."

"I have to get the doctor!" the nurse exclaimed as she hurried off.

"I should go," Maggie said. "I should tell Ash that you're awake." His friends had been worried about him, too.

"I think he probably heard," Blaine pointed out, as the nurse's voice rang out.

"Then he'll want to see you," Maggie said. She tugged on her hand, trying to free it from his so that she could escape before she suffered even more embarrassment. But before she could leave, a doctor hurried over with the excited nurse.

But even while the doctor talked to him—telling Blaine how lucky he was—he wouldn't release her. While she loved the warmth and comfort of his hand holding hers, she dreaded the moment when they would be alone again. Because even though he hadn't died, she suspected he would still be leaving her.

BLAINE WAS GRATEFUL to the doctor for saving his life, but he couldn't wait to get rid of him and the nurse. He wanted to be alone with Maggie again.

But the doctor wouldn't stop talking. "You're going to need to take it easy for a while and let your body recover from the blood loss. We're going to keep you in ICU overnight. You really need your rest."

"I should leave," Maggie said again as she tried to tug her hand free of his.

He wouldn't let her go, though. He was strong enough to hang on to her. She gave him strength. Hearing her sweet voice had drawn him from the fog of unconsciousness. She'd made him want to fight. Had made him want to live…

For her.

With her.

"No," he said. "I need to talk to you." And he gave a pointed look to the doctor and nurse, who finally took his not-so-subtle hint and left them alone.

"It's okay," she said. "I understand. You don't have to explain to me that you were just doing your job— protecting me and Drew. I know that you don't feel the same way about me that I do about you."

He reached out again and covered her silky soft lips with his fingers. "Sweetheart, you do talk too much." She'd said it herself, but until now he hadn't agreed with her.

"Sweetheart?" She mouthed the word against his fingers.

"But that's the only thing you're right about," he said. "You're wrong about everything else."

She stopped trying to talk now, and she waited for him to speak. That had never been easy for him—to share his feelings. He'd been hiding them for too long.

And obviously he'd hidden them too well from Maggie because she had no idea how he felt about her.

"You were never just a job to me," he said. "If you

were, I wouldn't have had to protect you myself. I would have trusted you to Truman or someone like him way before I had to—"

"But you did," she murmured against his fingers.

"I had to," he said, "or I was never going to figure out who was trying to hurt you and the baby. But it killed me to not be with you every day." And when he'd had to leave them again—after Drew had been born—it had literally nearly killed him. "I don't want to be away from you and Drew again."

Tears began to shimmer in those enormous brown eyes of hers. "Blaine…?"

He knew what he wanted to say, but he didn't know how to say it. "I don't have a ring…"

He couldn't forget the size and shine of the diamond Andy had given her. But Andy was gone. She had accepted that; Blaine needed to accept it, too.

"And I can't get down on one knee right now…" Hanging on to her hand had sapped all his strength. If he tried getting out of bed, he would undoubtedly pass out at her feet.

"I don't need a ring," she said. "I don't need any gestures. I just need to know how you feel about me."

"I'm not good at expressing my feelings," he said apologetically.

"Just tell me…"

"I love you," he said. "I love your sweetness and your openness. I love how you worry and care about everyone and everything."

"You love me?"

He nodded. "I know I'm not your first choice and that you'd promised to marry another man. But Andy's gone. And I'm here. And I will love you as much as he would have—if not more. I will take care of you and Drew. I will treat your son just like he's mine, too, if you'll let me."

The tears overflowed her eyes and spilled down her cheeks. "I don't deserve you," she said. "And I didn't deserve Andy. Tammy was right about that. I didn't love him like I should have. I loved him because he was my best friend. I didn't love him like a woman should love the man she wants to marry. And I didn't want to marry him. But I didn't know how to say no to his proposal without hurting him."

And with her big, loving heart, she would have given up her own happiness to ensure someone else's. He didn't want her doing that for him.

"You won't hurt me if you tell me no," he lied. It would hurt him. But he'd heard what she'd said when she'd thought him unconscious. He didn't think she would tell him no. But he wanted her to say yes for the right reasons. "You'll hurt me if you say yes and don't really love me."

"I love you," she said. "I love you like a woman loves a man. I love you with passion. I love you like a soul mate, not just as a friend."

The tightness in his chest eased, and he grinned. "I love how much you talk," he said. "I really do…especially when you're telling me how much you love me." But then he realized what she had yet to say. "But you haven't answered my question."

"Did you ask me something?" she asked with a coy flutter of her lashes.

"I will get out of this bed," he said, but they both knew it was an empty threat at the moment.

"I don't need the bended knee or the ring," she said. "I just need the question."

So he asked, "Will you marry me, Maggie Jenkins? Will you take me as your husband and as Drew's father?"

"Yes, Special Agent Blaine Campbell," she replied. "I will marry you."

He used their joined hands to tug her closer, to pull her down for the kiss to seal their promise.

Someone cleared his throat above the sound of a baby crying. "Excuse me," Truman said. "But someone was looking for his mama…" The burly agent carried the tiny fussing baby over to Maggie.

She laid the little boy on Blaine's chest, and the baby's cries stopped. He stared up at Blaine as if he recognized him. "Here's your daddy," she said.

Blaine had a perfect record—every case solved with the FBI, every criminal caught—but this—his family— meant far more to him. This woman and their child was what made his life special now and for always.

* * * * *

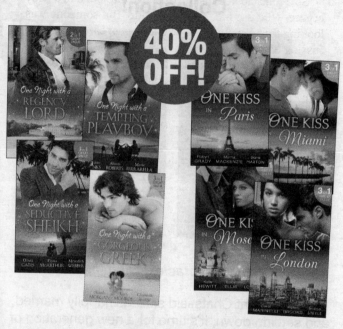

MILLS & BOON®

The Chatsfield Collection!

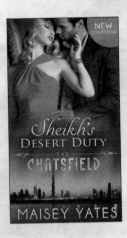

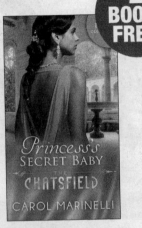

Style, spectacle, scandal…!

With the eight Chatsfield siblings happily married and settling down, it's time for a new generation of Chatsfields to shine, in this brand-new 8-book collection! The prospect of a merger with the Harrington family's boutique hotels will shape the future forever. But who will come out on top?

Find out at
www.millsandboon.co.uk/TheChatsfield2

215_INSHIP2

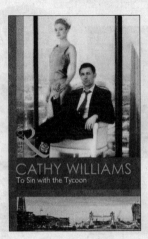
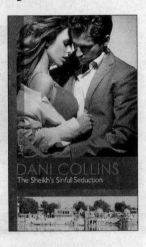